Books by Donna Anders:

The Flower Man
Another Life
Dead Silence
In All the Wrong Places

Published by POCKET BOOKS

DONNA ANDERS

IN ALL THE WRONG PLACES

POCKET BOOKS

NEW YORK   LONDON   TORONTO   SYDNEY   SINGAPORE

This book is a work of fiction. Names, characters, places and incidents are products of the author's imagination or are used fictitiously. Any resemblance to actual events or locales or persons, living or dead, is entirely coincidental.

An *Original* Publication of POCKET BOOKS

 POCKET BOOKS, a division of Simon & Schuster, Inc.
1230 Avenue of the Americas, New York, NY 10020

ISBN: 0-7394-3082-3

Cover art by TK

Printed in the U.S.A.

Acknowledgments

First and foremost, I am grateful to my family, my friends and to the various people who were so willing to share their expert advice and encouragement while I was working on this book. Special thanks to Nancy and Peter Crefeld who so generously helped with my East Coast research, to Heidi Kirsch who helped with my Atlanta research, to Steve Stroh who saved my half-finished manuscript from a computer glitch, and to Bryan Pearce whose computer savvy has saved my day more than once. And always, my love and gratitude to Ruth Aeschliman, Lisa Pearce and Tina Abeel, three great daughters who are always there for me.

Special thanks to my agent, Sheree Bykofsky. And yet again, sincere gratitude to my very talented editor, Amy Pierpont, at Pocket Books.

For Taryn Pearce and Ashlyn Pearce,
My movie buddies
And fellow Dove Bar junkies.

1

"**D**amn it!"

Carolyn stared in disbelief at the open glove box, and the papers that were scattered everywhere in the car. She ran a hand through her hair and sighed shakily. She must have forgotten to close the driver's window and her carelessness had allowed someone to break into her car and search it.

She reached into the open window and shuffled through the papers. Her car title and insurance certificate hadn't been stolen, nor had anything else as far as she could tell. Someone, probably a kid, had been looking for money, she decided, as she stuffed everything back into the glove box. Or had the tabloid reporters been snooping into her life again? A recent newspaper article honoring her father's philanthropic contributions to society could have sparked another flurry of interest in her, just as it had when he died a year ago. Whatever. She really hadn't needed this today.

After calling the company door guard from her cell phone to report the incident, Carolyn started her engine and headed for the interstate. The night commute into Atlanta from Marietta wasn't overly congested, a winter driving bonus for which Carolyn was grateful. As she turned south off I-75 onto I-285, she switched on the radio to easy listening music as she always did. It helped her relax after spending all day in front of the camera.

The haunting notes of *Somewhere in Time* filled the Volvo, bringing sudden tears to her eyes. She blinked quickly, wiping them away with her sleeve.

For God's sake, get a grip, she told herself. *Stop wallowing.*

She loved her job as a saleswoman at NNN, the National Neighborhood Network. It was a dream come true, her one anchor amid the losses in her personal life during the past several years. But after the stage lights snapped off and the cameras stopped rolling she sometimes felt drained, a letdown from the adrenaline high of performing before millions of television viewers across the country. And when her creative energy was at a low, Carolyn's memories crept in, like fingers of fog on a soggy night, relentless and all consuming.

Carolyn pressed a little harder on the accelerator, headed for a city exit. All she wanted to do was get home and close the door on the world, but she had a stop to make. Minnie was waiting for her.

And Minnie, her best friend in the world, was worth setting her fatigue aside for a few more minutes. Years ago Minnie had almost become her stepmom, but her dad, widowed since Carolyn was young, had married someone else. His sudden death had left Carolyn a thirty-year-old orphan.

Her father had died a year ago, today. She wondered if Minnie had remembered. The anniversary had loomed in Carolyn's mind for weeks, giving her nightmares. She had seen so much death. Her mother, her baby girl four years ago, and then her father. And her husband Rob might as well have died; he'd closed himself off completely after little Betsy died. Their divorce a year later came as a surprise to no one. Carolyn was startled out of her dark thoughts by the screeching of brakes behind her. Her glance shot to the rearview mirror.

"Oh, shit," she muttered.

A dark sedan, several cars back, had raced the caution light and nearly caused an accident in the intersection when it turned red.

"Stupid idiot," she told the vehicle as it caught up with her.

Steering onto a street that led to an area of dilapidated apartment buildings, another glance in the mirror told her that the dark sedan still followed her. Probably lived in the area, she told herself. A commuter anxious to get home and relax.

For the next few minutes Carolyn concentrated on finding the driveway to Anderson Youth House, a lane so obscured by shabby, 1920s-vintage apartment houses that she often missed it in the dark. She slowed her Volvo to a crawl, scanning the row of buildings that were cookie-cutter similar, down to the shrubs and flowers that lined the sidewalks.

She was almost on top of it when she braked and turned into the narrow blacktop approach to a small, poorly lighted parking lot squeezed behind the dwellings that fronted the street. Her headlights swept over the large two-story house, a pre-Civil War brick home that had been covered with stucco. Its square structure with its tacked-on addition looked like an albatross among the other buildings. The founders of Anderson Youth House had bought it dirt cheap fifteen years ago, saving it from the wrecking ball and converting it into a nonprofit facility for abandoned children and runaway street kids. Minnie donated her bookkeeping skills several nights a week.

Pulling into a parking place, Carolyn switched off the engine and lights. It was only then that she realized another vehicle had followed her into the shadowy lot. Her door was open and she had one foot on the ground when her gaze flew to the approaching car. Apprehension rippled over her.

It was the dark sedan. Was it following her?

Carolyn jerked her leg back into the car, slammed and locked the door. A moment later she felt stupid. The car circled the lot and headed back toward the street. The driver, hidden behind dark-tinted windows, had obviously made the same mistake she had in the past: taken the wrong driveway between old apartment houses. She watched the red tail lights disappear.

And—it may not have been the same dark sedan, she reminded herself.

But Carolyn felt uneasy as she got out of the Volvo and headed for the door, a wrapped package of old trade beads in her hand, compliments of the famous Lilly Lawton, an aging, if famous, actress who was a regular on NNN. Lilly was the spokes-woman for a line of primitive jewelry, created by ethnic artists in the southwestern United States. While they'd been chatting before the camera last month, Carolyn had told her and their viewing audience about her friend Minnie's jewelry creations, influenced by her Native American background. After the show, she'd mentioned that Minnie preferred old trade beads from the Far East and Africa but usually couldn't afford them. Lilly had immediately offered her a supply.

Her handbag swinging from a shoulder strap, Carolyn quickly crossed to the front entrance, stepped into the foyer and pressed the buzzer. Seconds later, the door was unlocked and she went inside, heading down the hall toward the social room where she was to meet Minnie.

The scarred hardwood squeaked under her feet, but Carolyn's thoughts were on the beads, not the floor. She smiled, thinking of Lilly, a genuine lady behind her face-lifts, false eyelashes and on-camera fibs about her true age. It was typical of Lilly to help a struggling artist by giving the antique beads, especially since she knew that Minnie worked a full-time job to subsidize her art. Minnie's offer of payment had been waved aside.

"Then what can I do to repay her?" Minnie had asked later when Carolyn had called her with the news.

"Send her one of your creations, along with the legend that goes with it." Carolyn had known that Minnie was reticent about accepting the gift. "Taking advantage of an opportunity is how to succeed.

Who knows, Minnie. One of these days you could be on NNN promoting *your* jewelry."

"Hey there girl! What you grinning about?"

Carolyn glanced up to see the object of her earlier phone conversation standing in the doorway to the social room, eyebrows raised in a question.

"Just feeling good about the end of the day, I guess." Carolyn smiled wider as she reached her. "And anticipating spring when it's not dark at five in the afternoon."

"C'mon, Carolyn. You can't fool me. No one feels that good in the middle of a work week."

For a moment Carolyn contemplated her friend: tall, slim, long straight black hair that was highlighted with streaks of gray, high cheekbones and wide, large brown eyes—a beautiful woman whose appearance belied her fifty years.

Carolyn held out the package. "Guess I'm smiling because the beads are exquisite. You're going to love them. Lilly claims that some are hundreds of years old."

Minnie stepped forward, her long wool skirt swirling around her black leather boots, and took the package, quickly unwrapping it to peer at the contents. "Jeez, Carolyn. They're beautiful, really special." She glanced up. "These have to be valuable. Are you sure Lilly won't let me pay her?"

"Certain."

There was a pause.

"Thanks, Carolyn," Minnie said. "For always being so thoughtful, for telling Lilly about me in the first place." She rewrapped the package as she talked. "I'll use a few of these beads to create something unique for her." She grinned. "And maybe a little surprise for you, my dear friend, something to emphasize those big green eyes of yours."

The moment was awkward, her praise reminding Carolyn of painful times in the past. Minnie had met Carolyn's father, a lawyer who was twenty-five years her senior and a well-known philanthropist in Atlanta, fifteen years ago when Anderson Youth House was being established in Atlanta. Minnie had been a board member; Arthur Langdon had taken care of zoning, licensing and certification issues.

Years later, after Carolyn's baby died, her dad had gently coaxed her into becoming active at Anderson Youth House, too. He'd believed that helping other babies would help her cope with her own loss. But since her father's death the place brought back sad memories. If it weren't for Minnie she might never have come back, even though she knew how much her father had believed in the place.

Thoughts of her dad triggered another urge to tear up, and she swallowed back a sudden lump in her throat. Silly, she chided herself. Get a grip.

Struggling for control, Carolyn told herself not to mention that today was the anniversary of her dad's death. Minnie was a private person who didn't share her feelings easily and had never revealed why Anderson Youth House was so important to her, although Carolyn knew from her dad that Minnie had been abandoned at age ten, and had lived in foster homes until she'd graduated high school. And Carolyn had never asked Minnie about her relationship with her father, sensing the older woman's pain. But she did know that Minnie believed that age shouldn't be a factor when you loved someone. Her dad had eventually married his secretary, Dolores, who was closer to his age and had taken care of all his everyday needs for many years. He never saw Dolores, who now lived in the family home where Carolyn grew up, as a fortune hunter, but as a caring, considerate woman. Carolyn had always suspected that it was Dolores who had undermined her father's confidence about marrying Minnie.

Carolyn gave herself a mental shake, bringing herself back to Minnie who stood watching, her beautiful eyes filled with affection, her full-mouthed smile revealing a perfect set of teeth. A natural beauty, Carolyn thought again. How could her father have been so blind, so closed to the one woman who had genuinely loved him?

Don't dwell on things you can't change, she told herself for the second time within an hour. Dolores was her stepmother, Minnie had become her best friend and her dad had been dead for months now. There was no changing the past.

"Hey, don't look so sad, Carolyn." Minnie stepped forward to hug her. For long seconds they stood embraced, Minnie's gentle pats on her back saying all the things that she would never put into words. "I know it's hard sometimes—" She broke off.

Carolyn was the first to pull away. She smiled, tremulously, knowing her eyes were brimming. It was her day for tears; somehow the deaths of her dad and baby were linked in her mind today.

"Thanks for understanding," she said, knowing their shared feelings didn't need to be spoken aloud. "I'm just—uh, a bit emotional tonight." She shook her head and quickly dabbed her eyes. "I shouldn't be so damned—"

"It's okay, Carolyn," Minnie said gently, interrupting. "We can't predict when something may trigger our emotions."

But it wasn't okay. It was one of those sudden, overemotional states she'd found herself in during the past year when she was stressed from the job, or fatigued from a night of insomnia, or sad with remembering. It was during sleepless nights that she thought about her perfect two-month-old infant who just died one night while she slept in the next room, oblivious that her child was in trouble.

"Yeah, you're right," she said finally. "Bed is what I need." Carolyn managed a smile. "So I'd better get going and have an early night."

Minnie nodded, watchful.

Maybe what I really require is Prozac, Carolyn thought, having lowered her eyes to pull on her leather gloves. Or more grief therapy. Whatever. She needed to get it together. She couldn't afford her state of mind to ultimately affect her job. So far, while before the cameras, she'd managed to hide her pain behind the outgoing personality her fans had come to expect.

"You okay?" Minnie frowned.

" 'Course. Like I said, just tired. It was a busy day."

"I expect every day is busy at NNN." Minnie hesitated. "I was going to suggest wine and pasta at Pasta da Pulcinella. It's only ten or so minutes from your condo, but maybe next time?"

"You know I'd love to, Minnie." She paused. "But can I have a rain check for next week instead?"

"Sure." Minnie's smile was soft. "I understand, sweetie."

"How about a rain check for me?" A deep male voice spoke from a short distance behind them. "All of us Italians love pasta. Wine, too."

Minnie rolled her eyes affectionately before she and Carolyn turned to face Barney McGill who was striding up the hall toward them.

His pale blue eyes were friendly as always, but Carolyn felt something sharp move between them when she met his gaze. She shivered. God, the man was attractive, in a dangerous sort of way.

He's not dangerous, she reminded herself. Only jaded by years of working crime scenes as a homicide detective. Barney was one of the good guys.

"Italian? I thought you were Irish," Carolyn said lightly, as though she hadn't noticed how lean and muscular he looked in Levis and a brown leather jacket.

"Only half. My dad's side."

He was staring at her. Carolyn fought the urge to glance away.

"My mother is Italian." His craggy features softened. Carolyn saw the smile start in his eyes before it touched his mouth. "And she was the cook who influenced my taste buds."

Carolyn looked away. She'd first met Barney a year ago but knew little about him, except that he coached basketball and baseball for the Youth House's kids, taking them to see the Hawks or the Braves when his schedule permitted. She'd often wondered about his personal life; he didn't seem to have one.

"Well, we'll keep that in mind," Minnie said,

breaking the tension between Carolyn and the detective. "If you're available next week you're welcome to come along." She turned to Carolyn. "Right?"

Carolyn pretended to adjust the strap on her handbag, feeling Barney's eyes on her. "Sure, Barney's welcome to our party."

"Great," he said, bringing her gaze back to his. "I'll plan on it." He was a model of seriousness, as though he hadn't invited himself to their dinner. "As a man with three older sisters, I'm used to hen parties."

"We call it girl talk," Minnie said, grinning.

"Whatever." Barney spread his hands, trying to look serious. "Gotta go. My guys are waiting for me." With a salute, and a final glance at Carolyn, he continued down the hall toward the gym, the addition that had been built onto the back of the building. "See you both next week for pasta," he added over a broad shoulder.

"He's kind of an enigma," Carolyn said, watching as his tall figure disappeared into the gym.

"I suppose so," Minnie said. "But then that's to be expected under the circumstances."

"The fact that he's a homicide detective?"

Minnie shook her head as they started toward the front entrance. "Because his wife and two little boys drowned. Remember, their boat capsized off Hilton Head two years ago last summer?"

"Yeah, I know that, but none of the details. You once mentioned that he never talks of it." Carolyn hesitated. "I figured that's why Barney helps the boys here, and why he seems reserved, closed off at times." She didn't add that he reminded her of her ex-husband in the way he never expressed his emotions. Not once had he mentioned his grief. And that same behavior in Rob had been fatal for her marriage.

"Uh-huh. By filling his spare time working with the kids he doesn't have time to dwell on what happened."

"What did happen?"

Minnie shrugged. "His wife and boys had gone for a visit with her parents, the grandpa took them fishing, and they all got caught in one of those sudden summer squalls."

They'd reached the door and Carolyn faced Minnie for her good-bye.

"You aren't leaving yet?"

Minnie flashed her toothy smile. "Since we aren't having pasta I'm going to catch up on computer entries."

"Not skipping supper because of me?"

"Nope. I'll eat later." She reached to open the door for Carolyn. "The trouble with volunteering my computer expertise here is that my knowledge is limited."

Carolyn gave a wry laugh. "We both need training, that's for sure." Neither her job, or Minnie's as a substance abuse therapist, required knowledge beyond basic computer skills. "Are we still on for that computer class?"

"Yep. Starts next week. Not soon enough for me if I'm to get this place on-line."

"Just let me know the time." Carolyn blew her a kiss and continued through the door, running to her car while Minnie watched. She was starting down the driveway when her cell phone rang.

She stopped at the street under a light pole and grabbed her phone. "Hello."

"Hey, Carolyn. Thought you'd be home by now."

"Not yet, Roberta, but I will be in a few minutes."

Roberta was her boss at NNN and she often called after hours if something important came up. Carolyn switched the phone to her other ear and waited.

"There's a vendor meeting in the morning and I'd like you to be there. Can you come in a half hour early?"

"Sure."

"Good." Her voice sounded relieved. "That's it then. See you in the morning." A pause. "And thanks."

"No problem." Carolyn was about to disconnect when Roberta said something else.

"What was that?"

"Oh, nothing really. Don't know why I mentioned it. Some wacko called the studio, said he was watching you."

"Me?"

"Yeah. Probably some guy with a crush. You know, we get those types from time to time. Okay, I'm going now."

Carolyn had the Volvo headed for home a few seconds later, but when she noticed the dark sedan behind her, a car that looked exactly like the one that had followed her earlier, Roberta's words about the phone call surfaced.

A wacko had said he was watching her.

She increased her speed, and turned at the next corner. The sedan followed. Her heart fluttered. She made two more right turns and the car behind her did the same. Clutching the steering wheel, she made a sudden left at the next intersection, her eyes glued to the rearview mirror. When the other vehicle kept going straight, she slumped in her seat and exhaled. Her legs felt like Jell-O. She pulled over at the curb until she could stop shaking.

She put her forehead against the steering wheel. *I'm going nuts.*

She stayed like that for a minute, then started home again, reminding herself that half of the cars in America were dark sedans. And the caller hadn't said he was following her. He'd said *watching*.

Of course he was watching her—along with millions of other viewers. It was time for bed and some badly needed sleep.

2

Ten minutes later Carolyn turned off Peachtree Street and headed toward an area of apartment lofts, some of which had been converted into pricey condominiums. She found herself continuously glancing at her rearview mirror. No one had followed her.

She was just being paranoid, again.

She needed to take herself in hand. It's what her dad would have wanted her to do.

Carolyn smiled, remembering. Her father had been the best dad: loving, sensitive, and proud of her. He'd complimented her often and told her that she was just like her mother: tall, slender and uniquely beautiful. She'd always felt close to the mother she'd never known because of his words.

"Oh, Dad. I miss you," she said, speaking into the silent car as she neared home.

Her street, lined with coastal Georgia live oaks, was deserted except for an occasional car. She was eager to curl up on the sofa with Mustard and Mayo, her yellow and white cats, and watch television in the peaceful quiet of her cozy family room. Her house was her haven, the walls of its rooms decorated with the collection of art that had once belonged to her parents, and the framed photographs of her family, now all dead.

Carolyn slowed the Volvo as she approached her duplex. Tucked between condominium buildings, the Victorian mansion had once been a showplace at the turn of the last century. A developer had transformed it into two elegant townhouses at the same time the apartment buildings had been remodeled into lavish condominiums. She could afford her place because of her job at NNN, and because of the inheritance from her father's estate.

She sighed. He'd been her friend and confidant as well as parent, and she still couldn't believe he was gone.

I'd give up this place in a second if I could have my dad and Betsy back, she thought as she turned into her driveway, hit the garage door opener, and drove into the attached garage on her side of the mansion. The two-car structure was an modern appendage that had been built to fit the Victorian design. It was an odd, almost disconcerting feeling to realize how the past could blend into the present—how the people of another time left their imprint for the future.

Grabbing her things, she went in through the laundry room, flipping the bolt lock behind her. Mustard and Mayo, her Angora-mix cats, ran to greet her, purring as she stooped to pet their long silky hair.

"My babies," she crooned, smiling. "I still have the two of you, don't I?"

She straightened, and still murmuring to her cats, moved into the kitchen, dropped her purse onto the marble counter, took off her suit jacket and stepped out of her pumps. She'd had the cats since the year before she'd been pregnant; they'd been a part of her perception of a successful marriage: loving husband, kids and pets. How wrong she'd been—at least about her husband Rob. Never overly expressive, his shutdown after Betsy's death had implied that she was responsible. When she'd started therapy he refused to go along, asking for a divorce instead. Rob had coped by avoiding the problem.

Then there'd been Tom Harrison, her first serious relationship since Rob. They'd broken up several months ago.

Don't think about them, she instructed herself, and turned on the music system. As a Mozart piece filled the house, she fed the cats, then moved from the kitchen to the wide vaulted hallway and front door where she pulled down the fringed shade. Then she went into the dining room, its walls a continuation of the mahogany paneling in the hall, and closed the drapes on the windows overlooking the veranda and driveway. After switching off the crystal chandelier, she crossed the hall to the sunken parlor filled with Oriental carpeting and French wallpaper, burgundy velvet drapes and matching silk cushions, crown moldings and a marble-trimmed fireplace. It had been her deciding factor in buying the place.

The peaceful ambience within her house enfolded Carolyn, as she surveyed the period furnishings she'd bought at estate sales and antique stores. She'd been seeing a therapist after the baby died, but shopping for antiques, giving herself a personal goal, had done more to keep her from dwelling on Betsy, who'd be almost four now. She'd already had her furniture by the time she found her place.

She hadn't seen her therapist on a regular basis for months, but now as Carolyn pulled more shades, she wondered if she'd made as much progress as they'd both thought.

Back in the hall Carolyn headed for the kitchen, passed the staircase that led to the open balcony above the entry, then closed the door to the small powder room that was tucked under the steps next to a coat closet.

At the refrigerator, she reached for a slim bottle of Chardonnay and poured the wine into a goblet. Sipping, she noticed the red message light was blinking on her phone. Sliding onto a counter stool, she pressed the button, figuring the message would be from Dolores, her step-mother, or from Dean, Dolores's eleven-year-old grandson, a shy boy Carolyn adored. Dean had recently interviewed her for a class project titled, "My Famous Aunt." He'd called her several times since with more questions.

Carolyn grinned as his voice filled the room. She'd been right. He had another question. She'd call him back before he went to bed.

She was about to take another sip when the second message sounded in the room and Tom Harrison's deep voice penetrated her sense of peace. She put down her glass too fast and wine splashed over her fingers.

"Hi, Carolyn," he said. "We need to talk about—

well, about this misunderstanding between us. How about getting together for dinner on the weekend?" There was a pause. "I've missed you. Even been watching you on TV. Give me a call back." Another hesitation. "No, scratch that. I'll get hold of you. Bye for now."

There was a brief silence. Then the automatic voice came out of the machine. "End of messages." For long seconds Carolyn stared at the phone.

Misunderstanding?

Like in using her to take over her dad's firm?—when her father was hardly cold in his grave? The only good thing about the whole mess was that she hadn't been madly in love with Tom, not like she'd once been with Rob. His actions had probably saved her from making another mistake—because she was lonely.

Carolyn sat listening to Mozart, remembering that day in her dad's office two weeks after his funeral. She'd come in the back entrance to find Tom going through her father's personal papers, the very thing she'd come to do.

"Darling," he'd said, crossing the room to pull her into his arms. "I thought I could do this job for you, save you from more distress."

She'd believed him, had allowed herself to be soothed by his deep calming voice, needing to feel connected to someone who loved her. Those feelings had lasted until a few days later.

Again she'd gone to her dad's office to meet Dolores who was considering an offer to sell the law practice. Carolyn had been appalled when Dolores had first told her, but after sleeping on the information, Carolyn realized it was the right thing to do. After all, her father had no successor to the firm. She'd gone to the meeting to affirm Dolores's decision.

Instead she'd walked into another private situation between Tom and her father's former secretary. Their conversation had been heated and neither had noticed Carolyn's arrival.

"You will not reveal this to Carolyn," Tom had said. His voice had been cold, final, a tone she'd never heard before. "As the man who'll soon be her husband, that's an order. You'll abide by my wishes or never work in this city again."

Out of respect for the woman, Carolyn had stepped back, out of sight. A few minutes later she'd made another entrance and there was no sign of animosity between them, no indication of what it was that Tom hadn't wanted her to know. She'd let it go at the time.

But she'd guessed the problem a few weeks later when a company audit, authorized by the firm as a matter of course to review her dad's estate, had turned up bookkeeping discrepancies, checks for bogus expenses supposedly authorized by her father. Then Dolores had announced that Tom was the buyer for the Langdon share of the firm. A little investigation by Carolyn revealed that the selling price had been devalued because of the missing capital. When she voiced concern to Dolores, her dad's heir to the business, Dolores had insisted the sale was fair, that the transaction forgave any discrepancies by Carolyn's father—and avoided a criminal investigation.

It was a stalemate.

As much as she'd wished otherwise, Carolyn no longer trusted Tom. He'd kept information from her, the woman he'd asked to be his wife, and he'd avoided talking about details of the sale, saying, "We'll talk about it later."

Why? she'd asked herself, confused. Because he was the person responsible for the missing funds? Was that the reason he wouldn't discuss it with her? Not for one moment had she believed that her dad was dishonest.

She'd finally come to a painful conclusion when Tom wouldn't discuss such an important matter with her, when he'd shut down, as Rob had once done. His interest in her may have been faked. Upon her father's death, and the subsequent cloudy financial issues that allowed him to buy into the firm, he no longer needed her. She'd ended their relationship.

Carolyn took another sip of wine and stood up. She was trying to relax after a hectic day. No way was Tom Harrison going to spoil that for her, too. She forced her thoughts to fixing supper. She'd think about Tom tomorrow.

The sudden ring of the phone startled her. About to pick it up, she hesitated, glancing at her caller ID first. She expelled her breath. It was Minnie's number, not Tom's. She grabbed the receiver.

"Hi Minnie."

"You knew it was me. You and that caller ID!"

"Yep, compliments of the phones we sell on NNN."

Minnie's contralto laugh came over the wires.

"You mean that *you* sell—by the thousands I'd wager."

"Yeah, quite a few." A pause. "What's up?"

"Nothing. Just checking to make sure you got home okay."

"I always do, Minnie." Carolyn pulled an earring off, then switched the receiver so she could remove the other one. "Did you think I wouldn't?"

"Well, I, uh, realized why today was especially hard for you, sweetie." A hesitation. "It was hard for me as well."

Carolyn ran her tongue over her lips. "So you did remember."

"Of course." Minnie's voice was lower. "I didn't bring up your dad's death because I didn't want to make you feel any worse."

"That's why I didn't bring it up either, in case you hadn't remembered."

"Not a chance."

A silence went by.

"Thanks, Minnie." Carolyn swallowed hard. "For caring."

"You, too."

They talked for a few minutes longer, then ended the call after deciding on a date the following week for Italian food. "We'll even take Barney along. Hold him to his claim of understanding girl talk."

"Sounds like a plan," Carolyn said, laughing. She was still smiling as she opened a can of soup and put it on the stove to heat. Maybe she'd take a nice warm soak after she ate.

She sat at the counter to eat, then placed the bowl and her empty wine glass in the sink, switched off the lights and went to check the front door lock before going up to her bedroom.

She heard a car start up out on the street. Her hand momentarily froze on the door shade. It sounded like it was in front of her house.

She peeked. The street seemed empty, but then she caught a glimpse of movement near the corner. She pressed her face against the glass. The darkness was still.

There was nothing.

But she felt uneasy.

Just a neighbor's car she couldn't see, she reminded herself, stepping back. It had nothing to do with her.

But the idea of a bath was no longer appealing. At the moment she felt too vulnerable. She'd have a shower in the morning, after her fear of a bogeyman had been dispelled by the bright light of day.

3

Slowly, Carolyn came awake and sat up in bed. A glance at the clock on the night table told her it was a little past 3:00 A.M. Mustard was also awake, standing at the bottom of the bed, her back arched, as though she were listening.

To what? Carolyn wondered, vaguely aware that something had also awakened her.

The house was quiet. She could even hear the ticking of the grandfather clock in the downstairs entry hall. Everything seemed normal.

Carolyn slipped out of bed, uneasy. Where was Mayo? The two cats usually slept together on the bed.

A yellow glow shown in through the bay windows from the garden lights below her room. She moved across the carpet on the balls of her feet and looked down at the flower beds, short rock walls, shrubs and stepping stones. A small dogwood tree grew in one corner, its leafless branches scarcely brushing the high wood fence that enclosed the whole small area. A three-foot statue of a garden fairy stood next to the trunk, one arm pointing to a water fountain under a magnolia tree. The faint gurgle of water was a soothing sound in the middle of the night.

"My secret garden," Carolyn whispered aloud. Another reason she'd fallen in love with her house at first sight. There was no access to the backyard other than through a door from the garage on one side and the paned, French doors from the family room. It was completely private.

And serene. A perfect place to escape from the real world. In summer, Carolyn often sat on the patio under its roof of wisteria, sipping iced tea on free afternoons, or white wine late at night before bed, unwinding, allowing her emotional well to gradually refill.

There was a faint sound downstairs.

Carolyn stiffened. The settling of the house timbers? The freezer's ice maker in the kitchen? Mayo having a snack of dried food?

She'd have to check. There was no reason to be afraid. No one could get into her house except through the front door, which she remembered locking. A glance through the side window over the driveway told her that the garage doors were still securely closed.

You're overreacting, she told herself. Because you went to bed feeling apprehensive. No one was following you. No one is watching you.

But Carolyn was careful not to make a sound as she glided out of her room and into the short hall that led to the balcony overlooking the lower entry area. She paused at the railing, scanning the shadowy staircase and lower floor that was within her vision. Nothing moved.

Go back to bed, she instructed herself. This is silly.

But what if something's wrong? her inner voice argued. And where is Mayo?

That settled it. Carolyn had no option but to go downstairs, make sure her house was secure.

Slowly, she moved down the steps, her hand on the railing, her gaze trying to penetrate the darkness below her. At the bottom she hesitated, glancing first through the open archway into the dining room, then opposite into the living room.

The shades were drawn on all the front windows, just as she'd left them. The air went out of her lungs in a gentle swoosh. Only then did she realize that she'd been holding her breath.

Everything was okay in the front of the house. She turned down the hall and faced the doorways to the powder room, kitchen and family room. The back of the house was slightly more illuminated by the garden lights that shown in through the curtained windows that lacked shades. She moved forward, suddenly feeling like a sleepwalker who'd just awakened to reality. There was no ominous presence in her house.

A quick walk through the rooms proved her right. She even found Mayo asleep on the family room sofa. After petting the cat, who had no interest in being aroused, Carolyn headed back to the front hall. She was about to start up the stairway when she heard a faint shuffling noise on the porch, then what sounded like running footsteps crossing the creaking boards to descend the steps to the side-walk.

Disbelief was a shock wave through her body, sagging her legs. She froze, one hand on the railing, steadying herself. For long moments her gaze was glued to the covered window on the door—and the slivers of glass on both sides where the shade didn't reach.

Had someone been out there? *Watching her?*

Her fear gave way to anger, and she leaped from the steps to the door, pulling back the shade, ready to confront the intruder.

No one was there.

By morning Carolyn was convinced that her fear in the night had heightened her sense of hearing—and her imagination. No one had been on her porch, unless it was her neighbor's dog. The elderly couple who lived in the other half of her house had a cranky old cocker spaniel—Mustard and Mayo's dreaded nemesis—who often prowled their mutual front yard. Being black, the dog could have darted into the azaleas and camellia shrubs and disappeared. Now, as she pulled into the parking lot at NNN and got out of her car, she grinned.

Your daddy always warned you about your over-active imagination, she reminded herself. Even Rob had thought she sometimes made mental leaps without much to go on.

The asshole. She hadn't seen him since that day in court three years ago when their divorce was final, and she hoped never to lay eyes on him again. He was a closed chapter in her life. She locked the Volvo and headed for the back entrance to the studio, mentally listing the things she had to do before her first show.

Oh, no. Carolyn stopped, her hand on the door. She'd forgotten to call Dean back last night. A glance at her watch told her it was too late now. He'd already be on his way to school. Pushing open the glass door, she stepped into the building and nodded to the guard.

"Mornin' Miss Langdon," he said, smiling.

She grinned back as he waved her past the electronic security gate that screened visitors for weapons. There had never been such an incident at NNN, but there had been occasional threats, which were taken seriously. The company had a fortune in the cubic zirconium jewelry alone, and a vast inventory of other products valued in the millions of dollars. The fake diamonds were one of Carolyn's favorite lines; she always sold out before her on-air segment ended and hoped that would happen today.

"Oh, Miss Langdon?" the guard called after her. "I almost forgot." He stepped forward and handed her a note.

She thanked him, then scanned a memo from Roberta. The meeting she'd arrived early to attend had been postponed, but Roberta still wanted to see Carolyn after the morning show. Relieved, she headed for the hair and makeup department, a daily ritual to ready herself for the camera.

A short time later, dressed in a clingy, black wool sheath dress, her thick hair falling in controlled waves over her shoulders, and her makeup accented to emphasize her large eyes and facial bone structure, Carolyn was ready. Even her fingernails had been filed, buffed and polished, so that her hands were perfect for modeling the rings and bracelets.

Once in the hall again she hurried to meet with NNN electronic technicians for last-minute instructions, and to go over the zirconium jewelry products she would be selling when the show aired in fifteen minutes. Her dress had been chosen with the brilliant gems in mind.

After a brief orientation, she walked down to the open sets on the floor below the control booths that rimmed the circumference of an open area the size of a football field. Above the many stages to showcase the products offered for sale over the television network was a ceiling of lighting equipment. The cameramen were ready to go when Carolyn arrived, as were the other floor technicians. Her props—black or red velvet backdrops to showcase the rings, bracelets, earrings and necklaces—were all in place.

Carolyn sat down on a scarlet overstuffed chair, a mahogany coffee table in front of her, and made sure that her yellow card prompt was within easy vision, as was the in-house TV screen. She placed her audio receiver in her ear, hidden from the camera by her hair. She was ready with minutes to spare.

"Hey, Carolyn." Roberta's voice sounded in her ear. "A quick reminder to stop by my office when you finish the show." A pause. "Just nod if you got my message. I'm above you in the control room."

Carolyn nodded just as the stage lights snapped on, followed by the sixty-second warning light. The set went quiet as everyone waited for the start of the show.

Once the program began Carolyn forgot everything else to concentrate on the product. As she demonstrated the jewelry pieces, twisting her fingers and wrists so the gems caught the light, she chatted with the customers who'd called in to order. She was also aware of her prompts beyond the camera's eye, cues that helped her keep the sales pitch going. She knew from the order numbers on her screen that the line was selling out fast.

The final call came from one of her regulars, a woman named Grace in Denver who ordered solitaire earrings and a matching bracelet. Between deciding which pieces she wanted, Grace updated Carolyn about her life, typical conversation from a customer.

"Nice visiting with you, Carolyn," she said after they'd chatted. "One last thing. How's Dean doing on his school project, you know, the one where he interviewed you, his famous aunt, about your likes and dislikes?" She laughed. "According to what you said, it was quite a list of things."

"Oh, thanks for reminding me, Grace." Carolyn knew the woman was talking about an earlier conversation they'd had on the air. Grace's daughter was Dean's age and Carolyn had mentioned his class assignment when Grace ordered a scrapbook kit for her child's homework. "I needed to call Dean back to answer some last-minute questions—and I almost forgot."

She laughed, glancing at the television monitor near the cameramen. For a moment she marveled that the animated woman many people described as beautiful, was really her. From the time she could remember, even her dad had complimented her beauty, calling her his little Miss America when she was a child. Carolyn accepted her looks, just as she knew they weren't the magic formula for happiness, a character balance her father had approved.

"I'll give my nephew a call when I finish up for the day," she told Grace.

Several minutes later Carolyn concluded the show and the camera was switched off. For a moment longer she sat in the overstuffed chair, relieved as the hot stage lights went out. Sighing, she relinquished the mental control she'd needed to process the barrage of information from the prompts while presenting a chatting, casual presence to her viewers. Then she stood up, pulled out the ear device and hurried to exit the soundstage, headed toward Roberta's office in the corporate wing of NNN.

"Come in." Roberta glanced up from her computer keyboard as Carolyn poked her head into a room piled high with possible product proposals, files and correspondence. She grinned, tossing her pen aside. "Good show. We sold out and were taking back orders for the final half hour."

"Great." Carolyn tucked a strand of hair behind her ear, unconcerned if she messed up the beautician's work. She was off camera for the rest of the day. "I felt it went well—fast paced, no time to take a deep breath."

Roberta raised black tweezed brows into an even higher arch. "You always do well, my friend." She shook her head, and her tight curls bounced like elasticized springs.

"Thanks. My customers make it easy."

"No, you make it easy, Carolyn. They talk to you like you're their personal friend, because you remember their names and share pieces of your own life with them."

"In a way they are my friends. Some of them order on a weekly basis."

A half smile pulled at the corners of Roberta's full lips. "Exactly. They love your enthusiasm and openness. But then that's why you're our star, not me."

"Oh, c'mon, Roberta. There's a bit of luck in the equation." She hesitated. "But I appreciate the compliment."

"Well deserved. You have an irrepressible zest for everything, and we love that quality at NNN."

Little do you know, Carolyn thought. Roberta was describing the person she was before Betsy and her father died, the facade she'd maintained over the past several years to hide her feelings of loss.

But seeming upbeat had helped her get on with her life, she reminded herself. She just hoped that repressed feelings weren't the reason she'd been overreacting lately, that the day would come when the facade would be her reality again.

"So, I thought you were the person to take home this line of makeup, see what you think of it and then report back to me." She paused. "That's why I postponed the meeting this morning, until I had your feedback."

Carolyn's thoughts were jerked back to the conversation, noticing the makeup case on the desk for the first time. "Uh, of course. You know I always evaluate a product before I try to sell it." She tilted her head. "Besides, isn't that NNN's policy?"

"Course it is, but this is a new line and not a slam dunk like others we handle, even though it carries the name of KAY, after the famous model. We want to see if it takes off before we agree to a long-term contract—such as we have with vendors like Lilly Lawton."

"Sounds like a good business decision."

"So, if everything goes well, NNN wants you as the hostess to launch the product." She closed the lid on the elegantly designed box and slid it across the desk toward Carolyn. "That'll mean we'll need to schedule a time slot and get it into the monthly program. I'll need your report in a couple of days, which should give you enough time to know if you like it or not."

"Yeah. If I'm gonna break out in a rash it'll be long before that."

They both laughed as Carolyn picked up the makeup kit and moved toward the door. She opened it and started through the doorway, but her glance had returned to Roberta for a final good-bye.

The barrier she walked into was unexpected, taking her breath. Her lashes flew up and her startled glance was caught by the dark brown eyes of the man she'd crashed into, whose arms now steadied her against his chest.

"I'm so sorry—"

"I'm not." His voice, deep and assured, interrupted her apology. "I can't believe my luck. I'm holding Carolyn Langdon in my arms."

Carolyn stepped back, pink-cheeked with embarrassment. She sensed his amusement by the slow crinkling at the corners of his eyes.

Roberta had come around her desk, her gaze darting between them. "I see you know Carolyn, Mr. Crawford."

"Who doesn't?" His smile reached his mouth, revealing slightly crooked teeth that contrasted with his dark complexion. "She's a national phenomenon."

"Carolyn, this is Richard Crawford, a possible vendor for NNN." Roberta's tone was dry, as though she was amused by the situation.

"Nice to meet you, Mr. Crawford." Carolyn managed to sound composed.

He inclined his head, his eyes still on her face, disconcerting her again.

With a final smile Carolyn stepped past him and closed the door behind her.

Almost by rote she scooted down the hall to the elevators, feeling absurdly flustered. There'd definitely been something about that man.

But she didn't have time to waste daydreaming; she had to call Dean back and leave a message for when he got home from school. She'd pretty much decided that he was the only male she wanted in her life anyway.

4

"**P**ardon me, aren't you Carolyn Langdon?"

Carolyn turned to the couple behind her at the bar of the Italian restaurant where she was to meet Minnie and Barney McGill, who were both late. She smiled, nodding.

"I am," she said.

"I knew it—I just knew it." The heavyset young woman turned to the slight man who was obviously her husband. "See, I told you I was right."

He fingered his long mustache, looking embarrassed by his wife's enthusiasm. "Pleased to meet you, Miss Langdon." He adjusted his glasses on a nose too thin to secure them. "Have to say, my wife has our whole house decorated with NNN special deals, all bought from you." He hesitated, uncertain. "Sorry if we've intruded. I'm Phil and this is my wife, Nina."

Carolyn went into her professional NNN mode, smiling broader. "I'm happy to meet you both. And you're not intruding at all. I'm just killing time until my party arrives." She held up the glass of Chardonnay she'd just bought. "Having some wine while I wait."

There you go again, she told herself. Too many words, revealing pieces of your personal life. But the couple beamed at her, obviously pleased by her attention.

"Like Phil said, we're sorry to bother you Carolyn, uh, Miss Langdon. It's just that I tune in every day to watch you on NNN and I feel that I know you." She grinned wider, revealing small, square teeth. "I cried when I read the article about you in that woman's magazine—that you'd lost your father after already having so many other troubles." She clucked her tongue. "How sad. I guess I just wanted you to know how very much I enjoy watching you. I feel like part of your family."

Carolyn only nodded, taken aback by Nina's sincere explanation, and a little uneasy as well. These people knew so much about her. She felt her stomach tightening and forced herself to relax, remembering that her viewers identified with her, tuned in to share their lives, expecting to hear bits of hers. They were by and large friends and genuinely sorry for her troubles, but she was starting to fear that between what she'd shared on the air, and what had been written about her in national publications, too much of her personal history had been made public.

"Oh, could I ask one more question?" Nina asked.

"Sure." Carolyn felt as though her smile was cracking. "Although I can't promise that I'll be able to answer it."

Nina seemed confident. "Isn't the velvet dress you're wearing the same one you wore this afternoon on your program that modeled the Alice Benson line?"

"You *do* watch, Nina." Carolyn glanced down at the emerald green, long-sleeved sheath dress, a favorite. "Yes, it is. One of the perks of my job is that I can keep the clothes I wear on the air."

"It looks great," Phil said, admiringly, then turned to his wife. "Maybe you should have ordered one."

"I did," Nina said. She winked at Carolyn, as if to say thanks for the endorsement, that it'd given her the courage to confess to one more NNN order.

Carolyn made small talk and then her excuses. Taking her wine with her, she left the bar and went back into the restaurant. After leaving instructions with the hostess to seat her guests when they arrived, Carolyn was escorted to their reserved table. Once settled, her coat and handbag on an extra chair, she sipped her wine and stared at the nearby fireplace where a fire took the winter chill from the room and added a cheerful ambience.

Deep in thought, and lost in the Italian music that was playing on the PA system, Carolyn marveled that many of her viewing couples had solid relationships, unlike her own former marriage. She was pricked with a sense of loss, and with her gaze fixed beyond her present reality in the restaurant, she didn't see Barney arrive.

He stood silently beside the table until she noticed him. For a moment neither of them spoke, as if he were giving her time to shift mental gears. An expression of—of what? Sympathy? Understanding?—

flickered on his face and was gone. Then he grinned, took off his black leather jacket and draped it over the back of a chair before he sat down across from her.

"Sorry if I've kept you waiting." The serious look in his pale eyes belied his light tone of voice.

"It's fine. I was only a few minutes ahead of you." She smiled, sensing that he was upset over something. "Besides, Minnie's late, too."

"Hope her delay isn't as unfortunate as mine." He glanced at her wine. "I could use one of those."

"Hard day?"

"Yeah, I guess you could say that." He motioned to a waiter. "Some guy went the mile in a domestic disturbance." He shook his head and the light from their table candle flickered over his craggy features, casting them into harsh lines.

She leaned forward. "And?"

There was a long silence.

"He shot his wife, then turned the gun on himself."

"They're . . . dead?"

He nodded, grimly. "They left two little kids behind who have now joined the ranks of orphans."

"Oh, God." Carolyn's words rushed out of her mouth in a shocked whisper. She knew Barney investigated murder cases, had seen him on television news when there had been a high-profile homicide in the city. But hearing about it firsthand was somehow more horrifying. She couldn't imagine what it would be like to actually see the death scene.

Barney turned away as the waiter approached and ordered a glass of Merlot. "We're not ready to order," he told the young man. "Still waiting for another person to join us."

The waiter inclined his head. "I'll just bring the Merlot for now and check back later."

"It's hard to understand why some people can go that far," Barney went on as the waiter left.

"Do the kids have a place to go?"

"The grandparents, mother's folks, are taking them."

Carolyn swirled the wine in her glass. "What a tragedy."

"Uh-huh . . . and then some."

Another silence dropped between them. Then the waiter was back with Barney's Merlot.

"A toast?" he asked when the waiter had moved on.

She nodded.

"To happier times for those kids . . . and for all of us," he said, raising his glass.

"Cheers."

They sipped, and Carolyn wondered if the second half of his toast referred to his own personal loss. Barney was able to discuss the tragedy he encountered in his work, but she'd never heard him talk about his dead family. Maybe the scar went too deep for words, she thought. Or maybe he was like Rob, who'd just shut everyone out of his grief. That was a little different, she supposed. After all, she wasn't Barney's wife, but she had the feeling that it wouldn't matter if she were. She sensed a distance in him and that was something she never wanted again in a relationship.

"Another toast," Barney said, holding up his glass

again. "For the color green. Anyone ever tell you that your dress matches your eyes?"

She nodded, uneasy with the flirtatious undercurrent. They toasted a second time.

Then the cell phone rang in Carolyn's purse, saving her from a reply to his unexpected comment. She'd forgotten to turn it off, her habit when she was in a restaurant. Shrugging an apology to Barney, she answered.

"Hello?"

"Carolyn, I'm so sorry I can't make it." Minnie's voice sounded in her ear. "I can't leave work. One of the counselors came down with the stomach flu and there's no one to take over her drug rehab session tonight except me. It's part of the program so we can't postpone it." A pause. "The court wouldn't take it kindly if we did."

"Minnie, it's fine. I took a rain check last week from you. It's your turn to postpone. We can try for next week instead. Okay?"

"What about Barney? I wasn't able to call him."

"He's right here, sitting across the table from me."

"Will you tell him what happened?"

"Of course."

"Thanks. I'll call you later. I've got to run."

"What was that all about?" Barney asked as she put her phone away.

Carolyn explained.

"Sure, we can all make it another night." A pause. "But you and I have to eat anyway." His light blue eyes seemed silver in the candlelight. "How about us ordering?"

She grinned, lightening the mood. "So glad you asked. I'm starving."

It was the first time she'd ever seen him laugh wide enough to expose his teeth, and she suddenly wondered how she could ever have thought him less than an extremely attractive man. One of those guys who was transformed from rugged looking to handsome by a smile.

"Me, too." He motioned to the waiter.

They both ordered the pasta and seafood special and a second glass of wine. The conversation had turned to happier topics: his childhood years with an Irish father and an Italian mother, hers growing up with only one parent, a father who'd been one of the most influential men in Atlanta. The evening passed pleasantly and they'd just finished after-dinner coffee when Barney's pager went off.

"Hmm," he said, glancing at the message. "As Joe Friday used to say on those old TV reruns, 'the city never sleeps.' "

"Aren't you going to call back?" Carolyn had pulled her wallet out of her purse and then reached for her cell phone to offer Barney. "You're welcome to use it."

"Thanks anyway, Carolyn. I'll call from my car."

She started to put two twenties down on the bill and he pushed her hand away. "This one's on me."

"Minnie and I always go Dutch—"

He flashed his smile. "I insist."

She put her money away, then stood to put on her long black coat and gloves. As they walked toward the front entrance he offered to see her to her car.

"No need. I have valet parking." She hesitated, smiling. "But thanks for offering."

They paused in front of the restaurant to say their good-byes. Abruptly, he dropped a kiss on her forehead, stepped back to give her a salute of thanks, and then strode off down the street. She handed the valet her car check, her eyes still following Barney's tall, lanky figure until he disappeared around a corner. Their time together had been surprisingly pleasant, although she'd noticed how he still avoided the topic of his deceased wife and kids.

"I can't believe my luck," a vaguely familiar male voice said from behind her, diverting her thoughts. "I come to a boring business meeting and meet Carolyn Langdon."

She turned, expecting to see another fan. Instead her gaze was caught by dark eyes that were already crinkling at the corners in anticipation of a smile.

"Richard, uh—" Her own smile was instantaneous. "I'm sorry I can't remember your last name. You're the man I bumped into as I was leaving Roberta's office."

"Uh-huh." He clucked his tongue. "I'm deflated. Forgotten so soon." His charming manner was so contagious that Carolyn laughed out loud.

"Uh, Crawford, isn't it?" she asked, suddenly remembering.

His gaze was warm with humor . . . and admiration. "That's right."

There was a silence as Carolyn considered what to say next. Richard Crawford was even more attractive than she remembered from their brief encounter at NNN. Although he was tall, maybe six feet, he wasn't as big a man as Barney was, or as intense. But he seemed dynamic in his own way, with a certain openness that Barney lacked.

"I could also make an extravagant comment," she said, finally. "Like you're unforgettable but—"

He grinned, interrupting. "But . . . it'd be a little white lie?"

"Goodness! I'd hate to get a reputation for telling lies. It'd be bad for my business." The wind had come up and Carolyn could smell rain in the air. "And I'm a professional saleswoman, Mr. Crawford."

"Richard."

She nodded. "Richard."

"That's better . . . may I call you Carolyn?"

"Of course. Everyone does."

Another pause, this time on his part. Then she saw his smile starting again.

"I didn't mean like all of your customers and fans. I was thinking more along the lines of friends, perhaps work associates." He hesitated, watching her face for a reaction. "As Roberta Singleton mentioned, I might become one of NNN's vendors."

"Then we would indeed be work associates. Have you heard one way or the other yet?"

He shook his head. "But I understand these things take time. NNN is very careful about what they choose to market, as they should be."

"That's very true. The company stands behind what they sell, because they believe in the product, a must for anything they handle."

"The very reason I want to be one of the lucky vendors."

"You know, Richard, I don't know what your product is."

"I'd love to explain, but it'd take too long right now when it's about to rain and the arrival of your car is imminent." He glanced at his watch. "Not to mention I'm already late for my meeting." A pause. "But I'd love to explain my product to you. Maybe we can have drinks one evening?"

"Maybe so," she said. Privately she doubted it. It might not be appropriate until after NNN made its decision.

"I'll see you at the studio in any case," he said.

Then, after a final wave of his hand, he strode into the restaurant for his business meeting. By the time the Volvo arrived a couple of minutes later it had started to rain. She slipped behind the wheel, her thoughts still on Richard Crawford. She would like to have drinks with him, she decided, get to know him better, see if her first impression of a friendly, open man was accurate. But was he married? She hadn't noticed a ring.

Go ahead, admit it, girl. Richard Crawford is a sexy man and you're attracted to him.

As long as he wasn't married.

5

Carolyn drove up the long driveway from the street, her eyes on the white, three-story mansion with its columned entrance, her family home until she went away to college. She loved the neighborhood of stately estates such as the governor's mansion, and Swan House that dated from 1929 and was now a part of the Atlanta History Center. Oh, to bring back those golden years while growing up, she thought, steering the Volvo into the half circle next to the front steps of the house.

About to switch off her headlights and wipers she paused, staring at the illuminated oak, magnolia, and pine trees lining the approach. They, and the shrubs, all glistening from the rain, had been invaded by the kudzu vine, a pointed leaf parasite that her dad's gardener never would have allowed on the property. The dreaded kudzu, if left to flourish, would smother every growing plant and bush. But Dolores had let the gardener go a few months ago and no one took care of the yard now.

Carolyn had noticed the overall neglect before but hadn't said anything. The Buckhead mansion was a sore subject for Dolores. The property had been in the Langdon family for three generations, and her dad had left it to Carolyn instead of to his wife, along with the assets he'd owned prior to marrying Dolores. Her father had worried that Dolores would squander Carolyn's birthright; her own daughter, Jessie, and husband Tony, were constantly in need of money. Although the will allowed Dolores to live there until she died or remarried, Carolyn sensed a little resentment.

Was she letting the lawn and flower beds go on purpose? she wondered, then dismissed the thought as silly. Dolores had always treated her like family. Her feelings had been hurt over the house, that's all, even though she'd inherited a sizable fortune herself, including the Lake Lanier cottage, an investment portfolio, and the law firm share which she'd sold to Tom. Dolores could afford to keep the place in top shape.

I'll have to mention the grounds problem before it gets much worse, Carolyn decided, hating the prospect. As she locked the Volvo and ran through the rain for the front door, a face-saving solution for everyone popped into her mind. She could point out that, as the property owner, the maintenance was her responsibility, maybe even apologize for letting things go. But she'd have to broach the subject carefully, so that Dolores wouldn't feel offended or chastised about the encroachment of the kudzu vine. The original deal had promised Dolores free rent in exchange for reasonable upkeep. For whatever reason, Dolores wasn't keeping the bargain.

Maybe I should sign the place over to her, restore family harmony, she thought, but dismissed the idea almost immediately. For a while she'd believed she'd never want another child, but when she considered giving up the house, she felt oddly reluctant. She might have a child someday who would inherit the house. That might have been the reason she'd resisted an impulse to forgo her rights after the lawyer had read the will.

Carolyn pressed the doorbell, hearing the sound resonate within the house. She smiled, reminded of earlier times. A succession of mental images surfaced: the days after her mother's death when her dad would hold her in his arms and cry, the years when their home was the meeting place for most of the philanthropic organizations in Atlanta, and after her father's marriage, when Dolores ran the Buckhead household.

The place has an interesting history, she thought. Although the five-acre property was valued at a million dollars, Carolyn knew she'd never sell it, not when she still hoped for marriage and other children. In the unlikely event of her death the house reverted to Dolores. If both she and Dolores died, it went to Carolyn's husband, and if she wasn't married, then to Dolores's daughter, Jessie.

Again, she rang the bell, another subtle change in her life after the advent of Dolores; Carolyn no longer walked in the door without knocking. After returning from college she'd no longer felt comfortable in the family home that had become Dolores's domain.

Stepping back, Carolyn glanced up to the second floor porch under the two-story roof of the huge portico, following the wood railing around its perimeter to the long windows on both sides, and her old bedroom on the right. The charcoal shutters were a startling contrast to the brilliant white of the clapboard siding. No light shown from her old room, now redecorated into a guest room.

The door opened abruptly, bringing her thoughts back to the present. Dean stood framed by the light that spilled onto the porch from the entrance hall. Instantly, his small face lit up with pleasure.

"Aunt Carolyn. You made it. I didn't think you would just to read my school assignment before I turned it in." He hesitated. "Especially since I kept bugging you for more information while I was writing it."

"Of course I was going to make it, even though I suspect that it's almost your bedtime." She hugged him, and didn't mention that she'd almost forgotten because her thoughts had been on Richard Crawford as she'd driven away from the restaurant. But she'd remembered in time to alter her route to the Buckhead area.

They went into the house and Dean closed the door. Carolyn followed him past the huge curved staircase, and thought she was probably the last person to slide down the banister. Dean wasn't a child who did such things.

"Do you mind being in the kitchen?" he asked over his shoulder. "I'm still doing homework on the table."

"Course not. It's where I used to do mine."

He shot her a glance, his bright blue eyes dancing with sudden humor. "My grandmother thinks it's the best place to spread out without hurting the good furniture in the dining room or living room." He shrugged. "You know my grandmother—she doesn't want anyone mussing up her house." The fondness in his tone canceled any censure from his words.

"Where is your grandmother? Upstairs?"

Carolyn knew from her own experience when she was a college kid how particular Dolores was about her house, even though all of the work was done by hired help. She also knew that Dolores loved Dean, and like tonight, had him stay with her when Jessie was working overtime or had to be away from home. No one counted on Tony who was often absent from his household.

Dean shook his head, and the light from the crystal chandelier above them burnished his red hair with fire. "No, she had to go over to my house with a heating pad and some other stuff 'cause my dad strained his back at work." He hesitated. "I would have gone home but you were coming here, and as Grandma said, eleven is old enough to stay alone for a little while."

They'd passed the high archways to the large formal rooms and the den, and moved through the open kitchen door at the end of the hall. The layout of the Buckhead house was very similar to the much smaller floor plan of her townhouse, another reason she'd loved her place at first sight.

"How on earth did your dad hurt himself selling insurance?"

"Dunno for sure. My mom told Grandma that he

was reaching for a file on a top shelf." Dean sat down at the table, then glanced up at Carolyn, his concern as evident on his pale face as the freckles that covered his nose and cheeks. "Sometimes it doesn't take much 'cause my dad has a bad back to begin with."

"Uh-huh, and I'm sure he'll be just fine in no time at all."

Carolyn pulled up a chair and sat down across the table from Dean, reassuring him, pointing out that if it had been really serious his dad would have been taken to the hospital.

"You think so, Aunt Carolyn?"

"Of course."

"That's what my grandmother said, too." He wiped a red curl from his forehead. "It's why she had me stay even though my dad was home, because she said he was okay, just needed the heating pad and some ointment that helps pain."

He visibly relaxed and Carolyn realized why Dolores had made a special trip. Jessie probably didn't have the money to buy the anti-inflammatory prescription at the drugstore. Because Dolores loved her red-haired daughter and grandson she always came to their rescue. In a similar situation I'd probably do the same, Carolyn thought.

"She'll be back soon 'cause she left two hours ago."

"I'll wait until she gets here then."

Carolyn was thoughtful as Dean leafed though his notebook for the class assignment he'd written about her. Jessie and Tony seemed to have consistent bad luck, were always behind on their bills and often borrowed money from Dolores. Although Jessie was hardworking and had a good-paying administrative assistant position, they couldn't make ends meet on her job alone. When Tony was out of work because of his back it often fell on Dolores to pick up the slack. Dolores resented Tony almost as much as Jessie loved him. Secretly, Carolyn sided with Dolores, because she suspected that Tony was a fraud. But since he was a good dad and Dean loved him, Carolyn forgave some of his failings.

Dean handed her his composition and Carolyn spent the next couple of minutes reading it. She was impressed. Dean had done an excellent job, not only in assembling the facts, but in the writing itself.

"What do you think?" He sounded anxious. "Is it okay?"

"Hmmm?" She glanced up.

"I mean, uh, do you like it?"

"It's wonderful, Dean. I hadn't realized you were such a good writer."

"Really?"

"Uh-huh. This is excellent. I'll be shocked if you don't get an A on this project."

He beamed, his face turning pink with pleasure. "You aren't just saying that, are you? You know, 'cause I'm your nephew and you love me."

"I really mean it, sweetie. This is terrific work."

He lowered his eyes. "Can you keep a secret, Aunt Carolyn?"

He glanced up, catching her nod.

"I'm going to be a writer when I grow up. I've been writing stories on the computer you gave me for Christmas."

"That's wonderful, Dean." Carolyn managed a smile, hiding her reservations. She'd meant to broaden his interests, and was pleased that he loved having a computer almost as much as Dolores who spent hours on hers each day. Dean had become the family technology expert, but he was also such a solitary boy that it worried her. She'd hoped that being on the Internet would help him interact with kids his own age. Instead it sounded as though he was becoming even more isolated. Jessie was too busy working to address the problem, and Tony pleaded health reasons for not being involved with Dean in sports and school activities.

They were still discussing Dean's writing a few minutes later when Dolores arrived, pulling off her leather gloves as she came into the kitchen.

"Sounds like you love what Dean's written, Carolyn," she said, grinning. "It's really good, isn't it?"

"Yeah, I'm impressed. I hadn't realized Dean was so talented."

She watched as Dolores bent and kissed Dean's freckled cheek. Her fifty-seven-year-old stepmother was an attractive woman, shapely if a bit on the stout side, her ash blond hair and blue eyes still her best features. Carolyn liked Dolores, understood that her penchant for shopping, beauty aids, and security stemmed from growing up poor out in Macon. Dean had confided that his grandmother was looking for another husband, was in regular E-mail correspondence with several men. Carolyn wasn't offended by how quickly she'd begun to look for another man. Dolores *had* loved her dad, but feared being poor again and having to do office work, like Jessie. Somewhere Carolyn had read that it was the happily married person who remarried quickly after the death of a spouse.

"How about a cup of tea?" Dolores asked. She put her handbag and coat on a chair and went to fill the tea kettle.

"Thanks, but I'd better get going," Carolyn said, standing. "It's been a long day and I have an early show in the morning."

As if to punctuate her refusal the mantel clock in the living room struck nine just as they stepped into the hall. After good-byes and Dean's promise to let her know after his paper had been graded, Carolyn went back into the night. Dolores and Dean waved from the doorway as she got into her car and started the engine.

She gave a light honk of the horn as she steered around the half moon of the driveway, her lights sliding over Dolores's late model Buick sedan. For a second her heart jolted.

Then she laughed at herself. Just goes to show, she told herself. Every other person in Georgia drives a dark sedan.

But the reminder of that other car was not a welcome thought as she drove home alone on a dark rainy night.

The next morning Carolyn arrived at the studio before seven, and was dressed, groomed and ready for her nine o'clock program. Today she was launching the line of cosmetics endorsed by the internationally renowned model, Kay. She had been using the samples Roberta had given her far past the usual several

days NNN recommended its sales hostesses to test
makeup, creams and lotions. And she'd fallen in
love with the whole line.

Kay, as she was known to her fans around the
world, arrived early, a six-foot tall, thin-to-the-point-
of-gauntness blonde who was the most beautiful
woman Carolyn had ever met. She was even more
gorgeous than any of her magazine cover photos
that emphasized her long hair, huge violet eyes and
wide, perfect smile. Carolyn was instantly drawn to
Kay's warm, down-to-earth personality. They got
acquainted, discussed the products, and were both
seated on the set, an elegant sitting room created by
NNN's carpenters, when the cameras began to roll.

The hour melted away and Carolyn knew from
the monitor that sales were fantastic. She'd endorsed
the makeup, demonstrating each item separately as
Kay explained why the viewers would benefit from
trying them. As the program wound down Carolyn
added a bonus sales pitch, one that had been approved by her bosses.

"Many of you know that NNN often donates
demo products used on our programs to worthy organizations here in Atlanta." Carolyn indicated Kay
as she went on. "Kay has generously donated some
of her line to a local shelter for battered women, in
the hope that women who are trying to get on their
feet will benefit from—" Carolyn smiled into the
camera—"feeling as good about themselves as both
Kay and I do using this wonderful makeup."

"And let me add that I'm delighted to help," Kay
said in her soft voice. "Once, long before I was successful, I, too, needed a hand up."

The program ended, the overhead lights went dark and Roberta spoke in Carolyn's ear mike. "After Kay leaves come up to my office." A hesitation. "And Carolyn, the show was a huge success, the phones are still ringing with orders."

A short time later after Kay, flushed with success, was led away by one of the company executives, Carolyn headed for Roberta's office.

"Hey, my girl, you did great!" Roberta said as Carolyn stepped into the room. "We sold out, and I've just heard that NNN will probably sign a contract for at least another show or two for the KAY line. Probably longer term after that if the makeup stands up with our customers."

"And they don't break out in a rash?" Carolyn asked, deadpanning.

There was a brief silence.

"Jeez, Carolyn, for a second I thought you were serious."

Carolyn grinned. "Seriously, I'm glad it went so well because I love the product, and I really like Kay. She's a regular person behind the glamour and glitz."

"And I noticed that Kay explained on the air that her line was hypoallergenic, but people with severe allergies should always test a product before using it."

Carolyn nodded. "That it?"

"Yeah, I think so."

"Good. Gotta run," Carolyn said. "I've got another segment coming up." She glanced at her watch. "In less than an hour."

She was opening the door when Roberta's next words stopped her.

"Uh . . . hate to put a damper on our recent success but—we had a rash of crank calls right after you mentioned the shelter donation on the air."

"And?" Carolyn's hand tightened on the knob.

"The caller—I think it was five calls—said the same thing each time and then immediately hung up."

"Which was?"

"A threat."

"From whom?"

"A person who said they'd been watching you. That's why the operators took it seriously—this person had called previously, and probably before anyone took the calls seriously. We don't know."

"What kind of threats?"

A silence went by.

"He said abused women aren't abused. They get what they deserve, just as Carolyn Langdon will get what she deserves."

"Shit!" A shiver of fear rippled down Carolyn's spine. "There was another caller who—"

"I know," Roberta said, interrupting. "The one I told you about on your cell phone, the same night you reported to the guard that someone had ransacked your car but didn't steal anything." Roberta stood up, dropping her pen on the desk. "That's why I'm telling you this, Carolyn. This person appears to be more persistent than most crank callers."

"You think he's a real threat?"

"Course not," Roberta retorted quickly—too quickly. "I'm sure he's just a wacko. Unfortunately there are lots of them in the world. Don't worry about it. They always move on eventually."

"I'm not worried," Carolyn said, faking. "I expect

that anyone who has their face on the tube as often as I do can expect a nut case from time to time."

But as she headed back to work Carolyn realized that she *was* concerned, especially when she thought about that last crank call Roberta had mentioned on her cell phone—the night she'd been so spooked.

Someone was watching her.

A creepy thought to think that hidden eyes were focused on her.

Maybe the calls were all random events, not the same person at all.

Somehow, she doubted it.

6

Carolyn sat forward on the chair, staring into the lens of the camera, knowing that it pictured her every gesture and expression. She listened to Audrey, a regular customer, chat about down comforters, one of the items from the bedding line on sale. Momentarily, Carolyn's mind shifted to her other million viewers. Was the watcher out there right now, looking back at her through the eye of the camera?

She gave herself a mental shake, and tried not to flash on her earlier conversation with Roberta. The wacko caller was probably looking for attention and wasn't a real threat, she reminded herself. Attracting a few oddballs was part of being a television salesperson.

"Carolyn, does NNN still have you travel abroad to evaluate possible products?" Audrey's direct question was an abrupt change of subject, bringing Carolyn from her momentary lapse back to her customer. "I remember when you went to Sweden to check out stainless steel utensils shortly after your divorce, and Switzerland to look at cotton undergarments a couple of months before your father passed away."

Carolyn managed a laugh, hiding her feelings. "Those trips were a few years ago, Audrey." A pause. "But, yes, I do still travel some for NNN."

"Have you been on one of those trips recently?" Audrey, who'd just ordered a feather bed and down comforter for her bedroom somewhere in Kansas, insisted on details.

"Not lately." Carolyn smiled brightly for the camera. Although she'd revealed too many everyday incidents about herself on the air in the past, it was the national magazine and tabloid articles that had sensationalized her whole life in recent months—so that people like Audrey knew details they ordinarily wouldn't have known.

"But soon I hope?" Audrey's tone was insistent.

Carolyn knew that Audrey meant well, probably didn't realize that business travel and vacations were two different things. "Well, I'm flying up to Toronto for the weekend," she said finally, hoping to end the questions.

"Ah, Toronto," Audrey replied. "What's the new product?"

"Well, Audrey, I can't say at this point."

"Okay, I get it." Audrey laughed, as though she'd finally realized she was being pushy. "You can't say until NNN decides to handle it."

"Something like that. And as always, the viewers will be the first to know when that happens."

Her camera persona restored, Carolyn changed the subject back to bedding and the program.

"I'll look forward to a Toronto update on Monday," Audrey said, and after a friendly good-bye, hung up.

A few minutes later the segment ended and the stage went dark. Carolyn stood, pulling out her ear mike. As the crewmen left the set she lingered, uneasy. She'd just told the world that she'd be gone for the weekend.

So what, she thought, forcing herself to shift gears to her next segment on kitchen gadgets in an hour. None of her viewers knew where she lived.

No one cared.

"Hey, kitties." Carolyn called to her cats as she came into the house from the garage. She was exhausted. It was already nine and she still had to pack her suitcase before going to bed. A glance at her answering machine told her that the red light was blinking, meaning she had messages. Hell with it for now. She'd check them after her shower. She wasn't expecting any special calls.

Mustard and Mayo sauntered into the kitchen from the family room to greet her. She talked to them while she dumped food into their dishes and refilled the water bowl.

"Don't like that damn computer class. It's turned my mind to mush," Carolyn told them. "Your mom doesn't have an aptitude for hardware, software and surfing the Net." She straightened up. "You kitties don't know how good you have it—sleeping, playing and eating all day."

It had been a long day. No, a long week, she corrected herself. She and Minnie had grabbed a bite to eat before heading to their first computer class, free instruction from the dealers who'd sold the system to Anderson Youth House. Driving home just now she'd decided to leave the high tech stuff to those who liked it, like Minnie and Dean. For now she was satisfied with word processing and sending E-mails.

"I'll tell Minnie I'm quitting the class after I get back from Toronto," she promised herself. Besides, her schedule was already too full with work and other commitments. It was like the plaque above her own computer in the family room said, "It's a violence to your soul to say yes to things when you should have said no."

She headed upstairs, grinning at her rationalization. When the phone rang several minutes later, Carolyn answered the call in her bedroom. Recognizing Tom Harrison's voice she berated herself. For God's sake, why hadn't she let her machine pick up?

Because your mind is mush, remember?

"Hello, Tom," she said, again. Only a fool would miss the sudden flatness in her tone.

"Hi there, Carolyn." He had one of those deep male voices that reminded her of sexy leading men in the movies. But his sex appeal was a thing of the past as far as she was concerned. "So glad I finally caught you," he went on, ignoring her chilly response. "Been trying to reach you for days now."

"Sorry about that. I've been extremely busy and haven't been here much."

"I left a message on your voice mail earlier." He chuckled. "So you probably know why I'm calling."

"As a matter of fact I just came in and haven't checked my messages yet."

What in hell did he want now? she wondered. Why wouldn't he take no for an answer? She traced the flower pattern on her bedspread. He wanted something from her, that had to be it. But what? He'd already taken over her dad's law firm.

"I'd like to take you out for dinner on Saturday night." A pause. "I have 9:30 reservations at Nikolai's Roof, so we'll have quiet, pleasant surroundings to talk, uh, about us."

A silence went by.

"I'm sorry, Tom. I'm going out of town in the morning and won't return until Sunday night."

There was a hesitation.

"I'm sorry to hear you can't make it," he began, his tone soothing, as though he was controlling his own disappointment. "But how about the following Saturday night then? I'll change the reservation."

"I don't have my calendar in front of me but I think I might already have something scheduled for that night."

"How about I call you back on Monday night, after you've had a chance to check your dates. You gonna be home?"

"Uh, yeah, I'll be here."

"Okay then. I'll talk to you the first of the week." Another hesitation. "And Carolyn, will you promise me one thing?"

She hesitated. "Guess that depends."

"Promise that you'll give my invitation some thought. For old time's sake if nothing else."

"Yes, I'll certainly give it some thought."

She deliberately did not thank him for calling, hoping to avoid being sucked back into the relationship in any way. Somehow his voice sounded condescending, not quite sincere. As they hung up she suddenly knew why he was inviting her out now, after all these months.

Carolyn plunked down on her bed, suddenly angry. Surely he wasn't pursuing her again because he'd realized that, although he now owned her dad's firm, he didn't have the prestige that went with it. She was willing to bet he'd lost many of her dad's old accounts. And what better way to regain their confidence than for him to reestablish his relationship with her.

And what about the woman she'd heard he was dating? Had they broken up? Or was she expendable in the face of Tom's ambition?

The hell with Tom. She headed for the shower, recognizing her grouchy mood. She wouldn't think about him now. Her answer on Monday night would be no. He'd never wanted to discuss her concerns after her father died and it was too late now. Shutting her out had been a death knell to their relationship; he'd never believed her when she'd told him, time and again, that a relationship had to be build on honesty and communication, not just exchanging telephone numbers, superficial trivia and house keys. The honest thing she could do for Tom was to avoid him.

The taxi ride home from the airport on Sunday night was long and hectic. A torrential rain storm was flooding the freeway, the windshield wipers kept stalling and the traffic had been stopped by a three-car accident. Upon reaching her townhouse, the driver carried her bag as they dashed to the front door. Carolyn paid him and he waited while she fumbled in her purse for her key, unlocked the door and opened it. He inclined his head, set down her suitcase on the Oriental rug in the hall, and then ran back through the downpour to his cab.

As she stepped farther into the entry both Mayo and Mustard came from the family room to greet her. Bending, she patted each one on the head, appreciating their affection for her. Although her trip had been successful, and the paintings she'd gone to see had been exquisite, she was happy to be home again. Carolyn intended to shower and get into a nightgown, then pour a glass of wine to sip while she watched the news. She'd wait until tomorrow to give Roberta her full report, but knew NNN would agree to exclusive rights to sell the limited run of prints. The artist had even agreed to fly down to appear on a two-hour TV segment.

"Hey," Carolyn asked the cats, walking them toward the kitchen. She'd left her suitcase in the hall to take upstairs after she'd checked their food and water dishes. "Did Thelma and Carl pamper you while I was gone?" She smiled, picturing the elderly couple next door. They loved it when she left Mayo and Mustard in their care. She'd often offered to do the same for their aging Sammy-dog, but her neighbors never went anywhere overnight.

She stepped into the kitchen and immediately noted that the cat dishes were still partly full. The Ashtons were dependable, if a little forgetful at times. Between them they remember everything, she told herself.

Gradually, she became aware that something was different. Glancing around she saw that the door from the laundry room to the garage was ajar. Why would either Thelma or Carl have opened it? There was nothing in there that they would have needed.

Quickly, she went to the door and peeked into the garage. Everything looked normal, so she closed it and flipped the bolt lock into place. She could've sworn it had been set when she left on Friday. Moving back into the kitchen she realized that something else was out of place. Dishes had been stacked in the sink—*clean dishes.*

Were her elderly neighbors losing it?

A finger of apprehension traced Carolyn's spine. Her tired brain went to full alert as her gaze scanned the room. A plant from the garden window above the sink now sat on the counter, and her oven light was on.

My God, how long had the oven been on? Turning it off, Carolyn couldn't remember the last time she'd used it.

Her gaze shifted to the key rack on the wall near the built-in desk in the breakfast nook. All of her extra keys hung in their correct slots: car keys, NNN keys and her one spare house key. Her neighbors had returned it today as promised.

She hurried into the family room. Again, little things were different: pillows moved, an afghan unfolded, a cup and saucer on an end table, as though someone had been sitting next to it. Her uneasiness grew, as did her annoyance with her neighbors with whom she'd entrusted her cats and her house. Thank God they hadn't let Mayo and Mustard escape.

The other downstairs rooms were not quite as she'd left them either. Nothing appeared gone, only disturbed, her things moved, just enough to let her know that someone had been there. She headed for the steps, wondering if Thelma and Carl had also gone upstairs. Her foot was on the bottom step, her eyes on the shadowy darkness of the upper floor when she hesitated, suddenly afraid.

What if the intruder hadn't been either of her neighbors?

The thought paralyzed her. Her chest felt as though it was swelling into her throat. For long seconds she could not go forward and she could not turn and run.

Wait, she instructed herself. No one has been in the house since you left but your cats and two old people. No one else has a key and the doors haven't been forced open. Nothing had been stolen, her cats were safe. In fact they seemed completely undisturbed. Didn't that indicate that no one was waiting for her upstairs?

Still she hesitated.

Stop acting like a coward—an alarmist. This is your house and there is no phantom trying to scare you.

With a burst of bravado she ran up the steps, glanced into the guest room which was undisturbed and then stepped into her bedroom and switched on the light.

The covers on her bed had been neatly turned down.

She went cold all over.

There had to be a rational explanation for what was happening. No one was in her house now, of that she was certain. It could only be the work of Thelma and Carl. Holding her terror in check, Carolyn went to the phone and called them. Thelma answered on the first ring.

First Carolyn thanked them for taking care of the cats. Then, tactfully, aware of hurting their feelings, she began to explain. "I just wondered if it was you who turned down my bed, who—"

"My dear, we never went upstairs," Thelma interrupted Carolyn, then covered her receiver to speak to Carl. After a momentary pause she spoke again. "We'll be right over, Carolyn. We can't imagine why anything was disturbed. It wasn't when we fed the cats this morning."

Carolyn dropped the phone, turned and flew down the stairs to the front door.

Someone had been in her house.

Who?

7

Carolyn's hand was on the knob when she realized that Thelma and Carl were already on her front porch. She took a deep breath, trying to calm herself, conscious that the Ashtons were in their early eighties, that she should not scare them by assuming someone else had been in her house.

She opened the door and her neighbors stepped into her entry hall. Thelma was short, round and had wavy gray hair and bright blue eyes, a woman who had once been the typical Southern beauty. Carl was a slight man who had a twinkle of humor in his hazel eyes, a retired bookkeeper who kept up with the stock market on his home computer, but who also asked Thelma the same question several times an hour. At the moment he looked concerned about Carolyn.

"My dear," Thelma said, frowning. "What's happened here?"

Carolyn forced a weak smile. She'd never felt so relieved to see another human being. "Follow me. You can see for yourselves."

As they walked through the rooms she pointed out the dishes in the kitchen sink, the plant that had been taken from the garden window to the counter, the cup and saucer, moved pillows and afghan in the family room. Upstairs she showed them the turned-down covers of her previously made bed.

"It's so strange." Carolyn shook her head, even more puzzled. "It's just dumb little things. Nothing's been stolen, none of the doors or windows were forced open, and there is no damage."

"My goodness." Thelma twisted her hands together nervously. "We didn't even go upstairs. And I don't remember dishes in the sink, or where the other things in the family room were, let alone if they were moved."

"And we don't know how anyone else could have gotten into your house," Carl said. "We left your key on the rack this morning, and made sure your door was locked on our way out."

"Does anyone else have a key, dear?" Thelma asked. "A family member perhaps?"

Thelma sounded composed but Carolyn sensed that she was nervous—as though she were hiding something. What? Had the key been out of her possession?—been left anywhere else but on their hall table as usual? Carolyn knew that they never locked their own front door while they walked Sammy each evening after supper. But then they were never gone for more than a few minutes.

"No one. I only have two keys to the front door. I kept one and you had the other." Carolyn didn't feel a need to mention that her father had once had a spare right after she moved in. But that key had been misplaced in his house and assumed lost long before he died. Tom had also had one, but had given it back; it was her extra that she'd given Thelma.

The faint sound of Sammy barking could be heard from the Ashton side of the house. Thelma turned to her husband, put her hand on his arm and spoke gently to him.

"Carl, maybe you should go be with Sammy. You know how upset he gets when we leave him alone in the house." She smiled, hopefully. "We don't want him chewing up the furniture."

Carl nodded. "Maybe I should. That little rascal is probably getting into all kinds of mischief already." His pale eyes shifted to Carolyn. "Everything appears to be fine here. No one's in your house, and I'm guessing that no one was." His false teeth clicked as he spoke. "Between the three of us, you leaving in a hurry, us going in and out—hell, we probably did those little things ourselves."

They watched him move slowly to the front door and step onto the porch. A minute later, Sammy stopped barking.

There was a silence as Thelma stood contemplating her wedding rings, twisting them around on her finger. Finally she started talking, her words hesitant.

"Would you mind if I sat down, Carolyn? There's something I need to share with you."

"Of course not." Carolyn again sensed that Thelma was in a dilemma. Her apprehension returned as her mind sifted through possibilities. Had Thelma seen someone in her house, but hesitated to talk about it in front of her frail husband? Had the

key been out of their possession? Had she let someone into Carolyn's house? With growing concern,
Carolyn led the way to the living room where they
both sat down.

"I don't really know how to begin, Carolyn, or if,
uh, I even should," Thelma said. Her upset was now
obvious in both her words and demeanor.

"Why not just say what's upsetting you," Carolyn
suggested. "I promise I won't blame you for anything that went amiss here." She hesitated. "I just
need to know what happened."

"I know you'll understand." She met Carolyn's
eyes. "You're too sweet to be angry with us." A
pause. "I just don't want to be disloyal to Carl. I love
him, have always respected his judgment and don't
want to discredit him in any way."

"Of course I know that, Thelma. You've always
been a devoted wife for as long as I've known you."

Her little neighbor sat stiffly, perched on the sofa
like a bird about to take flight. "It wouldn't be fair to
you if I didn't explain. I can't let you go to bed worried and scared about these weird little things you
came home to."

A silence went by.

Carolyn's apprehension was sidetracked by Thelma's
distress. She reached to pat the older woman's hands
that were now knotted on her lap. "It's okay, Thelma.
Go ahead."

Thelma drew in a quivering breath. "Carl has gotten forgetful, as you know."

Carolyn nodded.

"But you don't know that he does strange little
things sometimes."

"Like what?"

"Oh, he's harmless." Thelma gave a nervous laugh, avoiding a direct answer. "The doctor says it's age related."

"Alzheimer's?"

Thelma's gaze veered away from Carolyn's. "The doctor said dementia, but yes, it could be early Alzheimer's."

"I'm so sorry, Thelma—"

"It's okay, Carolyn," Thelma said, interrupting. "It's just that Carl has been so sharp during his whole life that I don't want to say anything to discredit him, or to embarrass him." She wiped her long sleeve over her eyes. "He's always been such a considerate man who would never do anything in the world to hurt another person."

"I know that." Carolyn hesitated, forming her words carefully, aware of Thelma's deep affection for her husband. "But what does this have to do with what's happened here?"

Thelma held out her hands, as if in supplication. "When Carl gets a bug about something, like turning down our bed hours before it's bedtime, he does it and then forgets he did. Later he always believes that I did it, and thanks me for being so considerate." She hesitated, as though searching for words.

"And?" Carolyn said, prompting her.

"I think it was Carl, who, for whatever strange twist of his mind, thought he was being helpful." She went back to twisting her rings but her gaze was direct. "Carolyn, I believe Carl was the one behind all of these odd little incidents. In fact—" She gulped a deep breath. "I'm convinced of it. There is no other explanation."

"You think Carl stacked the dishes in the sink?"

Thelma lowered her eyes, nodding. "He's been doing that very thing in our kitchen for several months now. He's developed a fixation on dishes not being clean enough, and lately he's been putting them back in the sink for rewashing." Thelma licked her lips, and Carolyn could see how painful the revelation was to her, that she was finding it hard to adjust to her husband's deteriorating mental health. "And this morning he made an issue of your cats' dishes, was about to get clean plates from your cupboard when I stopped him." She sighed. "He must have put the dishes in the sink while my back was turned."

"I see."

"I hope you can understand, Carolyn. Carl does these things and then forgets that he did them. He doesn't mean any harm."

"I do understand, Thelma." Carolyn stood up. "And I'm so sorry. I had no idea."

Thelma got to her feet. "Thanks, Carolyn. And I hope you know that Mayo and Mustard were safe in our care."

"Of course I do," she said, hugging Thelma. "I'm just glad that I have such caring neighbors."

Thelma's eyes glistened as she walked to the front door where she once again faced Carolyn. "You're okay now? You realize that no one was in your house but me and Carl?"

Carolyn nodded, smiling. "You're right. Nothing else makes sense." She paused as she opened the door. "I'm tired, and now that I understand what happened, I'll sleep like a baby."

"I'm so glad, dear." With a grateful smile, Thelma headed for her own front door.

Carolyn locked up, knowing that Thelma had been completely candid. It had been Carl who had caused the disturbances in her house. Then why did she still feel unsettled?

Because my personal space was unexpectedly violated, she rationalized. That's why I feel so spooked. No one was in here aside from Thelma and Carl.

And no one even knew she'd been gone for the weekend.

Wrong.

Her limbs were jolted with a charge of adrenaline. She'd told Tom. And Barney, Minnie, Dolores and Dean. Hell, the whole country knew. She'd announced it on her last program.

It was time she took herself in hand. She had to stop spilling her guts to all and sundry.

Carolyn felt reassured that her house was secure after Thelma left, even fixed something to eat, had a long soak in the tub, and then went to bed to sleep soundly until sometime in the middle of the night when she sat upright in the bed, wide awake.

Something had awakened her. What?

She strained her ears, listening. Nothing disturbed the peaceful quiet except the faint rushing sound of water from the fountain below her windows. Her eyes scanned the room. The garden lights that nestled in the shrubbery sent a yellow glow upward. She was alone.

Not again, she thought. She'd been on this roller-coaster ride of waking up in the middle of the night before, first after Betsy died, when she'd thought her baby was crying for her, only to have reality crash down on her moments later: her infant was dead. And the pattern had happened again after her father died. Somehow, her mind had refused to accept what had happened, at least that was her shrink's analysis.

She lay back down, snuggling into the down pillows, careful not to disturb the sleeping cats at the bottom of her bed. It seemed that she'd only closed her eyes when she opened them again to sunshine and chirping birds. Mustard and Mayo were already up and about, nowhere in sight.

Waiting to be fed, she thought. Carolyn tossed back the bedding and got up to pad barefooted across the carpet, headed for the stairs. Starting coffee was her first priority. Then feeding the cats.

Once the cat dishes were filled and the coffee brewed, she carried a mugful back upstairs to sip on while she got ready for work. A glance at the clock told her she'd better hurry.

Turning to the closet, her mind sifting though various outfits to wear, Carolyn was about to open the door when she realized it was already ajar by several inches.

Fear tightened her stomach muscles. Her body went rigid with indecision. Hadn't she closed the door last night, right after unpacking her suitcase and hanging her few garments? It always closed and opened with a metallic click; she thought she remembered hearing the sound.

Had it somehow popped open? Maybe the mechanism hadn't caught because it wasn't all the way closed.

Maybe—maybe. Her thoughts spun with likely scenarios.

Whoa! Carolyn instructed herself. Get a grip. This is "stinkin' thinkin,'" Minnie's term for negative thinking that allowed left-field conclusions. Like—whether or not someone had been hidden in the space behind her hung clothing last night.

No one is hiding in your closet.

This is just left over from your talk with Thelma before going to bed, she reminded herself. Anyone hiding in the closet after she got home would have strangled her while she slept, or fled in the night. Reassured by her own rationale, she grabbed the knob and yanked the door open. As suspected, there was no intruder.

But her legs suddenly wobbled. She sat down hard.

Carolyn forced herself to take three deep breaths. Her heartbeats slowed and she got to her feet, glad no one had witnessed her panic, not even the cats. With quick precision, she pulled a black skirt, a white blouse and a Burberry blazer from their hangers. She did her hair and makeup in record time, knowing she could touch up at the studio, and was soon on her way down to the Volvo. She needed perspective. Getting to work and into the real world would give her that.

She was almost to Marietta when she allowed herself to remember waking up in the night—and the sound that had awakened her. Was that when the closet door had clicked open?

Carolyn had a few minutes between the hairdresser and getting down to the set, and decided to call Dolores. As the phone rang at the other end she reminded herself that she must be tactful about the grounds maintenance. She wished again that Dolores had kept up the place as she'd promised.

"Hello." Dolores's voice was hurried, anxious.

"Hi, it's Carolyn." A hesitation. "Is everything all right?"

"Sorry if I sound flustered. I was trying to answer my E-mail before having to leave for an appointment."

"I won't keep you, then. I just wanted—"

"Oh no," Dolores said, interrupting. "I have a couple of minutes and I'm almost done here." A sigh came over the wires. "My computer glitched this morning and I lost some important mail. But would you believe it?" Her voice brightened. "Dean, my very own little computer wizard, fixed it—before I had to drive him to school. Thank God he spent the weekend."

Carolyn laughed. "Yeah, I can. He's one smart little boy when it comes to technology."

"So, what's up?"

"Well, uh, I know you have a lot of things going on, Dolores."

"Yeah, I figured you'd probably noticed, knowing Dean has been with me so much lately." She expelled a long breath. "Jessie and Tony are having problems again. Mostly financial."

Carolyn glanced at her watch. She still had a few minutes to spare—and Dolores had just given her the perfect opening. Her stepmother always filled the financial gaps in her daughter's life, which was probably the reason Dolores had no money for landscape upkeep. Privately, she thought Dolores should butt out, allow Jessie and Tony to face their own problems.

"That's kind of why I called Dolores. I know because of, uh, that situation, it becomes hard to do the extras, like hiring a gardener."

Carolyn went on quickly, explaining that since she was the one who actually owned the property she should be the one responsible for maintaining the grounds. By the time she finished, adding that she understood what Dolores was up against, that they were all family after all, her stepmother finally agreed to let her pay.

"But I insist on being the one who locates the gardener and makes sure that he does a good job, even if you are paying—at least for now when I'm strapped."

"Sounds like a good plan."

After Carolyn hung up she felt good about letting Dolores save face. Surely schmoozing for a good cause wasn't being dishonest, she told herself.

She still had a few minutes to spare and decided to call Tom as well and get her refusal over. She didn't want that unpleasant task weighing on her mind while she was trying to concentrate on selling pots and pans to thousands of viewers. She quickly dialed the number.

When his voice mail picked up she felt the tenseness go out of her body. She left a message thanking him, her voice businesslike as she explained another commitment that precluded dinner.

Then she headed off for the set, relieved that two troubling confrontations had gone well. In the future she needed to be even more direct with Tom, so he'd finally get the message that she didn't want him calling.

Not ever.

Carolyn had just said good-bye to the door guard and was about to head out of the building to the parking lot when someone called her name. Turning, she faced the man who'd come up behind her . . . Richard Crawford.

"Well hello there," she said, surprised and a little flustered.

"Hello yourself." A shaft of fading sunlight slanting in through the glass doors caught in his eyes, and for a second they shone like polished ebony. Inscrutable eyes, she thought. Dark, direct and extremely attractive with his dark complexion and hair.

"Here on business I'll bet." Carolyn hoped her voice didn't sound as inane as her words. "Have you joined the NNN family?"

"Unfortunately, not yet." He sobered. "My product is a long shot in the first place, not typical of a shopping network." The sides of his eyes crinkled and then he smiled. "But I'm still hoping to be a first at NNN, although it doesn't look too positive at the moment."

Carolyn grinned back, her hand on the release

lever that would open the door. "I still don't know what your product is, uh, Mr. Crawford."

"Richard . . . please."

She inclined her head. "What is your product, Richard?"

"Basically, it's investments."

He'd stepped closer as he spoke and now he reached around her, placed his hand next to hers, and pushed open the door. She had no option but to continue through the opening to the sidewalk that bordered the parking lot.

"Investments in what?"

"Ah, that's too much to explain in a paragraph or two." He hesitated, glancing at his watch. "Hey, it's almost cocktail hour. How about I explain over drinks."

His invitation was tempting. But she'd already made plans to meet Minnie at the Youth House, so she could explain why she was quitting the class. And Minnie, who had an aversion to cellular phones, didn't have one, so Carolyn couldn't call and cancel.

"That would have been nice," she said, honestly. "But I have a meeting at a youth center."

He raised his brows but didn't ask the obvious question. "So, when will you finish up?"

"Not until six or six-thirty."

"Then let's make it supper—say seven or seven-thirty at somewhere convenient to wherever you live."

"Um, I don't know—"

"You don't know what?"

A little ruffled by his dominant presence, his obvious attraction to her, she blurted the first thing that came to her mind. "I'm in my work clothes and—"

"You're lovely," he said finishing her sentence.

Despite her hesitation, Carolyn grinned. He was so damned macho, in the best sense of the word. And, she admitted, charismatic, charming and hard to resist.

"Okay, I can definitely make it by seven-thirty."

"Great."

They settled on a small restaurant only a few blocks from Carolyn's house. He gave a wave, said his good-bye and headed for his car, a white BMW sedan.

Carolyn was smiling as she headed toward her meeting with Minnie. She hadn't felt so energized in a long time, not since those early days when she was falling in love with Rob. Just because her marriage to him hadn't worked out didn't mean her reaction to Richard meant another bad relationship.

Stop thinking relationships, she instructed herself. Just because an attractive man had asked her out it didn't mean anything important.

Or did it?

8

Driving into the Five Points area, Carolyn looked for a parking place near the bar and grill where she'd agreed to meet Richard Crawford. She was a little early—thank goodness. She could touch up her makeup and hair before going into the restaurant.

She'd made good time from Marietta to the Anderson Youth House, then spent a half hour with Minnie discussing why she was dropping the computer class. In the course of their conversation Carolyn mentioned that Dean had just fixed a big glitch in his grandmother's computer.

"He's an eleven-year-old computer nerd," Minnie had said, grinning. "Unlike his aunt."

"Who is?" Barney had come up behind them, a habit of his.

Carolyn had explained that her nephew was a natural techie, then added that he was also quiet and introspective, and she was worried about his not having friends his own age.

Barney had nodded. "Yeah, it's great for the kid to excel at something, but not if it's his only outlet for expressing himself."

Barney, always the astute cop, had expressed her fears exactly, and she'd sensed all the questions he'd been too polite to ask. Now, as Carolyn slowed her car for the turn into the restaurant parking lot, she realized how fortunate the kids were at Anderson's Youth House to have Barney.

She swung her Volvo into the last available space, quickly saw to her face and hair, and then got out of the car. She felt exactly as she'd felt on her first date at sixteen: hesitant, nervous and uncertain.

Grow up, Carolyn, she told herself. You've been around the block. You've already been a wife and mother and now you're a divorcée. The whole world believes you're a sophisticate. Act like one.

But her heart raced as she headed for the front entrance. This Richard, with his dark eyes that crinkled with amusement even before his lips smiled, seemed to have that kind of effect on her.

Pushing open the door, Carolyn strode into the reception area where a hostess was taking names for the waiting list. Then Richard stepped forward and took her arm. She noted instantly that he'd changed into black slacks and a cashmere turtleneck sweater, dress that was appropriate to the rustic motif of the place. Behind him a gas fire burned in a huge fireplace and lit candles in glass holders flickered on every table.

"A woman who's on time," he said. His gaze flickered over her, admiring. "We already have our table."

"And a man who takes charge," she said, countering.

His eyelids lowered slightly, screening his expression. His hand moved to her elbow, so he could steer her through the dining room to a table against the back wall.

"Privacy and quiet, where we can talk." He helped her out of her blazer, draped it over the chair which he then pulled out for her. She sat down, even more impressed by his smooth command of the situation.

As he took the chair opposite her, Carolyn smiled, trying to maintain a casual air. But his friendly, open assessment of her was disconcerting, if flattering. She forced herself to relax. He seemed such a nice man, the type all women dreamed of meeting, and falling in love with.

Oh my God, what was she thinking? She'd only met him a short time ago, hardly knew him, and was already considering—deeper feelings?

The waitress arrived with menus, diverting her thoughts. Although Carolyn had never been in this particular restaurant, avoiding it because she believed the attached bar with its live music would be too noisy for conversation, she realized the dining room was relatively quiet, although she could hear the band in the next room.

"How about some wine?" Richard's gaze, warm and friendly, flickered between her eyes and her mouth.

"Sounds good," she said, smiling.

"What's your preference?"

"Chardonnay."

"Mind if I order for us?"

She shook her head. "I'd love it if you would."
She didn't add that she always ordered the same
thing, not being a connoisseur of good wine.

He glanced away to the young waitress who'd
been watching the interchange, a half smile on her
lips, openly admiring Richard's charming manner.
He named a French wine which wasn't available,
then settled on a bottle from California. Carolyn had
heard of it, knew it was pricey, but had never sampled it. As the woman went to fill the order, Richard
turned back to her.

"You're going to like this Chardonnay," he said.

"I'm sure I will." She lowered her eyes, abruptly
too aware of his closeness, the magnetic current that
emanated from him. "You seem to know your wines."

"Only because I travel so much, often abroad, and
sampling wines everywhere I go is one of my hob-
bies." He leaned back in his chair, and the subdued
candlelight caught in his eyes, reflecting a sincerity
that she also heard in his voice. He appeared to be a
man with a broad scope.

"So, what is it that takes you to all of those far-
away places, uh, Richard? Work?"

There was a flash of white as he laughed. "That's
right, Richard," he said, correctly reading her hesitation over his name. "We're Richard and Carolyn
now. Right?"

Carolyn smiled, nodding.

"Good. And yes, to answer your question, *Carolyn*." His brows slanted upward as he enunciated
her name. "It's my work that takes me all over the
globe. I've sampled good and bad wines in many
countries."

Their eyes met and there was a brief silence.

"And what is this work, the product you hope to sell on NNN?"

At that moment the waitress returned with their wine in an ice bucket, which she set on a stand next to their table. With a smile for Richard, she uncorked the bottle and poured wine into a goblet for him to sample.

"Very good," Richard said, winking at Carolyn. He nodded at the waitress who then filled Carolyn's glass before topping off his. Then the woman plunged the bottle back into its bucket and said she'd return in a few minutes to take their orders.

"A toast?" Richard asked, his gaze so leveled at her that it took everything she had not to lower hers.

"Why not?" She was pleased that her voice sounded calm, that she hadn't come across as a woman infatuated with a man who seemed so confident, so unflappable.

"Then," he raised his glass, "to new friends."

Momentarily, she hesitated before clinking her goblet to his. "New friends."

There was silence as they both sipped.

"As you were saying?" he asked.

"Oh, about the product you hope to sell on NNN." She gave a short laugh. "Maybe I'll be the one selling it."

He swirled the wine in his glass, watching as the liquid caught the candlelight. She waited, wondering why he hesitated.

The suddenness of his uplifted gaze caught her off guard. "I'm not going to have a product on

NNN, Carolyn. They turned me down. Just got the word before meeting you."

There was another brief silence before she rushed into the void, sensing his disappointment.

"I didn't know," she began, slowly, uncertain. "I'm so sorry, Richard."

"Me, too." He hesitated. "But I'm not terribly surprised. I think I mentioned earlier that going for my product would have been a long-shot for NNN."

"Why so?"

He took another sip, and then gently placed his glass on the table. "For starters, I don't have something visual to demonstrate for the viewers, as Roberta pointed out." He shook his head slowly. "You know, like pots and pans, clothing, or jewelry."

"Uh-huh. The focus of home shopping on television is a visual concept."

"Yeah, of course. But I believe there's room for other products with a broader scope, with ways to give the viewers a visual look at optional possibilities for increasing their financial portfolio."

"I'm still in the dark about what it is that you have for sale, Richard." Carolyn leaned forward, intrigued.

"Would you believe reasonably priced time-share condominiums, at most of the best vacation spots around the world?"

"You're kidding?"

"Nope, I'm not."

There was a momentary silence.

"Okay, I understand why NNN was hesitant, why Roberta mentioned visuals." Carolyn sought for a tactful response. "The company has a perspective on how it chooses products. They must be visually and economically appealing to their vast television audience."

He shrugged. "I agree, to a point. My product would have had video clips of the actual places, testimonials from satisfied customers, cost breakdowns showing the financial feasibility of buying in, why it's actually a sound business investment."

"But not for average people who couldn't afford it in the first place, which is probably a good percent of NNN customers."

He spread his hands in a gesture of surrender. "Roberta's point exactly, although I don't completely agree with her. Time-sharing *is* affordable to middle America and it's a great asset on a financial statement. Actually it allows working people to experience upscale vacations that they couldn't afford otherwise."

"You may be right, Richard. Unfortunately, our market research shows that a sizable percent of NNN's customers are people who don't have a big income, probably would never have the money to buy into a time-share even if they wanted to."

"They aren't high rollers. Right?"

"High rollers?"

"That's what Roberta said her viewers would dub a person buying my product," he said, dryly. "That using up air time with it wouldn't pencil out."

"I'm sorry, Richard," she said, softly. "Roberta can be direct, but I'm sure she didn't mean to offend. She has to conform to the ultimate decision of her boss and the NNN board."

"Hey, I understand." His eyes crinkled at the corners, signaling a smile. "It's not the end of the world.

I make a good living without NNN, but being the ambitious fellow that I am, I thought I'd give it a shot."

"I'm glad you did," she said, impulsively. "Or we would never have met."

He reached to place a hand over hers. Instantly, a ripple of sensation coursed through her, a feeling she hadn't felt for years now, reminding her that she was still a woman before anything else.

"Thanks, Carolyn."

"You're disappointed, aren't you?" Her question was inane but it was the first thing that popped into her mind on the heels of her reaction to his touch.

He nodded. "But I also recognize that NNN is a down-home type of business, and they're wildly successful at what they do because they have a handle on the market."

She inclined her head, agreeing.

"And my kind of thing would be a first for them." He hesitated. "As Roberta said when she turned down my concept—and it was a highly developed concept of how they could market time-share sales— NNN focuses on middle America, not global high-rolling investments."

"Like I said, Roberta is only the voice that reflects a corporate decision."

Again, he nodded.

Carolyn hesitated, wondering if she should add her thoughts, then decided it was the honest thing to do. "You know, Richard, I've been selling products on NNN for a few years now and—"

"And selling them very well indeed," he said, interrupting, grinning wide for the first time.

"Thanks," she said, a little disconcerted by his compliment. "I was about to say that time-share selling has yet to catch on with the home shopping networks, and your turndown today doesn't mean a rejection in the future when the timing is better."

"I'll keep that in mind, Carolyn." He paused. "I can take business rejection, it's part of the game. It's only personal rejection that's hard to take."

He tilted his head, watching her, and she sensed he was about to add something, then decided against it. Carolyn lifted her glass and took a sip. She didn't know what to say. Thankfully, she was saved from a reply by the waitress who'd stepped to their table, pad and pencil in hand.

"Ready to order?" she asked, her attention focused on Richard.

"We need a couple of minutes more," he told her, flashing a smile. "We haven't even glanced at our menus yet."

"I'll come back."

Richard nodded, and as the girl left, handed Carolyn a menu. "Shall we decide before we drive our waitress nuts?"

Carolyn arched her brows in agreement but said nothing. She wanted to tease him and say: *before you drive our waitress nuts* but she held her tongue. She didn't know him that well yet.

Yet? she thought, bemused. She was already assuming she would see Richard again after tonight.

She ended up ordering a Crab Louie, Richard the sweet-and-sour calamari, with side dishes of garlic mashed potatoes and creamed corn. Carolyn suppressed a grin. He ordered what he liked, not what a gourmet chef would have recommended with cala-mari.

The conversation never returned to NNN and time-shares, but veered into their personal lives. He told her about his two older sisters, both married and living in California. He explained that he rarely saw them since their parents died, his mother eight years ago and his dad twelve years ago. "My busi-ness is based in Chicago where I grew up," he said, "but I have business associates in Atlanta, Los Ange-les, New York and in Europe."

She told him about growing up with her father, a man she'd adored, about her stepfamily and how much she loved her nephew, Dean. Carolyn sud-denly hesitated, realizing that she didn't know his marital status.

"You said your home is in Chicago. Are you—uh,"

"No, I'm not married," he said, interrupting, hav-ing anticipated her question. "And I assumed you aren't."

"Divorced."

"Oh, I didn't know that."

Obviously he hadn't read the magazine stories about her, she thought, pleased. It would be much nicer to establish a friendship by learning of their backgrounds from each other.

"Kids?"

Carolyn averted her gaze, uncertain. "An infant who died," she said, finally, not wishing to discuss it further with someone she scarcely knew.

They'd finished eating and the waitress had taken their plates and given them the coffee they'd or-dered in lieu of dessert.

"I'm sorry," Richard said softly, and then tactfully changed the subject to the soft music that flowed into the dining room. "Good band."

She agreed and they went on to talk about favorite songs. Carolyn was glad he hadn't pressed her.

They finished their coffee, exchanged phone numbers and the waitress brought the check. Richard put down a hundred dollar bill on the tray as they stood to go. He helped her on with her blazer, then put on his own jacket, and, with his arm loosely around her waist, led her back to the entry where the music was louder. Carolyn could see into the lounge where several couples danced on an open space in front of the band.

The musicians had been playing a lot of old Elvis Presley tunes all evening and now they struck the first chords of "Love Me Tender," a favorite of Carolyn's. As they walked toward the door, she paused to listen.

"You like Elvis?" Richard asked, stopping with her.

"I like this song," she replied. "I think it's one of his best."

Without a word, his hand dropped from her waist and grabbed her hand, gently pulling her into the bar to the dance floor. "Shall we?"

"Let's." Carolyn didn't protest when he held her close against him and they began to dance. She liked the spontaneity of his action. There was something boyish and appealing about it, yet manly. She felt young. Young and light, and she wished the evening didn't have to end.

"You're so sweet, Carolyn," he murmured, pulling her even closer, so that they were cheek to cheek. She was sorry when the music stopped, and for a moment longer, stayed locked in his arms.

He was the first to step back, peering down into her face, his eyes unreadable. But before he could speak a man spoke up behind him. Carolyn's gaze shifted to the couple who stood waiting for the band to play another song.

Tom.

She couldn't believe it. He'd invited her to dinner and she'd refused with a business excuse. Now, here he was, seeing her out with Richard on the very day she'd turned him down for good. A glance at his face told her that he was angry, even though he was with his own date.

"Hello, Tom," she said, aware that he must have seen her dancing with Richard. Her eyes shifted to the woman. "You must be—" She broke off, not remembering Tom's new woman's name, wondering if she'd ever heard it.

"Allison Peters." The woman was attractive, if a bit severe looking with her short brown hairdo, sparse makeup and dark business suit.

"Oh. I don't suppose you're related to Judge Peters?" Feeling awkward, Carolyn had blurted the first thing that came to mind.

"As a matter of fact, Judge Peters is my father." Allison's response was crisp, her chin tilted in a gesture of superiority. "I'm his legal secretary."

Carolyn couldn't stop her grin. It figured. Tom knew who to date to get ahead. She wondered when they'd announce their wedding plans.

"Nice meeting you, Allison." Carolyn glanced at Tom who stood emotionless, like a wooden statue. "You, too, Tom. Good seeing you again."

Then she headed for the door with Richard, the silent observer, beside her. Once outside he stopped her.

"What was that all about?" he asked, his expression a little more than curious.

"Nothing much," she replied, considering what to tell him. No reason to hide anything, she reminded herself. "I used to date Tom," she said finally. "He worked for my dad's law firm. After my father died I had second thoughts and we broke up."

Richard waited, his expression inscrutable, as though he hesitated to question a relationship that was none of his affair.

"But he still cares?"

"Why do you say that?"

"Another man can tell, that's all." A pause. "Are you in love with him?"

"That's an odd question," she said, surprised.

"More odd than you not introducing me?"

He was walking her to her car as they talked.

"Oh. I didn't, did I? I'm sorry, Richard. It isn't what you think." They'd stopped at her car and she'd opened the driver's door before facing him again. "I'm not now, nor ever will be, in love with Tom." She hesitated. "When, if, we become better friends, Richard, I'll explain Tom."

"We will."

"We will—what?"

"Become better friends." He only hesitated for a second. And then he pulled her to him, gazed down into her face for another moment before lowering his mouth to hers.

It was a brief kiss, soft and warm. He moved away slowly, until he held her at arm's length.

"And when we're better friends I'll be interested in hearing all about this Tom."

He gave her his slow smile, then turned and strode off, whistling as he made his way toward the other side of the lot where he'd said his own car was parked. For a moment longer Carolyn watched him go. Then she sat down behind the wheel and closed the door. All the way home her mind was filled with Richard.

Had he been jealous of Tom?

Was he attracted to her?

His kiss said he was. She wondered when she'd see him again. He taken down her phone number, said he'd call, but hadn't made a date.

But he had said they would become better friends.

That was enough for now.

9

"**H**ey, I got to thinking after you left the Youth House, about your nephew, Dean."

Carolyn had just come into the kitchen from the garage in time to answer the phone before the machine picked up the call. She'd been surprised to hear Barney's voice on the other end of the wire.

"What about Dean?" She was momentarily breathless from running to catch the call. "Could you wait a sec while I put down my things. I was coming through the door when you called."

"Sure. Take your time."

Dropping her handbag on the counter, she also scooped dry food into the cat dishes, as Mayo and Mustard were also demanding attention, rubbing against her ankles. Then she grabbed the phone again.

"Sorry, Barney."

"No problem. I know it's late but since I knew you had a dinner date I figured you'd still be up."

She didn't want to talk about Richard. He was too

new to her emotions to get into a discussion about him, however brief. "As you were saying about Dean?"

"Yeah, well, like I said." Barney sounded gruff. "I was thinking about his computer skills and what you'd said about him not having much of a social life with other kids and I got excited about my idea."

"Which is?"

"As you know one of our patrons donated an old computer and a printer to the Youth House, and none of us on staff are computer literate enough to teach our kids how to use it." He took a quick breath. "So I thought of Dean."

"You want Dean to be the teacher?"

"Why not?"

"Uh, I don't know. He's only eleven. His parents might not let him do something like that."

"But you have to see that it would be a great opportunity for everyone concerned. The kids here would learn how to use a computer and Dean would become the person they all look up to—a computer guru." A pause. "The kids here aren't juvenile delinquents, Carolyn. They wouldn't be a bad influence, if that's what you're worried about."

"Barney, how could you suggest that?" She couldn't keep annoyance out of her tone. "For God's sake, I know they wouldn't lead Dean astray." She gulped a breath. "I can tell that you don't know me at all."

"I think I do, more than you could guess."

"Then don't imply that I'm prejudiced."

She heard his muffled laugh. "Sorry. Didn't mean

to ruffle your feathers. Guess you're right. I don't know you very well—yet."

"Yet?"

"Uh-huh. I expect we'll be spending more time together if Dean is able to help out with the computer problem."

"I haven't agreed to anything, Barney. Are you forgetting? I'm not his mother, only his aunt, and stepaunt at that."

"But I can tell that you think it's a good idea."

Her sigh went over the wires before her words. "How in the world can you tell that?"

"I pick up on these things," he said, and she sensed that he was smiling. "Didn't you know that all homicide detectives are a little psychic?"

"Are homicide detectives also steamrollers?"

He laughed outright. "Course, when we have to be. Some things and some people are worth—"

"Rolling over to get what you want?" she asked, interrupting.

There was a brief silence.

"Yeah, I guess you could say that, Carolyn. But only in the finest sense of the word."

"That's an ambiguous statement."

"Give it some time, say a couple of months." Another pause. "Probably won't seem so damn ambiguous then."

She shifted the receiver to the other ear. Surely Barney wasn't flirting with her? No, impossible, she told herself. You're still under the influence of Richard's charm, reading romance into normal conversations.

"Okay, I will."

"A deal." He hesitated. "But of course you have to come to the right conclusion. I could become a real steamroller in certain circumstances."

"Good lord, Barney. Is that a threat of some sort?" She drew in a breath. "And by the way, what are we talking about? Dean or something else?"

"Both."

"Listen, I'm going to bed now but I promise to talk to Dean's parents tomorrow. I'll let you know what they say."

"Fair enough. I'll look forward to hearing from you."

"And Barney?"

"Yes?" He stretched the word into a long drawl.

"You were right about one thing. I think your proposal for Dean would definitely be good for him."

"And the other thing?"

"Sorry, I don't know what that is."

"But you will in a couple of months, remember?"

They hung up and Carolyn was left with the feeling that Barney had definitely been flirting in his own oblique way. She sighed. First Richard, then Barney.

It was pheromones, she decided. Her body must be secreting the magical substance that attracted the opposite sex.

You're nuts, she told herself as she climbed into bed. But she was smiling when she closed her eyes.

Carolyn stood as Jessie approached her table in the coffee shop near the Underground entrance on Alabama Street. Jessie had called her concerning Carolyn's suggestion that Dean donate his time to help kids learn computer skills at Anderson Youth House. She had some concerns which Carolyn thought was understandable.

They'd agreed to meet after work, several days after Carolyn had called her with Barney's suggestion. The first few days hadn't coincided with either Carolyn's on-air schedule or Jessie's overtime. To compensate, Carolyn had agreed to meet Jessie near her work. She was an office administrator for a national insurance company in downtown Atlanta.

"You look great, Jessie," Carolyn said as Jessie took a stool opposite her at the high, round table. She pushed one of the lattes she'd ordered in front of her.

"Thanks, Carolyn—for the compliment and the latte." She tried wiping back her unruly red curly hair that was so like Dean's, but it flopped right back onto her forehead. "I don't feel great. In fact I feel pretty damned lousy. Nothing seems to be going right these days."

Carolyn leaned forward. "What do you mean?"

Jessie's thin shoulders lifted in a shrug. "I don't want to burden you with my problems."

"You're not." A hesitation. "But you know I care, don't you?"

Jessie's blue eyes filled with tears. "Yeah, I realized that a long time ago, Carolyn." She paused. "You know that I don't have a biological sister, but if I did, I couldn't ask for anyone dearer than you."

Carolyn glanced away, allowing Jessie to compose herself. She'd never seen the so-together-Jessie so upset, so ready for tears. Nor had Jessie ever expressed her deeper feelings about Carolyn until now. She reached to place her hand on Jessie's. "What's wrong? I know we need to talk about Dean and Anderson Youth House, but that's not why you're so upset, is it?"

Jessie shook her head. "I know how much you adore Dean—and believe me—I appreciate that." She hesitated. "Of course I need to know that Dean wouldn't be among kids who use drugs and are prone to criminal activities, but I believe you would never suggest something that would put him in jeopardy." She paused again. "My problems have nothing to do with any of that, which is why Dean has been spending so much time with his grandmother."

"To be honest, I wondered about that."

Jessie shook her head, as if to clear it. "It's complicated—and embarrassing."

"We're family. Who else can you share the complicated and embarrassing stuff with?"

"Thanks, Carolyn."

To divert Jessie's upset, whatever it was, she brought the topic back to Dean, explaining the Youth House and that the children there were not delinquents, but orphans. Hesitantly at first, Carolyn explained why she thought it would benefit Dean to have a position that other kids admired.

"I agree," Jessie said, finally. "Dean has become too much of a loner and he needs a boost to his confidence." She sipped her coffee, as though trying to compose herself. "I just needed you to explain the situation, Carolyn. I wanted reassurance that he wouldn't be led astray." She hesitated. "Dean can be impressionable."

"I understand," Carolyn said. "But Dean is so computer literate that he'll be the one to do the leading in this situation." She took a swallow of her own coffee. "Did you know that he even fixed your mom's computer when it locked up the other morning."

"No I didn't." Jessie set down her cup. "My mother and her on-line pals is another concern of mine."

"What do you mean?"

"Only that I'm a bit alarmed by my mother meeting men on-line in chat rooms, and that after a few weeks of talking back and forth on the computer, she thinks she knows them."

Jessie's freckles looked stark against her pale complexion. Carolyn saw that she was more than concerned; she was downright worried.

"Surely talking to men is relatively harmless. I know your mother is lonesome since my father died and—"

"It's not that, Carolyn. I'm sure you know that my mother hopes to marry again."

"I know that and I'm not offended." Carolyn took another drink. "I hope your mother eventually meets a nice man she can care about."

"That's generous. And I agree. I just don't think she'll meet that person on the Internet. She has no idea who's at the other end of her post." Jessie sucked in a ragged breath. "It could be a serial killer."

Carolyn laughed. "That's unlikely. But I agree, the guy may not be who he says he is."

The conversation shifted to other things and

Jessie finally admitted that she and Tony were having problems, that because of their constant arguments, mostly about money and his not keeping a job, she was letting Dean stay with his grandmother more often. But she was hesitant to confide details and Carolyn didn't push her.

They finished their coffee and stood to go, having agreed that Dean, if he wanted to, could spend Saturday afternoons at the Youth House giving computer instructions.

Once on the street they each went their separate ways and Carolyn was happy to be headed home. She had her own worries, the main one was that Richard hadn't called her as he'd said he would. It had been three days since she saw him.

All the way home she thought up different scenarios as to why he hadn't contacted her. By the time she reached her house she'd come to a conclusion. If he didn't call it was because he didn't want to, because he'd had second thoughts about her. She hoped she was wrong.

She drove into the garage, grabbed her things and went into the kitchen as the automatic door closed behind the Volvo. In the middle of the kitchen she stopped in mid-stride.

Something was wrong.

Where were Mayo and Mustard? They always ran to meet her, without fail.

And then she heard something from the family room. Cautiously, she went to check, wondering if her cats were in some kind of trouble.

They weren't in the room.

Movement outside the glass doors to the backyard

caught her eye. She turned, facing the garden where the subdued light from among the flowers and shrubbery illuminated her two cats rubbing against the windows, meowing for her to let them in.

Shock took her breath.

Who'd let her cats outside?

10

It took a moment for reason to reassert itself. Her house appeared untouched since she left it that morning. But still Carolyn stood uncertain, taking deep breaths to calm herself, trying to mentally picture her routine that morning, knowing she'd been rushing.

It had been beautiful weather: sunshine, birds chirping and unseasonably warm for February. She'd let Mayo and Mustard outside, knowing they had never found a way out of the walled garden. Then she'd gone back upstairs to finish getting ready for work. She'd been running late when she came back downstairs.

Carolyn stared at the cats beyond the doors. She could swear that she'd let them in that morning, but she couldn't remember actually doing it. Recently, she'd been doing her daily chores mindlessly. She'd been busy, focused on other things, like the product she'd be selling on NNN within several hours.

Everyone forgets little things when they are stressed or in a hurry.

No one else had been in her house. How could they have been? No one had a key, and it was obvious that there hadn't been a break-in. She didn't usually forget her babies, but maybe this was a sign that she needed to slow down and concentrate on what she was doing.

Having reassured herself, Carolyn headed for the French doors and found them unlocked, just as she suspected. If she'd forgotten her cats outside that morning, she'd also left her house open.

Mustard and Mayo rushed into the house, ignored Carolyn and headed for their dried food, the dishes still full from the morning. Carolyn made sure to secure the door this time and then gave her cats fresh water.

"Poor babies," she crooned. "Mommy's so sorry."

Smiling at their indifference to her amends, she went upstairs to change clothes before fixing something to eat. Again her thoughts turned to Richard. Why hadn't he called? Maybe he'd gone back to Chicago.

Dean called later in the evening, expressing interest in giving computer instructions at the Youth House, although he also had reservations. Again Carolyn sensed his shyness among kids his own age. After they hung up she pledged to get him involved with people other than a grandmother who spent hours a day in Internet chat rooms. Dean's casual comment that Dolores was "looking for love" had shocked her into momentary silence. It was a strange remark for an eleven-year-old boy to make about his grandmother.

She was watching the late news, about to turn out the light when the phone on her nightstand rang. She grabbed the receiver.

"Hello?"

"It's Richard. Not too late to call, is it?"

For all the thinking she'd been doing about Richard lately, Carolyn was surprised to hear his voice at that moment.

"No, it's fine." She cleared her throat, suddenly nervous. "I was only watching the news."

"Good. I figured you wouldn't have gone to bed yet."

"Well, I confess to watching TV in bed." She gave a laugh. "I often do. It puts me to sleep—sort of like reading does for most people."

He chuckled. "Sex, violence and natural disasters puts you to sleep?" He clucked his tongue in mock censure. "Watching the news keeps me awake."

Carolyn heard the teasing note in his voice. "Yep, I'm a strange one all right."

"Wouldn't you know, I find strange women charming, especially the pretty ones."

"And what about you? Do you have any odd tendencies? Are you as perfect as you seem?"

"I'm far from perfect, but as for strange tendencies, I'll just let you find out on your own."

Carolyn laughed lightly, but then there was an awkward silence. Was he thinking of their kiss? She was.

And she enjoyed it.

"Hey, I'd better get back to the subject at hand. It's getting late and I did call for a reason," he said, almost as if he'd read her mind.

"Uh-huh."

"How about a night out on the town this Saturday?"

She smiled at his old-fashioned way of asking for a date. "What did you have in mind?"

"I guess I should find out if you're free of work obligations first. I know you have shows on certain Saturdays."

"That's true, and I do have a two-hour segment on Saturday from noon to two." She was pleased that he knew that much about her programming. "Then I'm free for the rest of the day."

"Are you saying yes?"

"Yes."

There was another pause.

"I thought we could have an early dinner and then take in the show at Punch Line, if I can get tickets. I've heard that some of the comedians are famous, that they often try out new material that has the audience rolling in the aisles. You up for it?"

"Yeah, I sure am. I can vouch for the place. I've been there before and know it can be hilarious." She switched the phone to her other ear as she shifted position. "Who's performing?"

"Don't know yet." She heard the smile in his voice and could picture his eyes crinkling at the corners. "A business associate suggested the place." He hesitated. "I'm going on his word, and now yours. Remember, I'm not a native of Atlanta."

"It's a good choice, Richard. You'll see on Saturday night."

"So it's a date." His words weren't a question.

"It's a date. I'm looking forward to it already. It'll be fun."

"Me, too." A pause. "I almost forgot to explain why I hadn't called sooner. I had a business emergency in Chicago and had to fly up there, just got back tonight."

"I did wonder," she said, honestly.

"I'll tell you about it when I see you."

They settled on a time, and after saying good night, hung up. Carolyn turned off the news, then the lamp and slid deeper under the covers. She stared out through her windows at the night sky, her mind already on what she'd wear Saturday night. She wanted to look her best. Maybe she'd even buy a new outfit—if she could find time to shop between now and Saturday.

"You've got it bad," she whispered into the dark room.

She fell asleep with a smile on her lips and Richard on her mind.

That damn phone!

Jolted out of her sleep, Carolyn grabbed for the receiver, her eyes on the illuminated clock on the nightstand. It was past two in the morning.

"Yes?" she said, still half asleep.

"I'm sorry to wake you, dear." Thelma's voice sounded apologetic. "I just wanted to make sure you were safe."

"Safe? I was asleep. It's the middle of the night."

Carolyn sat up, suddenly wide awake. "Why would you think I wasn't okay?"

Thelma's sigh came over the line. "I'm relieved."

"About what?"

There was a brief silence.

"Carl went to check on Sammy barking downstairs, said he saw someone on the front porch—on your side."

"When?"

"A few minutes ago. But you're fine and I'm sorry to wake you up."

"But Thelma, where did this person go? Did Carl have a description?"

Another pause.

"My dear, there was no person." Her voice lowered to a whisper. "You remember our conversation about Carl?"

"Uh, of course."

"Well, I'm sure there was no one there. But you understand, I had to make sure you were all right, just in case."

A minute later they hung up. But Carolyn found it impossible to go back to sleep. Even after she'd slipped through the darkness of her house, checking door locks, she felt uneasy, as though someone out there was watching.

Silly. It was only the middle of the night heebie-jeebies. Carl was losing it, imagining things.

She hoped that was it.

Carolyn was running late when she arrived home after her last show. She'd had to substitute for a two-hour jewelry presentation featuring Lilly Lawton's latest creations. After the cameras were off, Lilly mentioned hearing from Minnie and how impressed she was with the prayer necklace Minnie had made for her as a thank-you gift for the beads. The contact for Minnie pleased Carolyn, especially when Lilly said she was going to talk to Minnie about her jewelry.

Oh, God, she thought, glancing at the clock as she went through the kitchen. How will I ever be ready in time? What if Richard hadn't gotten the message she'd left on his voice mail explaining the change in her schedule, that she had to change the time for an hour later?

"What if?—what if?" she mumbled, heading upstairs to shower and change. At least she'd laid out her clothes before going to work that morning. A premonition of her crazy day?

Then she remembered her answering machine and ran back down the steps to check it. She'd asked Richard to leave a message that he'd received hers. The red light was blinking and she pressed the button. Richard's voice filled the room.

"We'll play it by ear," he said calmly. "If we have to make a change in plans it's fine. Don't worry, honey. These things happen."

Carolyn was relieved, and his use of the endearment didn't elude her. She saved the message, knowing she'd want to hear his words at least one more time before she erased it. She'd learned another thing about Richard: he was flexible, a trait she liked in a man.

A shower revitalized her. After drying her hair and applying makeup, she slipped into a basic black wool sheath, a long-sleeved go-anywhere dress. Then she headed for the stairs; she had time to make sure her house was in order before Richard's arrival. She'd bought two bouquets of spring flowers, one each for the living and family rooms.

You're trying to impress him with your sexy dress and attractive home, admit it. You want to dazzle him with your fancy footwork, she told herself, dredging up a saying her dad had often used when he'd talked about how to impress a jury.

So what? Carolyn asked herself. She was allowed to be attracted to him. She could like a man and enjoy his company without thinking of love.

But she did like him. Very much.

Carolyn turned on several lamps in the living room, and the small glass Fenton on the hall table. The glow from the tiny light bulb illuminated the antique mirror that hung on the wall above it. She glanced at her reflection, noticing that her cheeks were slightly flushed. Smoothing her hair she was glad she'd decided to leave it down, not pinned up as she'd planned. All in all she felt ready for Richard's arrival, confident that she'd never looked better.

Back in the kitchen she checked on the wine she had chilling in the refrigerator, then filled a small glass dish with mixed nuts. She took the nuts and cocktail napkins to the family room and placed them on the coffee table, in case they had time for a glass of wine before leaving. She didn't know how her change in time had affected Richard's reservations for dinner. As an afterthought she switched on the gas fire in the fireplace. Carolyn glanced around, satisfied. Her place seemed elegant but cozy.

The doorbell caught her momentarily off guard. Richard was exactly on time. After taking a deep breath, she started toward the front door and opened it.

"Hi," she said, brightly.

Richard, dressed in tan slacks and a deep brown sports jacket, stood on the porch in momentary silence, his dark eyes admiring and strangely serious. But then he smiled and it dispelled the intensity of his gaze, and deepened the flush in her cheeks.

"You look gorgeous, Carolyn." He shook his head. "Don't think I've ever seen such green eyes on anyone. If I didn't know better I'd think they were contact lenses."

She spread her hands in denial and then laughed. "Thank you, Richard," she said, not knowing what else to say.

"You're welcome."

"Please come in."

She stepped aside, pushing the door all the way open. He was about to move forward when there was a commotion behind him. The azalea bushes rustled as a black shape darted forward to spring up the steps. Sammy, the neighbor's cocker spaniel, lunged at Richard, grabbed his trouser leg between his teeth and yanked at the fabric.

Richard kicked at the dog. It yelped and backed away to stand growling at the edge of the porch, his ruff standing straight up on the back of his neck. The incident happened so fast that Carolyn had no chance to intercede before the dog had torn Richard's slacks.

Horrified, she ran onto the porch, getting between Richard and Sammy. "Go home, Sammy!" she said, firmly. "Go home now!" She advanced on him. He'd gone after her cats but she'd never known him to attack people.

Sammy only growled defiantly, as though waiting for a chance to resume his attack.

Then Thelma came running, followed by her husband, Carl. "Bad dog!" Thelma cried, hurrying up the steps to snap a leash onto Sammy's collar. With the spaniel under control, her gaze shifted to Carolyn and Richard. "I'm so sorry. I can't imagine whatever got into Sammy to do such a thing." She hesitated, her eyes on Richard. "Did he bite your leg?"

"Luckily, no," Richard replied, dryly. "But he did ruin a perfectly good pair of slacks."

"We'll gladly replace them," Carl said, coming up behind Thelma. "Our Sammy is getting old and cranky." He cleared his throat to get more volume from his voice. "I know he didn't mean to be bad."

Carolyn knew Carl was also referring to himself and she suddenly felt sorry for the old couple. "Look," she said, kindly. "Why don't you take Sammy home now and we'll discuss this tomorrow. Okay?"

"All right, dear," Thelma said. "But Carl and I insist on paying for your friend's trousers."

"We'll talk about that later." Carolyn gave them both a gentle nudge toward the steps, and with a reluctant Sammy, they took the sidewalk around to their side of the porch, and went inside. Carolyn and Richard went into her part of the house and she closed the door.

"Not the welcome I'd intended," she told Richard

as she led the way down the hall to the kitchen and indicated that he sit down on a chair. "Let's look at your leg, make sure the skin isn't broken."

"It's not. I already checked it out."

About to bend down, she straightened, meeting his eyes. "How about a glass of wine then, to calm our nerves."

His eyes creased, but he sounded perfectly serious when he replied. "Sounds like a plan, Miss Nightingale."

She grinned.

He grinned back.

"I really do want to replace your slacks."

He shook his head. "No way. You didn't ruin them."

"I know but I don't want my old neighbors—"

"I wouldn't dream of having them replace them either," he said, interrupting. "However, they do need to keep that dog on a leash. It has a mean streak."

She nodded. "I hate to admit that you're probably right. Although Sammy has chased my cats I always thought he was harmless." She hesitated. "Thanks for being so understanding, Richard."

She went to pour the wine and he moved to a stool by the counter to watch, chatting about his plans for the evening, that he'd probably have to change his slacks first.

"When I changed the dinner reservation for later they didn't have a time until eight, and since I couldn't get tickets for Punch Line I thought we could try for that another time and take in a late movie after we ate."

While he'd explained they'd taken their wine and moved into the family room, sitting down on opposite sofas in front of the fireplace. Carolyn put down her glass on the coffee table between them, and then voiced the suggestion that had been growing in her mind since the Sammy incident.

"How about canceling our dinner reservation and having dinner here instead?" She shrugged. "It probably wouldn't be as good as the restaurant but it would give me a chance to make amends, and save you from having to change clothes."

His dark brows arched into a question. "But you're dressed to go out."

"I'm dressed for dinner with you," she said, honestly. "Here or there."

"Then let's make it here. If it's no bother."

She tilted her head. "It's not. Actually, it gives me a chance to use up some of the food in my freezer. I think I have two steaks, and I know I've got rice, vegetables and the makings of a fabulous salad."

"Hey, it sounds better than eating out. And staying put is probably a lot safer."

"What do you mean?"

He shrugged. "Just that the whole evening has been a comedy of errors. One of my new tires had a flat, the garage guy said it looked like a vandal had hammered a nail into the side of it, and then the dog attack."

"And that was after the plan changed because of my schedule." Carolyn managed a grin. She forced her thoughts away from the vandal reference. Things like that happened in Atlanta. It had nothing to do with Richard seeing her.

They went back into the kitchen where Carolyn put an apron on over her dress. She took the steaks from the freezer, the rice cooker from the cupboard and enlisted Richard to make the salad. Visiting as they worked, Carolyn learned more about Richard's work, that his foreign business associates were in Paris and London. She told him more about Dean and her own childhood with her dad.

The evening passed pleasantly, the steaks were broiled to perfection and dinner, complete with candlelight, was eaten in the family room by the fire rather than in the more formal dining room. She walked him back to the front door when it was finally time for him to leave.

"This has been the most perfect date I've ever had," he told her softly. "You are truly an amazing woman, Carolyn." His grin was slow and his dark eyes reflected the subtle light from the lamp on the hall table. "I hope we'll have many more great times together."

She nodded, not trusting her voice at that moment. He was so damn attractive, so vital with suppressed sexual energy. For a wild moment she wanted him to stay, to go upstairs with her, undress and spend the night. But she knew she wasn't ready for that. She needed to go slow, and make sure her feelings were real. That the man was as wonderful as he seemed to be. She couldn't afford another mistake.

And then he took the charged moment out of her hands, pulling her into his arms, holding her close against his body, his eyes intent on hers. Seconds passed, and in slow motion, his face lowered and he took her lips in a kiss that deepened until Carolyn felt as though she was melting into him. His hands tightened on her and she ached to press closer. When he lifted his head she would have stumbled backward but for his arms that still held her.

"Sweetheart," he whispered. "We have to wait."

Again, she could only incline her head.

"We must, you know." He feathered her face with kisses. "I don't want to spoil anything. You're too important to me."

"Yes, I know," she said, softly. "You're right."

Seconds later she opened the door and he stepped onto the porch where he turned back to face her.

"I'll call you, okay?"

"Okay." The words were a promise.

He raised a hand in farewell, then bounded down the steps to the sidewalk. Moments later he disappeared, headed to the white sports car parked on the street. She watched until his headlights disappeared.

After locking up and turning out the lights she went upstairs . . . alone.

11

During the following week Carolyn and Richard managed to see each other almost daily, their schedules permitting. Both were careful to keep a lid on feelings, she sensing he was as cautious about commitment as she was.

"We think alike," he'd told her several times when they'd been discussing personal likes and dislikes, an observation she'd already realized. "And it sounds like we have similar family goals." He'd grinned. "NNN might be the best thing that ever happened to me. I met you."

Now, as they sat together on the sofa in her family room, she remembered his words as they began to kiss. Within seconds the television movie they'd been watching was forgotten.

"My sweet Carolyn, I don't think I can leave you this time," Richard whispered against her mouth.

Carolyn's lashes fluttered open and she was caught by the passion she saw in his eyes. "I don't think I want you to go," she murmured, helpless to do anything but give herself to the moment.

His arm tightened around her, pulling her even closer as he tilted her backward so that they were lying side by side on the sofa.

"I've wanted you from our first meeting." His low voice hesitated. "Did you know that, Carolyn?—that it's taken every ounce of my willpower not to become a caveman with you." He feathered her face with kisses.

"Thank you for respecting me, Richard," she said, knowing her softly spoken words sounded inane. But the quaver in her voice gave away her own need of him.

He lifted his head, staring down into her face. "Are you sure?"

She nodded, and as his head lowered again, forgot everything else, closing her eyes, giving in to the sensation of his touch as he helped her undress. In seconds they lay naked. Again he hesitated.

"Yes," she whispered.

Her fingers traced invisible lines down his body as she answered his unspoken question. With a low moan his lips reclaimed hers, and this time his rising desire precluded gentleness. She met his mounting passion with a need she'd never felt before.

And then she forgot everything else.

Carolyn turned over in bed, not ready to wake up. Beyond her windows a late winter sun shone into her bedroom, giving her the illusion of spring which was less than a week away. She stretched, remembering that it was her day off, that she didn't have to rush to the studio for an early morning show. She could relax. Sleep in if she chose.

But the day beckoned. Carolyn threw back the covers and got up, humming as she went downstairs to make coffee, her two cats trailing at her heels. I've been singing a lot lately, she thought. And she knew why.

Richard.

She smiled as she headed for the front door, opened it and retrieved her morning newspaper. Taking it back to the kitchen, she sat on a bar stool, waiting for the coffee to drip. "Having time to read the paper with my coffee is pure luxury," she told the cats.

A half hour later Carolyn took her second cup and went upstairs to made her bed and put on jeans and a sweatshirt. She'd decided to weed her back-yard garden, a job she loved when time permitted. She spent the next couple of hours outside, again humming as she worked, her mind replaying the night Richard had first made love to her, the many hours she'd spent with him over the past two weeks since. It was surprising how quickly they'd bonded, how fast their feelings for one another had grown. He'd even postponed his return to Chicago, and curtailed some of his travel to be with her.

Love? she wondered, suspecting it was, as least from her perspective. Neither of them had spoken of love. She'd hesitated to commit herself that deeply and guessed he felt the same way, too, having been divorced.

She finished her outside work and was walking toward the open French doors when she heard the front doorbell ring. Tossing her gloves aside, she ran inside and down the hall toward the door where she could see a woman on the other side of the glass.

Reaching it, the door began to open before Carolyn could grab the knob. She froze, her body spasming with fear. She'd flipped the bolt lock after getting the paper this morning. Then the door swung wider and a woman stood framed in the opening.

"Dolores!" A long breath of relief whistled out of Carolyn's mouth.

"Hi, Carolyn." Dolores pulled off sunglasses to reveal puzzlement in her blue eyes. "I was surprised to find your door ajar. Did you forget to lock it?"

Carolyn shook her head. "I always keep it locked." She hesitated. "For a second I thought you'd found the key Dad misplaced. Did you?"

"I've never even seen a key to your place," Dolores replied. "And your door wasn't just unlocked, it wasn't even closed all the way."

"That's impossible. I made sure the bolt was flipped this morning. Since then I've been in the garden, not even in the house."

The thought sent a chill through Carolyn's stomach. Had someone come into her house? Her glance flew to the steps, traveling up them to the quietness of the second floor. She had to check the house. Now, while Dolores was with her.

But nobody had a key; the spare still hung on the hook in the kitchen. Still, in the light of the other incidents, she had to make sure. After asking Dolores to wait there, she looked into the first floor rooms, then headed upstairs and did the same. Once back in the lower hall she managed a shaky grin.

"Guess I'm jumpy," she said. "Because I can't imagine why that door was unlocked."

"Maybe you only thought you set the bolt. It's the only logical answer since you say there are no spare keys floating around." Her expression was suddenly defensive. "And even if I'd had a key I certainly would never have come into your house without permission."

Carolyn shook her head, as if to clear it. Something *was* wrong, but maybe it was her. Maybe Dolores was right; she hadn't really locked the door in her haste to read the paper with her morning coffee.

"I was about to make another pot of coffee," she said. "Care for a cup?" She reached behind Dolores and closed the door.

"I'd love one." Dolores followed her back to the kitchen. "I left in such a hurry this morning that I didn't get my usual quota."

In only minutes the coffee was dripping and Carolyn had set out two mugs, knowing they both drank it black. As they sat down on bar stools across the counter from one another Carolyn asked the question that was on her mind.

"So, what brings you to my place?"

Dolores sipped the coffee. "Wow, that's good." Then she glanced up to answer. "I had an early appointment with my hairdresser. If you remember, her shop is only a few blocks from you. I knew from Dean that today was your day off, and since I couldn't get you on the phone I figured you might be in the shower and chanced coming by and catching you at home." She indicated the blinking answering machine. "I left a message."

Carolyn grinned. "I didn't hear the phone over the radio I had playing. Guess I was really into my day off."

"As you should be, Carolyn. You work too hard."

Carolyn glanced away. She did put in a lot of hours, substituting when necessary at NNN. But work had been her lifesaver; it had kept her from thinking about the losses and failures in her personal life. Her job had become her life—until Richard.

"So, what brings you here, Dolores?" Carolyn realized something had to be on her stepmother's mind; Dolores had never just stopped by to visit.

"Well, two things."

Carolyn sipped her coffee. "Which are?"

A silence went by.

"I have qualms about Dean spending time at Anderson Youth House. Because he's been alone so much I don't think he has a grasp of the realities of the world. I'm worried that Dean could be influenced by the wrong type of kids." She put up a hand to stop Carolyn's retort. "He's my only grandchild and I want the best for him." Her eyes were suddenly direct. "Can you understand my concern, Carolyn? I know you love Dean, too."

"Of course I understand," she replied gently, then paused to gather her argument. "It's because I love Dean—and because I know the kids at the Youth House, including their sponsor Barney McGill—that I believe this experience will be a positive one for him." She drew in a deep breath. "Dolores, we both know that Dean lacks the confidence to make friends in his own age group. I think this may be his opportunity to gain that confidence."

Dolores glanced away, looking suddenly unsure. "You could be right. It's just that I worry about Dean. He's such a good boy and I want the best for him." She spread her hands. "I don't know how to go about helping him, and his parents are too busy—with one thing or another."

Carolyn knew what she meant. Jessie worked long hours to support the family and Tony was simply inadequate. Dean was getting lost somewhere within their shuffle.

Quickly, Carolyn explained her own concerns about Dean, and her recognition of his technology talents. "I promise you that he won't be exploited by the faculty or the kids." She hesitated. "And the experience could be important to his future."

There was another brief silence.

Finally, Dolores nodded. "All right then. You have my permission. I know you love Dean and will look out for him."

"You can be assured that I will."

Dolores sipped more coffee. "So that brings me to my second reason for stopping by."

Carolyn smiled, waiting for her to go on.

"I want to invite you to a little get-together I'm having for the family," she said.

"Someone's birthday—or something?"

"No, just because we've let such things slide since your dad's death, and I know he wouldn't like that."

Carolyn nodded. "You're right. Dad would have wanted family traditions to continue."

"So, are you free on Sunday evening?"

"Yeah, I am. Only working in the morning."

"Good." Dolores drained her mug and stood up. "I thought we'd have dinner at 6:30. Okay?"

"Fine with me." Carolyn hesitated. "If I can bring Richard with me. He'll be in town for the weekend and we've planned to spend it together."

Dolores raised her carefully plucked eyebrows. "I've heard about your new friend through Dean." She smiled. "Of course bring Richard." A pause. "Is he a serious suitor?"

Carolyn put down her mug, her gaze direct. "I think he might be, Dolores. I like him very much."

"I see." Dolores glanced away, headed for the hallway. "In that case we'll all look forward to meeting him." Her laugh sounded forced. "We'll check him out."

"Thanks, Dolores. I know everyone will like him as much as I do."

Dolores nodded, stepped onto the porch and glanced back to Carolyn. "I know you'll look out for Dean." A pause. "He'll be at my house after school tomorrow. You can pick him up and bring him back after his class. Will that work for you?"

"Of course. I'll be there a few minutes before six. His class will be from seven to eight-thirty. I should have him back to your place by nine."

"Great." Dolores went down the front steps. "We'll see you then."

Carolyn waved, watching as her stepmother got into her car and then headed out of the neighborhood. An odd encounter overall, she thought shutting the door. But then weren't most of her meetings of late with Dolores? She didn't understand her dad's wife, but it was enough that they got along and had the same goals in common.

But did they? Things were different now that she and Dolores had become her father's heirs. She'd often felt that Dolores resented her, because she'd inherited the assets typically given to the wife.

Foolish thought. Because of her dad Dolores was a wealthy woman. She wouldn't resent protocol for the offspring, no one would. Everyone knew that previous assets should go to the rightful heirs.

My mind is running away with itself, she thought and closed the door. She stood there for a moment, looking at her distorted reflection in the shiny brass lock, then slowly she reached out and turned the bolt. She could've sworn she'd done the same thing this morning.

But she must have been mistaken.

12

"**H**ey, would you believe it, Carolyn?" the on-air customer said. "I recently had the same experience you had a few weeks back."

Carolyn smiled at the camera. "What was that? Something to do with the makeup?" She gave a laugh, indicating the line of model's cosmetics she'd been demonstrating, and the kit of basics the woman had just ordered. "Did I wear the wrong color lipstick and rouge?"

"Oh no." The woman was a regular customer from Sarasota, Florida. "Your makeup is always perfect." A pause. "I was referring to the incident when you found your registration and insurance certificate on the front seat of your car. You didn't remember leaving your driver's window open after you'd locked the door and someone ransacked your car."

"Oh." Carolyn was momentarily taken aback but she managed to hold her smile. That was the last confidence she'd shared with her customers. "So you had one of those overload episodes, too," she replied, contriving a light tone. "They seem to happen when we have too many things on our mind and then do everyday actions by rote."

"Yeah," the woman said, laughing. "And then promptly forget we did them." Another pause before she switched the subject back to her order. "I know I'm going to enjoy my makeup—can't wait to get it. Thanks, Carolyn."

"You're welcome."

They hung up and Carolyn continued her spiel, talking to several more customers who'd called in to order the cosmetic kit. She had almost forgotten the earlier incident when Grace, another regular buyer from Denver, called in to chat and order.

"You know, Carolyn, the strangest thing is that I also had that same experience as you and your Sarasota customer."

"What do you mean?" Again Carolyn kept her cool, and her smile in place.

"Well, I'm a travel agent and I should know better, but I left my purse in the locked car when I ran into a drugstore to pick up a prescription. When I came back ten minutes later, my registration was on the passenger seat along with my emptied purse, and I figured I'd left the window open. I think I surprised the thief before he stole anything."

"Are you sure you're not calling from Sarasota?" Carolyn asked, joking to lighten the mood. But her inner antenna was on full alert. She couldn't control what was written about her, like her baby dying, but she knew it was imperative to turn the on-air conversation positive, or risk the ripple effect of many viewers' innate fear to call in and talk. She would lose customers, their orders and NNN's confidence in her saleswoman abilities.

Grace laughed. "No, as you know, my home is in Denver, lived here all my life."

"So it sounds like you and I and our friend from Sarasota are being a little absentminded."

"I guess so, Carolyn." A laugh came over the air. "I just wanted to share my own dumbness—because it was so similar." A hesitation. "And I want the makeup kit."

Her customer went on to talk about the product and Carolyn answered all of her questions. Shortly thereafter they hung up and the models' makeup segment was over a few minutes later. It was a relief to Carolyn when her stage went dark, and the lights went on for a salesman who was selling yard equipment on another set.

After disconnecting all of her ear and vocal devices, Carolyn left her set and headed for Roberta's office upstairs. Although the experiences of her viewers were probably random, they were too close to her own recent scary incidents to ignore. What if there was a crazy out there, a person who was zeroing in on her? She knew that such a thing was probably remote, but she also knew that it did happen to television personalities on occasion. She owed it to herself to make sure, and to her viewers who'd given their names and cities on the air. If they hadn't blocked their personal information, their addresses and phone numbers would be listed in local phone books—and they could become vulnerable to a stalking creep.

* * *

"Carolyn, are you all right? I mean, is everything okay in your life?"

"What do you mean?"

Carolyn's meeting with Roberta had gone differently from what she'd expected. Roberta's concern hadn't been for the callers but for her. She'd listened patiently while Carolyn had explained the incidents her customers had experienced that were so similar to her own.

Roberta came around her desk to grab her hand, and look intently into her eyes. "I'm your boss—" She hesitated, as though formulating her words into a way to express herself without offending Carolyn. "But I'm also your friend and I'm concerned that you might be reading more into this than you should—because you're upset about something else." She shook her head. "The last thing I'd ever do is pry into your private life, because it's none of my business—unless a personal problem affected your job at NNN."

A silence went by.

Was Roberta telling her that she felt a personal problem was affecting her on-camera performance? Carolyn wondered. Warning her to keep her work and private life separate? God! Thank goodness I didn't confide all the other things that have gone wrong in my life lately, she thought. I could lose my job.

"Everything is good in my life, Roberta," Carolyn said. She decided not to update her about her relationship with Richard, uncertain how Roberta would react to a romance that had begun in her own office. "I believed I should bring this issue to your attention, in the remote possibility that there was some connection between the viewer's incidents and my anonymous caller." She managed a smile and tried not to feel rebuffed. "Wouldn't I have been remiss if there was a creep out there and I hadn't reported it?"

"Of course." Roberta stepped back, smiling. "That caring is the very trait you display to your viewers, which is why they love you so much."

"Thanks, Roberta. I appreciate the compliment." Another pause. "So, we'll just disregard these latest incidents, figure it's only part of the job?"

Roberta moved back around her desk and sat down. "Yeah. I think that's wise—the way to handle it." She wiped her hair back and fixed it behind each ear. "As I told you the last time you had a concern about your viewers, they copy you, want to think their lives mimic yours, because that gives them a connection to the famous person they admire."

"You're probably right, Roberta," Carolyn said, moving back to the door where she faced her boss again. "I appreciate your input." She gave a laugh. "Part of your job, right?"

"Right. Among a multitude of other things."

"So thanks, Roberta."

"You're welcome, as always, Carolyn." Another grin. "You know you're our biggest gun in selling products. NNN loves you and wants you to stay happy with us."

"Thanks," Carolyn repeated, and then closed the door behind her as she left.

In minutes she was out in the employee parking lot, heading her Volvo for the exit, her thoughts on her conversation with Roberta.

"You're wrong, Roberta," she said into the quiet of her car. "Something is going on."

What? she wondered.

She didn't know. It was beyond comprehension.

And almost beyond belief.

"Hi, sweetheart. I was missing you so much I just had to call." A brief pause. "Hope it's not a bad time."

Carolyn smiled, pressing her cell phone to her ear, so pleased to hear from Richard that she'd almost rear-ended the car in front of her that was stopped at a red light. "It's never a bad time to hear your voice, Richard." She switched the receiver to her other ear in order to shift gears when the light changed.

"Glad to hear it. Exactly how I feel about you."

"A mutual admiration society?"

"Something like that."

There was a long silence as Carolyn drove through the intersection.

"So, where are you tonight?"

"Driving home to my place—in Chicago of course, after a long, hard-driving meeting today."

"And was it successful?"

His chuckle came over the line. "Of course. How could they resist my luxury condominium proposal on a South Sea island, or my devastating charm?"

She laughed, too. "How indeed? I certainly couldn't. Were your adversaries women?"

"'Course not, sweetheart." His laugh came over the wire, a deeply satisfied macho sound. "In this case everyone at the table were men, but I love it that you worry about women." A pause. "You don't have to worry about other women you know."

Carolyn shifted position on the car seat as she accelerated through another light. "Thanks for saying that," she replied, inanely, hating it that he'd guessed her fears.

"And—do I have to worry about other men?"

"No," she said, sincerely. "You don't."

"Good." A silence. "Then we can talk about our future when I get back to Atlanta."

Her emotions soared but she kept her voice in a normal range. "And when is that, Richard?"

"In a few days. I'll have to let you know."

"I'll be here."

"And I'll be in touch, okay?"

"Okay."

"I love you, Carolyn, you know that, don't you?"

"Yes," she whispered.

"And?"

"I love you, too."

"Good, sweetheart." Another brief pause. "I'll call you tonight, before you go to sleep. Will you be there?"

"Of course."

"Until then."

The phone went dead and Carolyn continued on to Dolores's house where she was to pick up Dean and take him to the Youth House. With Richard's words in her head, she felt like she was flying on wings rather than maneuvering in rush-hour traffic.

Had she ever loved any man more? Rob, her former husband? Tom, the boyfriend she'd almost married?

She didn't think so.

She turned off the street into the driveway that led to Anderson Youth House, and felt Dean tense in the passenger seat beside her.

She glanced. "You okay, honey?"

He nodded.

"You know," she said, as she swung the Volvo into a parking space. "These kids are probably trembling in their boots because they think you're a computer genius. They might even be a little scared to meet you, worried that you'll think they're dumb."

"But I'm not a genius, Auntie Carolyn. I'm only a kid," he added as his voice faded.

"Well, you know how they feel then, Dean," she said, grateful that he'd given her the opportunity to turn his feelings around. "They're intimidated by you just as you are by them. It's up to you to see to it that they don't feel inadequate by all of your computer knowledge—that they're able to feel safe enough to ask questions. You'll have to guard against seeming like an expert."

"Oh, I'd never do that."

"I know you wouldn't, Dean." She reached to squeeze his knee. "These kids will benefit so much by what you can teach them. They're computer illiterate at this point."

"Really?" He sounded incredulous.

She had his attention. "Yep."

Carolyn continued the conversation in the same vein as they walked to the back entrance. By the time they went into the Youth House, Dean's confidence was almost restored, although his darting glance told her he was still nervous.

"You'll really like Barney McGill," Carolyn said, as they headed down the hall toward the recreation room where two donated computers had been set up for the kids to use. "I know you've talked to him on the phone but he's quite a presence in person."

"You like him, Auntie Carolyn, I can tell," Dean replied, grinning. "I know he's single. Do you think you'd ever date him?"

Having reached the doorway, Carolyn stopped short to face Dean. "Barney and I are only friends." She hesitated. "You remember that I've been seeing Richard Crawford, the man I met at NNN?"

He nodded. "Grandma told me that the family would meet him soon."

"That's true, next Sunday."

"Do you like him as much as Barney?"

His question gave her pause. She'd always recognized Barney's attractiveness, but had felt he had some personality traits that were too similar to Rob's, that he was too closed about his personal feelings. But I'll never know that for sure now, she thought, as a mental picture of Richard flashed into her mind.

"Yes, I do, Dean," she said. It was a relief that they'd reached the recreation room. "But on a man and woman level, my feelings for Richard are stronger."

"What's all this about feelings?" Minnie said, turning from the small group of teenage kids just inside the door.

Carolyn grinned at her friend. "Nothing much. Just a few comments about Richard."

"Uh, the great and wonderful new man in your life." She paused, her expression curious. "So when do your friends get to meet him? And, um, pass judgment as to whether or not we think he's good enough for you."

Carolyn sensed that Minnie was halfway serious

even though her tone was teasing. "As I said when we talked on the phone, Richard lives in Chicago and isn't always in town. I plan to have a little dinner party soon, his schedule permitting."

"Good. I look forward to it. Can't wait to finally meet this paragon."

"Paragon?" Carolyn raised her brows.

Minnie laughed. "My impression from your description of him."

"I didn't know I sounded that enthused. I must have it bad."

"I think you do, kiddo." A pause. "I just hope you go slow."

"Think you do—what?" Barney asked, stepping into the room in time to hear Minnie's comment.

"Just telling Carolyn to take it easy with the new guy she's dating," Minnie said.

He raised his brows, his eyes shifting to Carolyn. "Sounds like good advice. You gonna listen?"

Carolyn smiled a hello. "I'll explain later, okay?"

"Sure, look forward to it." He held her gaze for a few seconds longer, his steely eyes unreadable. It was a relief when he turned their intensity onto Dean. "You must be our new teacher." He put out his hand. "Aside from our phone conversations, glad to finally meet you, Dean. Heard lots of good things about you."

Dean beamed as they shook hands. Carolyn watched as Barney introduced him to the half dozen kids who waited to learn the mysteries of the computer from Dean.

"Barney sure has a way with kids, doesn't he." Carolyn shook her head at Minnie. "You'd never believe that Dean was so scared only a few minutes ago."

"Yeah, Barney has a knack." A pause. "I hope he gets to be a dad again one of these days."

"Uh-huh. He's a natural."

"Want to hear something funny?" Minnie tapped the toe of her booted foot against the planked floor.

Carolyn nodded.

"I had this wild thought that you and Barney would be perfect for each other."

"Good God, Minnie," Carolyn said, startled. "How long have you been harboring that thought?"

"A few weeks."

"What on earth would ever give you that idea?"

Before they could talk more Barney raised his hand for quiet, then announced that the class would be a hands-on instruction, that Dean would explain the steps as he went along and anyone could ask questions. "I want you to take notes that you can refer to when it's your turn at the computer," he told them.

By the time the class was over an hour and a half later, Dean looked happy and satisfied. He had definitely made new friends and looked forward to the next class in a week. He talked nonstop all the way back to his grandmother's house where Carolyn hugged him and saw him safely inside. Then she turned toward home.

Her sudden awareness of the black sedan behind the Volvo jolted her with adrenaline. She pushed her foot down on the accelerator, shooting through a caution light. The other car didn't follow, stopping instead.

Carolyn sucked in a breath, then let it out in a long sigh. No one followed her. She was becoming a crisis junkie, and she needed to take herself in hand before she lost it completely.

Maybe, as Roberta had implied, she was buying into the weirdo scenario because something wasn't right in her personal life.

But what? Certainly falling in love with Richard was a positive thing. The negative events of the past—her dad and child dying, her divorce and the breakup with Tom—were all behind her.

There was nothing she could pinpoint. Just like there was nothing she could identify as a threat.

But she knew there was one.

13

"I love you, Carolyn."

Richard's words, spoken in her shadowy bedroom, fell against the soft backdrop of the water fountain below the windows. He had propped himself up onto his elbow that rested on the mattress, so that he could look down at her as she lay against the pillows, sated from their lovemaking. For long moments neither spoke.

"You're so beautiful." He lowered his lips to feather her flushed cheeks in kisses. "So sweet and kind and . . . sexy. You're every man's dream come true."

Carolyn's lashes fluttered open as he lifted his mouth, propping his face once more only inches above hers. Their eyes locked, brown and green, and she was unable to look away.

"I love you," he said again.

"I love you, too, Richard," she whispered back.

"I want you—no, I need you, to be my wife." He reached to pull her closer to him. "Will you marry me, Carolyn?"

Her arms encircled him, drawing him down on top of her, so she could hold him close, feel his heart beating against hers. For long seconds she clung to him, knowing her answer would alter her life, was in fact the most important decision she might ever make.

They clung together, gently, lovingly, the aftermath of their recent passion. Her mind replayed their times together since the day they'd met in Roberta's office almost three months ago. After the first date they'd been together almost constantly when Richard wasn't traveling. They'd exchanged family histories in depth: she knew everything about his background and he knew all of hers. It seemed as though they'd known each other forever, or at least a year, not just a few months.

But is length of time that important, she asked herself. She'd known Rob for several years before he'd proposed, but she'd spent far less time with him than she'd spent with Richard in three months. Richard had even shown her his computerized business setup that accessed the universal market, and she'd been impressed. He'd wanted to prove his legitimacy, a thing she had never doubted. He had to have a real business even to be considered by NNN.

"If you love me, too, it'll work," he said, gently prompting her, even as he sounded suddenly unsure of her response. "Because we both believe in marriage and—and having a family." He stared intently into her eyes. "We both made a mistake the first time but—" He broke off to control his emotions. "Oh my God, Carolyn, you *must* marry me. It won't be a mistake this time, for either of us."

Carolyn swallowed back the tightness in her throat, too close to tears to speak for a moment. "I will, Richard," she whispered. "There's nothing in the world that I want more than to be your wife."

For a second longer he didn't speak. Then, with a low groan, he lowered his lips over hers. After a few minutes Carolyn was able to utter a few words.

"Mrs. Richard Crawford. It sounds right."

"And it feels right, sweetheart."

Carolyn couldn't concentrate on anything else but him as he demonstrated his words. She knew that she'd made the right decision. And then she forgot everything else.

It was much later when Carolyn came awake as Richard sat up in bed. As she was about to speak, he motioned her to silence.

"Shh," he whispered. "I thought I heard something downstairs."

Her pulse quickened, and she held still, listening.

The quiet of the house was complete. A glance around the room told her the cats were gone. Then she remembered. They'd left them downstairs. She leaned closer to Richard and reminded him.

He shook his head. "Sounded like the front door."

Quietly, Richard stood up. Still whispering, he told her to stay put, then disappeared into the hall. Seconds later she followed him, too scared for his safety to do otherwise.

At the top of the stairs she hesitated. Richard had already disappeared into the darkness of the lower hall. She held her breath, straining her ears.

The silence was complete. Nothing moved. She

had no idea where Richard had gone. Panic knotted her stomach.

Then the hall light snapped on below her. "It's okay, Carolyn." Richard stepped into view, looking up at her. "No one's here. Must have been the cats."

"Where are they?"

"Asleep on the sofa in the family room."

She held onto the railing, weak with relief. Yet she still felt . . . what? Doubt that her cats would have gone back to sleep so soon after causing a disturbance loud enough to wake Richard up?

Stop it! she commanded herself. It's only nerves. Richard wasn't used to hearing the night sounds typical of her house. Her cats wouldn't have been so relaxed if there'd been an intruder.

Back in the bedroom Richard announced that Mayo and Mustard had done him a favor: awakened him or he might have slept until morning.

"I have to go, sweetheart, overseas business calls to make. Unfortunately that means I have to hustle or I'll miss their business day." He hesitated. "You okay to be alone?"

She nodded. Although she'd mentioned a few of her recent fears, Carolyn had avoided going into detail. She hadn't wanted to spoil their times together, maybe have him wonder about her state of mind, as Roberta had.

From a front window she watched him go out to his car, heard him try to start the engine. In minutes he was back at the door and she let him in.

"The damn car won't start." He tossed his jacket on a chair. "Guess I'm staying. My calls will have to wait."

"What's wrong with it?"

"Dunno. Might have something to do with the fuel line because it acts like it's out of gas, and I have a full tank." He shook his head in disgust. "Could even be the battery. I'm beginning to think it's a lemon."

They went back to bed. Carolyn lay awake, listening to Richard sleep, glad he was there, wondering if the BMW was really a lemon, or if someone had tampered with it.

The next morning the car was towed to a garage. Richard had been right; it was a clogged fuel line. The mechanic had said it happend a lot in older cars, as the gas tank gets rusty, but that it shouldn't have happened in a car as new as Richard's.

"Could someone have poured something into the gas tank?" Carolyn asked, prickling with apprehension.

"Not possible," Richard said. "I have a locking gas cap."

But Carolyn still couldn't help but wonder.

They hadn't told anyone about their engagement since Carolyn wanted to tell her family first. When Dolores called and reminded her about Sunday dinner, the date having been postponed once because of Dean's parents, she explained that Richard would be with her. It would be the perfect time to announce their engagement.

Carolyn, with Richard at her side, rang the front doorbell at exactly three in the afternoon.

"Nervous?" Richard asked, looking handsome in his dark slacks and pale blue cashmere sweater.

She grinned and shook her head. "Should I be?" she asked, teasing.

His lashes lowered slightly, and she knew he would have kissed her had they not heard movement on the other side of the door.

For a moment Carolyn had almost admitted that she was nervous. Sudden apprehension had descended upon her as they drove up the driveway. She wanted everyone to like Richard as much as she did, to accept him as a future family member.

Dean answered the door, swinging it wide and embracing Carolyn as she and Richard stepped into the entry hall. She hugged him back, and resisted an urge to smooth down the red rooster tail on the top of his head.

Then Dolores, dressed in a red silk, long-sleeved blouse and matching slacks, came from the living room to greet them, giving Carolyn a peck on the cheek before stepping back to look at Richard. Carolyn made the introductions, including Jessie and Tony who stood under the archway behind Dolores.

"Hey," Dean said, as they went into the living room and sat down. "Richard seems pretty cool, Aunt Carolyn."

Carolyn shot him a grin. "Thanks, Dean."

Dolores had the house polished and perfect, spring flowers in vases and light hors d'oeuvres on china serving dishes that had been arranged on the coffee table. She ushered them to seats on the sofas in front of the fireplace, then served a choice of Merlot or Chardonnay.

"Perfect bouquet," Richard told Dolores, as he sampled the Merlot. And a moment later as he swallowed a bacon-wrapped oyster, "Incredibly good."

Dolores smiled, pleased by his compliment. Carolyn could see how drastically her persona changed when she was in the presence of an attractive man. Dolores needed a significant other; she was really lost without a husband.

The next hour was pleasant, with Dean talking about his computer class at the Youth House, bragging about his new friend, Barney McGill, and about how much the kids loved learning about the Internet. It was obvious that Dean had a big case of hero worship for Barney.

"Everyone loves going on-line," he told them, his tone as serious as a headmaster's in a private school.

Carolyn suppressed a grin. "Even us adults."

"Like my grandma," Dean added.

Dolores nodded, without comment. Carolyn figured she didn't want to elaborate on her Internet interests: finding single men. Carolyn knew she wouldn't.

Richard tried to engage Tony in the conversation several times but Jessie's husband didn't appear to have a wide range of topics that interested him.

"I'm between jobs rights now," Tony said in response to Richard's generic question about his occupation.

Jessie glanced down, embarrassed, while Dolores's lips tightened. Tony's chronic unemployed status was a serious issue.

"Oh." Richard looked awkward, as though he sensed he'd accidentally hit on a sensitive subject and wished he hadn't asked. "I know how that feels, Tony. Happens to me when I'm between projects. I often wonder if the next one will really work out, or if I'll end up out of work."

"But it sounds like that can't be too big a worry for you, Richard." Dolores refilled his wine glass. "Not when those projects are multimillion dollar deals."

There was an instant silence.

"On the contrary, Dolores. Some are, some aren't," Richard said. His eyes darted to Carolyn, as though hoping she could help change the subject. "I'm always at the mercy of economics, interest rates, and my investors' perception of the stock market."

Carolyn set down her empty glass, then casually directed the conversation to the fragrance of Dolores's dinner that was cooking in the kitchen. She sniffed the air. "Smells like roast beef."

"It is," Dolores said, smiling, diverted from the conversation. "Prime rib to be exact." She stood up. "And I should check on it. Don't want it overcooked."

"Neither do we," Richard said, including Tony in his appraisal. "Us men usually like our beef rare."

"Or medium rare," Tony added, grinning, won over by Richard's friendliness.

A few minutes later Dolores ushered them into the dining room, explaining that there were name cards to show them where to sit. Carolyn couldn't help but feel the silliness of arranged seating for a family dinner party of six. She hoped Richard would overlook such pretension.

Once they were seated Dolores served the food: baked potatoes with her special cheese sauce, sliced prime rib with creamy horseradish, broccoli, green salad, and hot rolls. She placed the serving dishes on the table to be passed around. Then she poured white wine into their goblets and requested a toast.

"To family," Dolores said, lifting her glass.

"And prosperity for all of us," Jessie added.

Everyone sipped, including Dean who had water.

"Another toast," Carolyn lifted her glass again.

Everyone did the same, looking at her expectantly.

"To engagements." She'd decided a toast was the perfect way to announce their plans. "Richard and I have decided to marry. We wanted you to be the first to know."

There was a hesitation.

"That's great, Aunt Carolyn," Dean said, and clinked his glass against the others.

After that everyone offered congratulations. Questions flowed—where did they plan to live?—would he move to Atlanta if Carolyn was keeping her job?—when and where would they marry? Richard and Carolyn took turns answering. By the time Dolores started the food dishes around the table, the conversation had switched to other topics, but kept coming back to their announcement. When the meal was over, Carolyn felt drained, grateful that she and Richard could leave soon. But it was still another hour in the living room before they could make a gracious exit.

"Thank you for a wonderful time," Carolyn told Dolores as they were leaving. After good-byes and a kiss for Dean, she and Richard went out to his BMW. Once headed down the driveway, Carolyn breathed a sigh of relief. She hadn't realized how exhausting it could be to announce an engagement.

* * *

"So, who is this Barney McGill," Richard said as he drove along the street toward her townhouse. "The way Dean talked about him you'd think he was God." He chuckled, glancing at her. "You must know him."

"Yeah, I do know him. Barney's a great guy, even if he has some hard edges."

"How so?"

"For starters, he lost his wife and little boys several years ago in a boating accident. It left him pretty shattered." She paused. "And then there's his profession which can be pretty grim at times."

"What does he do?" He glanced again, interested.

"He's a homicide detective."

"You're kidding." Richard's surprise registered in his tone. "The guy works murder scenes, then spends his spare time with orphans? Fascinating."

"Uh-huh, it is. The kids all love him. Barney always keeps his promises and expects them to do the same." She gave a laugh. "Amazingly, they do. Barney is a father figure to them. They know he's there for them."

"Sounds like you have a case of hero worship, too."

"Nothing so drastic. But I do admire him immensely."

A silence settled around them. Richard was the first to break it.

"Have you ever dated Barney?" His words sounded stilted.

"Hey." Carolyn reached to pat his hand on the steering wheel. "You're not jealous of Barney, are you?"

"That depends." He didn't look at her but she sensed his seriousness.

"On what?"

"Whether or not you dated him, if you had a relationship—*if you were ever in love with him.*"

Unable to stop herself, Carolyn laughed.

"What's so funny?" His tone told her he was upset.

"Oh, Richard." She leaned against him, resting her head against his shoulder. "This topic is only funny because the thought of a romance with Barney is, and has always been, nonexistent. I'm not interested in him other than a friend, and he's not interested in me." A pause. "I think Barney is too wounded to be interested in any woman at this point."

"But have you dated him?"

"Of course not." She hesitated. "Do you remember the night we ran into each other outside of the Italian restaurant?"

He nodded, his eyes on his driving.

"We had dinner that night because my friend Minnie, who also donates time at the Youth House, was unable to join us as previously planned. It wasn't a date, even though we ended up eating together."

"I think I saw Barney that night. Is he a big man with dark hair?"

"That's him. You probably saw him leave to get his own car. I was waiting for mine when you turned up."

Another silence went by.

"I'm sorry. I guess I felt a little threatened."

She patted his hand again. "It's okay, Richard. I'd feel the same way about you."

It was his turn to laugh. He was still chuckling when the BMW suddenly veered toward the edge of the street.

"Shit!" Richard cried. "The steering wheel feels like it came loose." He slammed on the brakes, just as the car wheels left the street to angle into a shallow ditch. They came to an abrupt stop.

"At least the brakes still work," Richard said, turning to her. "Are you all right?"

She nodded. "What happened?" Her voice quavered. "We could have been in a serious accident."

"But we weren't, thank God." Richard sounded shaken. He fumbled in his pocket for his cell phone and then called 911. "One thing for sure," he told her. "We aren't riding in this car again until a mechanic tells me what happened this time—that it's not a fucking lemon."

A short time later a police cruiser pulled up behind them, followed a few minutes later by a tow truck. It was determined that the steering had failed. After the policeman took a brief report, arrangements made to tow the BMW to the nearest dealership, Richard called for a taxi to take them home.

All the way home Carolyn was unsettled but tried to convince herself that, odd as it was, the incident was accidental. But it was very strange, wasn't it?

Very strange.

14

Carolyn never did find out exactly what went wrong with the BMW. "A connection came loose, might be a flaw that goes back to something not being done right on the assembly line," Richard told her. "Whatever it was, the manufacturer is taking care of it free of charge."

"That's the least they could do," Carolyn said. "In different circumstances we could have been killed."

"Agreed."

Richard left town on Tuesday, having delayed his scheduled departure from Monday in order to take care of his car. The strangeness of the situation struck Carolyn as odd and she couldn't get it out of her mind. Common sense told her it was just as the dealer said, a freak accident. But in the light of all the other freaky things that had happened lately, she couldn't completely dismiss it as such.

When Dolores called and invited her out for dinner on Wednesday, Carolyn accepted, glad of the diversion. She wondered what was on her stepmother's mind. She suspected something to do with Dean, as Dolores had said it was important that they talk.

Carolyn walked into the restaurant at six-thirty on Wednesday night and was surprised to see Jessie sitting at the table with Dolores. Her heart sank. Was something wrong with Dean?

She'd only greeted them, been seated next to her stepmother, and exchanged greetings when Dolores ordered a bottle of Chardonnay from the waiter who hovered at the table. Carolyn waited, engaging in small talk until the wine was brought and served. But her stomach churned; something was wrong.

"Mom asked me to join you," Jessie said, opening the topic Carolyn had been dreading. She raised her brows and then looked away. "I'm still undecided as to whether or not I should even be here." She shrugged and then met Carolyn's eyes, her own open and honest. "I just want you to know you are a very important person in my life—and in Dean's life—and I want the best for you, because I care."

Carolyn smiled, suddenly confused, uncertain of what Jessie meant. So she nodded, and waited for either Jessie or Dolores to clarify.

Dolores reached to give Carolyn a hug, a gesture uncommon to their relationship. "I have a surrogate mother's need to intervene here, Carolyn," she began and then hesitated. "I loved your dad and I know he'd want me to speak up for him." She broke off. "It's about your engagement."

"What about my engagement, Dolores?" Carolyn's first reaction was relief. The meeting wasn't about Dean.

There was a long pause. They all sipped their

wine, as though no one wanted to jump into the vacuum left by Carolyn's question.

"I feel like I have to say something, Carolyn, because your father isn't here to say it for himself," Dolores said, finally.

Another pause.

Carolyn set down her glass. "And what's that, Dolores?"

Dolores exhaled a deep breath. "I'm concerned, and I know that your father would have been as well, that you've committed to marry a man you've only known a couple of months. I want to ask you, in place of your father, to reconsider, to put off such an important decision until you know Richard better."

Carolyn raised her eyes from her glass, meeting Dolores's steady gaze. "Thank you for being concerned, but it isn't necessary in this case. Although I've only known Richard for a relatively short time, *I know Richard*. NNN would never have considered him as a vendor if he wasn't legitimate. I've been with him almost constantly in the weeks I've known him, heard about his background, that his parents are dead, that his two sisters live on the West Coast, that he conducts much of his business on the Internet, that he is worth a great deal of money." Carolyn glanced away. "The money part means nothing to me aside from the fact that he doesn't need mine."

"But how do you know that for sure?"

"Trust me, I know."

Another silence.

"What about Tom?" Dolores asked.

Jessie kept her eyes lowered, obviously uncomfortable with the conversation.

"What about him?" Carolyn made an effort to keep her voice calm, to stay polite. The whole thrust of the conversation was none of Dolores's business.

Dolores took a drink from her wine glass. "I know that he still cares about you, Carolyn. And I know that you once cared deeply for him."

Carolyn controlled her need to lash out about Tom, the man who'd taken over her father's respected practice of many years. "I no longer have much regard for Tom, Dolores."

"You can't hold him responsible for your father's actions before he died, Carolyn."

"I don't."

"I think you do." As Carolyn opened her mouth to protest, Dolores waved her to silence. "I think you need to consider the possibility that you've transferred some of your pain regarding the loss of your father to Tom."

Instant anger shot through her. Carolyn pushed back her chair, indignant, ready to bolt from the restaurant. "And I think you don't know what you're talking about, Dolores. Aside from his personal integrity, his sense of right and wrong that he'd established long before he ever met you, he was a rich man and he didn't need to manipulate company funds." She leaned toward her stepmother. "Why is it that you keep bringing up this subject? And why don't you stick up for my father in this matter?"

"No reason, Carolyn. I always stuck up for your father, and I agree that he was a man with sterling integrity, one of the reasons I loved him so much." Dolores's eyes were suddenly direct. "But for now I only have concern for your welfare, believe it or not, Carolyn. I don't want you to make a mistake."

Before Carolyn could respond Jessie jumped into the conflict. "Hey guys, remember? We're family."

Another long silence went by and Carolyn wondered why she was even there. She wished she'd never agreed to meet Dolores and hear her stepmother's misguided attempt to be a confidant, a role she'd never assumed while Carolyn's father was alive.

"Mom," Jessie said finally, "you have no right to interfere in Carolyn's decisions about her life." As Dolores sucked in a shocked breath, she turned to Carolyn. "And Carolyn, I believe my mom's heart was in the right place to be concerned about you, especially in light of your losses in recent years." Nervously, she wiped back her red hair, looking frazzled. "But I agree with you that it doesn't give her license to tell you what to do, even if she has serious reservations."

Another silence.

"Thanks, Jessie. I know your feelings are genuine and I appreciate your being candid," Carolyn said finally, fighting sudden tears. "And I know you realize how much I love Dean. You're the only family I have and I love all of you."

Tears welled in Jessie's eyes. "I know Carolyn. I don't have a blood sister either, but you're *my sister*." She laughed. "Would you believe I've been almost jealous of Dean's love for you—because you're such an idol to him."

Carolyn shook her head, too emotional to respond.

And then they were all hugging, until the waiter interrupted with a request for their orders. The dispute was forgotten for the moment.

Later, over coffee, a variation of the topic surfaced again after Jessie confided Dean's new confidence in himself. She attributed the change to his computer class at the Youth House.

"Yeah, the computer is a great ice-breaker," Dolores said, agreeing. "I've found some wonderful friends on-line."

Jessie's features tightened momentarily. "Men friends? Like this person who calls himself Jock but who says his real name is Will Millgard from Paterson, New Jersey?"

Dolores swallowed her coffee wrong and choked. "Yes, that's right, Jessie," she said when she finally stopped coughing. "He's a widower who is lonely and hopes to remarry in the future." Her tone sharpened. "He's like many of the people who've lost a spouse, lonely and—"

"Looking for love?" Jessie finished her sentence.

Carolyn sipped her coffee, determined to stay out of yet another family conflict.

"Jessie!" Dolores's cheeks flamed. "That was uncalled for."

Jessie exhaled a long breath. "I'm sorry, Mom." She spread her hands, glancing at Carolyn. "I'm just concerned. You don't know who you're really talking to on those dating forums and singles chat rooms."

"They're perfectly safe, I promise. All of us have been checked out, have had to supply proof of identity."

"How do you do that?" Carolyn asked, curious

despite her resolve not to be involved in a mother-daughter dispute.

"I e-mailed a copy of my birth certificate." Dolores sounded defensive. "Everything is held in strictest confidence."

"What?" Jessie leaned forward. "Don't tell me you also gave them your Social Security number?"

"'Course not. But even if I had there is no way the information is shopped elsewhere." Dolores hesitated. "Besides, no data is completely private anymore. Everything—personal, financial, medical—is all on the Web somewhere."

"And there are people out there who know how to access that information," Jessie snapped. "Mom, you have to use good sense, not place yourself in a vulnerable situation. You'd be nuts to trust the men you meet on-line. Even when you know them in person they can fool you."

Dolores sat in stunned silence. Carolyn quickly drained her cup and gathered her handbag and jacket, making the move to end their evening. Better to go, she thought. Before things got any worse. Jessie had just alluded to her own unhappy situation with Tony, and Carolyn didn't want the conversation to go there next. They'd be here all night.

"Bed calls," she said, trying to sound cheerful. "I have an early morning at work."

"Me, too," Jessie said, glancing between her mother and Carolyn. "I'm sorry the conversation got heated but maybe these things needed to be said."

"Maybe. I'll think about that." Dolores put down several bills, refusing Carolyn's offer to pay. "My treat, such as it was," Dolores said with a hint of black humor.

They went outside, said their good-byes and then headed in three directions, each one toward her own car. Carolyn breathed a sigh of relief when she reached hers.

"Carolyn, I think we should consider going away to be married without the family."

They were sitting snuggled together on the sofa in Carolyn's family room, a fire in the fireplace and soft music playing from the sound system. She had just explained Dolores's position on their engagement, that they wait until they'd known each other longer. In one way she wished she hadn't shared that information because she sensed that his feelings were hurt; but in another, she knew that she couldn't keep such matters a secret, not if they were to be man and wife, a part of each other's families.

"I don't know. They might feel left out, offended."

Richard leaned away from her, so that he could look down into her face. "Or we might be saving them a lot of trouble, especially if we had a nice reception for family and friends when we came back to Atlanta. Sometimes family members make a bigger deal of things than they should." A pause. "And after all, we've both been married and divorced."

She nodded, thoughtful.

"Just think about it, sweetheart. We don't have to make a decision right now."

"I know."

"There's another possibility here concerning Dolores, one you might not have thought of, because it's not anything you would ever consider anyway."

"What's that?" She met his eyes, suddenly more curious than amorous.

"The Buckhead house."

"My dad's house?"

He inclined his head.

"What do you mean?"

"She might think that because the house is really yours you'll want it if you get married. Maybe her whole argument has less to do with what she said to you than her fear of losing her home."

Carolyn straightened, pulling away from Richard. "I'd never do that to her."

"Of course you wouldn't, Carolyn." He pulled her back against him. "And I wouldn't want you to. But she might be feeling insecure right now."

But the more she thought about his words, the more they made sense. The house did belong to her—unless she died, in which case Dolores inherited everything. Basically it was Carolyn first, Dolores second, and Carolyn's spouse or Dolores's family third.

A nutty will, she thought, and yet she understood her dad's wish to protect Dolores for her lifetime. Her dad had assumed that Carolyn would outlive her stepmother. But it might also be a threat to Dolores if Carolyn suddenly wanted to get married.

Left-field thinking, she admonished herself. Richard knew nothing about the details, only that the Buckhead house belonged to her, so he had no idea of the chord his perceptive observation struck in her. It was possible that he'd found the crux of the problem.

"You may be right," she said, softly, loving him even more for his understanding. "I'll give your suggestion some thought over the next few days."

But she already knew her answer. They should go away to marry, avoid any conflicts. And then Richard was kissing her. And she forgot everything else.

The decision could wait.

15

The early morning sun was already warm as Carolyn stretched her arms upward. She was enjoying her interlude in the garden putting in geraniums and petunias. In a couple of minutes she'd have to shower and get ready for work, but in the meantime, she allowed herself the joy of luxuriating in the peace of her little garden. Mayo and Mustard had settled onto a patio chair, already snoozing in the sun.

She wished Richard were here. They could curl up together like the cats, only they would do something more interesting than nap.

After a few minutes more in the garden, Carolyn prodded her two reluctant cats back into the house. She closed the French doors, and then ran to answer the phone that had begun to ring.

"Hello?"

"It's me, sweetheart." Richard's voice came over the wires from Chicago. "I'm so glad I caught you before you left for work."

"Hello," she said, pleased.

"Hearing your voice is a great start to my hectic day," he said, and she could hear the sincerity in his words.

"So, how's it going?"

"Moving along, but busy. I've listed my house and I'm in the process of closing my office here." His sigh came over the line. "And that's a bigger job than I thought it would be."

"I would love to have been there to help."

"That would have been lovely, for several reasons." His voice lowered. "I miss you—God, how I miss you." There was a hesitation. "But I know you can't be here—there are your job obligations and your other commitments." Another pause. "But I can't help but wish you could have been with me for these days."

"I know, and I'm sorry I couldn't." She sighed. "But I know you understand, Richard. My schedule at NNN is locked in stone for at least a month before airing our programs, and that doesn't include the times I have to substitute when there's an emergency."

"Of course I do, honey. I don't mean to bitch. I just love you so much and—" his voice lowered even more—"and I miss holding you, making love to you." He gave a laugh. "You've become my addiction."

"I love and miss you, too."

"I know. We'll make up for lost time when I get back." Another hesitation. "We'd better get married soon, sweetheart. The way I'm feeling I think our family might start right away." He gave a laugh. "When I even think about you I can't contain myself. *I want you all the time.*"

"Oh, Richard. I feel the same way."

"Did you talk to the judge, that old friend of your father's, the one who might agree to perform our marriage ceremony?"

"I did."

"And?"

"He's agreeable. We just have to give him a date so he can schedule us."

"Great. Let's do that when I get everything tied up here and get moved to Atlanta."

"When do you think that'll be?"

"No more than another week."

"Oh, Richard. I can hardly wait."

"Me either, honey." A hesitation. "And I was thinking about Savannah for our honeymoon. What do you think? We could take a longer, more exotic vacation in the fall."

"Sounds great to me." Carolyn paused. "It'll be paradise to be married whether or not we have a honeymoon."

There was a long silence.

"I love you, Carolyn."

"I love you too, Richard."

And then they hung up. She made sure the French doors were locked and then went to get ready for work. She couldn't stop humming. Not even the dark sedan that often seemed to be following her could dampen her spirits today.

She would soon be Mrs. Richard Crawford.

* * *

But when Carolyn was followed on her way to meet Minnie for supper that night she confided the progression of scary incidents to her friend. "At least I think I'm being followed, although I'm not positive." She gave a shaky laugh. "There are lots of black sedans in Atlanta."

"You say this has been going on for a while now, Carolyn?" Minnie's expression was concerned. "The first time you noticed the car following you was before you met Richard, right?"

Carolyn nodded.

"And the feeling that someone had been in your house?"

She nodded again.

"Do these things happen when Richard is in the city?"

"Not as often, but then the person—if there really is one—would be crazy to hang around when I'm not alone." She hesitated, thoughtful. "But that type of car is sometimes behind me even when Richard is in town."

Minnie lowered her eyes, sipping her drink. "Have you told him about all of this?"

"Only a few of the incidents. They all sound so silly when I try to explain them, because it's all so vague. I come off sounding a little paranoid."

"And maybe the dark sedan isn't following you. Maybe the car is, as you said, many cars."

"Believe me, I've thought of that, Minnie. Sometimes I wonder if I need to explain this to a doctor. It's possible that my mind is blowing these incidents out of proportion, in which case I might have some sort of mental disorder."

"Hogwash! You don't have a mental disorder, girl." She paused. "Just keep a log of what's going on and then we can determine if there's a pattern to all of this."

Carolyn agreed and their conversation moved on to Minnie's jewelry. Once they'd finished their meal and had coffee, she stood to go.

"Promise me you'll be careful, Carolyn," Minnie said before they got into their cars. "It's probably nothing serious but keep that log anyway, okay?"

Carolyn drove home and no one followed this time.

Richard called every night after she was in bed, listening to her daily update, giving her his—and then whispering endearments, until they both had to hang up, or go nuts over their need for each other.

But in the rational part of those conversations Carolyn learned more about his background, and sensed that his childhood had not been easy; Richard had worked hard for his position in life. Most important to her, she heard how much he wanted a family himself, how anxious he was to have roots. "Like you have, sweetheart."

"But have you known him long enough to make such a decision," Minnie said when Carolyn explained their wedding plans over the phone.

"I have, Minnie." She took a deep breath, willing her friend to understand. "Believe me, he's everything any woman would give up their single status for in a snap."

"He sounds wonderful."

"He is, Minnie, and much more."

"Then you have my blessings, Carolyn." A hesitation. "But let me know when you're back in town."

"You'll be the first to know, and the date of our reception." Carolyn switched the phone to her other ear. "You will come, won't you?"

"Wouldn't miss it." Another hesitation. "And take care, Carolyn. But have a wonderful honeymoon in Savannah."

"I promise, I will."

"Good. Bye for now."

Richard returned to Atlanta after closing his office in Chicago, temporarily moving his work into her spare bedroom until he found proper business space to either rent or buy. But that was okay with Carolyn; they'd bought their marriage license and were scheduled to marry the following weekend in the judge's chambers. Immediately after the ceremony they planned to drive to Savannah for several days. Carolyn had managed to get three days off at NNN, even though Roberta had been hesitant at first to find a substitute for her air time—"because no one else sells as much product and our vendors know it. They want you."

"I'll make it up to NNN," Carolyn promised.

"You'd better," Roberta said, and then she grinned and hugged Carolyn. "Congratulations, dear friend. No one deserves happiness more than you do."

"Thanks."

"And tell Richard that we're expecting him to make you very happy." A hesitation. "And also—

give him my best wishes, because he's getting a prize—you."

They embraced and Carolyn left Roberta's office feeling uplifted. She no longer felt guilty about keeping her wedding news from the family. They would be invited to the reception next week when she and Richard returned from Savannah. The invitations were already in the mail, to be received after she and Richard were married. Down the road, once they really knew Richard, they'd realize how lucky she was. In the meantime, she meant to enjoy her wonderful, life-altering event.

She intended to be Richard's wife for the rest of her life.

16

They were married on a beautiful spring morning by Judge Adams, the old friend of Carolyn's father. Richard had stood beside her, strong and tall, and when the judge pronounced them man and wife, he had lifted her to her toes for a kiss filled with warmth and just a touch of wickedness.

They honeymooned in a two hundred-year-old hotel in Savannah. It had been lovely, though Carolyn had seen little but the inside of their hotel room. Her body was still humming.

During their drive back to Atlanta Carolyn and Richard discussed the type of house they'd like to buy together. She opted for a large two-story with a columned entrance portico, a main receiving hall with a sweeping staircase, and enough bedrooms to accommodate a growing family.

He grinned. "Typical pre-Civil War Georgia in other words." He glanced. "Much like the house you grew up in."

She was quiet for the next few seconds. "I guess

you're right, Richard. My father's house was a happy place, even though I grew up without a mother." A pause. "My dad made sure of that. I have wonderful memories and I suppose I want the same for any future children of mine."

He patted her knee, his eyes still on the freeway. "I know, my darling. I wish I could have known your father."

"He would have liked you as much as I do."

"You think he would have approved of a scoundrel like me?"

"As much as if he'd handpicked you himself. Wherever he is now, I know that he's very pleased about my choice of husband."

"Well," he said after a moment. "I'll try to live up to such a nice tribute, make sure his little girl is taken care of in the manner he'd approve."

"Oh, Richard." She laughed. "You sound stilted."

"But sincere, my love." A pause. "We'll start looking for the perfect house as soon as our schedules permit." He smiled. "Your dream home is exactly what I want, too." Another knowing glance. "Especially the kids part."

Then he was preoccupied with city traffic and the conversation veered away from personal feelings. When they turned onto Carolyn's street she was relieved, and anxious to see Mayo and Mustard. Her neighbors, Thelma and Carl were again feeding her cats while she was gone. Thelma had assured her that Carl would not be alone in the house. They hadn't spoken again of what happened last time, but Carolyn was content to let the incident pass.

Richard parked in the garage and followed her

into the house with their suitcases. This time there were no odd incidents to disconcert Carolyn; everything was as they'd left it. Still, she did a walk through the rooms to make sure, pausing momentarily in the doorway of the spare bedroom that was still cluttered with Richard's office equipment and files. He hadn't had time to get settled before the wedding.

"Takes time to set up an office," he said, having come up behind her. "At least I've unpacked my clothes." He stepped around her and put his bag down. "Good thing you had an extra closet so I could put everything on hangers and then shut the door," he added with a laugh.

"Hey, it's no problem, Richard." She went to him and offered a kiss, which he took at once. "I just feel a little guilty that I made so much work for you."

"You mean because I married you and moved my office from Chicago to Atlanta?" He held her at arm's length, his eyes creasing at the corners, although he was trying to look serious. "Do you have regrets already?"

"Regrets? Oh God, no!" She hesitated. "Do you?"

He kissed her again, this time long and hard. "What do you think, sweetheart?" he murmured against her lips. "Do I seem regretful?"

Her answer was to press closer, because she couldn't talk with his lips against hers. For seconds longer they clung together, until Richard finally protested that their lovemaking must wait a short time, until he'd checked calls and E-mails.

"You're right," she said, sighing dramatically. "But not too long or there'll be a damsel in distress."

He grinned. "Can this damsel manage for a half hour?"

She raised her brows, as if she were a courtroom judge considering a life and death situation. "She thinks so, because she also has calls and E-mails to check." Carolyn laughed. "Seriously, Richard, I'm going to shower and change after that, so take your time."

He nodded. "Thanks. You know how it is with work. It's always waiting for you." He waved a hand at the packed boxes. "At least I've left most of my stuff in storage until we move into a bigger place," he told her, surveying the room. "As you know I'm selling my house in Chicago furnished, which eliminated the problem of storing or shipping all of it here. Besides, my stuff was too modern for the type of place we want."

She agreed, then gave Richard a last peck on the mouth and left him to his work while she went to see to hers.

Over the next week they settled into a routine; she went to NNN each day, he worked from home, having set up his own business phone line so "her personal line was not tied up for hours on end with his modem, fax or long-distance conversations." Each night they cooked supper together, discussed their day and then went to bed and made love. Carolyn wondered how she'd ever survived her life before Richard.

"To happiness and marital bliss!" Dolores said, raising her glass in a toast.

"Hear, hear," the group around the table in the

small private room at The Dining Room restaurant said in unison. Glasses clinked and everyone sipped.

"Can I say something, too?" Dean glanced at everyone, from his grandmother and parents to Minnie, Barney, Roberta and her date, Mike. "Even if I only have soda in my glass?"

"Of course you can," Carolyn said, smiling.

Dean stood up, looking very serious in the first dress suit he'd ever owned, compliments of his grandmother. He raised his glass and turned his head toward Richard and Carolyn. "I love my aunt Carolyn because she's the best aunt in America," he began, and hesitated. "She deserves the best husband in America. I hope she found that."

There was a momentary silence. Then everyone took a sip of the wine Richard had chosen from the restaurant's famous wine list. Dean sipped his soda and sat down, unaware that his words had raised a question in the minds of some members of the party.

Then Richard stood up. "I want to toast my wife." He looked down at Carolyn who sat next to him at the table of ten people at the Ritz-Carlton in Buckhead. "I'm the luckiest man alive to have won the heart of a woman like Carolyn." A brief pause. "I love you sweetheart."

"I love you, too," she whispered just before they all toasted again.

With the toast over, two waiters hired for the occasion began to serve the courses Carolyn and Richard had chosen together, although Richard had insisted upon footing the bill. "My pleasure," he'd told her, his tone brooking no argument. They had both specified that no one give them a gift.

Gourmet appetizers were served with the wine, then a salad of greens, followed by the main course of medallions of lamb in a brown sauce with sweet and sour eggplant, chickpeas and beans. Each course was presented with a special wine chosen by the chef to compliment the food being served. While everyone waited for dessert and coffee, Carolyn excused herself and went to the ladies room. As she headed back toward the private dining room someone called her name behind her. It was Tom Harrison. Carolyn winced, then turned slowly to face him.

"Hi, Tom," she said, simply. "What a surprise to run into you at The Dining Room."

"I don't know why it would be, Carolyn. As you'll remember, I often dine here."

There was a silence.

He was dressed in evening clothes, as though he'd just attended the opera or the symphony. His eyes swept over her ankle-length green velvet sheath, down to her high-heeled matching pumps, and then back to her face. Carolyn shifted, uncomfortable with his perusal.

"You're exquisitely beautiful tonight, Carolyn."

"Thank you, Tom."

She searched her mind for a polite way to end their encounter, and then came up with a response that wouldn't lead into why she was there.

"Guess I'd better get back to my group," she said, lightly. "It's dessert time. I don't want to miss that."

He nodded and she turned away, about to leave him.

"They make special efforts for special occasions,"

he said, his voice soft but stilted. "Like they're doing for your wedding reception."

She turned back. "How did you know?"

"How wouldn't I have known, Carolyn? Everyone in my office heard about you getting married."

She was taken aback. Dolores, she thought. It was her stepmother who'd spread the news. Was that why he was dining in the same place tonight?—because of her small reception? The thought was disconcerting. But she managed to seem casual about their encounter.

"I guess news travels fast," she said, contriving amusement.

He nodded again, his dark eyes probing.

"So I'd better get back to my guests," she said, trying to keep their conversation light, hoping he wasn't as disturbed about her marital status as he seemed.

He spread his hands. "Okay."

After a moment's hesitation, Carolyn left him, restraining the urge to look over her shoulder. Vaguely upset, she was grateful to take her seat next to Richard again. He made her feel safe.

They were the last of their small group to drive away from the Ritz-Carlton, having waited to make sure no one had to pay for valet parking. Richard, and his concern for others, made her feel secure. He valued her so much that she suspected he would pawn his last asset to maintain his personal integrity in an area he believed was his responsibility.

She snuggled next to him, thinking she was the luckiest woman alive.

"So," Richard said. "How do you think things went tonight?"

She smiled, gazing at his profile as he drove. "Wonderfully well, thanks to you, Richard."

"You think everyone enjoyed themselves, even your friend Minnie and Dean's idol, the detective?"

"Barney," she said, adding the name he'd forgotten. "Yes, everyone loved tonight. I'd bet none of them have had such a nice evening in ten years."

"You're serious?"

She laughed. "Of course, Richard. I wouldn't fool you."

"I know that, Carolyn. I was just trying to get a fix on your friends and family—because I don't know them as you do." A pause. "Unfortunately, neither of my sisters could make it."

"I'm so sorry that they couldn't, but I understand. We're on opposite sides of the country." She hesitated. "Would you mind if I wrote to them, maybe called them on the phone, told them about the wedding?"

"That would be nice, Carolyn, but it's not necessary. They'll both be in contact, and when they are, we'll invite them out for a visit, so they can meet you." He steered the car through an intersection, then onto the street that led to her townhouse. "My family is different from yours, my love. There's not much significance placed on family tradition."

"Is that how you feel, Richard?" She felt a moment of indecision. "I believed you were committed to having a family and everything that stood for."

He glanced, grinning. "Of course you believed

that. Because I am committed to having a family." A pause. "My sisters are older, with a different father, and happily, my upbringing created a whole other mindset from how they were brought up."

"What does that mean?"

"Only that the father of my sisters was very different from mine. Theirs had no family foundation. Mine did."

"Oh." She sensed his upset and changed the subject to a more positive place. "Well, whenever your sisters can visit, they're welcome here. We'll show them just how happy a good relationship can be." She snuggled even closer to him, ignoring the restrictions of bucket seats.

He reached an arm around her and pulled her even closer. They rode like that for several blocks before he needed his arm again to negotiate a turn.

"So, what did you think of Dean tonight?" he asked.

"Only that he fears our relationship will change now that we're married." She paused. "You know that I already have concerns about Dean because he's too much of a loner."

"I know," Richard said. He was silent for a few seconds. "Do you think Dean would feel more secure about our marriage if he spent time with me, got to know me so to speak?"

"Oh, Richard. I think that would be wonderful for him."

"Okay, then I'll make an effort to do that. We have computer interests in common. I overheard pieces of his conversation with Barney tonight. The kid is talented, especially when it come to technology."

She was so pleased. Richard was willing to step into the place that should have been occupied by Dean's dad. But then Tony didn't take fatherhood, or family finances, seriously, a sorrow for Jessie who had no time in her mad-dash schedule of working to pay the bills, to see to many of Dean's emotional needs. Even Dolores seemed to have less and less time for her grandson, too busy on-line trying to find a possible husband. Richard will be a great father, Carolyn told herself.

And then they were turning into their driveway and Carolyn forgot everything but Richard. In only minutes they would be in bed together.

Two mornings later Richard flew back to Chicago to tie up more loose ends in his business. Carolyn dropped him off at the airport, and on her way to work realized that she needed to know more details about Richard's business now that she was his wife. They were both so busy there just never seemed to be enough time to discuss it.

Carolyn sighed as she went through security at NNN, and then headed for makeup to get ready for her first show. Her beeper went off before she got there. It was Roberta; she obviously didn't know Carolyn was already in the building. Veering for the elevator, she went upstairs to Roberta's office.

"Oh my God! I'm so glad you got here." She was agitated and pale as she jumped up from her chair and came around her desk to greet Carolyn.

"What's wrong?"

"Carolyn, you'll never believe it."

"What?"

"The impossible happened."

Carolyn stood rooted in the doorway, uncertain. Roberta's words didn't sound as dire as her expression indicated. "What are you saying, Roberta?" she asked finally.

"Someone hacked into NNN's computer banks and stole our records."

"What?

"I just said—"

"I heard you," Carolyn said, interrupting. "But how is that possible?"

Roberta shrugged. "I only know that it did happen and NNN could be in big trouble. The ramifications are immense—names of our credit card shoppers, their card numbers and other personal information such as addresses and phone numbers. The hacker even accessed personnel files, getting all the personal information on our employees, including Social Security numbers and other confidential data." She gulped a breath. "The network bigwigs are in a flurry—scared to death of lawsuits."

"Have the appropriate authorities been notified?"

Roberta raked her fingers though her hair, anchoring the loose strands behind her ears. "The police were called and are on their way out here to take a report. They said even Microsoft, government files and international corporations have been breached through computer systems, that these things are possible." She hesitated. "But our cyber theft has to stay confidential."

Carolyn nodded, understanding. "Or our whole financial foundation could be at risk."

"That's it."

She plopped down on a chair. "How can something like this be kept secret?"

"It has to be or—"

"NNN could cease to exist?" Carolyn asked, finishing Roberta's thought.

Roberta glanced down.

Carolyn didn't need to hear the words. The situation was bad.

17

"It's perfect, just what we've been looking for."

Richard's words echoed in the big empty living room where sunlight streamed in through the long windows that overlooked the veranda. He turned to Carolyn, dropped an arm around her waist and pulled her to him.

"Hmm." She tilted her face, thinking. "Buckhead's a great neighborhood."

"So, what do you think, my sweet. Is this your house, or isn't it?"

"It costs a lot of money and I don't—"

"Trust me, we can afford it," he said, interrupting. "Just tell me what you think about the house, because I thought it was exactly what you wanted—what we wanted." He hesitated. "Unless you feel its location is too close to Dolores."

"'Course not." She grinned. "I love it."

"Thought so." He pulled her into his arms and kissed her, long and hard. When he finally raised his face he was smiling. "Our first kiss in our new house."

"Oh, Richard," she murmured. "It is perfect, isn't it?"

He nodded. And then they walked outside to talk to the realtor who had waited by his car, so that they could get the feel of the house without his sales pitch.

They agreed to sleep on a decision, but made an appointment to meet the salesman the next afternoon after Carolyn completed her work for the day. By the next morning they'd decided to go ahead with earnest money and Richard told her that his transfer of funds from some investments to his personal checking account in Atlanta should be complete by noon. But when Carolyn arrived back home around four Richard was annoyed; his funds hadn't arrived yet.

"We may have to postpone signing the earnest money contract today, until my money arrives," he said, looking embarrassed.

"This isn't a problem, Richard. I'll write the check."

"No way."

"Why not? We're married. Don't married couples share responsibilities?"

"That's true, Carolyn. But I have every intention of buying this house for my wife and future family."

There was a silence.

"Okay. You can pay me back then—when your funds come through."

He hesitated. "All right. I'll agree to that on one condition."

"What's that?"

"You take my check when I give the earnest money back to you."

"Oh Richard, you silly, lovable man." She laughed. "I agree."

Two hours later they bought the house.

"Son of a bitch! The damn car shit is really getting to be an annoyance," Richard told her a few days later as they ate supper. "First it was the faulty steering, then the flat tire because of a nail, then the clogged fuel line, and now failed brakes. What the hell next?"

Carolyn nodded. She didn't want to add her own fear of riding in his BMW. The rash of repairs was beyond coincidence; the car had low mileage and was in perfect condition. She hated to jump to the conclusion that someone had tampered with it. She preferred to believe his two-year-old car was a lemon. Besides, to suggest the problems were deliberate sounded crazy, especially in light of the mechanic not finding evidence of vandalism.

"We can count our blessings that the brakes failed where they did and not in traffic," she said, soothingly. "That they went out when you were about to park was a blessing."

"Yeah, you're right." He hesitated. "But it makes me wonder what'll happen next to the damn thing. I—or we—might not be as lucky next time. As the mechanic said, sometimes a car comes off the assembly line looking perfect but is off kilter somehow and then has nothing but problems."

"A lemon?"

"Uh-huh."

"Maybe you should get rid of it, Richard. Trade it in."

"That's what I've decided to do, when my cash flow loosens up."

"How about me giving you a loan?" She paused, knowing how fiercely proud he was about borrowing money, a trait he'd brought with him from his impoverished childhood. Even though it had been only a short time since she wrote the check for the earnest money, she knew it bothered him, that he was trying to expedite the release of monies owed him from several business deals. "I really think you should, Richard, because I'm worried about that bucket of bolts. It's unreliable and not safe."

He was silent for long seconds.

"Okay, I'll do it, but only because I have a lot of money coming in soon. It should have been in my account by now." He shrugged. "There are always delays with money transfers."

"Why is that?"

He grinned. "Have you ever thought about the interest made on large amounts of money? In big transactions everyone tries to hang onto their funds for as long as possible to make the interest income. I admit that I've done the same thing. The difference right now is that I need the ready cash that's owed me."

They changed the subject, finished their meal and then watched a television movie. The next morning Carolyn went to work as usual and Richard bought a new BMW four-door sedan, surprising her when she returned home. He took her for a drive and then bought them dinner at a catfish restaurant on the outskirts of the city.

"I'm glad that you chose another white car," she told him over coffee. "It's my favorite color on a vehicle."

His eyes crinkled at the corners. "I know."

Her eyes widened in a question.

"You mentioned that to me once." His expression relaxed into a full smile. "I'm happy that you're pleased."

He put down several twenty dollar bills on the table to pay for their meal, then led her outside to the car. "I feel like getting home," he said, gruffly. "So I can hold you properly, and in private."

Carolyn grinned, wishing she could snuggle up closer to him, that they didn't sit on bucket seats. Once home they went straight to bed and made love. Long after Richard had fallen asleep Carolyn lay next to him, smiling into the darkness, listening to his even breathing. She had never dreamed that she could be so happy.

Several days later when he gave her the check for the earnest money and his car, Carolyn hesitated. "You do know that my money is your money, and vice versa," she said softly. "It really isn't necessary to give this back, especially since you're bankrolling our new house."

He pulled her into his arms, holding her close as he looked down into her face. "Yes, it is, sweetheart. I want you to save your money for our future kids, because I intend to pay the family bills."

"But—"

"No buts," he said, interrupting. "When my

Chicago property sells I'm using that money for the downpayment on our house. If it doesn't sell in time I have other recourses." A pause. "I won't accept any argument on this issue." His grin softened the finality of his words.

She only nodded.

And then he feathered her face with kisses, until their passion mounted, and they forgot about who was paying for what.

The next day at work she had three telephone conversations right in a row. The first one was with Barney, who explained that he needed to contact Dean because the Youth House's computer had crashed and classes had to be canceled until they could get it fixed. As they talked Carolyn expressed an idea that had been growing in her mind since Dean had started his instructions for the Youth House's kids.

"Hey, Barney. How about I buy a new computer and printer and donate it to the center? According to Dean, what you have is a dinosaur." She paused. "I know the thing probably isn't worth fixing, and Dean said you need at least two new computers for the kids to use, but maybe this is a good start."

"True," he said. "And thanks, Carolyn. "Your nephew has generated such interest in going on-line, in opening up the world, that the kids have to take half hour turns."

Carolyn smiled into the receiver. She could only imagine Dean's pleasure and boosted confidence. "I'm going to call Dean's grandmother and pitch her on donating another computer—so that you'll have two new ones. Plus the printer that can be connected to both."

"Jeez, Carolyn, that'd be great. You can't imagine what that'd mean to these kids."

"Including Dean, Barney," she said. "These classes at the center have worked wonders on a very lonely little boy."

"I know. And I've noticed." A hesitation. "He's very lucky to have such a caring aunt."

"No more lucky than the Youth House is to have you, Barney."

A silence went by.

"Thanks," he said finally. "So we can depend on two new computers?—before Dean's next class?"

"You have my promise, Barney. They'll be there. Don't cancel anything."

"Gotcha."

They hung up and, with a few minutes to spare before the next show, Carolyn called Dolores who answered on the first ring.

"Oh," she said, recognizing Carolyn's voice. "I thought you were someone else."

"A hot date I hope," Carolyn said, cheerfully, trying humor to offset the stilted tone of Dolores's voice.

"My friend, Jock."

"Jock?"

"My Internet friend, I think I've mentioned him. His real name is Will Millgard and he lives in Paterson, New Jersey." A pause. "He's also a widower and he's become a very important man in my life."

For long seconds Carolyn didn't know how to respond. She didn't approve of Internet romances, not because the people at the other end of the keyboard might be con artists, but simply because anyone could say anything, misrepresent themselves to honest, needy people looking for real relationships—like Dolores.

"He's going to call you, on the phone?" Carolyn asked finally.

"Yeah. We've talked a number of times on the phone." A pause. "Jock wants to come down to Atlanta and meet me in person." Dolores's voice had gained emotion. "We've gotten to know each other very well and—and our relationship is serious, Carolyn. We'll probably eventually get married."

Dolores's revelation took Carolyn's response. For a moment she didn't know what to say. "But you don't even know what he looks like, Dolores," she said, finally.

"Oh, we exchanged pictures a long time ago, and we send snapshots of the current events in our lives—over the Net, of course." She gave a laugh. "I even sent Jock the photo of you and Richard kissing at your reception."

Carolyn was shocked silent. Somehow, in some way she couldn't explain, she felt that her privacy had been violated.

"Do you think that's wise?" she managed to ask finally.

"Of course," Dolores said at once. "It's perfectly safe." Another laugh. "Do you know Carolyn, many couples have married after meeting on the Internet. If not for the Web they would never have met, might never have had a new mate at all."

Carolyn sat down, forgetting that she didn't want

to wrinkle the skirt and blouse outfit for her upcoming segment on camera. "I have no idea about the statistics, Dolores."

"Me, either. But I know they're in favor of us single women."

Another silence.

Carolyn didn't ask how she knew that. Dolores was a lost cause at the moment, Jessie's worst fears confirmed. She just hoped that her father's wife would use good sense with the Jock person, and wasn't a prime candidate for being conned into a bad relationship, and out of the security her dad had left for her future. Only time would tell.

"I called about Dean's computer class at the Youth Center," Carolyn said, changing the subject. "You know how much teaching those classes to the kids has helped him gain confidence in himself."

"Yeah, that's true," Dolores said, her voice reverting to its earlier flat tone.

"To make a long story short," she began, "their old computer crashed and they need a new one. I offered to replace it and the printer." Carolyn took a deep breath. "Dean has generated so much interest in going onto the Web that the kids are lined up for cyber time. The center needs at least two computers and I thought you might like to donate one, too."

Dolores's sigh came over the wires.

"They're tax deductible," Carolyn added.

"I would do that gladly, Carolyn." A pause. "But I can't right now. I'm, uh, a bit overextended at the moment and my cash flow is low."

"Oh," Carolyn said, surprised.

"But I can next month. Stay in touch about this and I'll see what I can do then, after my funds are replenished."

They talked for a minute more and then Carolyn hung up, puzzled. Maybe Dolores was making excuses to not commit to the Youth House. She had once been poor and Carolyn knew money was very important to Dolores.

Don't jump to dumb conclusions, she told herself. Her stepmother might have just overextended herself in investing. In any case it was none of her business. But next month she'd ask again for the computer. In the meantime, she'd buy two for the center. I can afford it, she reminded herself. Didn't she have Richard insisting on taking care of everything else? She smiled. Lucky her. She had Richard.

She had five minutes left before going to the set when the phone rang again.

"Hello?"

"Carolyn?"

She switched the receiver to her other ear, giving herself a moment, recognizing Tom's voice.

"Hi, Tom. What can I do for you?"

"First, don't sound so formal. This is a friendly call to an old and dear friend."

"Okay," she said, at a loss for anything more literate.

A silence came over the line.

"I wanted to apologize, Carolyn."

"Apologize?"

"Uh-huh. For the other night when I ran into you at your reception. I acted like—like a poor loser." A pause. "I'm sorry for being such a bastard."

"It's okay, Tom. You didn't know that I'd be there. I understand."

"No, you don't. I did know you'd be there. Dolores told me the day before, when I gave her the final balloon payment on the practice."

"You were talking about me?"

"No, not directly. Dolores just mentioned your having gotten married and that the reception would be the next night." A pause. "I just couldn't resist, Carolyn." He gave a dry laugh. "I had to eyeball the groom—to compare him to me, I guess."

"And?"

"He looks like a nice guy." Another hesitation. "Seriously, I apologize again for my bad manners. And I wish you happiness in your new marriage, Carolyn. No one deserves that more than you."

She was taken aback. Tom sounded more sincere than she'd ever heard him. She wished he'd revealed that side to her during their relationship.

"Thanks, Tom. I am very happy and expect to remain so for a long time to come."

A silence.

"I'm glad, Carolyn. I just wish the lucky guy could have been me." He cleared his throat. "I hope you accept my apology, because I do wish you well."

"Thank you, Tom. And I do."

After a few more words they hung up, leaving Carolyn pensive, wondering about his motivation, if he'd really been sincere.

As she hurried to the set she also wondered about Dolores who'd just gotten the final payment from the sale of her dad's law practice. Carolyn knew it was sizable. So why was Dolores having a cash flow crunch? Had she invested it all in her portfolio, leaving her short for the month?

Carolyn was puzzled. And then the stage lights went on and she seated herself on the set, prepared to sell fashions for plus sizes. She forgot Tom, Dolores, even Dean and new computers as she blocked everything but her product from her mind.

She'd think about her own concerns later.

18

After the show Carolyn's thoughts bounced between her earlier conversation with Dolores and Tom's unexpected apology. She appreciated Tom's candid words but he still had not retracted the implied accusations about her father. He was so different from Richard.

The purchase of their house moved forward and Carolyn hoped that the deal would be finalized soon. Although she loved her townhouse, her dreams had shifted to the home she intended to spend the rest of her life in with Richard. For another thing, Thelma and Carl's old dog seemed to hate Richard, going into a barking frenzy each time they came face-to-face. Sammy had become a problem.

"You know I hate that mutt," Richard told her one night after another incident on the front porch. "Old dogs need to be put down when they start threatening people."

"I agree that Sammy is old and cranky and not used to having you live here, but Thelma and Carl

would be devastated if anything happened to him."
She kissed him lightly on the mouth. "We'll just
have to put up with Sammy for the few weeks until
we move."

"You're right, Carolyn. We'll be gone soon." He
raised his brows. "I just hope he won't terrorize the
people who'll live here next, especially if they have
small children."

"We'll hope for the best. Sammy has always loved
kids."

But Sammy was the least of her worries. The
black sedan always seemed to be behind her for
short sections of the commute to NNN and back.
You're becoming paranoid, she told herself each
time the dark car veered off. But somehow, a feeling
she couldn't define, Carolyn felt intimidated, *that
someone was following her.*

And then there were the incidents at home when
she felt as though someone had been in her house. A
chair pulled out, a sofa pillow moved, subtle things
that may have been normal. Those were the times
when she longed for Richard to return from his out-
of-town business trips, and looked forward to when
he could be in Atlanta on a more permanent basis.
He'd reassured her that he'd be completely relo-
cated soon. She'd resisted the urge to confide her
fears, knowing they were unsubstantiated and could
sound manipulative—even crazy.

Was she? She sometimes wondered.

It helped to confide in Minnie. Carolyn had
brought Dean for his class at the Youth House, the
first one since the new computers had been delivered. Everyone had been excited, including Barney

who'd thanked her several times. He'd lost his inscrutable expression to his delight for the kids.
While she waited for Dean, she and Minnie had coffee in the tiny employee lounge.

"So how you doing with the log?" Minnie asked.
Any new incidents to report?"

"Just more of the same little things. Nothing tangible." Carolyn explained, adding all the strange
breakdowns on Richard's car before he bought the
new one.

"And the new one has been okay?"

Carolyn nodded. "But he keeps it in the garage
where it's safe." She spread her hands. "And the old
one was probably just a lemon. There was never any
indication of vandalism."

Minnie digested her words. "The good news is
that the situation, if it's more than coincidence,
hasn't gotten worse."

They finished their coffee and Minnie walked her
back to Dean who had finished the class for the
night. The kids were already taking turns on the two
computers. After good-byes, she and Dean went out
to the Volvo and drove home through the warm
spring night.

The next afternoon Carolyn's show featured fine
china. She loved the product so much that her enthusiasm created even more sales than usual. "I
don't know which pattern I'd choose for myself,"
she told one of her regular callers. "But when I move
I intend to buy a set of these dishes."

"Oh, are you moving, Carolyn?" the woman
asked. "I thought you loved your townhouse."

"I do love it, Pam," Carolyn said. "But my new husband and I just bought a larger place in the Buckhead area."

Pam's laugh went out over the airwaves. "I get it. You're already thinking about expanding the family."

Carolyn didn't miss a beat but she quickly brought the focus back to the dishes. The next caller had a low, scratchy voice and Carolyn thought it was a woman who had gushed over the china with a rose pattern.

"What did you say your name was?" Carolyn asked, as she held up a cup and saucer for a better camera view.

"Rich bitch!" The altered persona was sudden. "You won't last in Buckhead!"

The caller was disconnected.

Startled, Carolyn managed to regain her equanimity almost immediately. She knew there was only a three-second delay on the calls, which meant a caller could make a short obscene remark before being cut off by the network. But this was a first for her. It had never happened before.

"I guess that person needed a book on manners, not a set of fine china," she said, making light of the incident.

She raised her brows, shook her head, and then she went on with the show, relieved that the segment was almost over. Once the cameras stopped rolling and the stage lights snapped off, she had a message from Roberta complimenting her on how she'd handled the caller. "Stop by my office in the morning, Carolyn. I'll have a full report on the incident by then." The crew was still talking about "the wacko" when she left for the day.

Once home, Carolyn changed out of her suit, poured herself a glass of Chardonnay and took it out on the patio where she sat on the chaise lounge and relaxed in the evening shade of her trees, missing Richard.

He'll be here tomorrow at this time, she reminded herself. Don't be a big baby just because of a psycho caller.

What in the hell was going on? She didn't have a clue. It didn't make any sense at all.

The phone rang and she jumped up. It would be Richard calling with his flight information. Running back into the house she caught the phone on the third ring.

"Hi there." She smiled into the receiver.

"Rich bitch!" The voice sounded more male than female this time. "Your days in Buckhead are limited. You won't last, bitch. Get it?"

The venom in the snarled words leaped out of the phone, striking her like the fangs of a snake.

"Who are—"

The dial tone sounded in her ear.

Carolyn flung the receiver onto its cradle. Then her knees buckled and she sagged against the counter, her eyes on the instrument that had delivered the threat. It lurked there, an inanimate object with a malevolent presence all of its own.

The person behind the voice knew her home number.

Oh God! Something—*someone* was getting closer.

Adrenaline sent her flying across the room toward the patio. She shooed Mayo and Mustard into the house, left her wine glass outside and slammed and locked the French doors even though it was still daylight. Then she closed the drapes and quickly checked out the rest of the house.

After a while she went upstairs to bed but didn't expect to sleep. It was no comfort to know that the caller ID on her phone had listed the call as private. When she tried *69 a recording told her the number was unavailable, to hang up. She dismissed calling Dolores or Minnie, or the police. What could she tell them? That she was being terrorized by a crazy sounding voice on the phone?

But she was.

"You think it was the same person who got on the show yesterday?" Roberta asked the next morning.

Carolyn nodded, and tried to sound calmer than she felt. "I'm sure of it."

"Even though you say that the caller last night sounded more like a man than the woman who managed to get her voice on the air?"

"I know that sounds odd but everything else about the voice was the same." She drew in a ragged breath. "This person went to a lot of trouble to get my home phone number, probably had to call a dozen listings before reaching me." Carolyn sighed. "I'm glad we're moving and getting a new one."

Roberta frowned, looking worried. "I hope this isn't somehow connected to that hacker who broke into NNN's computer banks."

"Are you wondering if that's how this person got my phone number?—from my personnel file?"

Roberta glanced away. "It's a slim possibility."

"Slim? How slim?"

Her eyes were suddenly direct. "The police, experts, our own security guys only know that someone cracked our codes and accessed our records. No one can tell if the information was actually stolen." She waved a hand nervously. "It's a mess, but if nothing ever comes of it then we might be able to assume that it was a teenage nerd out to prove his or her computer brilliance. Of course, whatever the case, we'll prosecute if we ever catch the creep."

"The records have been secured?"

"You bet. No one will ever hack their way in again."

"So we're back to square one with the caller." Carolyn felt exhausted and she hadn't even started work yet. As expected, she'd hardly slept last night. Somehow she needed to be revitalized before Richard's arrival.

"No, we do know a few things. The NNN operator could tell that the call came from a phone booth in the city, and our security guys think a phone synthesizer was used."

"Synthesizer?"

"Yeah, one of those gadgets that change phone voices from male to female, from young to old and vise versa."

"The bastard was covering his ass, wasn't he— she—it, whatever."

"And there's more," Roberta said, wiping a hand over her forehead. "There's been another rash of anonymous calls to the station demanding that NNN fire you."

"Shit!" Carolyn had been standing in front of

Roberta's desk and now she slumped onto a chair. "This is incredible. I didn't think I had an enemy in the world. And now this."

Roberta came around her desk and put a hand on Carolyn's shoulder. "What we've got here is some kind of a pervert who's fixated on you." She sighed. "These things happen to celebrities and it looks like you drew the unlucky straw."

"What does this person say when calling the station?"

"That you're a whore whose only reason to appear on television is to tease men."

"You're kidding?"

"I'm afraid not. But we aren't rolling over and playing dead on this situation either. We've made a report to the police." She hesitated. "One thing we do know is that this person will never get through our operators again."

Carolyn glanced at her watch and then stood to go. She still had a show to do.

"One last thing, Carolyn."

She inclined her head, waiting for Roberta to continue.

"It wouldn't be a good idea to mention this caller thing on the air, or get involved in a conversation with a customer about yesterday's incident."

"I wouldn't dream of it, believe me."

And then she went to get ready to sell porcelain statues, her only scheduled program for the day. Somehow she had to project herself into an upbeat frame of mind. And forget about who might be watching her.

* * *

She was meeting Richard at the airport in front of Baggage at 8:00 P.M. It was only six when Carolyn left home, intending to swing by the Youth House and drop off the computer instruction books. She'd forgotten to leave them and the extended warranty she'd bought for all of the new equipment. Minnie was meeting her there.

"Hey Carolyn, how you doing?" Minnie said, coming to meet her in the hall. She grinned as Barney stepped out of a room and joined them. "You'd think none of us had regular jobs, since this is the place we always seem to be meeting."

"Hi there," Barney said, addressing them both, his pale eyes inscrutable as usual. "I don't know about the two of you, but I'm outta here. I've had a long day on my regular job and I'm ready to crash."

"Yeah, me, too." Carolyn managed a smile. "But I still have to pick Richard up at the airport."

"Hey, you do look bushed, kiddo." Minnie cocked her head. "Have anything to do with that wacko caller yesterday?"

Carolyn's eyes widened. "How did you know about that?"

"Didn't I ever tell you that several of the women in my office are big fans, hooked on NNN. Several of them were watching and told me what happened."

"What's this?" Barney asked. "Clue me in."

Quickly, Carolyn explained, then added the incident with the caller on her home phone.

"Jeez, I don't like the sound of this," Minnie said. "What do the powers at NNN say about it?"

She told them.

"I have to agree with Roberta," Barney said.

"Sounds like the typical pervert who get his kicks from scaring people. Unfortunately, these types like to zero in on one person, until they get the urge to move on."

"I wish the creep would move on soon." Carolyn managed a laugh. "I'm sick of it already."

"I would suggest one thing," he said, abruptly serious.

"Which is?" Minnie asked, interrupting, obviously concerned.

"Carolyn needs to curtail any discussions about her personal life on camera," he answered. "So the wacko can't collect any more information."

"Roberta and I have already discussed this and have come to the same conclusion." Carolyn didn't add anything about the computer hacker. That situation was probably separate from her caller.

"Good." He saluted them both and turned to go. "I'd better get myself home while I'm still awake enough to drive."

They watched him go, then Carolyn handed Minnie the paperwork that went with the new computers. After more words of caution from Minnie, Carolyn went back out to her car, mindful of picking up Richard on time.

She pondered the events of the past few days while he'd been gone, and wondered how her career would be affected when she stopped sharing her life with her customers. Her openness had always been the marker of her success.

But she had no choice. Someone out there had taken away that option, at least for now. She could no longer share the books and movies she liked, the people she loved, the neighborhood where she lived, that she was a devoted Braves fan.

She kept glancing in the rearview mirror as she drove toward the airport. No dark sedans in sight. But she felt exposed, as though someone watched nevertheless. Carolyn didn't like the feeling.

Then she thought of Richard. Her foot pressed the gas pedal a little harder, increasing her speed. She couldn't wait to see him and feel safe again.

19

There reunion was wonderful. To Carolyn's amazement, she lost her tiredness once Richard was home. But later that night she slept the sleep of the dead until she awoke at eight the next morning to a steaming cup of fresh coffee that Richard had brought to her.

Her day at work passed quickly and uneventfully. NNN was keeping its promise; the crazy caller would not get through a second time. Once home again, Carolyn found Richard still busy at his computer, corresponding with European business associates. She kissed him, told him she was preparing a wonderful supper and then left him to his work.

She hummed as she placed New York steaks on the gas barbecue grill that stood outside just beyond the French doors. Then she put two baking potatoes in the microwave oven and made a green salad as the food cooked. Once the table was set there was still a few minutes to wait on the steaks. She turned on an Enya CD and for a moment her thoughts flashed to Barney. Enya was his favorite Irish singer.

She called up the stairs to Richard in the spare bedroom-turned-temporary office that dinner was about to be served. "Be right there," he called back.

As she waited, the phone rang. She picked it up and was surprised to hear Dolores's voice. Her stepmother rarely called and never at supper time since her marriage to Richard.

"Carolyn," she began and hesitated. "I have to renege on my promise to buy a computer for the Youth House." Dolores's words ran together in her haste to say them. "I still have a cash flow crunch and I can't see it being better for another month or so." A hesitation. "But when it is I'll certainly help out."

"I and the Youth House appreciate that, Dolores," Carolyn said, maintaining a light tone even though she wondered again what was going on in her stepmother's financial picture. None of your business, she reminded herself. Dolores was capable of making her own decisions.

"Thanks, Carolyn." Dolores took a quick breath. "I want you to know that I'm not in financial jeopardy." Her explanation sounded ambiguous. "I'm only securing my future."

"That's good, Dolores." Carolyn propped the phone between her chin and shoulder so that she could take the potatoes out of the microwave. "For a minute there I admit to being concerned, because I know you aren't a poor woman." She dropped the potatoes onto a plate. "But I also know if you're short of cash it's probably because you're reshuffling your investment portfolio."

There was a momentary silence.

"I think you've just described my position," she said with a laugh. "But I do intend to make a donation to Anderson Youth House when I can. Even if it's for something other than computers."

"They may need another computer by then," Carolyn said, and explained that she'd donated two, assuming Dolores already knew that from Dean. "But if not, there are many things they could use."

As they hung up Carolyn noticed Richard hesitating in the doorway, as though he'd hated to interrupt until she'd finished the conversation.

"Let's eat," she said, grinning. "That was just Dolores, worried as usual about something insignificant."

"Are you being unkind?" he asked, looking surprised.

She shook her head. "I don't think so."

He grinned. "Sorry. I came in on the last part of the conversation and that's how it sounded."

She met his eyes. "No, I was only being realistic. Dolores is a worrier, and she has a tendency to blow issues out of proportion."

"And of course, she may be resentful of you." He pulled a chair out from under the table and sat down. "That would explain why she seems on edge around you."

Carolyn had just put the food on the table and was pouring the wine. Startled by his observation, she put the bottle down without filling her glass. "Why would you say such a thing, Richard?"

He glanced up. "Did I say something wrong, sweetheart? I thought you were aware of Dolores's feelings." A pause. "It's pretty obvious, you know."

"No, I didn't know." Her eyelashes fluttered. "Maybe I didn't want to know."

He got up and took her in his arms. "I'm sorry, Carolyn. I'm too new to the family to express myself on this. I could be completely off base here." He tilted her face so he could look into her eyes. "Am I forgiven?"

She smiled. "Of course, because—"

He raised his brows.

"Because I love you—and you were only being honest."

He dropped a kiss on her lips, then stepped back, smiling. "Making love to you can wait until later." His black brows arched again. "Dinner's getting cold."

Carolyn stepped back, grinning. "Forsaken for food already." She sighed dramatically and he laughed.

The night came down in the back garden beyond their windows as they ate, leisurely discussing their day's work and their plans for the new house. Finally, Richard glanced at his watch and grimaced. "I've got to E-mail an associate in London. He'll be waiting for my figures on a merger we're working on."

He stood up. "Sorry, darling. We can talk later." He dropped a kiss on her forehead.

She stood, too. They'd finished their meal an hour ago, had just sat there sipping wine and talking. "Sure, we can talk later. In bed."

He grinned. "After we get a few things out of the way."

She waved him away.

After he'd gone upstairs to his computer she cleaned up the kitchen, pulled the garbage bag from under the sink and tied it off. Then she went out through the garage to dump it into the garbage container before dragging it to the curb for the morning collection.

Humming the notes of the latest Faith Hill song, Carolyn lifted the lid. Something flew at her face, startling her. She dropped the garbage bag and screamed.

A bat.

It swooped into the beams of the garage, flying erratically, diving toward her again. She screamed even louder, arms raised to protect herself, paralyzed by the thought of being bitten.

Richard came running. "For God's sake! What's wrong, Carolyn?"

She pointed, unable to talk.

"Jeez! How in hell did that thing get in here?"

"It was in the garbage can." she said, shakily. "It flew into my face when I opened the lid."

He looked startled. "It was inside the can with the lid closed?"

She nodded, her gaze on the bat that'd landed on a beam in the darkest part of the garage. She was afraid to move for fear of disturbing it again. The garage door to the house stood open. She'd never sleep tonight if it flew inside and hid somewhere. She tried not to think of horror stories about bats and rabies.

"Were you bitten?" Richard edged slowly toward the open doorway, his thoughts obviously in tune with hers. The bat mustn't get into the house.

She shook her head.

With a sudden movement, Richard grabbed the

knob and closed the door. Then he hit the button to open the garage door, and as it lifted, the bat was again flying erratically, guided by the broom he'd grabbed to swat at it. The creature suddenly swooped into the night and disappeared. Quickly, Richard closed the door.

"It's okay now, Carolyn. It's gone." He folded her to him, crooning words of comfort, seeing how scared she'd been. "C'mon, let's go inside. I'll see to the garbage in the morning."

He led her inside and they went upstairs to bed. Richard certainly knew how to calm her, Carolyn thought a long time later. She wouldn't think about how the bat came to be in the garbage can. That could wait until tomorrow.

"I don't feel right about going," Richard said.

Carolyn handed him his briefcase as she stepped out of the car at the airport. "You have to, Richard." She smiled, reassuringly. "I'll be fine."

His return smile seemed forced. Several days had passed since the incident with the bat, but he was still worried about her. He'd wanted to call the police, especially after she'd confided the earlier episodes, but she'd persuaded him to wait, that there was nothing tangible to report, nothing provable. Besides, NNN had already filed a report about the harassing calls. But she'd omitted telling him that someone had broken into NNN's computer banks. Damage control was in full effect, and that meant telling no one, not even a trusted spouse.

But yesterday he'd called the police anyway and an officer had come out to take a report. "Sorry, Carolyn. In all good conscience I can't fly off and leave you without having first alerted the police," Richard had said. "At least they can have a patrol car swing past a little more often."

As Carolyn had expected, the young officer looked skeptical even though he took down her chronology of incidents. Although polite, he explained that it could all be coincidence, but in the light of her high-profile job and the harassing calls to the studio, she should be extra cautious. "Lots of nuts out there these days," he'd told them as he'd left.

Now, as Richard kissed her good-bye, Carolyn wished he could have postponed his Los Angeles trip. But she restrained herself from expressing apprehension and putting even more pressure on him. Five days would pass quickly. She watched him stride into the airport, then turn and blow her a kiss before he disappeared.

She got back into the Volvo and drove to work. The day was busy with three two-hour segments on camera. Carolyn was dragging by the time she finally headed for home. There was a message from Richard that he'd arrived in LA and would call later. She changed out of her work clothes, fed the cats, then headed for the front porch to check the mailbox.

Opening the door, she reached into the wall-hung box and pulled out a stack of mail. Checking again, her fingers brushed a soft furry mound at the bottom of the box.

Carolyn yanked her hand back. *It felt like a small animal.*

She tapped the box. Nothing moved.

Gathering her courage, she stood on tiptoes to look inside. A long tail lay against the metal side, but the gray body, eyes wide open, was lifeless.

She screamed, leaping backward. It was a dead rat.

In her mailbox.

Someone had lifted the lid and dropped it inside. There was no other explanation.

Thelma came running out of her side of the house. "Carolyn! Are you all right?"

Carolyn took deep breaths. She hated rats, bats and snakes equally.

"There's a dead rat in my mailbox!" Her voice was shrill. "Who would do such a thing?"

But she knew. The same person who'd put a live bat in her garbage can, the phantom who was out there terrorizing her.

Why? she asked herself. Why would anyone care that much about her life? She had no answers.

Thelma stared wide-eyed. "Did you say—a rat?"

Carolyn nodded and pointed. Thelma could lift the lid and see for herself—if she wanted to.

Carl came up behind his wife. "What's going on?" He glanced between the women as Thelma explained. "Like Carolyn, I can't look."

Carl shrugged and peered into the mailbox. "Goodness," he said. "It *is* a rat."

Then he reached inside, grabbed the end of the tail and pulled it out. With it dangling in front of him, he moved away toward his own half of the house. "I'll take care of this," he said, and left them staring after him.

"How did a rat get in your mailbox?" Thelma's question seemed redundant.

Carolyn shook her head. "I don't know. I was gone all day." A hesitation. "Did you see anyone on the porch, Thelma? Was anyone here today looking for me?"

"I didn't see anyone on our porch except the mailman this morning." A pause. "And of course Carl who watered our flower planters."

They stared at each other in silence.

Carl was responsible.

He'd been acting strange lately. But would dementia motivate him to drop a dead rat in the mailbox, a live bat in the garbage can? Could he have made a duplicate of her house key, so that he could wander around her house when she was gone? But why would he do such a thing?—even if he wasn't in his right mind?

Then Thelma spoke with a possible answer to her question.

"Carl has been upset over Sammy." She glanced away. "Sammy doesn't like your new husband and Carl senses that Richard hates his dog." She hesitated. "Therefore Carl doesn't like your husband." Her face crinkled with worry. "But Carolyn, Carl would never try to frighten you."

Carolyn nodded agreement, for Thelma's sake. But she wasn't sure about Carl. His reasoning was becoming more distorted all the time.

Then Thelma turned to go. "I know you'll be fine," she said, and Carolyn wondered how she knew that. Because her husband was the perpetrator of some of her scary incidents?

Carolyn thanked her for coming over. In a way it made sense to her that Carl, in his befuddled way, was saying: leave my dog alone.

It seemed plausible . . . and then it didn't.

When Richard called later Carolyn didn't tell him about her latest horrifying experience, listening instead to his list of scheduled meetings in Los Angeles. She'd decided to spare him details until he returned. There was nothing he could do about it anyway from so far away . . . except worry.

Again, her next day at the studio was busy but uneventful, and she was able to leave just ahead of the rush hour traffic. But the thought of going home to that empty house had her cringing. She crossed the parking lot to her car and was about to unlock the door when she looked though the driver's side window. A magnolia blossom lay on the bucket seat.

Her body went rigid, poised for flight. The next moment she realized that no one was in her car, that no one lurked in the parking area, and that her doors were still locked.

Then how had the flower gotten on her front seat?

Carolyn turned and ran back inside the building, her skin rippling with goose bumps. She felt hidden eyes watching her reaction to the blossom that was exactly like those in her own garden.

The guard behind the desk glanced up as she approached, then got to his feet. "Carolyn? You okay?"

She shook her head, catching her breath. "Someone was in my car." She quickly explained.

His concerned expression relaxed as she talked. "You say your car was locked?"

She nodded. "I can't understand how someone was able to get in. No one has a key."

"Well, getting into a locked car isn't hard. Thieves have the same flat device that cops, tow truck drivers and automobile service clubs have. It slips down the side of the window to flip the lock. Works good on cars without the safety feature to prevent that kind of break-in." He came out from behind his desk. "I'll walk you outside, make sure everything's all right."

Once outside and standing by the Volvo, he shook his head. "You know, your car should have that safety feature."

She swallowed hard. Again, she had the sense of being watched. But nothing moved anywhere, except a gentle rainbow of spray from the sprinkler system in a shady area of the grounds. Its soft fht-fht-fht sound blended with chirping birds in the trees beyond the strip of grass. A peaceful, serene setting.

Then why did she feel scared?

She opened the door while the guard waited, then pulled out the magnolia blossom. It fell apart in her hand.

"I'll be damned," the guard said, taking it from her. "Someone pulled all the petals off, then placed it on the seat like it was still all together."

Symbolic? She wondered. Was her watcher trying to tell her something?

"Hey, you be careful," he told her as she slipped behind the wheel. She nodded, thanked him and drove out of her parking place. A glance at her rearview mirror told her that the guard still stood where she'd left him, making sure that no one followed her.

She headed for the freeway, making a conscious effort to relax. Everything was okay. Nothing was going to happen.

As she drove into her driveway everything seemed fine. But she knew something was wrong from the instant she stepped into the house. Scatter rugs were skewed on the kitchen floor, pillows in the family room were on the floor and there was a sudden barking from the front of the house.

There was a dog in the house. A big dog from the sound of it.

Mayo and Mustard! Without hesitation she ran toward the sounds. Oh God, let my cats be safe, she prayed silently, momentarily oblivious to her own danger.

Reaching the living room, she jerked to a stop, her mind slow to register what she was seeing. Mustard, hissing and spitting, was perched on the high windowsill next to the fireplace. Mayo, body arched, was on the mantel, barely out of reach of the snarling dog who kept leaping upward, trying to get hold of the cat. Then, hearing Carolyn, it spun around and lunged for her.

By reflex, Carolyn grabbed a straight-backed chair, turned it upside down, and then held it between herself and the animal. Backing into the hall, she inched toward the front door. The dog, teeth bared in a low growl, followed. She wondered how long she could keep it at bay.

"Don't panic—don't panic," she chanted. Or it could kill her. She wasn't going to give it that chance.

Cautiously, she took one hand off the chair so she could feel behind her for the bolt lock and knob. In seconds she had the door open, her hand back on her weapon, as she stepped aside. Quickly, she brought the chair down on the animal's backside.

It yelped in pain. Another hit and it fled through the doorway to the porch. She slammed the door before the dog could turn and attack. Through the window she saw it leap from the porch and run down the street.

Shaking uncontrollably, she calmed Mayo and Mustard. Then, with her eyes on the shadowy area at the top of the stairs, she called 911 from the hall phone. She'd wait to search the second floor after the police arrived.

She needed to report the latest crazy incidents, get them on record. Because someone was definitely out to do her bodily harm.

And they had a key to both her house and car. Getting the locks changed would be a priority tomorrow. She should have done it weeks ago. Instead she'd been in denial.

Time to move, she thought, watching the police cruiser pull up to the curb in front of her house. Her once perfect Victorian home had become a house of horrors.

20

It had been a different officer who came out in response to Carolyn's 911 call than the one who'd responded to Richard. He'd listened to her story about the dog in her living room, that she didn't know how it had gotten inside because all of the doors had been locked. He'd raised his eyebrows and taken down her account in silence. After walking through her house, garden and garage he'd left with the same caution as the first officer, that she should be careful. He'd added that she might consider having her locks changed.

Duh, she thought, again on her way to work the next morning. The only good thing about calling the police was that all of her crazy incidents were now documented on police reports. Just in case . . .

Of what? she wondered. Her mind boggled.

Frank, the morning security guard came out to meet her when she drove into the employee parking lot a few minutes later. Surprised, she got out of her car, locked it and walked inside with him.

"Roberta wants you to stop by her office before you head to Makeup," he told her. "Says it's important."

"Thanks for—for everything," Carolyn said, not completely understanding what was going on. She suspected it was more than a magnolia blossom on the front seat of her car yesterday.

Roberta confirmed her worst dread. "I'm so sorry about all this, Carolyn. Please remember that none of this is your fault." A hesitation. "It seems we have more than a fixated viewer on our hands." She wiped a hand over her forehead. "We have some kind of a psycho." A pause. "I don't want to scare you but we think this person, whoever he or she is, could be dangerous."

Carolyn sank onto a chair in Roberta's office. "What exactly are you saying?"

"Have you checked your in-box lately?"

Carolyn shook her head. "As usual, once or twice a week—because there are never any significant messages in it. Anything work related comes through NNN's direct channels."

Roberta nodded. "So I checked your in-box, after the series of calls."

"What calls?"

Roberta glanced away. "They were brief, anonymous, untraceable calls that came in with negative comments about you."

"But I didn't do anything."

Roberta shrugged, but not indifferently. "I don't think you have to."

There was a silence.

"So what was in my in-box?"

Roberta's answer was to shove three pieces of lined yellow paper across her desk to Carolyn. She picked them up, noticing that the black felt pen messages were scrawled in an distorted pattern of printed letters.

"Carolyn hates bats and rats."

"Carolyn loves magnolias but she better check her garden."

"Carolyn is afraid of killer dogs."

She sat staring at the cheap paper with the terrorizing words. Who? Why? What had she ever done to offend someone, something so bad that the person had taken a terrible revenge on her.

Or was the person deranged, someone who'd fixated on her and imagined a whole crazy scenario out of a distorted mind.

Carolyn felt fear ripple down her spine. She was a target and she didn't have a clue as to who was taking a bead on her. She updated Roberta on the incidents mentioned in the notes, and briefly explained.

"It's obvious that each time this person tries to scare you, Carolyn, they place a note in your in-box."

"How did they gain access?"

"We don't know." Roberta pushed her chair back and stood up. "Anyone who could do that has to come through security. It's a mystery to all of us. And believe me, Security is on it."

Carolyn stood up, too. "I admit, Roberta. I'm scared."

Roberta came around the desk and hugged her. "Just be cautious. Believe me, we've got the top people on this and we'll get to the bottom of it." A pause. "NNN isn't going to throw you to the wolves. We can't in any case. This could happen to any of our salespeople. You happen to be our celebrity and consequently the obvious target of this psycho."

"Thanks, Roberta. I appreciate NNN's stand on this. But it doesn't make me feel a whole lot better. This person has invaded my personal life."

Carolyn headed for Makeup, then detoured to a telephone, pulling out the slip of paper with the locksmith's telephone number. First things first. All of her locks needed to be changed, as soon as possible.

And then she went to work, hoping she could act out the part of Carolyn Langdon, top saleswoman on NNN, known for her outgoing, candid personality, the woman loved by all for sharing her personal life with the public . . . because she'd once trusted the people out there.

That afternoon Carolyn had a two-hour segment of selling camping equipment. She'd familiarized herself with all of the sales items, and fallen in love with the products.

"You know I've had this fantasy since childhood to go on a camping trip to Yellowstone National Park in Wyoming or the wilds of western Montana," she told a customer who'd just ordered a tent, two sleeping bags and miscellaneous cooking equipment.

"Why don't you just do it then?" the woman named Gail asked, laughing. "Could be a second honeymoon for you and your husband."

Carolyn quickly changed the subject, knowing

she'd again moved into personal information. The pace of the show was fast and her sales brisk. Near the end of the segment a grandpa ordered three Swiss army knives for his three grandsons. "They look like good ones," he said.

"I believe they are," Carolyn countered, and then demonstrated all the various devices on the knife. As she was refolding it, closing the last blade, she accidentally cut the tip of her finger. "Darn!" she cried.

"Oh, I'm sorry," the grandpa said, his voice going out to her millions of viewers. "That must hurt."

Quickly regaining her composure, Carolyn smiled into the camera. "It's really just a prick, doesn't hurt at all." She tilted her head and shrugged. "It was my own fault. Even your three grandsons would have known better."

Then she continued her spiel about the safety of the knife, that people such as herself should respect their potential for harm and treat them with care. While the camera panned to a summary of the products, all narrated by Carolyn, her finger was wrapped in gauze. When the lens were turned back to her she held up her finger and joked about it, hiding the fact that she hated the sight of blood.

Oddly, there was a rush of sales for the knife after her minor accident and the Swiss Army knife sold out, then racked up hundreds of back orders. After the show ended Roberta again congratulated her salesmanship.

Neither of them mentioned that the incident might have been noted by the person they now referred to as "the watcher."

When it was time to leave the studio, Frank the

security guard was still on duty. He insisted on walking her to the Volvo. "A commandment from the big boss," he told her, meaning Roberta. He grinned. "Her word is law."

"Thanks, Frank," she told him as she got into her car.

She really was relieved to have him there even if it was still broad daylight. The last few days had been rough, but she'd made an appointment for the locksmith to change the locks the day after tomorrow when she was home in the morning. The timing worked out; Richard would arrive that night, in time to get the new keys. She just wished they were changed already, so she didn't feel so damned apprehensive about going home. And after reading the notes left in her in-box she meant to check her magnolia tree, make sure it was okay.

She was approaching the freeway when her cell phone rang. "Hello?" She slowed the car and stopped in a parking place on the street. The traffic was too heavy for one-handed driving.

"Hi, Carolyn. It's Dolores."

"Oh, Dolores." She was surprised. "Is everything okay?"

"We're all fine. I just realized I hadn't talked to you in a while. Dean is here and he just told me that Richard was out of town." A hesitation. "I know it's spur of the moment, but I thought maybe you'd like to join us for supper."

"I'm sorry, but I can't tonight," Carolyn began, improvising. The last thing she needed today was listening to her stepmother's small talk.

"Oh, darn," Dolores said. "I have good news and

I thought you and Dean could help me celebrate."

"Good news?"

"Great news. My friend Will Millgard from New Jersey is flying down soon to see me. I know Jock, that's his E-mail name, as well as I knew your father."

"That's hard to believe, Dolores."

"But it's true, Carolyn. Somehow, getting to know people on the Internet is less inhibiting than in person. We can type the things we wouldn't dream of saying in the early days of a relationship." She laughed. "Of course I'm not suggesting anyone should marry someone without first meeting them."

"I would hope not, Dolores."

"And lately we've been talking on the phone," Dolores went on. "It's serious, Carolyn. We've even discussed marriage." She giggled. "If we still like each other after we meet face-to-face."

Momentarily, Carolyn was struck dumb. "But won't meeting only be the beginning of getting to know this uh, Jock?"

"Sure, but us women know when a guy is the right one. Wouldn't you agree? Isn't that how you felt about Richard?"

"I didn't meet Richard on the Internet, Dolores."

"That's true." A hesitation. "Well, let's take a rain check for next time Richard is gone. Dinner at my place."

It didn't escape Carolyn that Dolores had changed the subject, but she let it go. She wanted to get back on the road, get home before it was any later. A few seconds later she was able to end the call. Then she headed back into the traffic.

* * *

Frank met her the next morning when she arrived at work, then walked her to her car when she left midafternoon. Carolyn felt better. Last night had been peaceful at home. She'd spoken with Richard and couldn't wait until he got home tomorrow evening. The locks would be changed by then so she wouldn't have to worry about any incidents. The one thing she hadn't done yet was check her magnolia tree. From the window it had looked okay.

The sun dappled the driveway with leaf patterns of shade as Carolyn drove into the garage and closed the door. Once inside the house, she moved cautiously through the laundry room to the kitchen door, aware that the locks had not been changed yet—that someone had a key.

Everything seemed okay—until she stepped farther into the room. The sweet, sickly smell hit her first, then she saw the red mass congealing on the inlaid wood floor.

Blood.

Her knees threatened to buckle, her heart took wing in her chest, and she stood paralyzed in another nightmare. Someone had been in her house again, while she was gone.

Could still be in her house.

Her darting glance told her that there was nothing dead—at least within her visual range. Oh God! Please let Mayo and Mustard be alive. They were nowhere in sight, just as there was no blood on the ceiling that could have dripped onto the floor.

Someone had put it there.

She backed out of the kitchen, her eyes on the

shadowy areas beyond. When she reached the door to the garage, she hit the garage door button, and as it lifted she ran to her car, got inside and locked the doors. A second later she was backing out of the garage, tires squealing. At the end of the driveway, she braked hard, stopping with a jerk.

No way was she being forced out of her own house.

Grabbing her cell phone, Carolyn called 911, trying not to sound hysterical. After explaining, they said an officer was on the way. Then she called the police, said it was an emergency, and got Barney's cell phone number. He answered after the first ring.

"I'll be right there," he said, cutting off her disjointed story of what had happened. Three minutes later a police cruiser pulled up behind her.

She lowered her window and the patrolman confirmed that he'd gotten a call for her address. She quickly explained the incident. His expression remained inscrutable but she sensed his ambivalence. He instructed her to stay parked where she was, but to press the door opener so he could enter the house through the garage. She got out of the car and followed him.

They went into the house, she showed him the blood, and then he searched the house. He found the cats in her bedroom, meowing behind a closet door.

Barney arrived as the officer returned to the kitchen, Mayo and Mustard at his heels. "What's going on here?" he asked, his pale eyes shifting from the officer to Carolyn. He reached for his I.D. and identified himself as an Atlanta homicide detective. "This lady is a friend of mine."

She managed a brief smile and then indicated the pool of blood.

His glance did what she'd done, surveyed the ceiling and floor, determining that the blood was in a perfect pool, no drops or smears. It had been placed there, not left from something dead.

Barney and the officer talked for a few minutes, substantiating that the house was secure. After a few more minutes Barney indicated that the patrolman could go, that he'd see to the blood on the floor. With a nod at Carolyn the young cop went out through the garage to his car. A moment later she heard the engine start and the car back out of the driveway. Barney punched the door button, closing the door after the officer.

"So what's really going on here, Carolyn?" he asked again after they were back in the kitchen. He was dressed in Levi jeans, a navy windbreaker, and a Braves baseball cap tipped over his forehead. He was off duty.

She raised her brows, about to speak when he went on, explaining.

"I checked with the dispatcher who accessed our computer database. It came up with all the recent reports from this address, and—" He hesitated. "And also some other reports from NNN concerning you."

"But the NNN incidents are private."

"Not to me, or any other law enforcement officer who might be checking out related infractions connected to the subject."

"Subject? Meaning me?"

"In this instance, yes." He leaned against the counter, his eyes slightly hooded over the directness of his gaze. "But our information is confidential, a cross reference of facts that helps us build a case."

She sagged against the counter. It was hard to believe that she was part of a police case.

"Don't worry about it," he said softly, guessing her feelings. He stepped around the counter and led her away from where she could see the blood. "Why don't you start from the beginning and tell me everything that's happened."

She glanced away. "Some of the things seem too odd, Barney. Too—paranoid."

"Trust me," he said as they sat down on kitchen chairs on the opposite side of the counter from the spectacle on the floor. "By the way, have you called Richard?"

She shook her head. "He'll be home tomorrow night and I don't want to worry him any more than he already is."

"He's in LA?"

"How did you know?"

He grinned for the first time. "Remember, I checked the computer on my way over here? Seems Richard made a report before he left, was very concerned about what was going on."

She nodded. "That's true."

"So why did he go?" Barney's tone was deceptively low, his eyes level.

"He had to, Barney. He's been trying to tie up things, move his business to Atlanta so that he won't have to travel so much."

His gaze barely wavered. "You have a phone number for him?"

"Yes, I do, but he usually calls me."

"You want to give it to me?"

She stared at him. "Why? Please don't call and scare him, Barney. What good would that do?"

"I promise not to." He grinned again. "But give it to me anyway, just so someone else has it, okay?"

She hesitated, then went to the pad by the phone and copied the number for the Westin Bonaventure Hotel in Los Angeles, handing it to him before sitting back down.

"Thanks." He put it in his pocket. "Okay, let's hear your version of what's been happening. I've already heard a little from Minnie, but start from the very first time you sensed something was wrong."

"I'm warning you, Barney. This is going to sound nuts."

"You're entitled."

"It started months ago, weeks before I met Richard."

He nodded. "Go on."

She drew in a deep breath and started with the first time the anonymous caller left a message about her with the NNN operator, and a black sedan followed her, then the other strange incidents, including her neighbors, down to the bat, rat, dog and blood on her floor.

"What color was the dark sedan? Black?"

"I couldn't tell for sure. Just a very dark color."

He'd pulled out a pad and pen while she talked and made some notes. Now he looked up. "That it?"

"Uh-huh. Isn't that enough?"

A silence went by.

"You think NNN's computer hacker has anything to do with any of this?" he asked, casually.

"Barney, that's confidential. NNN can't have that information get out. It would—"

"I know what it'd mean, and it's still confidential. I happen to be privy to the information, that's all." A pause. "So, what's your take on that?"

"I just don't know," she answered at once.

His brows arched but he didn't comment further. "Okay, I'll wait here while you pack a bag."

She stood up. "What do you mean?"

"You aren't staying here tonight." He shrugged. "Tomorrow's different when Richard is back."

"But—"

"No buts. You're staying with Minnie. She's already expecting you."

She stared, wide-eyed. "I'm fine here, really. Once I'm in the house I use the extra locks."

"Get your bag," he said again. "If you'll trust me with a key I'll make sure the mess is cleaned up." A hesitation. "And I'll have the blood analyzed at the lab, find out what we're dealing with here."

"I'm off in the morning and the locksmith is coming at nine."

"I'll have you back by then."

It was an impasse. Then the phone rang, startling them both. She reached for it.

She half expected Richard's voice on the other end of the wire, but it was Roberta. She spoke so fast Carolyn couldn't get past uttering her first hello. She listened in silence, feeling the fear gather in her stomach. A minute later she thanked her boss and hung up. Then her gaze locked with Barney's.

"It was Roberta. The caller left another brief message."

Barney slipped off the stool. "And?"

"He said, 'Carolyn hates knives and blood.' "

"Shit. Did Roberta call the police?"

Carolyn nodded. She had no further arguments and went to get an overnight bag. Minutes later as they drove away, she was relieved that Barney had taken the decision out of her hands.

What in hell was happening? Someone was terrorizing her and she had no idea why.

21

Minnie stepped out the front door and onto the porch of her pink stucco cottage as Barney pulled up in front of the house. Carolyn got out of the car, ran up the steps and straight into her old friend's arms.

"Oh, Minnie," she said. "I've never been so scared in my life. I don't know what's happening." She fought sudden tears. "Why would someone do these awful things?"

"I don't know, kiddo." Minnie spoke softly. "But you're safe here."

"And you can bet your life that we'll find out what in hell's going on." Barney had come up behind her, and his cold tone was one she'd never heard him use before.

Carolyn turned around and their eyes locked. For the first time she faced the full impact of the professional Barney. His features were set into hard lines and his pale blue eyes had gone as flat as a slate-gray sky. She'd hate to be the focus of his investigation, she thought. He'd be a formidable enemy.

"What we need to find out is why this creep is zeroing in on you—focusing beyond your professional
life to your personal life," he added.

Minnie nodded, her expression troubled . . .
angry. "I just wish you weren't going through this
alone, Carolyn, that Richard was here for moral support."

"I wish that, too." Carolyn tried to hang onto her
composure. "But as I explained to Barney, he's upset
about this and is trying to get his business in order
so that he doesn't have to travel so much." She hesitated. "And I haven't told him about what's happened since he left."

"Some things take precedence, my dear," Minnie
replied, her voice and expression noncommittal.
"It's my experience that nothing is more important
than the people we love."

Carolyn nodded, unsure of how to answer.

Although Barney was silent, Carolyn sensed his
agreement with Minnie. She suddenly realized they
disapproved of Richard leaving her, felt he should
have postponed his trip after the recent incidents.

Don't jump to conclusions because you're upset,
she instructed herself. Of course they liked Richard.
They were just reacting out of their fear for her.

"Come on inside," Minnie said, including Barney
in the invitation. "I'll pour us a drink."

He shook his head. "Can't, but thanks anyway.
I'm meeting a guy from forensics back at Carolyn's
place. He's gonna test the blood, determine if it's
human, animal or what."

Carolyn shuddered involuntarily. It was a nightmare, one with no logical reason for anything that

was happening, but one that left the dreamer terrified and gasping for breath. Only she wouldn't wake up from it. Her nightmare was real.

Barney started back to his car, then hesitated and faced them again. "When did the locksmith say he'd be there?"

"Nine."

"Pick you up at eight. Go on inside and—be careful."

Carolyn followed Minnie into the house. She heard his car take off down the street, after he'd made sure the door had closed between the women and the gathering darkness.

"I'll have a drink, Minnie." Carolyn's voice wobbled. She cleared her throat and tried again. "If you'll join me."

"Of course," Minnie said. "We both need a little artificial courage right now."

Barney arrived ten minutes early the next morning, in time to grab a cup of coffee. Carolyn left with him a short time later, after promising Minnie that she would keep her updated on what was happening.

"I should hear from the lab about the blood by the end of the day," he said, pulling into her driveway. "By the way, your kitchen floor is back to spotless. Didn't think you'd want to look at that mess when you got home."

"Thanks, Barney. I can't tell you how much I appreciate all—"

"No problem," he said, interrupting. He switched off the engine and shot her a grin. "We're friends, right?"

She nodded, wondering how she could ever repay him. His friendship, and his help, meant a lot to her. She'd have to be careful or she'd end up with a case of hero worship just like Dean and the kids at Anderson Youth House.

He waited until after the locksmith had changed the locks before he turned to go himself. When she'd worried aloud that he'd be late for work he'd only shrugged and said it was his day off. Then, after another admonition to watch her back, to call him if anything else happened, he left her to shower and change for work.

She was relieved when she drove away from her house. Richard would be with her when she returned that evening. She didn't notice the traffic as she drove to the studio. Driving gave her a chance to think about all the things that had happened in the days since Richard had been gone.

It was almost as though the person behind all the cruel incidents knew he was gone and had accelerated the terror tactics accordingly.

But the only people who knew he'd left Atlanta were Dean and Dolores and a few close friends like Roberta, Minnie and Barney.

Was someone keeping track of her every move? Somehow that thought was too overwhelming to think about. She shivered even though the day was sunny and hot. The concept of being that intimately involved with a faceless phantom, someone who knew so much about her, had taken the joy from her life.

She could no longer rationalize her fears. Someone was out there.

* * *

She was on the way to the airport when Barney called on her cell phone. "I got the results on the blood," he said, a note of disgust in his voice. "You ready for this?"

"Probably not, but I'm prepared to hear whatever you have to tell me."

"It's chicken blood."

"Chicken blood?"

"That's what came up."

"That's weird."

"Uh-huh." A pause. "But chicken blood can be bought at a butcher shop. I'm not saying it's not creepy, but at least I don't think he killed a chicken to get it." Another pause. "Gotta go, but keep me posted, Carolyn. And for the umpteenth time, be careful."

Carolyn promised and was about to disconnect when she heard his voice again. "A patrolman will be swinging past your house every so often to check on it. Okay?"

"Thanks, Barney."

"No thanks needed. We're friends, remember?"

And then he hung up and she drove on to the airport. Thank God Richard was coming home.

But Richard was not in a good mood when he met her outside the baggage claim area and got into her car. He kissed her long and hard, explained that he was happy to be home with her, but that he hadn't been able to tie up all the loose ends on a time-share condominium deal, a property located on the Pacific Ocean south of San Diego. He seemed upset, and was brooding over the fact that he'd probably have to make another trip out to California in the near future. She had never seen Richard so disturbed.

"So what's been happening in my absence?" he asked when they were almost home.

"Um, just the usual," she replied, not wanting to upset him further. "I'll give you an update on everything tomorrow."

She glanced at his profile. Sensing her scrutiny, he faced her and smiled. "Sorry, I'm out of sorts, Carolyn. I just get so damned mad when I'm faced with incompetence, when all I really want to do is be here in Atlanta with you."

"It's okay, Richard." She hesitated. "Maybe you should have stayed on for a few days, concluded your business."

"I would have done that but the fools had a legal problem that couldn't be resolved in a few days." He wiped a hand over his forehead, as though to erase the troubling issue. "I wasn't about to hang around while they tried to figure out how to handle a property line dispute."

Once home, she poured him a Scotch, then went upstairs to shower and get ready for bed. By the time she was out of the bathroom, he, too, had showered and was waiting for her. Mellowed by the drink, he made love to her. And then she went to sleep in his arms, feeling safe for the first time in days.

A week later, as Carolyn was reducing speed for her exit, the brakes suddenly failed on the Volvo. She pumped them frantically as she steered onto the off-ramp. She pulled the emergency brake and the car slowed, but she realized she'd never be able to stop at the end of the ramp. Twisting the wheel, she managed to drive off the road and onto the median which sloped slightly upward from the side of the highway. The car came to a gradual stop.

She sat with her hands on the wheel, shaking from reaction, and realized how lucky she was to have escaped injury. But her nerves were shattered.

She heard the approaching siren before she saw the police car pull up nearby. The officer requested her driver's license and she could only nod, still shaken. She grabbed her purse, rummaged through it to find her wallet and pulled it out. Abruptly, she sat up straighter. Her license was gone. And her insurance certificate wasn't in the glove box.

Her explanation fell on deaf ears. The more she tried to explain, the tighter his expression became. She finally gave up.

"Sorry, lady," the officer said. "I realize that your brakes failed but that doesn't exonerate you from driving without a license or an insurance certificate. The statutes are explicit. You must have a valid license to drive, and proof of insurance must be in the vehicle. Ma'am, those are the rules."

He wrote her a ticket, called for a tow truck and her car was taken to the nearest Volvo repair shop. She rode with the driver and called Richard once they arrived. He'd been at home working on his computer and was able to come get her right away.

"Christ almighty!" he told her as they drove home. "Something has to be done about all of these so-called incidents and accidents. Some wacko is out there laughing at us."

"I agree." Carolyn felt exhausted. "But what else we can do? We don't even know who we're looking for."

"Why haven't the police figured that out?"

"I don't know. I suppose because they have nothing to go on, no evidence, no suspect." She paused. "At least that's what they're telling the bigwigs at NNN."

"And in the meantime some crazy maniac is stalking my wife." He pounded the steering wheel with his hand. "That's unacceptable."

Carolyn was silent for the next few seconds. When she'd finally explained what had happened while he was gone, Richard had been enraged. He'd called the police and insisted that something be done before someone was hurt, namely his wife. On one hand she'd been heartened by his concern for her; on the other his reaction had left her hesitant to share her own fears and worry him even more.

They drove into the garage, got out of the car and went into the house. Richard had decided to call the police again about her missing license and insurance certificate. "The least we can do is get everything documented on a police report."

He was still talking about it as they walked through the kitchen and up the front hall to the stairs. Carolyn was headed to the bedroom to change clothes, Richard to his office to call the police and check phone messages.

About to start up the steps, Richard waited as Carolyn opened the front door to get the mail. Upon retrieving the small pile of envelopes, she backed into the hall again, her gaze on the material in her hand.

"My God!"

Their eyes met and locked. Then she slowly raised the top two items from the stack of mail.

Her driver's license and insurance certificate.

He went directly to the phone to call the police.

The next afternoon Roberta drove her from work to the Volvo shop and let her off.

"Let me know the verdict," she told Carolyn. "Sure the car is ready to drive? Should I wait and see?"

Carolyn shook her head on both counts. "No, the office girl who called said it was all done."

Roberta nodded. "You have my cell phone number if it's not. I'll come back and get you."

Carolyn went into the shop as Roberta drove away. She could see her Volvo parked in the lot and knew it had been fixed. The mechanic came out of the work area where he'd been seeing to another car that was up on the lift.

"It's ready to go," the small lean man told her. He scratched his head. "But it's a puzzle as to why the brake lines under the car failed. Shouldn't have in a new car."

"What do you mean?"

"Well, if the lines that carry the fluid are severed, then the brakes fail."

"Were my lines deliberately cut?"

He hesitated, as though he considered what he should or shouldn't say. "Don't know. I only know they look like they've been cut. You could've driven over something that had the same result."

"But I didn't."

He stared for a moment, unwilling to offer a further opinion. "Don't know what to tell you, lady. But I can assure you that your car is safe to drive now. You won't have any more problems with your brakes."

There was no further conversation. It was obvious that the mechanic didn't want to get involved in her problems. She paid her bill, took possession of her car and then drove out of the shop. She hadn't gone far when her cell phone rang.

"It's Roberta."

"What's up?"

"The caller left another message. The operator saw that the call came from Atlanta but it was a public phone and therefore untraceable back to a person."

"What did he say?"

"Carolyn, like before, we're not sure if the caller is a man or woman. The voice could be either."

"But what did *it* say?"

"I don't want to scare you more, but I feel that I have to tell you." She paused. "So you know, so you're warned about this crazy lunatic."

"But what was the message?"

"It was brief. 'Carolyn hates driving on the freeway. I tried to put her out of her misery.' "

She veered off the street and into a grocery parking lot. Her fingers shook so hard she barely managed to turn the car off. It had been for real. Someone had tried to kill her.

22

"**Y**our brakes went out, too. Remember?"

"I've already thought of that, Carolyn," Richard replied. "And, yes, the circumstances were similar. My mechanic said the line had been severed." He propped himself up on an elbow so that he could look down at her in the bed. "But we don't know that both brake failures were caused by the same reason—a fuckin' psycho."

"But we do know that both were unusual." She hesitated. "I hope I haven't put you in danger, Richard."

"Don't worry about me. I can take care of myself." His expression softened. "It's you I'm worried about."

She glanced away. "I just wish I knew why, of all people on television, I'm being targeted by this person—this crazy nut."

"Crazy nut or not. He, or she as Roberta has indicated, appears to be pretty damn smart. A wacko would be oblivious to being discovered. This person is one step ahead of everyone, including the police."

His voice lowered with his face as he suddenly kissed her. "Promise me you'll be careful, Carolyn. Promise that you'll stay safe."

She smiled under his lips. "I promise."

"Maybe the police patrol of our house will deter this pervert from doing anything more," Richard said. "And it's possible our move to another address will end this whole thing very soon."

Carolyn nodded. "Maybe." She had her doubts. How had the person known all of her personal information in the first place? She wasn't sure they could hide, that a simple change of address would stop the problem. But she hoped Richard was right.

She smiled, sensing his frustration, wanting to somehow make things right again. "Maybe we'll never come up against this—this watcher-person again," she said. "Maybe he'll give up."

"I hope you're right," he replied.

But she was wrong.

Two days later as she was on the freeway from work a back tire suddenly blew out. Veering across several lanes of rush-hour traffic, scattering vehicles with screeching brakes and honking horns, Carolyn managed to bring her car to a gravel-skidding stop on the shoulder.

She dropped her head onto her arms that circled the wheel, gulping long, deep breaths, striving to slow her heart rate, willing the sudden tremors that shook her body to stop. "I won't faint—I won't faint," she whispered. But her wavering vision, and the sensation of her chest swelling against her throat, told her that she might do just that. Desperately, she lowered her window to allow fresh air into the car.

She could have killed someone.

Or herself.

By the time she felt revived enough to get out of the car and view the damage to her tire, a highway patrolman had pulled up behind her.

"Looks like you had a blowout, miss." The tall uniformed man was lean, had craggy features and a concerned manner, unlike the officer who'd assisted her when the brakes failed.

She nodded and managed a smile. "I've never had one before and—and it really shook me up." She sucked in a ragged breath. "I'm so glad that I didn't cause a wreck, maybe kill someone."

"Yeah, you were real lucky." He glanced at the river of traffic behind him, then down the driver's side of the car to the flat tire. "You have a spare?"

"Uh-huh."

"I'll give you a hand, have you fixed up in a jiffy."

He stepped back and she opened her door to pull the trunk release lever. Then Carolyn and the patrolman walked to the back of the Volvo.

"Here, let me," he said as she struggled to retrieve the spare tire and jack.

"Thanks." She managed a smile. "I appreciate your help."

"You're like my wife," he said. "She's helpless when it comes to anything about a car except driving it." His grin softened his words and she felt no offense. When he took over and changed the tire himself, she was relieved.

"You know, this is really a strange blowout," he

said, staring at the tire he'd just removed from the car. "The tire is not shredded."

"What do you mean?"

"It has an obvious hole in it, but there's no nail—nothing."

"Then what caused the hole?"

"Dunno." He shook his head as he examined the flat. "Something hit the tire, then exited through the opposite side. Resembles a bullet hole."

"You mean, someone shot my tire?"

"No, not at all." The officer straightened. "I'm just saying that this is an odd type of hole for a tire that's almost new. The flat was probably caused by a projectile that spun out from under a truck wheel. I've seen that happen a time or two."

"And that can look like a bullet hole? You can tell the difference?"

"Yeah. We once had a freeway sniper who shot at cars from an overpass. The drivers heard nothing and didn't know what hit them." He shook his head. "Don't think that's the case here but I'll include my observations in my report."

A few minutes later she was ready to go. Carolyn thanked him, he gave a salute and then drove off into the traffic. She followed in the slow lane, conscious that anyone who could shoot with such precision could take aim on the driver and not miss.

All the way home she considered the possibilities. Maybe the incident was accidental this time; the officer hadn't been alarmed. Oh God, she no longer knew what to think. Her peace of mind, her very life was being destroyed.

No dark cars had followed her but Carolyn felt

eyes watching her. It was only when she was safely in her garage that she realized she'd been taking short breaths, was on the verge of hyperventilating. She sat for a minute, until she was composed enough to face Richard without breaking down.

The whole damn mess was getting old.

"Hey, your commute took longer than expected."

Richard turned from the sink as she came into the kitchen. "I was beginning to worry that our steaks would turn to shoe leather before you got here." His words were tempered by a smile and a kiss. "Bad traffic, huh?"

"You cooked supper?"

"Yep. It's our anniversary." He paused, stepping back and cocking one dark eyebrow. "Don't tell me you forgot?"

Her mind went blank.

"Our six-month anniversary—since we met in Roberta's office."

"Oh, Richard. How thoughtful."

"So quick, go change into something comfortable." He scooted her toward the hallway. "Dinner will be served in five minutes."

She grinned, suddenly feeling uplifted. She planted a kiss on his lips, then scurried off toward the stairs, looking forward to their romantic evening.

And maybe the blowout had been an accident.

Maybe.

Whatever the reason she wasn't about to allow it to spoil Richard's surprise. She'd wait to tell him about it. Or just take care of getting the tire repaired and forget the whole thing.

* * *

The decision was taken out of her hands the following evening as she drove home from an especially successful day of sales at the studio. Carolyn was listening to a Puccini CD as she moved with the flow of traffic under an overpass.

The splash of black fluid on the windshield was so sudden that she slammed on her brakes by reflex. Tires screeched behind her, but fortunately no one ran into her trunk as she strained to see where she was going.

Luckily, she'd been driving in the slower, right-hand lane and was able to get off the freeway and onto an exit ramp. Once on a side street she stopped, leaving the engine running while making sure no one had followed. Cautiously, she stepped out of the car, but her legs threatened to fold under her.

Motor oil, she decided, recognizing its odor. Someone had thrown it onto her car from the overpass. Random vandalism? she wondered.

Grabbing a box of Kleenex from the car, Carolyn tried to clear the windshield enough so that she could see to drive. She wondered if the paint job was ruined.

Possibly. She kept up a running dialogue in her mind, trying to divert her thoughts from the obvious: someone had attacked her again.

Why? she asked herself for the umpteenth time. Who hated her so much that they would subject her to this? What had she done to warrant these attempts on her life?

Staying calm was hopeless. She couldn't deny the facts, just as she couldn't pretend the oil had landed on her car by accident. Just get home, she told herself. Richard was there.

Once she'd cleared the windshield enough to drive she got back into the car, glancing around the light industrial area where she'd parked. Hundreds of cars were passing on the nearby freeway, but there wasn't a person in sight on the side road. Her glance stopped on the overpass which wasn't far away. Even though no one was there now they could still be close, watching. She needed to get out of there.

A black car came out of a nearby street. She floored the gas pedal, taking off in a spray of gravel. How had anyone known when she'd be on that section of road? She'd just driven back onto the freeway when it hit her. At the close of her last on-air segment, she'd mentioned going straight home after work.

"You must be tired after three consecutive two-hour programs," her customer had said. "I'd be exhausted."

Carolyn had reminded the woman that she'd substituted at the last minute for one of them, that three in a row was not typical.

But the phantom viewer must have been listening—and already knew her route home. She'd inadvertently given the time she'd be driving it.

"Stupid!" she shouted at herself. "Don't you know better after all the crap that's been going on? *Personal chitchat is out!*"

But what about last night? She hadn't mentioned when she was leaving yesterday—and someone had shot her tire.

"Dear God," she prayed, hands clenched on the wheel. "Please tell me what's happening."

Richard stood in silence as Carolyn showed him the oil-streaked Volvo, after she'd driven into the garage and immediately closed the door. Pretending a calmness she didn't feel, Carolyn explained what had happened.

Without responding, he circled the car, checking for damage, smelling the black sludge to verify it was motor oil. Finally he met her eyes, unable to hide the apprehension in his own.

"Have you told me everything?" he asked.

She stared. "What do you mean?"

"Only that you didn't tell me about what was going on while I was gone. Is there anything else I should know?"

Carolyn lowered her gaze, unable to lie.

"What?" he said, prompting her, seeing her hesitation.

Slowly, almost reluctantly, she told him about the blowout on the freeway the night before, that the patrolman who'd changed the tire had wondered about the hole, that it seemed like a bullet hole.

"Why didn't you tell me?" he demanded.

"Because I didn't want to worry you."

"For Christ's sake, Carolyn. What do you think I am now?—a person who is calmly listening to a Sunday School report?"

Tears brimmed her eyes. "You'd fixed supper and—"

"And—" His hands came down on her shoulders. "I'd fixed supper for who?—the woman I love, the person I cherish—my wife who means everything to me." He gave her a shake. "So why wouldn't you tell me?"

She glanced down. "I'm sorry, Richard. I hate putting all of this on you." She hesitated. "If only I knew why this person has zeroed in on me in the first place."

"I don't give a shit why at this point!" His angry outburst was a drastic contrast to his earlier calm. "I just want NNN, the police, someone, to stop it."

"Oh, Richard. I'm so sorry that you've been sucked into this insanity." She gulped, willing herself not to break down. "I don't want you to be in danger along with me. You're an innocent bystander."

"Does that mean you think you're guilty of something?"

"'Course not." She paused. "But apparently someone out there thinks I am."

Richard drew in a sharp breath. "We may as well get it all out on the table."

"What do you mean?"

"Did you know that the magnolia tree in the garden is dead?"

"No." Her mind flashed on the note that had been left in her message box at NNN, about checking her magnolia tree. "It can't be. It was healthy, no bugs or blights and watered daily."

"Someone sawed it off at the trunk, Carolyn, left it propped up so that it would look alive until the leaves and blossoms drooped."

"Oh my God, no. How did someone get back there?"

"Probably through the house before the locks were changed. Our neighbors wouldn't have noticed the sawing."

"Then it was already dead before—" Her voice faltered. "Before the blood."

Another silence.

"I'm afraid so."

She sagged against Richard who'd stepped forward as he'd spoken.

"Come on, sweetheart, let's go inside." His tone was softer and she realized he was controlling his anger, for her sake. "I'll see to getting your car cleaned tomorrow."

Carolyn allowed herself to be led from the garage and into the kitchen, watched as Richard locked the garden doors and closed the drapes, so that she couldn't see her dead magnolia tree.

"It's as I've said before, one of your fans has a grudge against you, Carolyn," he said.

She nodded. It was the only reasonable explanation. But what could she do about it? Quit her job? And would that do any good anyway? As her dad used to say, "It's too late to shutter the house after the hurricane has already blown out the windows." The watcher already knew where she lived.

Sighing, she plopped down on a kitchen chair, too shaky to face the stairs at the moment. The cold grip of terror that had knotted her stomach all the way home would not let go.

"Why don't you have a nice warm bath, change into something more comfortable," Richard said. "When you come back down we'll fix a great supper together." His dark eyes narrowed. "While you're relaxing I'll report this latest incident to the police, and then we'll forget all this bullshit for a little while." He nudged her to her feet. "Let's not allow an awful situation to get to us, sweetheart, spoil our life together. Okay?"

Her smile met his, the one she loved so much, that started at the corners of his eyes before it curved his lips.

"Something sexy?" she asked, answering the first part of his suggestion.

He nodded. "I'll look forward to it."

Raising her brows suggestively, she headed upstairs.

When Carolyn returned a half hour later Richard was talking on the phone and she hesitated in the doorway to the kitchen.

"I've just talked to the police, Roberta." Richard's fingers drummed the counter, expressing his upset. "They can't give me any answers but I expect some from NNN. This is a life and death situation, and Carolyn has done nothing to bring this down on herself, or me, for that matter." A hesitation. "Surely NNN has a security plan to protect its stars from stalkers." Another pause. "You're saying you don't, then. And I'm telling you that you'd better get one. Pronto."

He turned and saw Carolyn in the doorway.

"Wait, tell Carolyn. She just came downstairs."

Carolyn stepped forward and took the receiver which he'd held out to her. "Hello?" she said.

"It's Roberta, Carolyn. I'm so sorry, and terribly upset about what's going on."

"Richard told you the latest?"

"Yeah." A pause. "Off the record, it's pretty scary, Carolyn. Nothing like this has ever happened at NNN."

"I know, Roberta. And I can't tell you what's happening now. Whoever is behind all these terror tactics never shows himself—or herself, for that matter." She drew in a wobbly breath. "But I admit, I'm terrified. And I don't know how to protect myself. I feel like a sitting duck."

"I understand completely." Roberta's sigh came over the wires. "All I can say is that NNN is working on it with the police." A pause. "And we're adding extra security at the studio, not just for you but for all of our on-the-air salespeople."

"You think the harassment could spread to them?"

"We have to be prepared for that, because we don't know who this person is, or what's motivating these incidents. We do know that our computerized company information was accessed and the attacks on you are getting more frequent and serious." Another pause. "It's all a threat to NNN in the home shopping network competition."

"Roberta, do you think that's what this is all about?—competitors trying to discredit NNN?"

"We don't know, Carolyn. We're open to all possibilities, but the first concern is your safety."

A long silence went by. Carolyn switched the receiver to her other ear, so that she could watch Richard rummaging in the refrigerator for salad parts.

"—so we've arranged for the limo," Roberta was saying.

"What's that about a limo, Roberta?"

"I said we've arranged for a limo to pick you up and take you home for the next week."

"What?" Carolyn's response was sharp and loud, and Richard turned to face her. "That's not necessary, Roberta."

"Richard and I agreed that it was, Carolyn. Topic closed." Her drawn-in breath sounded in Carolyn's ear. "In any case, the network doesn't want anything happening to our star."

After another minute of talk, Carolyn hung up. There was no point in arguing with Roberta about the limo, but she knew that if the craziness didn't stop she might not be NNN's star for long. Anyone could be replaced.

And maybe that was what the watcher person wanted.

23

Everything was quiet for the next week. Carolyn gradually fell back into a normal pattern, except for the limo service. She was uncomfortable with such attention. She didn't want people to think she was a prima donna.

The bright spot on the immediate horizon was the imminent closing of their new house. Hopeful again, Carolyn felt that the move might exorcise the dark presence in her life for good. She tried not to think she was deluding herself.

The limo brought her to the studio on the last day it had been scheduled, and Richard was picking her up at eight that night, after her three-hour special on Diamonique jewelry. Carolyn was relieved by his plan; walking to the car after dark, even with the security guard, was a scary proposition right now.

By the time she was ready to leave Richard hadn't arrived. It was a first. Richard was never late.

Carolyn waited another fifteen minutes, thinking he'd gotten delayed, then tried calling him on his

cell phone and their home phone. There was no answer on either one. She tried not to feel alarmed
when she spoke to the door guard, asking him if
he'd seen Richard.

"I haven't, Carolyn," he said. "Are you sure he
isn't waiting in the car?"

She shook her head. "He stated emphatically that
he'd come in and get me, that I wasn't to wait outside."

The guard came out from behind his desk and
strode to the glass front doors. "You stay here while
I have a quick look around the lot. Your husband
drives a white BMW, doesn't he?"

She nodded.

The guard headed toward the employee parking
section, the door swinging shut behind him. Carolyn
watched him go, saw him pause under one of the
pole lights, then dart between some cars and disappear. A minute later he stepped back into the light,
his arm around another man, propping him up as
they headed back toward the studio entrance.

It was Richard and he was hurt.

Carolyn ran out to help, shocked by his appearance. His face was smudged with dirt, his lip was
cut and bleeding and his clothing was torn.

"For God's sake, what happened?" "Did you
have an accident?—what?"

Richard shook his head, as though trying to focus
on her questions. "I was mugged." His voice wobbled. "The guy took my wallet."

As they went into the building Carolyn told the
guard to call for help, then helped Richard lie down
on the sofa in the reception area. In minutes the

lobby was alive with activity. A police car pulled up outside and two officers strode into the group, followed by medics who'd arrived seconds after the patrolmen.

Richard couldn't describe his assailant, aside from knowing the person was tall, muscular and wore gloves; he'd been attacked from behind. One of the officers took down his statement as the medics examined him; the other policeman secured the parking lot. Richard's injuries seemed superficial, but because he was dizzy and slightly disoriented, the medics insisted he be checked out at the hospital.

"For God's sake, what's happened now?" Roberta asked, arriving on the scene. Her question was to Carolyn, but her gaze was on the medics attending to Richard.

Carolyn was hovering as close to Richard as the medics would allow, and she stepped back to talk to Roberta. She explained what she knew, pausing between phrases to clear her throat, a futile attempt to calm her quavering voice.

Roberta hesitated, digesting the latest frightening incident, but her expression said she was thinking along the same lines as Carolyn. That whoever was behind the attacks was getting closer. "Jeez, I'm sorry, Carolyn," she said. "What in hell can we do to stop this?"

Carolyn glanced away. She didn't have a clue. But now was not the time to discuss it; she was too near breaking down and she needed to stay strong for Richard.

"Let's talk about it tomorrow, try to come up with something."

Roberta nodded, understanding.

"Mrs. Crawford?" The medic had snapped his medical bag closed and stood up. "As we said, we want to take your husband to the hospital, make sure a doctor sees him to determine if he needs more tests."

"Of course. I want that, too."

They put him on a gurney to transport him to the aid vehicle and the hospital. Richard protested and Carolyn grabbed his hand, bent over and kissed him. "This is what you'd insist upon for me, isn't it?"

He managed a smile. "Okay, but you'll have to follow in my car, so you can take me home after they realize I'm okay."

She kissed him again. "Agreed."

The next few minutes were chaotic as the medics, accompanied by the police officers, scattered the crowd and wheeled Richard out to the aid car. Seconds later they were headed out of NNN's parking lot, Carolyn following in Richard's BMW.

No one followed.

"Minnie?"

"Carolyn? Is that you?"

"Uh-huh." Her voice was unstable. "I'm at the hospital. Richard was—"

"Are you okay?" Minnie's rapid-fire questions interrupted, her instant concern obvious in her tone. "What happened?"

"I'm okay, Minnie, really." A pause. "Richard came to pick me up and was mugged in the NNN parking lot."

"No!" A pause. "You weren't with him, were you?"

"I was still inside waiting for him."

"Is he hurt?"

"He seems okay, but since he complained of dizziness and seemed disoriented, they're keeping him overnight for observation, even though the doctor checked him out and feels that his head wound is superficial. I was told that I might as well go home."

A silence came over the airwaves.

"You aren't planning to, are you Carolyn?"

"Yeah. I have to. My cats need to be fed and—"

"And nothing," Minnie interrupted again. "This whole screwy mess is getting worse instead of better. I'm not letting you go home alone with that wacko on the loose. I insist that you come here, spend the night, and then see to the cats, Richard and work in the bright light of day."

Carolyn didn't reply.

"Are you there, Carolyn?"

"Yes, I'm here."

"And did you hear what I said?" A pause. "I'm not just speaking as your friend, I'm speaking for your father who's not here to give you the same advice."

"Thanks, Minnie," she said, finally. "I appreciate your concern. I just wanted you to know what I was doing, so I could check in with you once I was in my house—because I am scared." Another pause. "I forgot that I'd be putting a big worry on you as well. I'm sorry."

"Okay, so you're coming over here for the night?"

Carolyn breathed deeply. "No, I'm not, but I'll call you when I'm safely in the house." She hesitated. "Minnie, please understand. I have to go home. I can't let some wacko dictate my life. It's my house, my cats, my future and no one is going to grab that away from me no matter how much they threaten me."

There was a long silence.

"Okay, kiddo. You know that I'm a backup for you. I'll even go feed your cats."

"And have you become a target in my place? No way."

"Are you leaving right now?"

"Yeah. I should be home in fifteen minutes."

"Call me on your cell phone before you drive into the garage. Agree?"

"Yes, I'll call from the street."

"I can't change your mind?"

"No."

"I'll be waiting then, for your call. If I don't get it in sixteen minutes I'll be calling out the cavalry."

"I'll call."

The sound of the tires on the blacktop was ominous as Carolyn turned onto her street. Her senses went to full alert.

Then she saw the low sports car that was parked in front of her house—and the shadowy shape of a man behind the wheel.

An icy cold chill momentarily shut off her breathing. As she stopped at the bottom of her driveway, a tall, lean man stepped from the other car. Then she recognized—Barney.

He tapped on the passenger window, she unlocked the door and he opened it, swinging his body onto the passenger seat. "What in hell's happening,

Carolyn?" he asked, meeting her gaze. "You lost your mind—or something?"

Even in the faint light from the street lamps Carolyn saw the glint in his pale eyes—wolf eyes that missed nothing even though it was the dark of night.

"How did you know?"

"Minnie called."

"And told you—"

"Everything she knew, that Richard had been attacked, that she was terrified for you."

"So you came over?"

"Yeah. Someone has to do the right thing here."

"You sound mad, Barney. At me?"

There was a silence.

"Just drive into the garage, Carolyn. We'll discuss this once we're in the house, okay?" A pause. "I'm glad Richard's injuries aren't serious. And just so you know, I hadn't heard about your tire blowout, or the motor oil on your windshield. There was no police report but you should have let me know . . . under the circumstances."

She didn't know how to respond, and pressed the garage opener and then drove slowly forward. Once inside, she punched the button again and the door closed behind them. She switched off the motor and turned to Barney.

"So, what's the script from here, Mr. Detective?"

"Are you being sarcastic, Carolyn?"

She shook her head. "Just sensitive, and very scared."

His expression changed at her words, and without answering, he opened the car door and stepped into the garage. She followed suit, and then moved to the laundry room door that led into the house.

"Wait."

She turned, her hand on the knob, waiting for him to join her.

"I want you to stay here," he said. "Until I check out the house."

Her eyes widened.

"Just in case," he said, and pulled out his revolver.

She shrunk away from him. "Surely that's not necessary, Barney."

His gaze shifted from the door to her. "Only a precaution. Better to be cautious than find yourself in a bad situation."

She nodded and he went on into the house. A few minutes later he reappeared. "All clear." He grinned briefly. "Come on in."

"To my own house." Her voice was filled with jaded humor.

Mayo and Mustard were immediately rubbing her ankles and she raised her brows at Barney. "Duty calls. My cats are hungry."

While he propped himself up on a bar stool, she took off her jacket, dropped her purse onto the table and then grabbed the bag of dried cat food from the cupboard. She dumped a generous portion into the cats' bowls and then refilled their water dish. Her immediate duties completed, she turned to Barney. "Coffee, tea or wine? What can I offer you?"

"Wine. I'm off duty."

She smiled a little too brightly, went to the refrigerator and pulled out a bottle of chilled Chardonnay.

Uncorking it, she poured it into two wine glasses. Then she handed one to Barney, her brows raised in a question.

"A toast?"

He nodded. "You give it."

She raised her glass. "To a good friend." A pause. "I appreciate you, Barney."

His eyes glinted as he raised his glass. "Good friends," he said.

And then they both took a sip.

"I need to check my messages," she said, glancing at the answering machine. Do you mind, Barney?"

He shook his head and sipped more wine. "Go ahead. Want me to go into the other room?"

She laughed aloud. "I don't have secrets. You can hear my messages."

She punched the button. The first one was from Dolores, again inviting her for supper. The second one brought Barney straight up on the stool.

"I know how much you hate dark parking lots, Carolyn." A hoarse snort of laughter sounded on the recording. "Next time it could be you."

There was a beep.

The last call was from Roberta. "Security found Richard's wallet in a trash barrel. His driver's license and credit cards are still in it, but any money he might have had is gone." A long pause. "This is so bizarre. Talk to you tomorrow."

"End of messages," the voice on the answering machine said into the stunned silence of Carolyn's kitchen.

"Play it again," Barney said.

She did, so glad that Barney was with her. Otherwise she'd be a basket case.

He glanced at the caller ID that was attached to her service. The watcher's call came in at 7:54, a few minutes before Richard's attack. Barney met her eyes.

"This guy just made a mistake. We have the time of his call, and we can have the phone company trace the origin of the call—because it came into your line." He looked grim. "And the caller left the message *before* the attack.

"Guy?"

"Man or woman. Maybe we'll get lucky and find out."

She slumped down on another stool, her eyes on her glass, again glad he was there. If she'd heard that message alone she would have—

He reached to place his hand over hers. "Don't be upset," he said. "We'll stop this."

"We?" She glanced up.

"The police—me."

"But you're a homicide detective, Barney. This isn't a homicide case."

Something flickered in his eyes and was gone. "That's true but the captain has assigned it to me, at my request."

"Do you think someone could—could die?"

He sipped his wine, not meeting her eyes. "We won't let that happen."

"But you think it could?" she asked, pressing the point.

"Not necessarily. We only know that we're dealing with what seems to be an unstable person who has fixated on you for some reason." He hesitated. "I've taken the case because I have a vested interest in doing so."

"Which is?"

His gaze was suddenly direct. "I don't want anything happening to you."

She was the first to lower her eyes, unwilling to read the deeper meaning of his words.

He finished his wine and stood up. "Time you were in bed," he said. "And time for me to go."

She stood, too. "Thanks for everything, Barney."

He grinned. "Welcome." A pause. "By the way, I checked with the Humane Society about the dog you found in your house. It was bought that morning by a man they couldn't describe and picked up that evening by the dog catcher."

He walked toward the front door, then turned, his eyebrows arched in a question. "One more question, Carolyn."

"Shoot."

"Who would have anything to gain if something happened to you?"

"What do you mean?" A pause. "Surely you don't think Richard—"

He put up a flat silencing hand. "Didn't this all start before Richard?"

She nodded.

"Then, who else."

"This is ridiculous."

"So, humor me."

She hesitated a moment longer. "Well, if I died my estate, which really means the inheritance from my father, reverts to Dolores, if I'm childless."

"Not Richard?"

She shook her head. "According to my dad's will, any husband I might have is third in line after me and Dolores. If I have children neither would inherit, and the estate would revert to a trust fund for my father's grandchildren."

"Can I ask you a personal question, Carolyn, one that only has significance to me as a police officer investigating a case?"

She nodded.

"Would your estate be significant?"

She hesitated. "How so?"

"In thousands?—millions?"

"I don't think of myself as rich, Barney. The money is in investments and I never think about it. I live on my own salary."

He grinned. "Don't be so sensitive. The answer is important to the investigation."

She glanced away. "A few million."

He blew out his breath. "So Dolores is the one to gain if, uh, something happened to you."

"I don't want to think such things, Barney. It's destructive."

He'd reached the front door and turned to face her. "I've authorized a tap on your phone."

"A tap?"

He inclined his head. "A tap will keep track of all of your in- and outgoing calls. Give us a picture of who might be calling your number, and from where."

"But Richard has his business calls."

His gaze was suddenly penetrating. "I want you to promise that you'll tell no one about the tap, Carolyn, not even Richard. Legitimate calls have nothing to hide, and of course you'll not be privy to the conversations, only the origin of the calls."

She hesitated. What was Barney saying? That they couldn't trust anyone at this point. But she trusted Richard. Any calls to or from him were legitimate.

"Okay, I promise." The words were out of her mouth before she could edit them. Richard had nothing to hide. She could promise, for the sake of their future together.

"Good." His eyelids narrowed and she shivered a little at the flat expression in his eyes. "And keep the doors locked and a sharp eye out for anything unusual." A pause. "Call me even if you think it's nothing."

She nodded, glad he was on her side.

He put two fingers to his mouth and then planted them briefly on her lips, as though his gesture sealed a pledge between them.

So be it. Barney was someone she could trust. She'd stake her life on that.

24

"Well, let me know when Richard is out of town again. Maybe you can have supper with Dean and me."

Dolores's voice sounded brittle, and Carolyn wondered if she was annoyed because of her recent invitations being turned down. Dolores didn't know what had been going on and Carolyn wasn't about to tell her. There was no point for Dean and his family to worry, too.

"I will," she replied. "But I miss everyone, and I've heard great reports about Dean's class at the Youth House."

"Yeah, we're all proud of him. Dean has become a different boy lately, confident and more outgoing."

"Our new house in Buckhead is about to close, and after we've moved, we'll all get together more often."

A deep sigh. "If Richard approves."

Carolyn was taken aback. "What do you mean, Dolores?"

There was a silence.

"I, that is, we got the impression that he wasn't too fond of us, that's all."

"I'm so sorry you feel that way," Carolyn said. "But it's not true. Richard looks forward to being a part of the family, especially when we have children."

"Are you pregnant, Carolyn?"

She laughed. "Unfortunately, no. But we're hoping I will be in the near future."

Another silence.

"Let's get together soon," Carolyn said. She hated feeling that Dolores disapproved of her life with Richard.

"You call when you're free. We'd love to see you."

They hung up and Carolyn turned from the phone to face Richard who stood in the doorway.

His smile was hesitant. "What was that all about? I gather that Dolores feels we're avoiding her."

"Yeah, something like that."

"Ridiculous." He moved into the kitchen and poured himself a cup of coffee. Then he faced Carolyn again. "She may be annoyed with us but that doesn't mean she's lusting after your inheritance, as your friend Barney intimated."

She stared, silenced by his words, wishing she hadn't shared that part of her conversation with Barney. "Barney was only asking questions, trying to make some sense of what's going on, including you getting hurt."

"I know that, Carolyn. I just don't want you to start doubting your family, unless you have concrete evidence to the contrary."

Carolyn glanced away. She'd wanted to be honest

about everything with him, because she'd avoided telling him about the tap on her phone line, as Barney had requested. But it didn't feel right to keep secrets from her husband.

Another byproduct of the reign of terror.

"I know that, Richard. Barney just wanted to know who would gain anything if something happened to me."

"For God's sake, don't tell me he suspects me because I'm your husband?" He put his cup down, suddenly frowning. "He doesn't, does he?"

She shook her head. "No, he doesn't. He knows you have nothing to gain, except the few assets I've accumulated on my own."

His frown deepened. "What do you mean?"

She drew in a deep breath. She hated talking about her inheritance, which was probably the reason she'd never discussed that part of her background with Richard. She'd give it all up to have her dad back.

She explained the will.

He digested her words. "So you told Barney all this?"

She nodded. "But that doesn't mean he thinks Dolores is orchestrating this whole scary mess."

"Maybe not. But I can see why he's looking into it." A pause. "So how much are we talking about, Carolyn?"

She glanced down. "A few hundred thousand," she said. And then she hated herself for fibbing— again. She'd tell him the truth later, after things had calmed down.

"Whew! That's a relief."

She lifted her gaze. "Why?"

He grinned. "I couldn't be a suspect. My worth is much, much higher, sweetheart. Thank God!"

He felt better but she didn't. She'd just lied to her husband about the amount, hadn't mentioned that he'd be third in line after Dolores, because she didn't want him to worry about Barney's investigation. And she didn't want him to think she suspected Dolores. And . . . .

And what? she asked herself. There was no other reason in the world that she didn't want him to know her net worth.

"I've taken out a life insurance policy on myself," Richard told her that night as they lay in bed talking.

"What?" She propped herself on an elbow so she could meet his gaze. "Why did you do that?"

"Don't be upset, Carolyn. I gave this a lot of thought and I want you to be protected." A pause. "You're the beneficiary."

"But I don't need it, Richard. I'm okay financially, as you know."

"Yeah, I know you are and that's how I want it to stay if something happened to me. Inheritance tax on my holdings could wipe out your portfolio, Carolyn." A pause. "And depending on where I am at the time, there may not be ready cash to pay the tax. Then you'd lose my assets, too.

She was silent, trying to read his face. She sensed that he wasn't being entirely truthful.

"Is there something you haven't told me?" Her voice wobbled. "Are you sick, Richard?"

"For God's sake, Carolyn. Get real. Think about

what's been happening. Someone out there is determined to do both of us bodily harm."

"You mean—kill us?"

He shook his head, as if in disbelief that she would even ask the question. "I sincerely hope not."

She sat up straighter, trying to read his expression in the shadowy room. "What's the value of the policy?"

"Five hundred thousand."

"Good God, Richard. The premium has to cost the earth!"

"It's worth my peace of mind."

"Okay, then I'll take out a policy, too."

He took hold of her, tipping her body so that he was peering into her face. "No, this is my gig, not yours. I don't need insurance money because what I'd have to pay would be nominal. The bulk of your estate would revert to Dolores."

She had no words.

"Agreed?"

She nodded.

"It's a moot point anyway," he said. "We'll be together for another fifty years, right?"

She smiled.

"And by then we'll have had three or four kids and a half dozen grandkids, right?"

She managed to nod again.

And then he made love to her to seal their bargain.

Much later, after Richard was asleep, Carolyn lay wide awake. She snuggled closer to him, appreciating his concern about her future. She wouldn't take out a new life insurance policy and offend him. But she could change the beneficiary from Dean to Richard on her current $250,000 policy at NNN, a part of her work contract he didn't know about.

Just in case she met an untimely end before he did.

She sighed, sated and content, and without further thought went to sleep.

Two days later they received the call that their house deal was closing, which meant the full downpayment was due.

"Jeez, wouldn't you know it," Richard said, combing his fingers through his thick dark hair. "My deal in Germany is delaying transfer of funds for another couple of weeks." He slumped onto a kitchen stool, looking upset and stressed.

She got up from where she sat at the kitchen table and went to him. "It's no problem, Richard. Really."

He glanced up. "I'm sorry about this, Carolyn. In my business the assets are there but cash flow fluctuates." He hesitated. "And I believed I'd synchronized everything to close together."

"It's okay." She spoke softly, hoping he wouldn't feel emasculated by her offer. "I can put the money in your account and then you can write the check."

A silence went by.

"Remember, we did this before and you paid me back," she went on. "This is no big deal, Richard. Aren't we married?—in our commitment together?"

"Yeah, you're right, Carolyn." He met her eyes. I'm being a macho pig, aren't I?"

"Macho?—maybe." She grinned. "A pig?—no."

He laughed. "Okay, you cover the deal and I'll pay you back in a week or two." A pause. "How was I so lucky to find you, sweetheart? You're everything I'm not—sensitive, caring and loving."

"C'mon, Richard. Let's not get melodramatic." She grinned back. "I just love you, that's all."

Something flickered in his eyes. "In any event, I'll pay you back. I insist. It's always been my intention that our new home is my gift to you."

"Agreed."

She dropped a kiss on his cheek, then went upstairs to get ready for work. She hummed as she showered, dressed, and applied her makeup. No matter what was going on she was the luckiest woman in the world.

The pace at NNN was busier than usual. Along with two on-air segments, she had a meeting with Roberta who was still upset about Richard's mugging, and worried about how to prevent bad publicity for NNN.

Carolyn also made time to transfer funds from her investment portfolio into Richard's bank account. Then a real estate agent called with a possible buyer for her townhouse. The sale proceeds could repay her portfolio, with interest, if Richard's funds were delayed again. She was about to leave for the day when she had a message that someone was waiting for her at the security station by the front entrance.

Grabbing her things, Carolyn headed downstairs, anxious to be on her way home. She hesitated as she stepped into the reception area and saw Barney waiting for her. He was dressed like a detective today: slacks and sport jacket.

What was he doing here?

He faced her as she approached.

His eyes flickered over her, from her green leather heels to her short black skirt, emerald silk blouse and long flowing auburn hair. Slowly, he shook his head, a slight smile curving his lips.

"Jeez," he said. "It's hard to believe that all the psychos in the country aren't hooked on you, Carolyn. You're drop-dead gorgeous today." A pause. "This is what you wore on-camera?" He spread his hands, indicating her outfit.

It was but she didn't admit it. "What does that have to do with anything?" she asked, softening her question with a smile.

He shrugged. "Just my offhand compliment." He sobered and indicated the empty reception area. "Can we talk for a few minutes?"

"Of course." She followed him to the sofa where Richard had lain a couple of nights earlier. She appreciated his professional interest, and wondered why his expression had gone from admiring to serious.

They sat facing each other, the guard hovering in the background, waiting to escort Carolyn to her car.

"So," she began. "What prompted this visit? Did you find anything?"

"Business," he said. "Your welfare I should say."

"What?" Carolyn was suddenly apprehensive.

"Who is Tom Harrison?"

It was the last thing she expected him to say. "Tom? Why do you want to know that?"

His eyelids lowered slightly—his dangerous look—but his gaze didn't waver. "Remember, I had a tap put on your phone line?"

She leaned forward on the sofa, nodding.

"His number has come up several times, as hang ups when the receiver on your end was picked up."

"I've had no one hang up on me, Barney."

"Then it must be after Richard or the machine picks up." A pause. "Who's Tom Harrison?" Barney asked again.

"I was once engaged to him, when my dad was alive. He was a member of my father's law firm."

A hesitation.

"What can you tell me about him?"

For long seconds she was silent, then decided that she must explain everything. If Tom was connected to the frightening incidents in her life they needed to know. She gave him a synopsis of Tom's part in her life, and why they'd broken up—because there'd been a cloud on her dad's integrity, enabling Tom to buy out Dolores's share in the firm.

"Dolores always sticks up for Tom," Carolyn added. "She couldn't see why I was no longer interested in a man who had implied that my father had covered up shady financial matters."

"I see."

"Just what is it that you see, Barney?" she asked.

He shrugged. "Only that Dolores is connected in many ways to your life." He stood up. "But I'll look a little deeper." His smile seemed contrived. "And I'll let you know what I turn up."

"But what about Tom?"

He shrugged again. "He might just be a jilted

boyfriend who carries a torch for you, wants to hear your voice, even if it's on an answering machine."

"You don't believe that for a moment, Barney." She got to her feet and faced him. "What are you really fishing for, detective?"

He grinned at her display of authority. "Hey, nothing in particular." His features tightened so slightly that she wondered if her perception was off. "Let's wait and see, okay?"

She managed a nod, even if she still had her doubts. "Will you let me know if you come up with something?"

"You'll be the first to know."

And then he waved the security guard away and escorted her out to her car, watching as she drove away.

What was Barney up to? she wondered. What did he suspect?

He was on to something. She also knew he would keep his own counsel until the facts were in. She hoped that would be soon. Before either she or Richard were really hurt.

25

"This place is really beginning to shape up," Richard said. He'd come up behind Carolyn in the dining room where she was unpacking dishes for the china cabinet. "You have an artist's eye for what goes where."

She faced him, smiling. He'd given her the same compliment many times since they'd moved into their new house a week ago. While he'd set up his office in the front part of the second floor, she'd unpacked their bedroom first, and then the kitchen, the rooms they needed right away. She had one more week of the two-week vacation time she'd taken from NNN to get settled.

"Thanks. I want us to love our house, because I hope we'll live here for the rest of our lives."

His gaze wavered momentarily before he grinned. "And bring up a slew of kids?"

"Slew?" She raised her brows. "That sounds ominous."

"Not romantic?"

"That, too."

The silence was suddenly a presence between them. Richard was the first to break it, pulling her into his arms, nuzzling her neck. "I wish I believed as you do, Carolyn."

"How so?" she whispered.

"In happy ever after."

"You make it sound like a fairy tale."

"Isn't that what life really is, a fairy tale?"

Surprised by his cynicism, she took a step back, then saw his amused expression. "Stop teasing, Richard."

"You sure I'm teasing?" He couldn't control the twitch at the sides of his eyes.

She punched his arm playfully.

"Okay—okay," he said. "I promise, with one condition."

She waited.

"You stop work for the day and let me take you out for a cheeseburger."

"Richard!" She wiped a long strand of hair back under the clip that held her ponytail. "For a moment I thought you were serious about the fairy tale thing and all you are is hungry." She glanced at her watch. "It is supper time, isn't it."

"Past. So how about it? You up for a greasy dinner?"

"Can I go like I am?"

"C'mon, let's go." He grabbed her hand and pulled her away from the packing box. "Didn't I ever tell you how sexy you are in Levis and a tank top? Maybe after I get my strength up from some food we can try for that first kid." A pause. "Besides, we can celebrate my news at the burger joint."

"Your news?"

"My house in Chicago sold and the funds from the German deal have been transferred into my account."

"Oh, Richard." She threw her arms around his neck. "That's great news. I know how stressed you've been about your cash flow."

He nodded. "My house didn't sell on the first day it was listed as yours did." A pause. "But now I can transfer the money we used from your portfolio back into your account."

"There was never a rush for that, Richard." She hesitated. "I still think we should split the cost of our new house, half from my sale and half from yours."

"Not on your life," he said. "We already agreed about that. Whatever you inherited goes to our kids some day."

Carolyn lowered her eyes, and decided to change the subject . . . for now. She planted a light kiss on his lips, and then went to freshen up. She'd never been happier. Her life was almost perfect.

Except for the watcher person who was still out there. She tried not to think about that, even though she knew NNN continued to get threatening phone calls. For now she meant to enjoy her new home.

"My vacation's up tomorrow, Dean." Carolyn sighed. "Two weeks just aren't enough to get moved and settled into a new house."

Dean grinned. "I'm sure glad summer vacation for us school kids isn't over." He wrinkled his nose, momentarily blending his freckles into a solid splash of brown. 'Course I'm still spending one night a week at the Youth House. There's always more to teach when it comes to computers."

She turned away, pretending to adjust the living room drape, controlling her urge to smile. When it came to computers, or the Youth House, Dean was completely hooked, and as Barney had told her recently, "The kids think Dean's their computer guru." She'd been even more pleased when Dean began sharing Internet updates with Richard.

Facing him again, she saw that his expression was suddenly serious. "I guess I should go," he said. "My grandma hasn't been in a very good mood lately, not since my mom and dad asked for the loan to save our house and she couldn't give it to them."

"What?" Carolyn hadn't heard anything about Jessie and Tony's house being in jeopardy. "Surely your parents aren't in danger of losing their home?"

"Aunt Carolyn, Grandma made me promise not to tell you." He looked guilty. "I better not say any more. My parents and grandma will be mad at me."

"Aren't I a part of your family, too?" Carolyn spoke softly. She tried not to show that her feelings were hurt.

"You're my favorite person in the world," he said. "It's just that my grandma gets embarrassed. 'Cause she never has enough money lately." A pause. "Can you keep a secret, Aunt Carolyn?"

She nodded.

"I've wondered if my grandma made poor investments, lost a lot of money when the stock market went down so bad." He met her eyes. "My grandma would never want to admit that, but that might be why she couldn't help my parents save our house."

"Your parents didn't really lose the house, did they Dean?"

He nodded. "The bank foreclosed."

"But how could that happen? Your parents both work and—"

"My dad lost his job a few months ago and couldn't find another one." He shook his head. "I'm just the kid so I only know what I overhear. I guess they already had big bills and were way behind on them, and my mom couldn't pay everything on her salary."

Carolyn listened, stunned.

"I sure wish I was grown up and had my own computer business, Aunt Carolyn. Then I would have paid and we'd still have our house."

"And your grandmother couldn't help?"

Dean lowered his gaze to his feet. "I don't think she had any money or she would have."

Poor kid, Carolyn thought. If only she could sign over the Buckhead house to Dolores, but the stipulation in her father's will forbade it. The house became hers only if Carolyn should die before Dolores, and without heirs.

I need to be pregnant soon, she thought, even as she grieved for Dean. She'd always take care of him. School, college, whatever, she'd be there for him.

But as she followed Dean to the front door, Carolyn felt a flash of anger. Dolores had inherited a fortune, and if she'd squandered it, Carolyn couldn't feel too sorry for her. Her father had seen to it that his wife would have intelligent financial advisers.

Dean reached the front door and faced Carolyn again. "Guess I should tell you the rest since I already broke my promise." He seemed close to tears. "My parents and I have moved in with Grandma. But only until my dad gets a job and my parents find another house."

Carolyn felt like crying herself. What in hell was Dolores thinking of? She had to be financially strapped or she'd have come to Jessie's rescue, a thing she'd done so many times in the past. Where had her money gone?

She kissed Dean good-bye, then reminded him of how well liked he was at Anderson Youth House.

"I love teaching them." He managed a smile. "Most of all I love having so many friends." He stepped onto the porch and then turned back. "Another good thing about living at my grandma's house is that it's close to yours now that you've moved." His expression brightened. "And I'll get to see you lots more."

She watched him go, feeling sad. As she closed the door Carolyn realized how wise her dad had been. Dolores couldn't manage money and he'd made sure that Carolyn wouldn't be tempted to throw good money after bad.

She went upstairs in her new house that was twice as big as her townhouse, to shower and change, anticipating Richard's being home in a half hour. Richard was her rock.

"I'm having a twelfth birthday party for Dean at the lake on Sunday," Dolores told Carolyn a couple of days later on the phone, her chatty conversation omitting her personal problems. "It'll be a barbecue and we sure hope you and Richard can join us."

"Of course we'll be there," Carolyn said. "Wouldn't miss it."

"Good."

"What time?" Carolyn mimicked Dolores's up-beat tone, remembering that her stepmother had a lot of things to cope with right now.

Dolores told her and they hung up. Carolyn shrugged and went on preparing supper, her mind on possible birthday presents for Dean. She tried to forget that she'd seen the dark sedan again.

Richard steered his car up the road that was lined with underbrush and small pine trees, toward Lake Lanier. Carolyn smiled when Richard glanced at her, and didn't let on that the place her dad had left to Dolores didn't have happy memories for her. She'd almost drowned when she was nine. Instead, she pointed out landmarks, and then the turnoff to the property. At least the day would be a diversion from her other worry. The watcher.

The dirt driveway led to the lake and a tepee type house with open beams, a glass front that opened onto a huge deck, and a spacious open living area. The two bedrooms were on the second floor under a sloping roof.

Dolores met them at the door, then led them through the house to the back deck where Jessie, Tony and Dean sat on beach chairs. Excited to see them, Dean jumped up as they stepped outside.

"Happy birthday, birthday boy!" Carolyn said, hugging him. "Twelve years old—you're grow-ing up!"

"Yep." Dean's freckled face flushed with pleasure.

"Hi, Carolyn," Jessie said, and took the layered salad Carolyn had brought for their picnic. "I'll put it in the refrigerator."

"Thanks," Carolyn said. She placed the wrapped present of computer programs and games down with the other gifts on a table by the door. Tony seemed subdued as he waved a greeting from across the deck.

Richard stepped next to him, looking out over the lake. "This is a great setting, Dolores," he said, turning back to their hostess. "Prime real estate."

She nodded, her gaze fixed on the foliage beside the lake. "But we never come up here now that Arthur is gone and—and I've decided to sell the property."

Carolyn felt her smile freeze and moved out of hearing range. She couldn't bear to hear more. Although the place had bad memories for her, her dad had loved it, and he and Dolores had spent every weekend in the summer at the lake. And now, less than two years after his death, it was being sold. She wondered if Dolores was spiraling out of control, desperate for money. What had happened to her? she wondered.

"Aunt Carolyn?" Dean stepped next to her.

"Yeah?" She managed a smile.

"Would you like to go for a walk down to the dock?" He hesitated. "I saw snakes swimming down there earlier this morning."

She suppressed a shudder. Another reason she'd been afraid of the lake as a child. No one swam near the shore because of the snakes. And she'd always been afraid of swimming off the boat in the deep water way out in the lake. But she nodded to Dean. She was no longer a child, she reminded herself. Water snakes and deep water need not frighten her any longer.

Glancing at Richard, she saw that he was still talking with Dolores and Tony, so she followed Dean down the front steps toward the lake. Maybe it's time Dolores did sell, she thought, noticing that the place was rundown.

"We'll join you shortly," Dolores called after them.

They followed a path to the narrow board dock that jutted fifteen feet out over the lake, Dean chatting all the way. "I feel bad that Grandma is selling this place," he said, stepping carefully on the planking. "But she says she has no choice."

"I guess your grandma has to do what she feels is right for her." Carolyn was on dangerous ground. She didn't dare express her real feelings to a twelve-year-old boy.

He nodded, his gaze on a speed boat that looped inland toward the dock and then back out into the lake. They both braced themselves as the wake rocked the dock. "I know," he said finally.

Carolyn noticed that the others had left the deck and were on their way to join them on the dock, Richard and Tony carrying folded deck chairs. She dropped an arm around Dean. "There are other lake places, honey. Some that are much better than here." She paused. "Up north they don't have to worry about alligators and snakes."

"Hey, isn't that boat going too fast?" Jessie asked, stepping onto the dock.

Everyone glanced at the boat that was making another loop toward them. Only this time it was coming in faster and closer than before. Scared for Dean, Carolyn jumped forward to pull him away from the end of the dock where he had bent over the water to watch a pair of water snakes.

"Someone needs to report that jerk!" Tony cried.

"Dean!" Jessie hollered as the boat passed within several feet of him.

Carolyn grabbed his shirt just as the dock began to rock, yanking him away from the edge. But the motion caught her off balance. She struggled to regain her footing, but each time she tried to steady herself, the dock moved in the opposite direction.

There was nothing to hold onto. Then someone fell against her and she slipped sideways off the dock. Her startled cry was smothered by a mouthful of murky water. She felt herself being sucked into the weeds on the bottom.

She kicked and paddled frantically, trying to surface. The harder she struggled, the heavier she felt. The weight of the lake seemed to hold her down.

Fighting panic, her mind filled with images of water snakes and trailing weeds that were trapping her. She was drowning.

Her lungs were about to explode when someone grabbed her long hair. She hardly felt the pain; she needed air.

"Carolyn!" Richard's cry replaced the soundless pressure in her ears as she broke the surface.

She tried to answer and began to cough up the water she'd swallowed. A few minutes later she was able to sit up.

"I think we should call 911," Jessie said. The family huddled around Carolyn nodded agreement. She managed to shake her head, tell them she was okay.

"I just need to catch my breath," she said, shakily.

"That bastard needs to be reported," Richard said. "I think that's exactly what I'm gonna do." He stood, then hesitated. "You sure you're okay, sweetheart?"

"You're right, Richard," Dolores said. "Someone could have drowned. I'll call them. The local patrol knows me and may give more credence to my complaint."

"Yeah, go ahead," he agreed. "The damn fool is still at it, circling the lake. Maybe they can catch him in the act."

She nodded and strode away toward the phone in the house. With Richard's help, Carolyn stood and they all went back to the deck. She felt stronger, but still shaky and weak.

But the day was ruined for her. She changed into clothes borrowed from Dolores, but as soon as the barbecue was over and Dean had opened his presents, Richard suggested they go. Gratefully, Carolyn agreed.

All the way home she thought about what had happened. No one remembered bumping into her, or saw her fall. Everyone had their eyes on the boat. But one thought kept circling her mind.

No one would have intentionally pushed her. Maybe it just felt like it once the waves hit the dock and rocked it so violently.

Maybe.

26

"This is quite the house." Barney stood in the front hall, looking around at the Victorian motif. He seemed even taller than usual in his casual khaki slacks and short-sleeved blue shirt, but he was still dwarfed by the high ceiling of the entry with its huge crystal chandelier. "Minnie said it was when she invited me to your housewarming shindig.

"Thank you, Barney. I love this place."

"Yeah, it's you all right." His eyes seemed almost silvery against his skin, darkened by the Georgia summer sun that had descended on Atlanta.

She tilted her head, grinning. "It is me. Sometimes I think I was born in the wrong century."

"I don't think so. Then you wouldn't be Carolyn Langdon now, and none of your friends would have had the pleasure of you in their lives."

"Crawford." Correcting him was barely out of her mouth when she regretted the reaction to his compliment. She'd been momentarily uncertain of how to respond.

"Crawford, of course." His gaze shifted away to nearby furniture. "Did I ever tell you that my wife and I were also Victorian buffs? Our favorite outings were to estate sales and antique shops."

Carolyn's eyes were caught by his when he suddenly glanced back. It was the first time he'd alluded to his former marriage. A silence went by, locking them into—into what? Mutual understanding?—intimacy?

He was the first to break it. "So, do I get the grand tour?"

"I'd love to show you my house." She glanced through the wide doorway to the living room where Richard was talking with several of her fellow NNN on-air saleswomen, one of whom was becoming almost as popular as Carolyn. Susan was a stunning brunette, about her age, and from Boston. Roberta and Minnie seemed to be in an animated conversation away from the others. Carolyn's family members hadn't arrived yet.

"Good," he said. "And I'd love to see it."

She grinned. "Shall we start with the upstairs first?"

"Sounds good to me."

Nodding, she led him up the wide, curving staircase to the second-floor hall, showing him the master bedroom suite with dressing room and bathroom. Then they moved on to the guest room, a hall bathroom and finally the front of the house that had once been a bedroom/sitting/bathroom suite.

"This is Richard's office." She indicated the computer station that had been set up in the bay window alcove above the portico. Filing cabinets lined one wall and a sitting area with a sofa, chair and coffee table occupied the opposite side of the room.

"Very professional. He even has a TV set so he can watch you on NNN." Barney stepped into the room. "And a great view of the street at the end of the driveway."

"Yeah, it's a pleasant place to work." Something had altered in Barney's manner but Carolyn couldn't put her finger on just what. Surely not resentment of Richard's office, she thought. Barney wasn't the type of man who'd enjoy sitting at a computer for hours on end.

"Do you share this office, Carolyn?" A pause. "I mean, do you share the computer?"

"'Course not. It's Richard's business tool and off limits." She shrugged. "I respect that. All of his business is on that computer."

"Really?"

Their eyes met again.

"Uh-huh." Carolyn glanced away and walked to the windows, looking out at the twilight that was quickly fading into night. "I don't understand all of the programs anyway." She gave a laugh. "That's aside from the fact that I have very little time to be on-line."

He raised his brows. "Unlike your stepmother?"

She nodded, and wondered if Dean had been sharing family concerns with Barney. "I'm afraid Dolores is addicted to the Internet. She's on-line many hours a day."

He paused, noticing the small narrow door on the wall next to the filing cabinets. "What's that?" He pointed. "Another closet?"

"Just an area under the eaves that connects to the crawl space above the breezeway." She grinned. "These old houses have lots of useless footage under their sloping roofs. Aren't even high enough to hang clothes."

"For sure. Fire traps if people load them up with junk and combustible materials."

"Which is why we don't."

They stepped back into the open hallway above the staircase. His eyes were suddenly obscure. What's he thinking? she wondered.

"Quite the elegant house," he said, as they went down the stairs.

"I like to think it's just homey, a place to raise a family, a nest where I can feel secure."

They stopped at the bottom and he faced her. "Don't you feel secure, Carolyn?"

"What a silly question," she said, evading.

He dipped his head, waiting.

"You know I don't. Not yet."

There was a long silence.

"Do you think the Lake Lanier incident is connected in any way to your other, uh, concerns?"

His unexpected question startled her. "How did you know about that?"

"Dean. He was quite upset that you could have drowned."

"So was I." She loosened her grip that had tightened on the banister. "It wasn't a fun experience, especially since I'd almost drowned off that dock when I was nine."

"Jeez, I didn't know that."

"But you obviously know other things."

"Yeah, I know what Dean confides to me, because he's an upset little boy who doesn't know where he stands in his family."

Another silence.

"I sense that you say this because you care about Dean and—and you trust me."

A slight smile touched his lips as he slouched against the banister post. "You've got that right, Carolyn."

"Would it surprise you if I agreed about Dean?"

"It would surprise me if you didn't."

"What does that mean?"

His smile was slow, attractive, and verged on seeming—what? Surely not sexy. "Only that you're a sensitive, caring and honest woman."

"Coming from you that's a huge compliment, Barney. I appreciate it."

He gave a salute, then switched the conversation back to the lake incident. "So, tell me what happened when you went into the lake?"

She glanced away, hating to resurrect those feelings of panic.

"I know it's upsetting, Carolyn." His hand came down gently on her shoulder. "It's important." He hesitated before going on. "Dean said you'd yanked him away from the edge of the dock, then felt someone hit against you when you were off balance. Consequently, you went into the lake instead of Dean."

She nodded. "That's basically it." She hesitated. "The dock rocked so hard that everyone was trying to stay on their feet, and no one remembers bumping against me."

Another silence.

"And no one saw anyone close to you?"

"Everyone was trying to stay upright, I guess."

She glanced into the living room, noticing that Richard was now talking to Susan alone, the others having drifted on to other clusters of people. She wondered why Dolores, Dean and family hadn't arrived yet.

"You're saying that none of the four adults on that dock saw what happened to you?"

"Uh-huh."

"But you believe that someone pushed you?"

She glanced away. "It felt like it."

"Like what?"

She hesitated, considering her answer.

"Like being shoved, Barney. But I know that wasn't the case."

"How so?"

"Because no one on that dock would do that."

His response was withheld because of the knock on the front door. Carolyn shrugged, grinned and went to answer. It was Dolores and Dean, she in a pink cotton sundress and he in white shorts and T-shirt. She welcomed them.

"Are Jessie and Tony on their way?" she asked, knowing that it was an hour past the time on the invitation.

Dolores shook her head. "They couldn't make it." She offered no excuse for them, or for why she and Dean were late. Barney moved away from the railing and walked into the living room to join the others, Dean by his side.

"This is a glorious house, Carolyn," Dolores said instead. "It reminds me of mine, where you grew up."

Carolyn smiled, realizing that Dolores had changed the subject on purpose. Jessie and Tony, living with Dolores, probably couldn't face seeing Carolyn's new place, not when they'd recently lost their own home. Carolyn understood that. But she again wondered why Dolores hadn't been able to help them financially.

"Yes, that's exactly why I loved it at first sight."

"And the fact that it's only a few blocks from my house, and any future children would go to the schools you attended."

Carolyn dropped an arm around her stepmother's shoulders. "You're right, Dolores. The roots that I have left mean everything to me."

Dolores was silent as they joined the other guests in the living room, but stopped Carolyn before they were drawn into a conversation. "I want you to know something," she said.

Carolyn smiled, waiting.

"I may be getting married soon. To my friend from New Jersey."

"The man you met on the Internet, the one you told me was coming to visit?"

Dolores nodded. "Will Millgard."

"Did he?"

"He had to postpone temporarily. A business crisis."

"So you've still not met him face-to-face?"

Dolores sighed. "I know it's hard for you and Jessie to understand, but I do know Will. We're talking on the phone every day now, as well as e-mailing." She repeated her story again and Carolyn listened politely, although she was in complete agreement with Jessie.

Dolores was fooling herself. If the guy had been serious, he'd have come to visit a long time ago.

Carolyn had no words. It was *magical thinking,* the pop term for people whose minds made the leap from reality into their own fantasy. *Wait and see,* she instructed herself. *You aren't a psychologist.*

So she just wished Dolores her best, and then went to see to her other guests.

"Thanks for doing all this." Carolyn said, as she walked Minnie to the front door.

"You're so welcome." Minnie laughed, and her face relaxed so that she seemed years younger. "Everyone kept asking me if there would be a housewarming party once you'd moved. Since I knew that there was no one else who might arrange it, I decided to. You know, something casual and fun."

"We really appreciate it, Minnie."

"We?"

"Richard and I." Carolyn glanced across the living room to where Richard stood by the fireplace, still talking to a small group of her co-workers from NNN.

"Oh, of course."

There was something in Minnie's tone that had Carolyn staring into her face. It was inscrutable. Did Minnie not like Richard? Why? Carolyn wondered, then realized she'd probably jumped to a false conclusion. She was imagining dislike where none existed.

"Where's Dean?" Minnie asked, changing the subject. "Haven't seen him for a while. Did he leave with Barney?"

"He went upstairs," Dolores said, turning briefly from a conversation about computer software with an NNN salesman. "Maybe to the bathroom."

"I have to go, busy Sunday tomorrow at the Youth House, and I wanted to say good-bye to him." Minnie hesitated. "Should I look for him or will you tell him I'll see him soon?" she asked Carolyn.

"C'mon, let's go upstairs and see where he is." Carolyn motioned toward the steps. "He must be playing with Mayo and Mustard. They're up there because they hate crowds."

Minnie grinned. "I can see a kid preferring two cats over the adult mayhem of a cocktail party."

They went upstairs and found Dean sitting in front of Richard's computer. Carolyn froze in the doorway, horrified.

"Dean!" she cried. "What are you doing in Richard's office?"

"Whoa," Minnie said. "The kid didn't rob a bank, Carolyn."

Carolyn took a deep breath. In a voice only Minnie could hear, she explained that no one used Richard's computer but him, that it was off limits because all of his business files were on the hard drive.

Minnie grinned. "Relax, Carolyn. All of my business is on my computer, too, including my fledgling jewelry company records. It's not that easily lost. Even a crashed hard drive can be restored. But I'm sure Richard would have backup disks."

Carolyn nodded, but was still apprehensive. She knew Richard wouldn't take kindly to someone on his computer, even if it was Dean who was knowledgeable about what he should and shouldn't do.

Dean had swiveled on the chair, facing them. "I was bored downstairs, thought Uncle Richard wouldn't mind if I checked out some games on his computer." Dean grinned. "I couldn't have disturbed anything even if I'd wanted to, 'cause I don't know the password to get on-line. Without it I'm locked out."

"I know, Dean," Carolyn said with controlled calm. She and Minnie stepped into the office, as Dean switched off the terminal. Swinging the chair sideways, his arm hit the keyboard, skewing it. A small scrap of paper fluttered to the floor.

"I'll get it," Minnie said. She bent to retrieve it, then frowned thoughtfully as she read what had been written on the small piece of paper.

Carolyn nodded, intent on getting Dean out of there before Richard came upstairs and found them. He'd always been emphatic about no one touching anything in his office.

Once in the hall, Carolyn breathed a sigh of relief.

"You aren't scared of Richard's wrath, are you?" Minnie asked. She'd followed a few seconds later, the scrap still in her hand.

"'Course not. Just respectful of his space, as he is of mine."

Minnie grinned. "Just checking."

"What was on that paper?" Carolyn asked. "I thought you were throwing it away."

"There's no wastebasket. So I'm tossing it in the kitchen garbage—because Dean might get in trouble if I leave it on the keyboard instead. It's just waste paper."

"Nothing important?"

She hesitated.

"I don't think so, Carolyn. Just a doodling of on-line tags."

She shrugged as they went downstairs with Dean who was oblivious to having done anything wrong. He felt his uncle trusted his computer abilities. But Carolyn knew she'd have to tell Richard later, after the party. He would understand. Especially since Dean hadn't disturbed anything in his office, or been able to get past the password prompt on the screen.

"Hey, that was a great shindig Minnie put on for us," Richard said after the last person was gone. "Jeez, she's some sexy woman. I bet men line up to fuck her."

"Richard! That's a disgusting comment to make about my best friend." Carolyn had never before heard him refer to a woman in such a crude manner. Then she realized he'd had too much wine.

"And," he went on, "some of your co-workers are interested in investing in the high-tech company in Germany which is about to float their stock on the European market." He wove around the furniture as he made his way to the stairs. "It's their opportunity to double their money." He stopped abruptly and she bumped into him. "Guess what?" he asked.

"What?"

"I also pledged a sizable contribution to the Anderson Youth House." He bobbed his head furiously. "I told Minnie that I'd take it from my own profits once the transaction is complete." He stumbled and she helped him regain his balance. "That's how much I trust this deal."

"That's good, Richard. I know the Youth House will appreciate anything you do."

She was pacifying him, seeing that he was really drunk. Once she had him in bed, Carolyn went back downstairs to straighten up. It was only when she was finally in bed, Richard sleeping beside her, that she remembered Dean being on his computer.

Not important after all, she decided. Dean was too computer savvy to have hurt anything. And as Dean had said, he didn't have the password to access Richard's files anyway.

Best to forget the whole thing.

27

The phone rang as Carolyn was rushing to complete the final cleanup the next morning. Richard was upstairs packing for a trip to Frankfurt where he was closing negotiations on a huge America/Germany condominium exchange deal. Each two owners, matched for compatibility, agreed to swap places between countries every six months, thus owning half a condo in Germany and half a condo in the States. She grabbed the receiver on the third ring.

"Hello?" she said.

"Carolyn, this is Minnie."

"Hi, Minnie." Carolyn was glad to sit down with the phone and her coffee before getting ready to take Richard to the airport. "Did you enjoy the party last night?"

There was a silence.

"Minnie? Are you there?"

"I'm here." Another pause. "Carolyn, I need to talk to you and I don't know how to begin."

"That sounds serious." Carolyn gave a laugh but

she sensed that her friend was stressed about something.

"I hope it's not."

"What's wrong, Minnie?"

"I don't know exactly, but I'm concerned about something I stumbled onto, something so bizarre that it probably couldn't be true." She drew in a breath. "But I'm compelled to run it past you—just in case."

"In case of what?"

"Tomorrow's Monday." Minnie didn't answer her question, but asked her own instead. "Will you be stopping at the Youth House after work? We could talk then."

"I hadn't planned on it, Minnie. My day at NNN doesn't begin until late morning and won't be over until seven. I'll probably come straight home after that." She switched the phone to her other ear in order to stack clean plates in the cupboard. "You could come over here. I should be home by eight."

"I have bookkeeping to do at the Youth House but if I skip supper I might finish up by then," Minnie said. A pause and Carolyn envisioned her friend's thinking expression. "Our conversation needs to be private so your house won't work."

"Richard is leaving for Germany in a few hours, so there wouldn't be anyone here but us. I'd love to have you for supper—probably something light."

"Okay, I'll be there around eight."

Carolyn was puzzled. What was so important that Minnie would go out of her way just to talk? "Can't you discuss this on the phone? I'll be here alone this evening after Richard is gone."

"I need to talk about this in person and I can't come over today." Minnie gave a short laugh. "Would you believe I have jewelry orders to fill for Lilly Lawton, after I finish up here at the Youth House."

"That's wonderful. I had no idea that you and Lilly had gotten together on some jewelry orders."

"It just happened last week, and she needs them right away. She likes my creations because they represent Indian legends." Minnie sighed. "This is a tremendous opportunity for me, so I can't blow it." She hesitated. "But I'm tempted. What I have to tell you may be more important."

"Nothing is more important than your filling those orders. I was prophetic when I said I might be selling your jewelry along with Lilly's on NNN," Carolyn said, laughing.

"Thanks to you if that should happen." Minnie drew in a sharp breath. "So, I'll see you tomorrow night at your place and—"

"What?"

"Please don't mention anything I've said to Dolores, or Richard, or anyone."

"But you haven't really said anything, Minnie. And why shouldn't I mention your concerns to Richard?"

"Just humor me for now, okay? And I won't mention anything about what I found at your place to Barney, at least until after we've talked."

"Talk to Barney about what? What could you have possibly found here that is so mysterious?"

"I'll explain when I see you. I don't want to talk about it on the phone."

"For God's sake, do you think someone might be listening?"

"I don't know. This may be nothing or—just be careful, Carolyn."

"You're almost scaring me."

"Hey, don't want to do that, kiddo." Her tone was more upbeat, but it sounded contrived. "We'll get this figured out." A pause. "See you tomorrow night."

"I'll look forward to hearing more about this mystery."

"Bye, then."

Minnie disconnected and Carolyn finished up in the kitchen. But she was disturbed. Minnie wasn't an alarmist. And she was alarmed.

"Carolyn, don't look so glum," Richard said, as she drove up to the airport terminal. "I'll be home in a few days."

She flashed him a smile. "I just miss you when you're gone."

Richard got out of the Volvo, pulling his small overnight bag and briefcase from the backseat. Then he bent back inside the car to kiss her. "Love you."

"Love you, too." She hesitated. "Sure you don't want me to wait with you at the gate?"

"No point. I know you have better things to do. Besides, I hate long good-byes, especially when I'll only be away for a few days."

She nodded, trying not to feel down. Confess, she told herself. Minnie's call depressed you.

His gaze was suddenly direct. "You sure everything's okay? You seem bothered by something."

She managed a smile. "Everything's fine. I just miss you already." She almost blurted out Minnie's earlier call but resisted the impulse. She didn't want to worry him. Maybe she was only imagining distress behind Minnie's strained tone of voice.

"Okay then. Guess I'd better go."

He stepped back and closed the passenger door. Then he came around to the driver's side, bent and kissed her again through the open window.

"Take care of yourself while I'm gone," he whispered against her mouth. "I'll call you."

And then he was gone, striding into the terminal. He didn't look back and that made Carolyn smile. It was his way; he hated good-byes because, as he always said, "I'm coming back."

She drove toward home but she couldn't shake the growing feeling that something bad loomed on her horizon.

Dumb, she told herself. She was jittery because of Minnie's call and Richard's leaving. It had nothing to do with anyone watching her.

The balance of the day was surprisingly pleasant. By bedtime Carolyn had admitted to herself that she missed her single life at times, when she could just hang out with Mayo and Mustard. She loved Richard, enjoyed being with him, but since he worked from home she no longer had down time. He wasn't demanding; he was just always there. She'd come to look forward to his trips as reprieves, even as she anticipated his homecomings.

Carolyn crawled into bed expecting to fall asleep immediately, and was wide awake, her thoughts on

Minnie's call, a concern she'd tried to avoid all day. Tossing and turning, she heard every creak and groan of the house timbers settling, the constricting of wall and floor boards as the night air cooled them, and faint scratchy noises in the crawl space above her. Even Mayo and Mustard were restless, changing positions each time there was a strange sound. Catching only small patches of sleep all night long, she was relieved when the first rays of light shown on the horizon.

She threw back the covers and got up, even though she didn't have to leave for a few hours. "I also miss my townhouse," she told her cats who'd gotten to their feet with her.

Downstairs, she started coffee, fed her cats and then the phone rang. She grabbed the receiver, noting that it was only seven.

"Hello."

"Hey, it's your husband from Frankfurt." A pause. "Are you out of bed yet?"

"Oh, Richard. So good to hear your voice."

"And yours."

"So, what's up?"

"Can't a man call his wife because he misses her? Does something have to be up?"

She smiled. "I miss you, too." A pause. "The coffee is dripping. Wish you were here to have a cup."

"I will be in a couple more days."

"I know. I'm counting."

There was a pause.

"Can I ask you to do me a favor?"

"Of course."

"It's afternoon here, but tomorrow I'll need some

information before I head into a business meeting. My Chicago banker will be sending a fax before the end of the day to my fax there. I need you to fax it on to me."

"Of course I'll do that. But I won't be home from work until around eight tonight. Is that too late?"

"It's fine," he said. "I'll have it in time for the meeting in the morning." A hesitation. "I'd have the bank fax it directly, but because I'm using financial figures from my Chicago bank as leverage for my deal here, I don't want them to read it as a conflict of interest."

She sat down on a kitchen bar stool. "Is it, Richard?"

"Of course not. It's how high-stake deals work." He chuckled. "Banks don't want to know all the details so long as they're legal. They just want to make the money."

"Okay, Richard. Give me the fax number and I'll forward the information when I get home tonight."

"Great." He gave her the number and she wrote it down. "I miss you, so much," he said. "I just wish you were here with me."

She sighed. "I wish that too, Richard. One of these days . . . ."

"Yeah. And in the not too distant future."

"I'll work on it."

They hung up on that positive note. And then Carolyn went back to her coffee and newspaper.

Carolyn had just walked into the kitchen from the garage a few minutes before eight that evening when the phone rang. She dropped her handbag and briefcase and ran to catch it before voice mail picked up.

"It's me," Minnie said when she answered.

"Hey, I know, you're gonna be late." Carolyn managed a nervous laugh. "But I'm looking forward to our conversation. It was all I could think about today."

A sigh came over the line. "I'm going to be worse than late, Carolyn." A pause. "I can't make it, too much to do here at the Youth House. I thought I'd be done by now but I still have lots more to do."

"Could you finish the job tomorrow?"

"Unfortunately, they need my financial numbers right away to submit for state aid. Tomorrow's the deadline so I have to complete the job tonight." She sighed again. "Sometimes I wonder why I always overextend myself for charitable causes."

"Because you're you, that's why." Carolyn pushed her hair back so she could hear better. "It's okay to cancel, Minnie. I have something to do for Richard anyway. We could make it tomorrow night instead."

"I don't know if we should wait that long. Are you free for lunch tomorrow?"

"I have a three-hour program from 11:00 A.M. to 2:00 P.M. Lunch won't work."

"Okay, let's plan on tomorrow night. What time?"

"I can be home by six."

"Will Richard be back?"

"No, I'm still alone for a couple more days."

"Okay, tomorrow night at six, your place."

"Minnie, can't you tell me what this is all about?"

"I'm not so sure anymore, Carolyn. Maybe I'm

reaching, maybe I have an overactive imagination, maybe my concerns are far-fetched." A pause. "But I need to show you something, let you decide."

"You have something to show me? What?"

"Something I found at your housewarming party, something I almost threw away. Let it be, Carolyn, until you can decide, as I said." She hesitated. "I hope that you'll forgive me if it's all nonsense and I'm out of line."

"Hey, whatever my dear friend. You'll never be out of line with me."

A sharp creaking sound pierced the quiet house. Carolyn whirled around to face the back staircase. Was someone on the steps, just out of her view? Minnie's words faded in her ear as she edged back around the counter, closer to the breezeway door that led to the garage. Her eyes were glued on the shadowy passageway to the second floor.

There was a flash of white and yellow. Then Mayo and Mustard ran into the room and headed straight for her.

The air went out of her chest. She grabbed the counter, supporting herself.

"I know, Carolyn," Minnie was saying, and Carolyn realized that only a few seconds had passed. "You know, that's what your father always said when I contradicted his opinion on something."

"My father loved you Minnie." Carolyn was amazed that her voice sounded normal. Her breathing sure wasn't.

There was a hesitation.

"How do you know that, Carolyn?"

"He told me."

A long silence went by, one Carolyn used to re-store her normal heart rate.

"You know that I loved him, don't you?"

"I've always known, Minnie." Carolyn took a deep breath and then proceeded into a territory she'd previously avoided. "Shortly before he died he confided that he'd made a big mistake, that he should have married you, not Dolores."

"Oh my God." Minnie's anguish came over the wires, and Carolyn had second thoughts.

"I shouldn't have—"

"No, you should have, Carolyn. Thank you."

"But I've upset you."

"No, dear heart, you've set me free. You've told me what I've needed to know for so long." She sucked in a quick breath. "Your father was the love of my life. Once he gave me a friendship ring, you know the lit-tle silver wire ring that ends in love knots, the one I've never taken off my finger since he gave it to me?"

"I didn't know it was from my dad."

"I know, honey, but we're telling secrets here." A long pause. "There will never be anyone for me but him."

"Oh Minnie, I'm so sorry—"

"Don't be. Your father and I will be together again, in another life."

Carolyn didn't question her friend's analogy. If more explanations were necessary they could wait until tomorrow night. All of a sudden she felt good about what she'd told Minnie. It had been time.

The next afternoon she went off camera, exhausted from a successful three-hour shopping spree of plus-size clothing. "The best segment yet," Roberta had said in her ear phone as the soundstage went dark.

She nodded. Roberta could see her on a monitor.

Carolyn stood up, pulled out her audio device, relieved that her day was over, and walked off the set. Barney was waiting for her outside the door in the hall. She stopped short.

"Barney?"

He nodded, his expression closed.

"What's wrong? Why are you here?"

He shook his head, and Carolyn felt her heart race. He suddenly looked upset. "Something's happened." His voice faltered. "Something bad."

"What?"

He took hold of her, pulling her into his arms. "I'm so sorry, Carolyn," he whispered against her hair. "Minnie is dead."

She pulled away, staring into his eyes. "What?" she said again, her voice rising.

"It's Minnie, Carolyn." His voice broke. "Minnie is dead."

Tears filled her eyes even as she denied his words. "Not Minnie. I'm meeting her at my house in a little while."

"Yes, Minnie."

She started to cry, and then she couldn't stop. He pulled her into the empty visitors' lounge where they had privacy. He held her so close she could feel him shuddering. Barney was crying.

If Barney was crying, then it must be true. Minnie was dead.

28

Barney offered to take her home but she refused, saying she needed her car, that Richard was away. He followed behind her, watched as she drove into the garage, then waited until she could let him in through the front door.

He immediately took her into his arms, holding her while she cried, the thing she'd been doing all the way home. Minnie was dead. It just couldn't be true. Instead of Minnie meeting her at home, Barney was trying to console her because Minnie was dead.

"How? How can this have happened?" she asked.

He shook his head, baffled. "I don't know but I intend to find out." He hesitated. "It's so out of nowhere, so unexpected." Another pause. "But then we both know all about that, don't we? Death doesn't ask permission from anyone."

She gulped air, trying to stem the flow of more tears. The shock of hearing about Minnie had brought back all the anguish and loss when her baby girl, and then her father, died. She could only imagine Barney's feelings. She often wondered how he could have continued as a homicide detective after the deaths of his wife and children. Maybe one day they would know each other well enough to talk about it.

Almost as though he guessed her thoughts, he stepped back, wiped his hand over his forehead and managed a faint smile. "You think you're up to making some coffee, Carolyn? I could use a cup."

"What about a whiskey or Scotch instead." She didn't need a stimulant; she needed something to dull her feelings temporarily, until she was ready to cope with her best friend's death.

"Okay. I think you're right." He followed her into the kitchen where she pulled the bottles from a cupboard.

"Which?" she asked.

"Whiskey."

She poured a double shot into two glasses, then added a little cold water and ice. She handed one to him and kept one. Wordlessly, they both took a drink.

They sat across from each other at the counter. Finally, as the whiskey began to calm her, Carolyn asked, "What happened, Barney? How did Minnie die?"

He swirled the ice in his glass. "Like I said, we don't know for sure yet."

"But you have an idea?"

"I can tell you what a preliminary examination revealed," he said, avoiding a direct answer.

"Please."

"It might have been a stroke, a blood clot hitting her brain." He swallowed more of his drink and she added a splash more whiskey. "You knew that she had chronic high blood pressure?"

Carolyn shook her head. "I didn't know that. But I know Minnie was a vegetarian, never ate salt, sugar or fat if she could help it."

He nodded. "She had her own herb garden, and I thought she'd had her blood pressure under control for years now." He hesitated. "The medical examiner will make the final determination of cause of death."

She gulped more whiskey. "But what do you think, Barney?"

He sipped from his own glass, then faced her. "Like I said, we'll see."

"For God's sake, Barney. This was our friend. Why did she die so suddenly? And why were you called?—you're a homicide detective."

He looked away and took another drink. "Procedure."

"Procedure, shit!" she cried. "There are questions here. Something is wrong."

A long silence went by.

"Okay," he said finally. "Something didn't look right, especially since it was Minnie who made the call."

"What?" She plunked her glass down so hard that it splashed on the counter.

"The 911 call came in but no one spoke on the other end. We presume that she was in fact dying and couldn't speak."

"Oh my God! My poor Minnie. She died alone."

"We'll know the cause of death once the medical examiner's report is back."

"When?" Carolyn's voice wobbled.

"Within twenty-four hours."

"I need to go over there, see if there's something else wrong that an outsider wouldn't notice. I—"

"No," he said, gently. "Her little East Point house has been cordoned off until it can be processed."

"Processed?"

He nodded, his expression grim. "It will be searched, dusted for prints, and vacuumed for evidence." A muscle in his jaw twitched. "If perpetrators only knew what modern science had in store for them. Advanced DNA testing, AFIS for identifying fingerprints, and other computerized options that leave them in jeopardy of being caught."

"AFIS?"

"Yeah. Automated Fingerprint Identification System."

"Perpetrators?"

"Yeah." He didn't meet her eyes. "In the event that someone caused her death."

"But you said Minnie's death was from natural causes."

A brief silence.

"No, I didn't," he said. His tone was low and intense. "I only told you a possible cause of death, one expressed by the medics."

She turned to face him, her eyes brimming. "You think someone killed her, don't you Barney." She swallowed hard. "I think so, too."

His pale eyes seemed to fog over, as though he didn't want to give away his own feelings. But he couldn't hide them from her. He agreed with her.

She gulped more whiskey but it didn't stop the tears. She plunked her head down onto her arms on the counter. In seconds, she was sobbing as Barney held her, trying to sooth her with calming words.

Nothing helped but after a while she managed to control herself, holding her tears in check. Barney saw her upstairs, turned his back as she undressed and slipped into a nightgown, then saw her into bed.

For a while he sat beside her, until she finally dropped into a restless sleep, her two cats dozing at her feet, as though protecting her. Vaguely, she was aware when Barney let himself out of the house, after a whispered assurance that everything was locked and secure.

Sometime later Carolyn got up, still groggy from the whiskey, her thoughts on Minnie. With tears wet on her cheeks, she wandered the house, fearfully rechecking the doors. A glance out of an upstairs window revealed Barney's car parked at the end of the driveway. She sighed in relief. He was making sure her house stayed safe, at least for the rest of the night.

Carolyn called Barney the next morning from work to thank him, and to ask if he had more information about Minnie's death.

"Not yet," he said, sounding tired. "I should have the report on my desk by noon." A pause. "How are you doing?"

"Okay, I guess." She managed a wry laugh. "I've managed to sell cedar chests already today, you know, the type they used to call hope chests back in the 1950s."

"Life goes on."

"Yeah, it always does." She switched the phone to her other ear. "How about you Barney, aren't you exhausted after staying up all night?"

"Naw, us cops are used to it. A hot shower and clean clothes work wonders."

She thanked him again and they hung up a short time later, after he'd promised to let her know when he heard anything. The day dragged after that, noon came and went. By the time she left for the day, Barney still hadn't called. She drove her route home automatically, trying to control the tears that were smudging her mascara. As she reached her street and pulled into the driveway, a glance at the rearview mirror reflected Barney's car behind the Volvo. She wondered how far he'd been trailing her.

She motioned for him to meet her at the front door, then went on into the garage she'd opened, quickly closing it behind her. Within two minutes she'd hurried through the house and opened the door for him.

"You have news, Barney?"

He nodded.

Carolyn ushered him back into the kitchen, wishing she'd had time to change out of the clingy long green dress she'd worn on television to sell the cedar hope chests. Somehow the Victorian gown and hair style didn't fit the hopelessness of her mood right now.

"Do I offer you coffee or whiskey?" she asked, meaningfully.

"Whiskey."

She got out the bottle, poured whiskey, water and ice into two glasses, the same procedure as last night. They both knew his information would not be pleasant.

"You had the medical examiner's report then?"

He nodded. "It's not pretty, Carolyn." He hesitated, his pale eyes silvered by the lights above the counter. "You really want to hear it?"

"I have to, Barney," she whispered. "You know that."

He kept his gaze level as he recited the medical examiner's report from memory, as though to put off the harsh verdict. "There was petechiae in the striated muscles of Minnie's neck, tiny pinpoint hemorrhages."

Carolyn gulped air. "Which means?"

"Death by suffocation."

"Oh my God! She *was* murdered!"

Barney took a deep breath, then a slug of whiskey. "There's more. A vaginal swab tested positive to the acid phoshatase test, evidence of semen." A pause. "Minnie was raped."

Carolyn's head tipped forward. "Poor Minnie. How horrible for her."

"For any woman," Barney said. "Fifteen or ninety."

She nodded, unable to talk.

"Just so you know, Carolyn, we'll catch this pervert. Her pubic hair was combed for pubic hairs of the rapist. Whoever murdered her tried to make it look like a natural death, down to redressing the body. This is unusual procedure for the typical rapist."

She met his eyes. "Will you really catch him, Barney?"

"You're goddamned right I will." His voice gained volume. "If I have to track him into hell!"

She poured them another drink. "We might become drunks at this rate, Barney."

They sat in silence until Barney finally broke it. "I need you to tell me everything you know, Carolyn. Anything that might shed light on what's happened here."

"I know." Hesitantly at first, she told him about her strange call from Minnie on Sunday morning after the housewarming party, their scheduled meeting the night before, and why Minnie canceled.

"So you didn't know what she was going to tell you?"

"No. But she asked me not to discuss it with Dolores, or Richard, or anyone."

"That's it?"

"Well, when she canceled, she said she'd found something here, that she'd leave it up to me to determine its significance, that she wanted me to forgive her if she was wrong."

"What does that mean?"

"She wouldn't say over the phone, said it might not be safe, that our conversation had to be private."

"Curious."

"What?"

"I'm thinking that she may have stumbled onto something that became her death sentence."

"Here? At my housewarming party?"

"It may be, Carolyn." A hesitation. "I want you to be prepared for that."

She took another drink of her whiskey, wishing it could erase the whole ugly reality of Minnie dying.

"So, what can I do?"

"Let's start by you telling me again about all of the threatening incidents over the past few months, who was involved, where you were and what you were doing."

She understood. She might have forgotten something. "It began last winter, before I met Richard," she began, and then proceeded to tell him the incidents she could remember in the sequence they'd happened.

"So, you still have no idea who this person is?" he asked, referring to the caller at NNN.

She shook her head. "As you know, we don't really know if the watcher person is a man or a woman." She mentioned the voice synthesizer.

Barney didn't reply, but she had the impression that he was forming his own opinion.

The phone rang, startling them both.

She grabbed the receiver, her eyes on Barney. "Hello."

"Carolyn, it's Roberta. I'm sorry to bother you at home but NNN has had another call from the wacko."

Carolyn got to her feet. "What did he say this time?"

"Jeez, Carolyn, I hate to tell you."

"You have to, Roberta. It's important."

"He said, 'Carolyn is afraid because a loved one has been murdered.' "

"Oh my God!" She sank back onto her stool, her eyes brimming, her heart fluttering with alarming speed.

Barney grabbed the receiver. "This is Barney McGill, Roberta. What's going on here?"

She told him.

He gave her a few instructions, then hung up and went around the counter to Carolyn. "It's going to be okay," he told her. "Please believe me, you're safe."

"No, I'm not, Barney. Whoever this creep is, I'm the intended victim. And somehow, Minnie got in the way."

He didn't dispute her. Instead he asked her when Richard would return.

"In two days."

"Too long. You need to call him, tell him to get back here now."

"I can't, Barney. He's in Germany." She hesitated. "And I can't worry him when he's so far away. All I can do is wait until he gets back to tell him what's happened." She clenched her hands together. "Besides, even if he knew he probably couldn't get here much sooner."

Barney was suddenly inscrutable, his eyes narrowed, his wolf eyes, she thought.

"Okay, then he won't mind if I spend the night in his place. You can't stay here alone."

Her eyes widened.

"On the sofa."

"I could go over to Dolores's house."

"No!" His voice suddenly boomed. He tempered it with a forced smile. "You can't do that under the circumstances, until I get a fix on what's going on here."

She stared, trying not to be even more upset, but knowing he was right. And then she made up a bed for him on the living room sofa.

And went upstairs to be with Mayo and Mustard.

29

Carolyn had planned to wait until after she'd driven Richard home from the airport to tell him about Minnie. She'd managed to maintain her control when Richard had called from Frankfurt to say he'd received the fax, thankful that the connection was bad and their conversation brief.

But as he strode out of the terminal into the fading evening, glancing over the cars and buses crowding the loading zone until he spotted her, she felt her resolve weaken. He waved, an instant smile lighting his face. He half ran to her Volvo, yanked open the door, tossed his bags in the backseat and then slid onto the passenger seat.

"I'm so glad to be home." He leaned across the console and kissed her. "Jeez, I've missed you."

She kissed him back. And then, unexpectedly, burst into tears, suddenly crying so hard she couldn't talk.

"For God's sake! What's wrong?"

He shook her gently, and when that didn't help,

folded her into his arms and just held her. When she was finally able to control the flow of tears, he let her go, wiped her face with his handkerchief, and then stepped out of the car and went around to the driver's side. He nudged her sideways to the seat he'd vacated.

"I'm driving," he said, and proceeded to get them away from the airport, but swung into an empty bank parking lot rather than get onto the freeway. He switched off the engine and then turned to face her.

"Okay, what's going on?"

Although his words were direct, his tone was soft, considerate.

"Minnie was murdered."

He stared, stunned. Instantly, she was sorry for blurting out such terrible news without preparing him. But she was so emotionally fragile, so unable to speak calmly, that it was the only way she could get it said. Minnie had been the mother she never had. That thought brought a new flow of tears, quiet tears that brimmed in her eyes and ran down her face.

"When?"

"Two days ago, at her house in East Point." Haltingly, she told him what had happened, that Minnie had been mysterious about something at their housewarming party, that she'd warned Carolyn not to mention anything to Dolores.

"Why?"

"I don't know."

"Do you think she surprised a burglar?"

She shook her head. "Nothing appeared to be

stolen." Carolyn took a deep breath. "She was raped. Barney didn't tell me all the details."

"Barney is involved in the investigation?" His expression was puzzled. "Is this his jurisdiction?"

She shook her head. "But all of the Atlanta counties trade information—and Minnie was his personal friend. They'd worked together for years at the Youth House." She hesitated. "I think Barney believes all the strange incidents that have happened to me, including the NNN caller, are somehow related to Minnie's murder, that someone from the Youth House or NNN might be the killer."

"He's said that?"

"Not in so many words."

"Then how?"

She shrugged. "Just an impression, nothing specific."

There was a long silence as he held her against him.

"So what do you think, Carolyn? That Dolores is a suspect, as Minnie sort of implied?"

"Of course not." She gulped a ragged breath. "Minnie didn't say that, only that I shouldn't mention it to her."

He stroked her tears away. "You've had a hard time since I've been gone. I wish you'd told me. I would have caught the next flight home."

"I didn't want you to worry when you were so far away." She paused. "There were times when I was tempted but I didn't have your phone number, only the fax."

"Shit. I can't believe that I forgot such an important detail." His jaw tightened. "I guarantee it'll never happen again." He feathered her face with kisses. "I need to make it up to you."

He removed his hands from her and started the engine. "And I'll do that once we get home."

As they headed for the freeway Carolyn felt a little better. Richard was back.

Carolyn had just opened the door to leave Roberta's office when she surprised Barney who was about to knock. "Hey, how you doing?" he asked.

"Better."

"Good. We'll talk later." He stepped around her and went into the room, his ID flipped open in his hand, his attention shifting to Roberta. "I have some questions," he said. "You have a minute?"

"Yeah, and you can put your ID away, Barney," Roberta said, dryly. "Remember, I know you? You're a homicide detective with the Atlanta Police Department, a friend of Carolyn's and you knew Minnie for years." She hesitated, standing up behind her desk. "So, what's with all this formality?"

"Procedure in a homicide investigation," he said. His gaze returned to Carolyn, obviously waiting for her to go.

"I'm staying," she said, moving back into the room. "Your business here has everything to do with me."

"Sorry, Carolyn. I'd like to talk to Roberta alone."

"I understand your concern, Barney, but I'm not leaving." Carolyn sat back down on the chair she'd just vacated.

"Hey, it's okay if she stays," Roberta said. "She knows everything I know about the problem."

Barney hesitated, as though trying to make up his mind about something. "Okay then, let's start from the beginning," he said. "I need to know everything you know about this guy."

Roberta leaned forward, her lips pursed in thought. "First of all, none of us here are certain that the caller is a male or a female."

"How so? Explain." He directed his questions to Roberta, so Carolyn remained silent.

"Just that. Some of the people taking the call have reported a woman, some a man. I think the person has one of those voices or—"

"Or, what?"

"Is using a voice synthesizer. We've even sold them, on one of our programs that sells high-tech gadgets."

He glanced at Carolyn and she nodded agreement.

"And NNN is now tracing these calls?" His eyes had returned to Roberta.

"Yeah. But so far all of them, including the one after Minnie died, originated at public pay phones from different parts of the city." Roberta sighed, showing her frustration. "No way to identify the caller. And the police haven't had any luck checking for fingerprints, nor have they found witnesses to interview."

He'd taken out a notepad and was taking notes. Now he glanced up. "I understand a computer hack accessed NNN records a while back. What's happened on that?"

She drew in a sharp breath. "How did—"

He waved her to silence. "Our computer system

tracks, and cross-checks, everything pertaining to a case and the people involved." He shook his head. "Don't worry. I know confidentiality is an issue here and the Department, which includes me, won't violate that trust."

"Thanks."

"So?" he prompted.

She held out her hands. "So, what?"

"Do you think the hacker really hijacked NNN's customer list? And if so, doesn't that mean he would have every customer's address and phone number and a record of how much they spend?" He hesitated. "And the personal information of all the women who have become Carolyn's television friends, who talk about their lives on TV?"

"It would, if the hacker really downloaded that information. We don't know that for sure and so far, thank goodness, we have no evidence that this person wasn't just a kid proving his computer genius."

"In which case NNN feels they're in the clear?"

"We're hoping."

He glanced down at his pad. "And this hacker, hopefully a kid, would also have had access to your employee files?"

"Good God, Barney," Roberta retorted. "Do you ever leave any question unasked?"

"Not if I can help it."

Carolyn glanced down, suppressing a smile. A silence went by as Roberta considered her answer and he waited.

"Yes, they would have had access to everything in our personnel files," she said, finally. "Mine, Carolyn's, anyone who works here."

"Jeez."

"I try not to think about it, Barney." Roberta paused. "But this is all included in our original report."

He stood up. "Guess that's it for now, Roberta."

She stood, too. "So, what are your conclusions?"

He put his notepad in his pocket. "I don't have any yet. I'll let you know."

"Are you being inscrutable, Barney?" Roberta asked, as Carolyn got to her feet, still watchful and silent.

He turned from the door, his hand on the knob. "No, I'm not Roberta. Only cautious."

"And that leaves a lot unsaid."

"There's a lot we don't know, Roberta."

"I have a feeling that we'd better find out quick, detective."

He saluted her, including Carolyn in his gesture. "I couldn't agree more."

And then he strode out through the doorway and disappeared down the hall.

"Whew, Barney seemed in a hurry," Carolyn said. "I've never seen him so—so preoccupied."

Roberta looked thoughtful. "Can't say that I blame him. He knows that time is of the essence."

Her words gave Carolyn an ache in the pit of her stomach as she went down to work. Someone was out there laughing at all of them.

"That isn't necessary, Roberta," Carolyn said into the phone receiver that night. "I don't need the limo again."

Roberta's sigh came over the line.

"NNN wants you to be safe, Carolyn. As I've said in the past, you're our star, we can't afford something happening to you."

"Roberta, are you telling me that you're afraid I'll be murdered—like Minnie?"

"Oh God, Carolyn, no. Her indecision was in her tone. "We're only trying to protect you." She hesitated. "Carolyn, can I level with you, just between us?"

"Of course."

"You won't quote me?"

"No."

"Because I'm going out on a limb here." Another pause. "But, goddamn it, you're my friend before this fuckin' job."

"I promise, Roberta."

"We, that is NNN, feel you're in danger. Statistics point to a stalker, but the network can't go on record here without explaining that our main computer banks were broken into, that our personnel and customers alike could be in similar jeopardy. That could put us out of business."

"I know all that, Roberta, and I appreciate the concern, but how long can I take a limo? Who knows when this wacko might go away." Carolyn gulped a breath and said what would have been unthinkable a few months ago. "Maybe, for the sake of everyone concerned, I should quit."

"Fuck—no!" Roberta's retort vibrated in Carolyn's ear. "The powers-that-be want to avoid that at all costs." A pause. "I won't fool you, Carolyn. It all has to do with ratings, and your popularity with customers."

Carolyn felt weary. Even Richard, once past consoling her about Minnie, couldn't understand her ongoing grief. She'd stopped trying to explain. But she'd become resentful. She wasn't a light switch. She couldn't turn her feelings off by a flick of a finger.

"Thanks for being candid, Roberta. I appreciate your friendship. But I'll be okay. Richard has insisted that he's driving me to and from work for now. He thinks I'm safer with him than with a limo driver."

A silence.

"Okay, he may be right. We'll go with that for now."

"And maybe it'll all go away," Carolyn said, trying to cheer her friend.

"Maybe. I hope so."

Carolyn hung up. But she knew Roberta and NNN were right in the first place. Someone out there meant to kill her.

The next day when she had a private minute, Carolyn called Barney and asked for an update. "For the sake of my sanity I need to be kept posted," she told him.

"I don't have much, except that the report is back from the FBI's NCIC computers."

"And?"

"Nothing really."

"Which means what?"

"Everyone close to you is clean, including your stepmother and husband, at least as far as recorded offenses are concerned. As you already know, Tony had a few minor arrests years ago, drug use, disturbing the peace, and so on."

"My God, Barney! How could you think anyone in my family was a killer?"

His sigh sounded in her ear. "Just doing my job, Carolyn."

She let her annoyance go. "What else is being done?"

"We're following every lead, long shots."

"What leads?"

"Anything that has even a remote significance to the problem."

"That's ambiguous, Barney. Give me an example."

"Okay. I'm waiting for a report on some of your recent customers, women who order on a regular basis."

"But they live all over the country."

"Yeah, I know."

"I don't get it."

"It's just a routine check on their status, making sure that—"

"Barney!" she interrupted, suddenly understanding. "You don't think some of my customers have been murdered, do you?"

"Of course not." His tone was stilted, as though he knew he'd gone too far. "We look at everything in a homicide investigation, and hope a pattern emerges."

"What possible connection would my customers have to Minnie?"

"Don't know. Like I said, just checking long shots."

But Carolyn could guess Barney's train of thought.

Minnie knew something, something that was incrim-
inating to someone. The caller? So she'd been murdered to shut her up.

What? And who? It was all she could think about
after they'd hung up. She wondered what else Barney suspected and wasn't telling her.

30

Minnie was cremated and a memorial service was held at Anderson Youth House. The kids served coffee and cookies afterward, looking subdued by the loss of the woman who'd been a mentor to many of them. Carolyn was surprised to see Lilly Lawton among the few dozen guests. She stood with Roberta and both women looked shaken by the service that blended Christianity with Native American beliefs.

"I'm so sorry," Lilly said, as she came over to Carolyn and Richard. "I was just beginning to know Minnie, and her art, and I can't express how shocked I am over her death."

"I know, Lilly." Carolyn said. She blinked quickly, attempting to stem another flow of tears. "Minnie was important to my life for so many years. I can't imagine being without her."

"And she was so talented," Lilly said. "I had plans for her jewelry." She shook her head sadly. "As it is, her completed work will sell well. I'm just sorry that there won't be more."

Carolyn glanced away, trying to regain her composure. Her poor, dear Minnie. If only she were still here to know what Lilly thought. Fragments of memory played on her mental screen, of outings and shared conversations. If only some perverted creep hadn't killed her. If only— She reined in her thoughts. She couldn't think of those things now, not if she wanted to get through the next half hour without breaking down.

Her eyes wandered the room, as she tried to focus on other people. Dolores was talking to Barney by the coffee urn, Dean was deep in conversation with several of his male computer pals and Richard was engaged with Lilly's description of her jewelry line. Carolyn turned away, looking out the window at a live oak that shaded the parking area. Minnie was dead. She was really dead.

"Don't look so sad, my friend."

She glanced, meeting the pale stare of eyes that could seem as cold as a predator's, or as warm as a sultry summer sky—like now.

"I am sad, Barney. At this moment, I don't know if I'll ever be happy again."

"I know." His voice was low, intimate, his words not carrying beyond them. "But I promise you, Carolyn. I intend to catch this guy. Someone is going to pay for what they've done, what they've been doing to you."

"So you do think Minnie's murderer is connected to this watcher person?"

He didn't hesitate. "Yeah, I do."

She turned her gaze out a window to the parking lot. "Then her death is my fault."

Instantly, his hands came down on her shoulders, bringing her eyes back to his. "No way!"

"And because she was raped, we know whoever is after me must be a man."

"Not necessarily."

"But Barney, a woman can't rape a woman as a man would, leaving semen."

"I know." He managed a brief grin. "But there could be more than one person involved here."

"What do you mean?"

He shook his head. "I don't know yet. We're still investigating."

She opened her mouth to ask more questions but he put a finger across her lips.

"No more questions. You'll be the first to know if I find out anything. Okay?"

She nodded. "Promise?"

His smile was slow to start, but then it transformed his face. "I promise."

And then Richard turned back to her and the unexpectedly intimate moment with Barney was gone. For the best, Carolyn thought. She was a married woman.

Barney sat forward on the sofa in Dolores's living room, his gaze fastened on Dean who was explaining about the housewarming party, when Carolyn and Minnie found him on Richard's computer. Dolores had gone into the front hall to answer the phone, and Carolyn sat quietly, watching. Barney had asked her to be there, as a silent support so Dean wouldn't feel intimidated by the questions.

"I'd only turned it on when Aunt Carolyn and

Minnie came in," Dean said. "I didn't think Richard would mind because he knows I wouldn't hurt his computer."

"But it was his business computer, Dean," Barney said. "You should have asked his permission first."

"I was wrong, I know that now." Dean glanced at Carolyn, then down at the Oriental carpet. "I only wanted to check out computer games. I was the only kid at the party and it was pretty boring."

"Did you find the games?"

"I couldn't get on-line. Richard has a password and I didn't know what it was."

"A password? Like to get on AOL?"

"No, to get into anything on the computer, before you'd even try to get onto one of the servers like AOL." His forehead creased. "Without it, people like me who try to log on are locked out of everything on the hard drive."

"So nothing unusual happened?"

Dean shook his head again. "Nothing." He hesitated. "As we were leaving Minnie picked up a piece of paper that was on the floor. I think it'd been under the keyboard but it looked like something intended for the wastepaper basket."

"What did she do with it?"

Dean shrugged. "I don't know."

"You don't know what?" Dolores came back into the room and sat down on a high-backed chair near the fireplace. Before Dean could respond, she went on, directing a question to Barney. "Care for something to drink, coffee, tea, maybe a soft drink?"

"No thanks." He smiled at her. "But I would like to ask you some questions."

She clasped her hands over her chest. "I wondered when you'd get around to me, since you've already talked to both Jessie and Tony."

"I'd like a Coke, Grandma," Dean said, standing. "May I go get one?"

She nodded. "'Course."

"You want one, Aunt Carolyn?"

"No, sweetie, think I'll pass." Carolyn remained seated, sensing that Barney wanted her to stay. She wondered about his real motivation for her being present. Did he think that something she heard might trigger a forgotten memory—one that could be relevant to his investigation? She'd realized that Barney had his reasons for everything.

"So, what were your perceptions of the house-warming?" Barney asked, opening the conversation once Dean was out of the room.

"Only that it was a lovely party," Dolores replied.

"You saw nothing unusual? Didn't feel that Minnie was upset about anything?"

"On the contrary. I felt that Minnie was upbeat, happy about Carolyn's new house. She was the one who organized the party."

He nodded. "You know that Minnie and Carolyn caught Dean on Richard's computer. Any thoughts on that?"

She shook her head, waiting.

"I guess you would have if he'd accessed your computer without permission, right?" Barney's tone was friendly, and he sat back, waiting for her response.

"Dean has often used my computer when he's stayed overnight." A pause. "Of course, as you know, he and his parents are staying with me temporarily. His own computer, the one Carolyn gave him, is set up in his bedroom."

"He's a real whiz when it comes to technology." Barney smiled again. "And like most kids his age, he probably talks too much."

"What do you mean?"

"Well." Barney spread his hands, as if to discredit his own words.

"Go ahead, Barney. I won't get mad at Dean. Believe me. I adore my grandson."

"I know you do, Dolores. That's obvious." He hesitated. "Dean only said you have a computer boyfriend, a Will Millgard who lives in New Jersey."

She sat up straighter. "That's true."

"And Carolyn told me that he's coming to meet you, that your relationship is serious."

"Yes, Carolyn is right on both comments."

"So, what does Will do?"

"He's into investments."

"Hmm, that's an interesting profession." Barney paused. "What kind of investments?"

"All kinds." Dolores's reply was instant, as though she was annoyed and trying not to show it.

"I see." He scooted forward on the sofa. "Just high-rolling types of investments, as so many are these days?"

"That describes it, big investments, big profits."

Barney stood up. "Guess that's about it, Dolores."

Carolyn stood, too, and wondered if Barney had realized that Dolores wasn't about to elaborate further. She could tell that something was bothering her.

"About time," Tony said from the doorway to the hall. "My mom-in-law doesn't like the third degree." His wink behind Dolores's back diluted the thrust of his words.

Dolores allowed Tony to see Barney and Carolyn out, after they'd said good-bye to Dean.

"She has a temporary cash flow problem because of a personal loan to a friend, a possible husband," Tony told them at the front door. "Dolores is desperate to find another husband."

Carolyn was momentarily taken aback. Dolores had lent money to Will Millgard, a man she hadn't met in person? How much? Surely Dolores hadn't been that stupid. Maybe she'd only told Tony that so he'd be motivated to get a job, make his own money and not expect hers.

"How do you feel about that?" Barney asked him.

He spread his hands. "My wife thinks she's vulnerable to a con artist, like this Millgard guy, that she could be duped into losing everything. I just think she's a little dumb, but not so dumb that she'd lose her assets."

"You think this Millgard is conning her?"

"Nah, he's probably harmless." He shot a grin at Carolyn, as if Dolores's love life was a storm in a teacup. "Don't worry about it, her computer dating phase will pass when she realizes how silly it is."

Carolyn lowered her eyes and restrained herself from answering. She'd have a private talk with Dolores later.

Barney thanked her for driving over, then got in his own car and headed back toward the city. As Carolyn drove home she wondered what Barney was thinking. One thing she did know for sure: Barney would be checking out another long shot in Paterson, New Jersey, to see what he could find out about this William Millgard.

"We're adding a few safety precautions," Richard told her several days after the memorial service.

Carolyn glanced up from where she was loading the dishwasher. "We agreed to the alarm system already."

"Yeah, but we need more than that." He paused. "I have an electrician coming out tomorrow to put in garden lights along the driveway, and floods on the corners of the house. The illumination will discourage anyone from getting too close."

She stared at him. "Isn't that a little drastic?"

"I don't think so. On the contrary, it'll make our property safer and more pleasing to the eye at the same time."

"And, there's more?"

He nodded. "All the outside fixtures will have light sensors, coming on automatically at dusk." He drew in a sharp breath. "And all exterior doors are being fitted with dead bolts."

She closed the dishwasher and straightened up, facing him, a little taken aback by such drastic measures. "We'll be living in a fortress."

"But a safe fortress."

"I have a problem with this."

He raised his brows, waiting for her to elaborate.

"Someone out there is terrorizing us. We react with these safety precautions." She drew in a sharp breath. "I resent a wacko controlling my life."

"Precisely the point, Carolyn. Your life. I want you to keep it." A pause. "Don't allow yourself to go into denial. You're not just dealing with a wacko, you're matching wits with a cold-blooded murderer."

His words silenced her.

They also brought home to her how limited her life had become: Richard driving her to and from work, having to be diligent about driving right into the garage, pushing the automatic door closure behind her before getting out of the car, and then using the inside entrance through the breezeway to the house. All spontaneity had disappeared from her life.

And I damn well don't like it. Something had to change. She had a sudden impulse to buy a gun and stalk the stalker.

Silly, she told herself. But if her life was being taken away anyway . . . she brought herself up short. As another famous Atlanta native had once written, "I'll think about that tomorrow."

She went to get ready for work.

She was driving herself to NNN by the end of the week. All of Richard's safety precautions were in place, and as she'd told him, "I can't be a prisoner to living. I have to be in control of my own life."

He'd hesitated, then agreed, but with stipulations. She had to call him when she got to work and when she left work. Also the NNN guard had to meet her car on arrival and escort her out to the parking lot when she left. Roberta agreed to all of Richard's safety requests.

It was the second week after Minnie's memorial service before Carolyn could face everyone at the Youth House. Now that the police crime lab had gone over Minnie's office and found nothing, she was free to box everything for sending to a brother up in Tennessee. The job promised to be painful.

She was able to leave NNN an hour earlier than expected; the guard walked her to her car and saw her leave the lot. Carolyn didn't call Richard, intending to call him when she left Anderson Youth House. This was one job that she had to do alone and it wouldn't take long. Her call to Richard would be at the expected time.

Upon arriving in Minnie's office Carolyn turned on the computer, to scan the index for projects she and Minnie had worked on together. She intended to copy them onto a floppy disk, so that the next person to use the computer could start fresh. Her scrolling stopped at her own name, and the entry date was two days before Minnie died.

Clicking the mouse, she entered the file which was titled *Big.Wind*. Her heart was suddenly beating twice as fast as usual. This was not something she and Minnie had worked on together. Was it the something she'd wanted to tell Carolyn?

But the file itself was a disappointment. It was only a list of unfamiliar computer tags: DPeaches, SylviaCozy, GretaSilklove, RMack, and a dozen or so more.

She stared at the screen, wondering what it meant. She had no clue. Minnie had died before she could explain.

Carolyn gulped air, disappointed, but tried not to

cry again. She'd done enough of that in the days since Minnie's death.

But she copied the brief information onto a disk and then dropped it into her purse. Then she pulled out her cell phone, called Barney and left a message for him to look at Minnie's computer again at the Youth House, and why.

She went out to her car, too heartsick to linger.

Minnie's information meant something, but she didn't know what. Maybe Barney could figure it out.

31

"I'm gonna skip this trip," Richard said.

"But I thought you said it was important." Carolyn reached across the supper table and took his hand. "Everything's been okay here, nothing out of the ordinary since Minnie's death." She didn't add that nothing would ever really be normal again, that her sense of safety had been altered forever. "With all of our safety precautions, you being gone for one night to New York doesn't seem like that big of a deal," she added.

"I don't know."

"I'll be fine."

"You sure?"

"Uh-huh." She was determined that they go on with their lives as usual. What was the alternative? Hiding out, fearful of anything that moved?

"All right then, but I'll drive myself to the airport and pay for parking since I'll only be gone for two days and a night."

She nodded. It was settled. He'd leave in the morning.

She wasn't scared to be alone, she told herself. But she was . . . a little.

July had been so hot that Carolyn relished the afternoon electrical storm and sudden downpour, a torrential dumping that produced minor flooding. As she drove home through the late afternoon, the day was still overcast and humid. She wished it would rain again, and from the look of the sky, maybe it would.

It was only as she drove into the garage that vague apprehension hit her. Richard was gone tonight. She would be alone in a big house. She'd just turned off the engine and the automatic door had closed behind her when her cell phone rang. She grabbed it from the passenger seat.

"It's Barney. You and Richard gonna be home?"

"I just got here and Richard is in New York."

There was a pause. "One of his trips?"

"Yeah, just overnight. He'll be home late tomorrow."

"Mind if I stop by?"

"No, I'd love you to. We could have a glass of wine, that is if you're off duty."

"I'm five minutes away. See you then."

She smiled. Typical Barney. He'd respond to the wine invitation when he got there.

But she felt strangely uplifted. She hadn't relished an evening alone. With Barney in the house she'd know it was secure. If she had any apprehension at all, he'd check out the whole place for her.

The house was strangely silent, no cats to greet her as she stepped into the kitchen. She glanced into all the rooms on the lower floor, calling for them. Still no Mayo and Mustard. As she was about to go upstairs, they came ambling down the steps, their long hairs dusting the treads, to rub against her ankles, their way of asking for food.

"Bad cats. You should answer your mom, not worry her." She smiled as she dumped food into their dishes, and refreshed their water.

The front bell rang and she ran to the entry hall, knowing it was Barney. She flung open the door and he stood there, in khaki shorts and a butter yellow T-shirt, the deep tan on his muscular arms and legs furred with dark hair that gleamed in the sunlight.

"Hey, you *were* only five minutes away."

"Wasn't lying, was I." He grinned and stepped into the hall. "I'm off duty, as you can see." A pause. "By the way, don't you check to see who's on the porch before you open the door?"

"Always." She lifted her long hair from against her neck, feeling the humid heat. "But this time I knew it was you."

"Because I'd said so? What if it hadn't been?"

She hesitated. "Okay, you're right. I won't do it again."

"Good."

He followed her back through the house to the kitchen where she opened a bottle of Chardonnay and poured a glass for each of them.

"You read my mind," he said. "I don't remember saying aloud that I'd love a glass of wine."

"Lately, it seems that's all we do when you come over." She raised her glass. "To good friends."

"And to remaining so for many years to come."

They both sipped to the toast, then sat down at the kitchen table facing each other. "So what did you want to tell Richard and me?" Carolyn asked.

His eyelids lowered slightly, hooding his eyes. "I mainly wanted to give you an update on something I've learned, something that has to stay confidential."

"I remember," she said. "You promised to do that at the memorial service."

He inclined his head, his gaze suddenly so piercing she had to look away. "That's right."

There was a silence and Carolyn filled it with another sip of wine.

"So, will you keep what I'm about to say to yourself?"

She nodded.

"I feel you need to know this, Carolyn, so maybe you can come up with some new thoughts on this watcher person."

"I'll try." She leaned forward. "I'm really curious now, Barney."

"What do you know about Dolores's finances?"

His words surprised her. "Nothing, really. I know what she inherited, that she's a very wealthy woman."

"Not anymore."

She put down her glass, even more startled. "What do you mean?"

"Only that Dolores has completely depleted her investment accounts, and the proceeds from the lake sale are gone."

"What? Good God! That can't be true."

"I'm afraid it is." A pause. "If it weren't for the monthly payment from your dad's law partnership, she'd be broke."

"What happened?" She stared at him. "Oh, my God. You don't think Tony was right, that she lent money to that guy on the Internet?"

"Will Millgard. I'm looking into that right now," he said. "Haven't heard anything back yet. I was hoping you could shed some light on that question. Figured you'd be having a talk with her after what Tony said."

"I planned on it but hadn't set anything up yet." She hesitated. "You know, I felt that Tony's revelation was a joke. That's how he acted about it. Surely Dolores wouldn't have given her whole fortune away."

"So you can't add anything to what we know, like how long this has been going on?"

"I can't, although months ago I'd noticed that the grounds around the house were looking pretty rundown, and managed to make arrangements with Dolores to have them maintained."

"Because you're the legal owner?"

She nodded. "I'm shocked. And I'm glad my father had no idea how badly Dolores would handle her assets."

"He might have had an inkling, Carolyn. He left the house to you."

She nodded. "Dolores can live there as long as she wants to." She sighed. "She'll always have a roof over her head."

He was silent, slowly sipping his wine. She had the impression that he had more to say but she didn't

push him. She was still horrified about Dolores's finances. Where had all her money gone? Barney's information clarified the reason Dolores had allowed
Jessie's house to be repossessed.

"I did a background check on Tom Harrison,"
Barney said, finally.

She was instantly alert to what he'd say next.

"I don't know if you realized that Tom had no
choice but to expose what had happened at the firm.
He now believes it was Dolores who authorized the
bogus checks, and once your dad found out, he tried
to cover it up until he could figure out how to handle the situation."

"Oh my God! Dad never shared any of this
with me."

"Probably too embarrassed. Tom thinks your father intended to repay the firm, but his death precluded it."

Carolyn glanced down, suddenly feeling so sad
about her dad. He'd chosen the wrong woman but
he would have tried to make the best of things.

"I guess it figures, Barney. Dolores was always a
big spender, always in trouble with her credit card
limits."

"I'm sorry kiddo."

She felt like crying. Her poor dad. Carolyn hated
to believe Dolores was dishonest. But it didn't look
good.

He sipped his wine, then ran his tongue over his
lips. His next question was direct. "Did Dolores
know that you were your dad's main heir, not her?"

"I honestly don't know." She'd never thought
much about the will, expecting him to be around for

many more years. "Even though more assets came to me, like the house, Dolores was left a wealthy woman, Barney."

"I know."

"So what are you getting at?" She gave a nervous laugh. "That something underhanded was going on?"

He glanced away, but not before she glimpsed the answer in his eyes.

"For God's sake, Barney. What?"

He shrugged, avoiding a direct answer.

"Surely you don't think Dolores has anything to do with the creep out there? Or that there's something suspicious about my father's death?"

"I didn't say that." His tone was guarded. "But as we know, the person with the most to gain by your demise is Dolores, just as she once believed about your dad before he died."

Carolyn swallowed hard, then got up to find the wine bottle and refilled their glasses. Barney was silent as she sat back down.

"I'm about to pull something together for supper. Have you eaten?"

"Nope." His brows shot up and down, in an attempt to mimic Groucho Marx, one of the characters from his classic movie collection. His gesture broke the somber mood between them. "What's on the menu?"

"I gather the Marx brothers must be in your library of old flicks."

"How'd you know about that?"

"Who else? Minnie."

She stood again. "I'll check out the fridge, see what

I can offer you." Carolyn went back to the original question rather than pursue another sad subject.

"I'm not picky."

"Good, then we'll have broiled steaks, a green salad and some broccoli."

"Sounds like a feast to me." He got up and came around the table. "Can I help?"

She put him to work on the salad. They chatted while they worked, topics ranging from the Youth House, to politics, to the stock market, even child rearing. Carolyn was surprised. She rarely talked about her views on raising children; in the past it had brought back sad memories, and she suspected the same was probably true for Barney. As they ate she realized how easy he was to talk to, even more so than Richard who was almost too coddling at times, a trait that suppressed her spontaneity.

Hey there girl, she told herself. Just because you like a little more give-and-take in a man doesn't mean you should be critical of your husband. What's come over you? When did you begin to think of Barney in a personal way?

The next two hours passed quickly and it was starting to get dark when Barney finally got up to leave.

"You put a great meal together, ma'am." He hesitated at the front door.

"And if you ever retire from the force you could get a job as a chef's helper."

They both laughed and he stepped out onto the porch, then faced her again. "Guess I don't need to tell you to lock up, and call me if there's any problem?"

"I've got the ritual down pat. Even the part about keeping my cell phone next to the bed."

His pale eyes seemed to flame against the gathering darkness behind him. "Good. And I have the local patrol keeping an eye on the house." He hesitated. "Go on inside now, while I'm still here."

She did what he asked. When she peeked from behind the blind a few minutes later she saw his car parked at the end of the driveway. She was relieved. He intended to stake out the place again, not have her unprotected for even one night. She shivered. Someone out there was waiting for just such a chance.

Fifteen minutes later Carolyn had straightened the kitchen, set the alarm, and was already upstairs getting ready for bed when the phone rang on her nightstand. She grabbed it, thinking it would be Richard.

"One more question." Barney was calling from his cell phone.

"Shoot." She smiled down at Mayo and Mustard who were settling in for the night on the cushioned window seat.

"Do you know the Internet name Dolores uses on the singles bulletin board?"

"I don't but Dean probably does." Sobering, she sat down on her bed. "Why do you need to know?"

"I just called headquarters and got the message that there is no Will Millgard from Paterson, New Jersey, or in any of the Internet chat rooms."

"How in the hell could you know who is or isn't in a chat room, Barney?"

There was a pause and she knew he was smiling. "Court orders do wonders for us lowly homicide detectives. Not to mention our sympathetic counter-parts in other cities."

She didn't completely understand but she took his word for it. She had come to see why Barney solved so many cases; he was tenacious.

"I'll talk to Dean tomorrow," he said. "Nighty-night again."

The dial tone sounded and she replaced the receiver. It rang again.

"Another question?" she asked. A glance at the clock told her it wasn't ten yet.

"Hi, Carolyn, it's Tom."

For long seconds Carolyn was struck speechless. Tom Harrison was the last person on earth she ex-pected to hear from at that moment.

"Hello, Tom." Her tone was cool, distant. "I'm surprised."

"Is it too late to call? I didn't think you folks would be in bed this early, and as you'll recall from your father's long hours of work, I just got home from the office."

"No, it's fine, Tom." She glanced at the cats. "We're not in bed yet." She wasn't about to tell him that Richard was gone. A random thought hit her. *Maybe he already knew that.*

Get real, she told herself. Don't project anything beyond what you know to be fact. Or you'll go nuts.

"Good, because something's been on my mind and I just got up my courage to talk to you about it." He sounded hesitant, awkward. "Do you think you could manage having lunch with me soon?"

She shifted the receiver into her other hand, turn-ing toward a slight noise near the doorway. Mayo had jumped from the window seat to prance across the carpet. "Can't you tell me what this is all about, Tom?"

"A Detective McGill talked to me several days ago and he explained that what I have to say wouldn't shock you."

"About my father?"

"Mostly about how I didn't handle the Dolores situation properly, that I should have trusted you with some suspicions I had. But you'd just lost your father and I didn't want to add more sorrows at that time."

"Yeah, you should have trusted me. There's a philosophy somewhere that says it's easier to deal with the truth than all the unknown possibilities."

"I know that now." A pause. "So how about lunch for old time's sake, so we can get everything out on the table and at least be friends again."

She hesitated, considering. He seemed sincere, his actions back then may have been well intended. Maybe she had misjudged him. He was right. It was time for honesty.

"Okay, Tom. My only free time would be tomorrow and it would have to be near NNN, so I could get back in time for my next program."

"That's good for me."

They agreed on where and when and she hung up for the second time. Then she climbed into bed, turned off the lamp and fell asleep within minutes.

Carolyn sat up suddenly, almost by reflex. What had she heard? The cats again? They weren't on the bed.

Her eyes scanned the dark room, identifying the

furniture, the doors and windows. Everything was normal. Stiffening with resolve, she grabbed her cell phone, slid out of bed and moved silently out to the hallway. Mustard and Mayo were both there, also restless.

She stood like a statue, straining her ears. There were only the usual sounds: the ice maker down in the kitchen, a discordant noise that went unnoticed during the day, wind that had come up while she slept, gently rattling a loose drain and fanning pine branches against the siding, and the faint rumble of distant thunder.

It was thunder, she decided. As though to add credence to her assumption, lightning flashed, like dancing strobe lights across the walls.

Go back to bed, Carolyn told herself, and started toward her bedroom. Then, pausing, she faced the hall again, uncertain. How could she relax when something had awakened her out of a dead sleep? She had no choice. She had to make sure the house was secure.

But why wouldn't it be? she argued mentally. The windows and doors on the lower floor were alarmed; no one could enter the house without setting off a high-pitched siren.

But the interior motion sensors weren't on because of the cats. No, she had to make sure. She'd never go back to sleep until she did. A glance into Richard's office, the bathrooms and the guest room told her nothing was disturbed.

At the top of the stairs, she hesitated. The lower floor was quiet, disturbed only by the ticking grandfather clock in the entry below her. The exterior lights shown dimly from behind the drawn shades and the red security system light glowed by the door, alarmed as she'd left it.

Still she felt uneasy. Something wasn't right. But what?

This was silly. She was allowing her imagination to work overtime. Not that it wasn't understandable, but she wasn't going to let this situation turn her into a lunatic. She slipped silently down the steps and through the house, rechecking the door locks, careful not to touch anything that might set off the alarm. An occasional flash of lightning lit her way, followed by a rumble of thunder. A storm was closing in on Buckhead—as surely as the presence she felt closing in on her.

Upstairs again she hesitated. A sucking fear in her stomach held her in its grip. She couldn't shake the feeling that someone was watching.

Paranoid, she thought again. It was that stinkin' thinkin' syndrome, those crazy thoughts that momentarily alter reality. She *knew* no other person was in the house.

And as she'd done as a child when she was frightened by imaginary bogeymen and closet monsters, Carolyn got back in bed and pulled the covers up to her chin.

And like that other time in her townhouse when she'd sensed another presence, Carolyn didn't sleep for the rest of the night. Instead she watched the storm as it intensified, and waited.

For what she didn't know.

32

Carolyn was a few minutes early to the small deli/restaurant but Tom was already there. Dressed in a gray Brooks Brothers suit, white shirt and tie, he looked attractive and professional, but out of place in a vegetarian café where customers wore shorts and sandals.

"Lovely, as always," Tom said.

They were directed to a small wrought iron table with two matching chairs in the back corner. Tom pulled hers out, and as she sat down, he took the one opposite. For a moment there was an awkward silence.

"Thanks for coming," he said. "I didn't think you would."

She raised her eyebrows and managed a smile. "I'm surprised that I did, too." She glanced down at her hands on the table. "I was very disillusioned when you closed me out. I'd always believed that two people who cared enough about each other to consider marriage didn't do that."

358 *Donna Anders*

"I'm so sorry, Carolyn," he said. "I believed I was protecting you. I was wrong."

A young woman in shorts and T-shirt stopped at their table and handed them a one-page menu. The interruption allowed Carolyn to avoid answering. They both ordered iced tea, a garden salad and roll. The waitress nodded and left.

"So, are you open to hearing what happened?" he asked.

She nodded. "Barney McGill told me about his conversation with you. I realize now that you believed you were making the best of a bad situation."

The waitress brought their iced tea, smiled and left.

"Yeah, but I misjudged you, Carolyn. I didn't give you the credit you deserved, that you had a right to know the truth."

She met his eyes. "Thank you, Tom. I appreciate your admitting that." A pause. "And I'm sorry if I treated you badly. I was terribly upset at the time. I came to the conclusion that you might have been trying to position yourself by discrediting my father."

"Christ almighty! That was never true." The words whistled out of his mouth. "I had no idea—" He broke off, shaking his head in disbelief.

The whisper of other conversations swirled in the room, dishes rattled, and traffic went past on the street beyond the front windows. But the silence that dropped between them was profound.

She was the first to break it, explaining why she'd come to that conclusion, then going on to relate her recent conversation with Barney. She paused. "I know my father was an honorable man and it makes sense that he would have protected Dolores." Carolyn lowered her eyes. "But it's hard for me to believe she could have been so dishonest."

"It was for me as well." He covered her hand with his. "I can't begin to express my regret, Carolyn. I knew the financial discrepancies that pointed to your father would be covered once Dolores was bought out of the firm."

"In other words, the differences were balanced by her taking less cash even though the paperwork showed the original price?"

"Something like that." He removed his hand. "I thought you would never have to know anything about it. Dolores was all the family you had left."

The waitress brought their salads and they began to eat. Carolyn was glad that she'd come, had finally learned the truth. But she also realized that she no longer had feelings for Tom and wondered if she had ever loved him. It was a moot point now; she was married to Richard.

They finished their meal and as Carolyn grabbed her handbag in readiness to end their meeting, Tom again covered her hand briefly, stopping her departure.

"I know it's too late for us, Carolyn," he began. "But I want you to know that I'd always hoped we'd get back together after the situation cooled." His gaze was direct, and honest. "I was shocked when you married another man because—" He ran his tongue over his lips, as though considering whether he should continue. "Because I admit it, I'm still in love with you."

An awkward silence went by.

He stood up first, obviously aware that his admission wasn't what she'd wanted to hear. His hand on her elbow as they walked toward the cashier precluded an answer. Carolyn was relieved. She had nothing to say.

Once outside in the midday sunshine she thanked him for lunch, expressed her gratitude that he'd explained and then said good-bye. Upon reaching her car down the street she glanced back. Tom stood where she'd left him, still watching her. The realization was unsettling and a random thought surfaced in her mind.

Could Tom be out to get even with her?—because she'd broken so completely with him?

Was he stalking her?

Quickly, she slipped behind the wheel and closed the door, removing herself from his vision. Then she called the security desk at NNN to alert the guard that she was on her way back, the safety procedure instituted by Roberta.

But she wasn't able to shake the fear that was dragging at her again. She had learned that people, even those who were close to her like Dolores, could deceive her.

A disillusioning realization.

"As I've said many times, I can't be a prisoner of a lunatic," she told Richard the next morning. "I have to live my life as normally as possible." She turned from the breezeway door. "Besides, I'll finish early today and be home by three." She didn't add that she'd sensed his stress when he had to drop his own work to taxi her back and forth to her job.

"I don't know, Carolyn. I think you should let me drive you."

"You have your work. Like I said, we can't run scared or we'll destroy our lives."

He sighed. "Okay, then. Call me when you get there."

She nodded and went out to the garage. Checking in and out was enough. She couldn't expect NNN to continue limo service. It was time to quit the job if it became that bad.

And she was considering that option.

Carolyn found herself glancing in the rearview mirror every few seconds as she drove to NNN and was relieved to finally arrive. Again, the guard watched her drive into the lot and escorted her into the building.

Her first on-camera segment was selling a line of mix-and-match clothing. Once the stage went dark she was summoned to Roberta's office.

"We've had another series of threatening calls to the studio while you were on the air," Roberta said.

"Oh, shit!" Carolyn sank down on the nearest chair. "What did the creep say this time?"

Roberta's worried frown deepened. "The same old crap. Threats about you."

"What're we going to do?" Carolyn wiped her hair back, tucking loose strands behind her ears. "You know, Roberta, maybe I have to quit my job."

"For God's sake, no!" Roberta jumped up and came around her desk. "If you go who's to say that this lunatic won't fixate on the person who takes your place. We've got to get to the bottom of this now. I've called the police and an officer is on the way."

Carolyn was silent, digesting her words.

"There's something more." Roberta indicated a letter on her desk. "Don't touch it. It may have fingerprints."

Standing, Carolyn bent over the desk to read the words that were printed in bold, black ink over a dried wash of red stain. "Carolyn is a selfish, greedy bitch and is going to die."

Her legs wobbled and she grabbed the desk for support, then plopped back onto the chair. "It's blood, isn't it?"

"I think so but the police will find out for sure."

Carolyn couldn't take her eyes off the drug store stationery, the same type that Dolores used, down to the roses on the top of the page. It couldn't be, she told herself. It was just a coincidence.

There was a tap on the door a moment before Barney strode into the room, nodding to them, surprising both Carolyn and Roberta.

"Are you here because of my call?" Roberta asked.

"Yeah, that's right."

"But you're a homicide detective," she replied.

"I'm investigating a homicide, Roberta." Barney's voice was deceptively calm.

"Oh, I'm so sorry." Roberta glanced away from his eyes that glinted like shards of steel. "I think I blocked thoughts of Minnie."

"Thank you for coming, Barney." Carolyn managed a smile.

He dropped a hand on her shoulder, gently squeezing it.

"Roberta can tell you what happened," Carolyn added.

He inclined his head, waiting for Roberta to begin. She related the whole incident again as Barney took notes. As she finished, he looked up. "Your station's caller ID system has again recorded that the calls were made from several downtown pay telephones."

"In other words, untraceable like the others were."

"Yeah, by the time anyone could get to the location the caller was gone." He stepped closer to the desk to examine the threatening note. At the same time he pulled a plastic bag from his pocket and carefully slipped the paper into it.

Carolyn watched, her thoughts spinning. Should she mention that the rose stationery was the type that Dolores used? Oh, God. What if it was just a terrible coincidence. But what if it wasn't? What if Dolores resented her so much that she was the person behind the reign of terror?

"Barney?" Carolyn's voice was hesitant.

He turned, meeting her eyes.

"There's something else."

He raised his brows, waiting for her to continue.

She swallowed, licked her lips and blurted out her observation. "The stationery is the same kind that Dolores has used for years. She buys it at the drug store."

There was an abrupt silence. They both knew what Dolores had to gain if she died: everything.

"Your stepmother?" Roberta drew in a sharp breath.

"Uh-huh." Carolyn felt terrible. "I'm sure there's no connection." She glanced at Barney, hoping for affirmation of her words. His expression was inscrutable.

"That's . . . interesting," he said, finally.

"I'm sure it has no significance," Carolyn said. "That stationery is sold everywhere. Anyone could have it."

"True," he agreed.

Carolyn glanced at her watch, then stood up. "I've got to get back downstairs." She gave an ironic laugh. "The show must go on."

"I'll be in touch," Barney told her. "Let you know what forensics comes up with on the note, okay?"

She nodded and fled the room, her mind on the rose stationery. Despite everything, Carolyn couldn't believe that Dolores was the maniac responsible for raping and killing Minnie. It was physically impossible. Her next thought stopped her cold. Tony? He and Jessie would also gain by her death.

Carolyn forced herself to take deep breaths. She needed to get herself together before she went on camera. She hoped that was possible.

Several hours later, after Carolyn called Richard to say she was leaving NNN, the guard accompanied her outside into the hot afternoon. She had decided to wait until she was home before updating Richard on the latest threats, unwilling to disturb his work day. A slight breeze ruffled her hair and caressed her bare arms as they walked, giving some relief from the bald Georgia sun. When Barney stepped from the shade of the flowering shrubbery, she was momentarily startled.

He grinned. "Sorry." Barney inclined his head at the guard, indicating that he'd see Carolyn to her car. "But I figured you'd want an update."

She stopped, facing him. "What?"

"I just got the call from the crime lab. They did a rush job for me."

"What?" she repeated.

"It was chicken blood again."

"Oh my God, Barney. This is so crazy."

They started walking again, and as they approached the Volvo, Carolyn saw the flat tire.

"Son of a bitch," he muttered. "Someone slashed your tire."

Barney took her arm, turned her around and directed her back to the lobby. He requested the car keys, then instructed her to wait while he changed the tire. He came back a few minutes later to get her. Then he followed her all the way home and didn't drive away until he was sure that Richard was there and she was safe.

It was then that she realized he'd never inquired about why Richard hadn't driven her to work in the first place.

The next day Barney stopped by the studio with the news of having talked with Dolores. As they sat over coffee in the lounge, he updated Carolyn on their conversation.

"She seemed surprised that a fan situation at NNN, difficult or not, could possibly be connected to Minnie's murder. She wondered how to help and I asked her about the rose stationery."

"What did she say?" Carolyn asked, trying not to show her upset.

"That she no longer used that type, switched to another style six months ago." He paused. "She also had an alibi for yesterday when your car tire was slashed—said she was looking at apartments with Jessie and Tony."

"Oh yeah. Dean mentioned that they were going to do that." She expelled a long breath. "I'm relieved."

"We'll see."

"You didn't believe her?"

"Hell no. She was hiding something. Time will tell what that is."

33

There were no further incidents at NNN for the next ten days and Carolyn began to hope that the crazy caller had lost interest in her. Oh God, she hoped so.

As she walked into the kitchen, Carolyn was about to speak to Richard when she realized he was on the phone. She hesitated in the doorway, noticing that the coffee was dripping and that he was in the process of making toast. She'd thought he was in his office checking E-mails while she got ready for work. Instead, he'd been making breakfast for them.

"No, I can't be in Chicago for two days and that's final," Richard said to the person he was talking to. "If that's not okay, then I'll just lose the money." He paused, allowing the person on the other end of the line to talk. "I know it's in the six-figure range. I still can't leave here now."

He listened, impatiently, the receiver pressed to his ear.

"So be it then. I'll write it off on my taxes."

He slammed down the receiver, then turned back to the toaster, the butter knife in his hand. When he saw Carolyn he stopped. "You heard?"

She nodded.

There was a brief silence.

"Sit down," he said, ignoring the phone conversation. "Breakfast is about ready." He indicated the covered frying pan. "An egg, vegetable and cheese omelet." He grinned, looking tousled and handsome in his terrycloth robe and slippers. "It's more like an open pan frittata—scrambled eggs and veggies."

She sniffed the air, smiling, acknowledging his considerate gesture. She sat down at the table he'd set in the kitchen, grinning as he dished up the food and poured the coffee. Then he took the chair opposite and raised his orange juice glass.

"A toast."

She nodded.

"To our lives together for the next fifty years."

They clinked their glasses, then sipped the juice and began eating. Carolyn didn't express the thoughts and questions that swirled in her mind. She didn't want to destroy the closeness between them at the moment.

As they finished eating, Carolyn put down her fork. "That was wonderful, Richard. Thank you."

He reached to place his hand over hers. "You're my life, Carolyn. I want to do nice things for you."

Carolyn glanced down, wondering why his words didn't sound quite believable. The phone conversation replayed in her mind. Richard was altering his life more than she'd realized. The situation was now influencing whether or not he could continue the trips that were vital to his financial success.

She looked up, meeting his eyes. "You should go to Chicago, Richard. It sounded important."

"Not as important as your welfare, Carolyn."

"Are you going to lose the money if you don't go?"

"Carolyn, don't ask. I have to do what I feel is right."

There was a silence between them.

"I don't want you to alter your business, jeopardize your income, Richard. If we stop our lives because of a crazy person then that person wins."

He took a swallow of coffee. "What are you saying?"

"You can't stop traveling because of your fear for me. While I appreciate your concern and love you for having it, I don't want our decisions to be based on fear."

He stared at his plate, considering her words.

"I want you to go, Richard. Two days won't make that much difference to me but you stand to lose a hell of a lot." She hesitated. "I don't want to live with knowing you forfeited a business deal you've worked hard to gain." She paused. "You have to go on earning a living, just as I do."

He cleared his throat, then stood up to pick up their plates and take them to the sink. Turning back to her he said, "Are you sure?"

She nodded.

He quickly closed the space between them, pulling her against his body. "It means I won't be here when you come home from work tonight."

She nodded again. "I know. I'm okay with that."

"All right then. But only because everything seems to be over. I hope to hell I'm right." He hesitated. "But I'll need your reassurance that NNN will see to all security precautions and that you'll adhere to them."

"I promise, Richard." She smiled, reassuringly. "Remember, everything is quiet. Like you said, the guy may have moved on."

"Maybe so, but don't depend on it yet."

"So, you're going?"

He inclined his head. "And I promise you, Carolyn. My business concerns are almost completely transferred to Atlanta. This is about the last time I'll need to go."

"Only thing is I won't be free to drive you to the airport," she said.

"I'll take a cab."

She kissed him good-bye. Then she went out to the garage and left for work.

It was dark by the time Carolyn went down to the lobby to head out to her car. She hesitated at the bottom of the stairs, glancing around. The guard was nowhere to be seen. Odd. She wondered if she should go out to the parking lot, then decided to wait a few minutes. The guard might have gone to the rest room.

Uncertain, Carolyn thought about calling Roberta who was still in her office. Don't be silly, she told herself. Roberta was already on edge over the state of alert at NNN and might react with alarm.

When the guard still hadn't returned a short time later, Carolyn went to the front entrance. Her car was right in front. Scanning the parking lot, she decided to risk walking the short distance without an escort.

But still she hesitated, knowing she shouldn't be foolish just because she'd begun to feel safe again. She went back to the guard's phone and quickly punched in Roberta's extension. Her voice mail picked up; she was out of her office.

Shit. Carolyn didn't know who else to call. It was past business hours and the daytime workers had gone home. Although programming was still being televised, the soundstages were soundproof and some distance from the lobby.

She made her decision and acted on it before her good sense surfaced. Key and cell phone in hand, she went back to the front door and hurried outside into the warm night. Within seconds she'd reached the Volvo, and stopped short, her eyes on the front tire. Adrenaline hit her nervous system and she grabbed the car, steadying herself.

Another slashed tire.

Carolyn whirled around and was running back to the entrance before her mind even registered the action. To her horror, the door wouldn't open.

It had locked behind her.

The guard was still missing and no other person was in sight. She turned, her back against the door, feeling totally vulnerable. She grabbed the door handle again, rattling it as she screamed for the guard. There was no answer.

Where is everyone? she thought, fighting panic.

She flipped open her cell phone and tried to call NNN's main number. There was no service; she was too close to the high-tech building. But did she dare move out into the lot to make her call? She'd be even more vulnerable.

She suddenly remembered there was a public phone at the corner of the building. Running, she plunged into the tiny cubicle, dropped her purse onto the shelf under the phone to search it for quarters and dimes. Half inside the booth, the open folding door bouncing against her elbow, she concentrated on dropping coins into the slot. Carolyn didn't see the person who shoved her forward and slammed the folding panels closed.

She squirmed around in the tight space, even as she realized there was no dial tone, and caught a brief flash of movement in the shrubbery. She pushed and struggled against the door but it wouldn't open. Something was jammed under it—from the outside and out of her reach.

Headlights of a car flipped on at the far edge of the parking lot. Then the vehicle started forward, headed toward the telephone booth that was on the walkway a dozen feet away from the building.

Carolyn tried to scream but her absolute terror held the sound in her throat. She gulped deep breaths and several high-pitched shrieks escaped her mouth. She watched the headlights move closer, and her shrieks for help grew stronger, suddenly attracting the attention of two men who were exiting the building from a side entrance. They rushed forward to help her, yanking the door open.

The approaching car veered off across the parking lot, headed for the exit. Glancing behind her, Carolyn saw that it was a black sedan. She didn't recognize the make. But she knew what it meant.

The two men, camera technicians, took her back inside where the guard was now on duty. The police were called and then the guard explained that he had been called away by an emergency phone call, a call that proved false. Before leaving his post for those minutes he'd made sure that the building was secure—by locking the doors.

"A Detective McGill is on the way," he told Carolyn. "He said you weren't to leave until he got here."

Carolyn only nodded, still too shaken to comment. But it figured. Barney was on call for anything that pertained to her, and to Minnie's murder.

Barney took her home after taking down the statements from all involved. He'd been upset, started to scold her for being careless, then stopped himself and was silent for the drive to Buckhead. "Someone can bring your car later, after forensics has checked for fingerprints," he'd told her.

He was noncommittal when she explained that Richard had gone to Chicago, then checked out her house before he allowed her to get out of his car. Once she was safely inside, he told her that an officer would be staked out near her house, so she didn't need to worry. Then he drove off, after mentioning he was checking out some things on Minnie's computer—such as deciphering the list of tags—and a "Mack," a person Dolores had met on a singles bulletin board.

Carolyn was disturbed to realize Barney was upset with her. He believed her decision to flaunt safety rules had been irresponsible. She couldn't agree more.

Carolyn came awake slowly, opening her eyes to the dark room. She lay on her side, her back to the door, not moving, listening. Had something awakened her? She separated the night sounds like flowers in her garden. A high-flying jet whined across the sky above her, bringing the image of Richard to her mind. The house creaked gently, as if settling more securely into its decades of existence. Even the warm current of wind blowing inland from the Atlantic Ocean many miles to the east was only a soft whisper in the pines.

She was about to shift position when she heard the thump from somewhere in the middle of the house.

Had one of the cats jumped off a chair in Richard's office? Tremors of fear began in her stomach and rippled into her limbs. That wasn't possible. She'd left Mayo and Mustard in the laundry room, so their night movements wouldn't activate the motion sensors and trip the alarm.

The squeak of a floorboard sounded close, in the hall near the bedroom door. *There were no motion sensors on the second floor.*

She fought a reflex to jump out of bed and face the door. There were more subtle sounds, like someone on tiptoes, someone who stepped carefully so as to not awaken her. The sense of movement stopped—at her doorway.

Every nerve and muscle in her body screamed at her to run. But where? The only way out was the hall door, the place where the phantom of her imagination stood. She felt its intense gaze, and the hairs on the back of her neck seemed to raise in defense.

But if someone was really there why hadn't they attacked? she wondered. Was it because they didn't want her aware of their presence? Must be. Otherwise she'd already be dead.

Pretend you're asleep, she instructed herself. Don't look unless the footsteps start into the room. Whoever it is mustn't know you're awake.

Her ears straining to hear, she squeezed her eyes closed, so terrified she was beginning to pant. Compressing her lips, she forced herself to take quiet, shallow breaths, and prayed she wouldn't start hyperventilating—and give herself away. Carolyn felt frozen in time, like someone had pushed the pause button on the ongoing frames of her life.

The seconds stretched until the silence was as heavy as the pressure that was building in her chest.

Then the movement began again, barely discernable, moving away. Seconds later there was nothing. Carolyn waited for several minutes before allowing herself deep breaths. Slowly, as quietly as possible, she turned over to face the doorway. No one was there.

Reason reasserted itself. How would anyone have gotten into the house when the security system was armed? Had someone bypassed it? And there was a policeman right outside. Surely he would have noticed someone breaking in. Unless someone had killed him.

Stop it, Carolyn, she ordered herself.

But self-talk couldn't quell her fear. Carolyn had

to satisfy herself that no one had been skulking along the upstairs hall. Still, she was unable to force herself to the doorway, even though she'd slipped silently out of bed.

She stood beside it, listening.

Finally, she was able to move. A glance into the hall told her it was empty. Forcing herself forward, Carolyn knew it was now or never. Or she'd lose her nerve.

Quickly, she glanced into the spare bedroom, both the back and main stairways, and then Richard's office in the front of the house. Again, there was nothing out of the ordinary.

As she stepped farther into his work place, her eyes were drawn to the tiny monitor light on the computer. Why hadn't she noticed that it had been left on? Richard was diligent about switching off his equipment.

But no one was there.

After turning on the hall lights, Carolyn went back to her own bedroom but she couldn't shake her apprehension. She hated feeling so vulnerable, so scared. She would not stay alone in the house again if Richard had to be gone overnight.

She glanced at the clock, saw that it was almost four in the morning. She punched her pillows into shape, then propped them up behind her. Half sitting, she was resolved that she'd never be able to sleep. She was right. Instead she watched dawn creep in through the windows.

While making coffee in the kitchen, Carolyn noticed that her answering machine was turned off. Last night she hadn't checked messages because the message light hadn't been on and she'd assumed there were none. Now she realized that, in her frightened state, she must have turned the thing off without thinking.

As the coffee dripped, she listened to Richard telling her that he'd arrived in Chicago and would call her the next day. The second message was from Roberta at NNN, left before Barney brought her home, confirming that a limo would pick her up in the morning, then asking her to call her at home. "I might have seen the person who slashed your tire and I need to talk with you before I call Barney—because maybe there's a logical reason for what I saw."

It was deja vu—Minnie's words.

The icy fingers of terror which had knotted her stomach during the night clutched at her again. She picked up the phone and called Barney before trying Roberta's number.

He answered, having only arrived at Homicide. "Yeah, I just got Roberta's message. She said she'd left a message on your voice mail but hadn't heard back from you. I'm just calling her back on the other line. Can you hang on a minute?"

"Sure," she said, then waited as she was put on hold.

"I gotta hang up." Barney's voice was suddenly in her ear. "Something's happened at Roberta's place. We'll talk later." Then the phone went dead.

34

Carolyn got out of the limo at the NNN entrance and froze, her eyes on Barney who waited for her by the door. Oh, no. Please God, she thought. No more bad news.

He stepped forward and took her arm, guiding her in through the doors to the lobby. Nodding at the guard, Barney led her to the empty waiting area and sat her down.

"I have something to tell you, Carolyn." He hesitated. "And it's not good news."

She braced herself, trying to ignore the alarming increase in her heart rate. "What, Barney?"

His eyes glinted as he formulated his thoughts. "When I hung up so fast on you I'd just gotten Roberta on the line. Before she could say much more than hello I heard what sounded like two gunshots, then the dial tone."

Carolyn gulped deep breaths, and waited for him to go on. She put off asking the obvious question, trying to brace herself for hearing the answer.

"I sent the closest patrol car to check her house, then raced out there myself. We were all too late." Barney moved closer and took her hands in his. "Roberta was already dead, murdered."

"Shot?" Her word wobbled.

"Twice." A pause. "You don't need to know the details," he said, gently.

"I do, Barney," she managed. "I have to know what happened."

His gaze shifted to the window, beyond which a flawless morning gave promise of another beautiful day. "Okay, I understand."

She waited, trying to hold back the urge to scream, as he again gathered his thoughts. Then he began.

"She was found on her living room floor, the phone lay next to her right hand. Whatever happened was sudden. She hadn't seen it coming." He shifted position. "The forensic unit is out there now processing the house, you know, the usual procedure as was done at Minnie's place."

"I've forgotten," she whispered.

His expression tightened and she wondered if he was thinking about the person who'd pulled the trigger. "They'll dust for fingerprints, analyze blood splatter for direction and velocity and—"

"Blood! Poor Roberta," Carolyn cried, interrupting. She tightened her stomach muscles, trying to control the trembling deep inside her. The thought of her friend bleeding jolted her with a new sense of loss—Roberta was dead, too.

"We don't have to go on with the details," Barney said.

"Please." She tried to pull herself together. "I need to hear that everything is being done."

He gave a short nod and continued. "They'll vacuum for threads, fibers and hairs that'll be examined in the lab by a laser-equipped spectrometer with a scanning electron microscope. The hope is to find solid physical evidence that can be matched to a suspect." He drew in a breath. "We have one break. There was a trace of blood on the broken glass door where the killer entered the house."

For a moment longer she held frayed nerves in check. "It's because of me—because she saw the person who slashed my tire."

"We don't know that for sure," Barney said. "As I've said before, it's not your fault this psycho has fixated on you."

"I tried to call her after I talked to you but her voice mail picked up. She must have already been—"

Carolyn's voice faltered again as great heaving, tearing, convulsive sobs rose up in her throat, taking her breath away.

Barney pulled her against him, trying to comfort her, and somewhere in the back of her mind she knew he must be devastated as well. This was not the homicide case of a stranger; this was another person he knew.

Finally, Barney's consoling words began to calm her and she was able to ask him if Roberta had named the person she saw slashing her tire."

"Unfortunately, no." He grabbed a Kleenex from a box on the end table and handed it to her. "I just wish she'd called me when it happened."

Carolyn glanced down, dabbing at her eyes, knowing her cheeks were smeared with mascara. "I think she was uncertain about something, wanted to make sure in case she was wrong."

"Yeah, that's my take on it. Maybe it was someone she knew, someone who is close to you." His eyelids lowered. "Maybe she couldn't believe what she thought she saw."

She shook her head, not wanting to think about that aspect, let alone talk about it right then.

He glanced down, pulling a notepad and pen from his pocket, and she wondered who he suspected, if anyone. Abruptly, his eyes were direct. "Let's go over things again, Carolyn." A pause. "You up to that?"

She nodded. Her friends were dying. She had to be up to it, ready or not. "But we've gone over everything before, Barney."

"I know, but we may have missed something." He hesitated. "Start at the beginning, when you first thought something might be wrong."

Carolyn took deep breaths, barely holding back the urge to cry again. Then she began, telling him about the dark sedan that followed her from NNN to the Youth House, the incidents at her condo. She explained the acceleration of events after her marriage, from the bat and rat to her brake failure, the tire blowout on the freeway and the motor oil on her windshield. She even mentioned her feelings of being watched while in her own house.

Barney listened without comment, letting her talk at her own speed until she finished. "So these incidents started way back, a few months after you broke up with Tom?"

She glanced down. "Yeah, that's right."

"Is that it?" Barney asked.

"There is one more thing, something that I'd sort of forgotten about."

"What's that?"

"It's the English class assignment Dean wrote about me. It's probably not relevant but it was around the time I first saw the dark car following me."

Barney leaned forward, waiting for clarification.

Carolyn explained it was a paper he'd written about her, including what she hated or loved, and the things she feared, including *bats, blood and knives.* She hesitated. "I discussed on the air what he was doing." She knotted her hands on her lap. "I used to talk with my viewers about my personal life." She shook her head. "Stupid me."

"Do you have a copy of it?"

"No, I don't."

"That's okay. I'll get it from Dean."

"What could you possibly learn from it, except that he got an A?"

He shrugged. "Interesting to read what your viewers already know about you, make sure there isn't a connection somewhere." He put his notepad away, not meeting her eyes. "I think you've realized that we check out every lead, however remote. We even verified Richard's trips." Abruptly, his gaze was direct. "All of them proved to be legitimate."

A flash of annoyance pierced her grief. But then she realized that Barney was only trying to protect her, doing his job. Richard wasn't a suspect.

Or was he? The thought came unbidden. She immediately dismissed it as a part of her own hysteria.

At that moment the elevator door opened and Bill Youngman, Roberta's boss, stepped out, saw Carolyn and Barney and strode over to them. "A terrible thing that's happened here," he said, his wiry frame stiff from shock, his words delivered like bullets from an automatic weapon. "I've just put the whole company on alert."

Carolyn only nodded, unable to talk as he went on to express his grief over Roberta's death.

"I've had a preliminary report," he said, turning his attention to Barney. "Anything else you can tell me?"

Barney told him what he could, that the forensic unit was going over the crime scene with every high-tech tool known to man. Bill nodded, then spoke to Carolyn.

"I've arranged for a substitute hostess for the next few days," he told her. "I want you to go home, maybe call your doctor and get a sedative." He shook his head. "This tragedy is a terrible blow for NNN."

She started to protest and he put up a flat silencing hand. "It's done. The limo will take you."

"No need for the limo," Barney said, interrupting. I'll take her, make sure she gets settled."

"And safe." Bill gave her a hug, then strode off to continue damage control. "I'll be in touch, Carolyn."

She wondered how it was all going to end. One thing was for sure. Her career at NNN could be over. She could never again risk anyone's life because of the obsession of a crazy viewer, even though she realized that the wacko could have latched on to anyone.

But no decisions today. Tomorrow or the day after was soon enough, when she felt emotionally ready for that loss, too.

The officer staking out Carolyn's Buckhead house was parked a few yards up the street. Barney drove past him and into the driveway, as Carolyn opened the garage door with the opener she'd put in her purse that morning.

Carolyn turned off the alarm system and waited in the breezeway while Barney went ahead to make sure the place was safe, despite the security measures Richard had installed. As he disappeared inside, she glimpsed him pull out his pistol.

Silence pressed down on her, and seconds became minutes. She wondered why it was taking Barney so long. On the drive home he'd updated her about the investigation, that he was still cross-checking NNN shoppers whose information may have been stolen by the computer hacker. He'd told her that the Carolyn file in Minnie's computer had turned up three matches, two women and *RMack*, a man who had been wooing them on-line on a singles bulletin board that Dolores used. RMack had requested face-to-face meetings with each woman.

"Sorry I took so long," he told her when he finally returned. He'd already put his pistol back into the shoulder holster under his jacket. "Everything is fine, but at first I had this itchy feeling that something was out of sync." He gave a laugh. "So I had to satisfy myself that no one was hiding anywhere."

Carolyn didn't reply, knowing the feeling. She habitually felt like someone was watching her, even when she knew it was impossible.

The phone was ringing as they entered the kitchen and Carolyn ran to grab it. "Hello?" Her voice shook.

"Hi, sweetheart." Richard's voice in her ear sounded surprised. "Didn't you go to work today? The operator at NNN told me you were at home."

"I had to leave early." She glanced at the wall clock, noting that it was still only late morning. Barney had moved closer to lean against the counter, listening.

"Oh, Richard." She slumped onto a stool. "Something terrible has happened."

"For God's sake, what?"

She started to explain and broke down. The more she tried to talk, the harder she cried. Barney took the phone, identified himself and then told Richard about Roberta, the reason Carolyn had come home.

There was a silence as Barney listened.

"Yeah, I agree. You need to catch the next available flight back here," Barney said, sharply. "Your wife needs your support."

Another pause.

"Glad to hear you say that, Richard." He glanced at Carolyn. "Under the circumstances, I'd feel pretty guilty about being gone, too."

Barney filled in a few more details, assured him that Carolyn had police protection and then hung up.

When Carolyn couldn't stop crying, Barney went to the cupboard and took out the whiskey. She watched him pour her a shot. If she hadn't been so upset she might have joked about their recent drinking habit. As it was, she only cried harder.

* * *

The phone rang several hours after Barney left, and Carolyn ran to pick it up in her bedroom, expecting Richard. She was hoping he'd managed to book an earlier flight than the one arriving in Atlanta at ten that night. Instead it was Dolores.

"The police have taken Tony in for questioning," Dolores said, sounding breathless.

"What?"

"You heard me, Carolyn." Dolores sounded upset, angry and close to tears. "My God, why would they suspect Tony, or me and Jessie? None of us are murderers. We have no motive in killing Roberta."

"How did you find out about Roberta?" Carolyn sagged down onto the bed.

"Barney was here and left. Then two other officers came a short time later to take Tony down for questioning. They said it was routine, that he wasn't being arrested or anything." Dolores suddenly sounded old. "But I'm scared, Carolyn. Barney said he'd gotten a ballistic report that the weapon used was a .38 caliber Smith & Wesson revolver—and Tony owns one, like lots of other people in Atlanta." A pause. "What have you said about us to Barney?"

"Nothing. I'm shocked."

"Then how did Barney know that Tony has guns in the house?"

"I don't know, maybe Dean told him." Carolyn felt a hopelessness settling around her. The watcher—caller—killer—whoever it was, was destroying every part of her life. It was a living nightmare.

"Then Barney found a .38 revolver in Tony's collection," Dolores said.

"You showed him Tony's collection?"

"I had no choice. Dean came in just as Barney mentioned guns and offered to show him his dad's. I tried to have them wait until Tony got back but Dean insisted his dad wouldn't mind." A pause. "I felt like I couldn't refuse after that, or I'd seem like I'm guilty of something, and I'm not."

Carolyn was struck dumb. She figured that there wasn't enough evidence for a search warrant when Barney had gone to question Dolores and her family. She knew that he'd probably known Tony owned a .38 if the gun was registered. He'd taken advantage of Dean's innocent offer when the opportunity presented itself. She felt sick. Barney was desperately seeking clues, but she didn't approve of his method.

"We're distraught, Carolyn. Jessie and Dean can't stop crying. Tony is innocent. He even volunteered to let them test his revolver. What are you going to do about it?"

Carolyn couldn't think. Her mind boggled. The only family she had left couldn't be guilty of this horror.

They just couldn't be.

35

When the front doorbell rang in midafternoon Carolyn hurried from the back of the house to answer it. But as she reached the hall, she hesitated. Who could it be? Barney would have called ahead and Richard was still in Chicago. He'd managed to get on a flight arriving in Atlanta around eight that night rather than ten, but he'd still have to drive home after that.

Apprehension dragged at her feet as she moved forward, slowly and quietly, to the long stained-glass windows that edged the entrance. She peeked out to the porch, saw who it was and quickly opened the door.

"Aunt Carolyn," Dean said, rushing forward to hug her. "I need you to help us."

Beyond the portico she could see his bike leaning against a support post. He'd ridden the mile or so from Dolores's house to plead for his family.

"The police have my dad," he said, his expression stricken with concern. "He has the kind of gun that was used to shoot your boss." His voice shook and tears welled in his eyes. "Do they think my dad killed Roberta, Aunt Carolyn?"

"I don't know what they think, Dean," she said gently. It broke her heart to see him looking so fragile. She kissed his cheek, holding him against her for a moment longer before closing the door. "I'm sure it'll be okay, honey."

Oh God, she thought. Will this nightmare ever end? Why is someone doing this? Why am I the target?—and my family?

"My dad isn't a strong man and he doesn't like to work, I know that, Aunt Carolyn," Dean said. "But he's not mean. He won't even pull down spider webs, because he told me that spiders work too hard to create them." He sucked in a deep breath. "My dad would never hurt anyone. Please Aunt Carolyn, make the police let my dad go."

Carolyn felt defeated. She couldn't bear to see Dean so devastated, having to confess his personal feelings about his father's weakness.

"Does Barney think my dad is a killer? Is that why he wanted to see the guns in our house?"

"I'm sure he doesn't think that, Dean. Barney was probably doing his job, eliminating my family as suspects."

Dean nodded. "That's what Barney told my grandma."

There was a momentary silence.

"Would you like a Coke?" she asked, seeing that he was sweaty from his bike ride. Carolyn hoped to divert his thoughts.

"I guess so." He sounded uncertain, but followed

her into the kitchen and sat down on a counter stool, waiting while she took two Cokes from the refrigerator.

"Did Barney tell you about the Youth House plan to connect with other similar shelters across the country, via the Internet?" She'd tried for an upbeat tone.

He shook his head, but his expression brightened.

"And Barney also said you'll be very much involved, that they'll need your expertise."

He set his Coke can down. "I'll probably have my own personal password then," he said. "Like Uncle Richard has to get into his computer."

"You mean his password for going on the Web to access his E-mail, don't you?"

"That, too." He grinned, pleased with himself, his worries temporarily forgotten. "Remember, I explained that the password for E-mail is different?"

She smiled back. "That's right. You said Richard has a personal password that he uses after he turns on his computer, so you couldn't get on-line?"

"Yep. And I might know what it is."

"How could you know?" Carolyn leaned forward.

"Well, I don't know for sure. I accidentally found a scrap of paper under his keyboard with a word on it." He took a swallow of Coke. "That was the night of your housewarming party."

"Why didn't you say something?"

"Because I'd just put it back and was never going to tell anyone, or try it." He glanced down. "The other piece that Minnie found must have fallen when I moved the keyboard. I didn't know it was there."

"So, the name you found might not be Richard's access password."

He shrugged. "I just figured Tornado was because almost everyone I know writes their password down at first, until they're sure they won't forget it. My grandma even taped hers, Peaches, to her monitor for the first week she had it."

"Tornado?"

His eyes widened. "Oh my gosh, I slipped."

"It's okay, honey. You didn't do anything wrong, and I won't tell Uncle Richard."

He looked relieved, then stood up to go. She followed him back to the front door where he turned to face her. The anxious expression was back on his face.

"You will ask Barney to let my dad go, won't you Aunt Carolyn?"

She kissed him. "Of course I will, honey. Everything will be all right. Your dad is only being questioned, not arrested. Don't you worry about it for now, okay?"

He nodded and went out to his bike, as thunder rumbled in the darkening sky. He waved on his way down the driveway, and she hoped he'd make it home before the storm broke. She watched him out of sight, then closed and locked the door.

She hoped Tony was home by the time Dean got there, for all of their sakes.

The inside of the house darkened as the clouds lowered over the late afternoon. Lightning lit the rooms every few seconds, followed by thunder so deafening that it shook the dishes in the china cabinet. Carolyn didn't dare turn on Richard's computer until the storm passed, the thing she'd decided to do right after Dean left. Then the rain came, a torrential deluge that had water running off the roof like someone had turned on a fire hose. It was so loud that even Mustard and Mayo were uneasy, pacing around her ankles.

But above everything else, Carolyn's mind was spinning with Dean's concerns, and his inadvertent revelation about *Tornado*. As the storm raged outside, Carolyn went up to Richard's office. It was immaculate as always, not even a scrap of paper in the wastebasket. She lifted the keyboard but there was no longer anything under it.

She bent closer. There was a faint impression on the top sheet of a legal tablet, as though he'd written something with a ballpoint pen on the page that had been above it.

Seven letters. Not a word.

But was it the password for Richard's E-mail? She'd have to wait until the storm passed to find out, and to confirm if Tornado was the access word for the computer itself. If it wasn't, then the seven letters became a moot point, unless they were the key to unlock the hard drive and Tornado was the E-mail password. And maybe neither would work.

Carolyn sat in Richard's chair in front of his computer, staring into space, confused by what it all meant. She remembered that Richard had been working in his office right up until their first guests arrived that day. He must have shoved the pieces of paper under the keyboard, never dreaming anyone would sit down at his computer.

A mental picture of Minnie picking one of them up flashed into her mind. As she remembered the tag list her memory was jolted. Was Peaches also in Minnie's file named Carolyn? She wasn't positive. Barney would know. She was sure that Tornado wasn't, but was there something else that was similar—with the word wind? She squirmed on her chair. The idea was unthinkable.

Suddenly she realized her skin was pricking. She froze on the leather cushions. Someone was watching, she felt it in the core of her being. She spun the chair around, her gaze darting around the room. No one was there.

Mustard rubbed against her legs. She glanced down. Both cats had followed her into Richard's office, but seemed restless, unable to settle down, as though they, too, sensed another presence.

The storm seemed stalled overhead, as though another front had joined the first one. What if there was a power surge. She wasn't sure she should risk it. She might crash the computer. How could she explain? That she was suspicious of him and had turned it on to prove he was innocent?

Carolyn forced her thoughts back to the file she'd seen on Minnie's computer, remembering that she'd made a copy on a disk. With lightning still flashing over the walls, she crossed the hall to her bedroom, grabbed her purse and dumped its contents onto the bed. The disk wasn't there.

Could she have taken it out at work and unthinkingly put it somewhere for safekeeping? Or had someone taken it?

She picked up the phone and called Barney, ready

to ask him about the Carolyn list. But his voice mail picked up, and she left a brief message, that she needed his advice. "I may have stumbled onto something, Barney, and I'm confused. Please call."

And then she made an instant decision. In the time it would take to drive to Anderson Youth House the storm should have abated. She needed to know if Dolores's E-mail name was really on Minnie's list—and make sure that the seven letters she'd found weren't, not to mention Tornado, in case that was the user name to access Richard's business information.

In minutes she'd set the alarm and was driving away from her house in almost blinding rain. As she passed the stakeout car she glimpsed the officer sitting behind the wheel, his head tilted back against the seat, obviously dozing. He didn't see her.

That's good and bad news, she thought. He wouldn't stop her, as Barney had probably instructed, but he also couldn't see anyone prowling her house if he was asleep. She put the disturbing thought out of her head and concentrated on her goal. Determining facts was her priority and it was now or never. Richard would be home in a few hours.

When she got to the Youth House, she parked, locked up and then dashed to the front door and went inside the building, hurrying to Minnie's old office.

With raindrops still dripping from her hair, she sat down at the desk and switched on the computer. She sent the cursor down the file index, stopping on her name, then clicking the mouse.

The file came up on the screen. But it was a disappointment, although the list of E-mail names did include a DPeaches, not just a Peaches. She printed out the page and then saved the file.

She went off line and then shut down the terminal and screen. A couple of minutes later she was back in her car, headed home, still uncertain, but resolved to learn the truth. She was convinced that the answer would be on Richard's computer.

The thought almost took her breath away.

Carolyn pushed back her own feelings and steered the Volvo almost by rote. The storm had abated, and when she passed the stakeout she saw that he still appeared to be asleep. She needed to tell Barney. A sleeping policeman was no help in a life-or-death situation.

Once back in the safety of her own house, Carolyn saw that she had a phone message and pressed the button. Richard's voice sounded in the quiet room, telling her he was about to get on the plane which should arrive a few minutes after eight. "I love you," he said and hung up.

Carolyn felt shattered, but determined. She had to hurry. The day was dark and night would come early.

She went upstairs to his office and switched on the computer, wondering if someone was trying to set him up, link him to the murders. Richard had nothing to gain by her death, only Dolores would. Or maybe someone was trying to gain access to his business deals and Tornado and Peaches and the other names had nothing to do with the deaths and other terrifying incidents that had been directed toward her. She placed the printout from Minnie's computer where she could see it.

As the computer screen came up with the instruction to type in the code word, Carolyn hesitated, staring at it.

Was she ready? Did she really want to know if the man she'd married, slept with and hoped to have children with was not who she'd believed him to be?

Oh, God. She dropped her face into her hands, her stomach churning, feeling sick.

Maybe Tornado wouldn't open Richard's computer to her. In that case her fears would be unfounded, and the other names on the list might not have anything to do with him either.

She typed Tornado. An hourglass appeared and Carolyn held her breath.

Instantly she was in, with full access to the files.

The phone ringing on his desk startled her so badly that she swung around and swept a container of pens and pencils onto the floor. She grabbed the receiver.

"Hello."

"Hi, sweetheart. "I'm on my way, calling from an air phone on the plane."

"Richard," she said. Her eyes darted everywhere, suddenly feeling like a kid who'd been caught stealing nickels to buy candy.

"Yeah, it's me. I've been worried about you. Just wanted to know that you were okay." A hesitation. "And tell you that I love you," he said, repeating his earlier message.

"I'm fine." Her voice sounded stilted even to her own ears.

"You don't sound yourself," he said. She could

hear a slight static on the line. "Sure everything's okay?"

She braced the receiver with her other hand. "Uh-huh. I'll explain everything that's happened when you get home."

"You sound scared, Carolyn." His concern was evident in his tone. "What's happened? Something more than Roberta's death?"

She didn't know what to say.

"C'mon, Carolyn, what is it? You're scared about something, I can tell."

"Yes," she admitted finally. "I am scared, but I can't talk about it now." She stared at his computer data which she'd just accessed. "I can't explain over the phone."

"Have you called Barney?"

She hesitated. "Not yet."

"I insist that you call him right now."

"You're probably right, Richard." She fiddled nervously with the phone cord. "I'll call him."

"No, I'll call him myself." The connection sounded distant, as if there was air in the wires. "I want a cop to be placed right in the house until I get there."

They hung up quickly and Carolyn felt even more uncertain—and guilty that she had doubts about Richard. But she decided to finish what she'd started on his computer, maybe find a clue to what Minnie and Roberta had both tried to tell her before they died.

The unsettled feeling of being watched crept up on her again, and before she typed in more commands on the computer she called Barney herself and left another message on his voice mail, that she was trying to verify the disturbing information she'd mentioned on Richard's computer. "Richard called from the plane and said he was calling you, Barney. He's concerned about me being so scared right now." She hesitated. "I didn't tell him that I'd found his password and accessed his files. Oh God, please call back soon, Barney."

Carolyn dropped the receiver back onto its cradle, and went back to Richard's computer. She tried to ignore the strange whispery sounds of movement in the house around her that didn't seem to have any real origin at all.

And then the phone rang again. For seconds she stared at it, like it had fangs and would bite if she reached to answer. With a quick motion, she did.

"It's Dean, Aunt Carolyn. For a minute I thought you weren't there."

"You okay, Dean?"

"I guess so." His tone was higher than usual, as though he were frightened.

"What's wrong, Dean?"

"Me and Grandma were here alone and she had a phone call." A pause. "She got real upset, but she wouldn't tell me what was wrong, only that a police officer had requested that she stay with you until Uncle Richard gets home."

"Let me talk to her, Dean."

"That's just it. She rushed out of here a few minutes ago for your place. I've never seen her drive so fast."

Carolyn had no time to digest his news when he continued. "I was about to call you when the phone rang and it was Barney. He told me that my dad's been cleared."

"That's wonderful, honey. I'm so glad."

"Yeah, me, too." He took a breath. "But when I told Barney about my grandma's call and her rushing out to your place, he just hung up." A pause. "What's going on?"

Carolyn reassured him, and then hung up herself. She just knew something bad was about to happen.

36

Carolyn sat at the computer, hurriedly surfing the Web to find the singles bulletin board that Dolores used before her stepmother arrived at her door. Another storm was approaching, but she hoped to find a connection between that site and some of the people on Minnie's list before it hit. She was annoyed at her own ineptness on the Internet, and vowed to have Dean give her private instructions—if the killer didn't get her first.

Then the doorbell rang.

She pushed back the chair and jumped up. Functioning on adrenaline, her nervous system barely above breaking down, Carolyn ran out into the upper hall where she paused to look down into the entry. She couldn't see who was on the front porch, but guessed it was Dolores. Continuing down the steps, Carolyn went straight to the door, glanced through the window and then unbolted the lock and flung it open.

Dolores stood there, wild-eyed, rain dripping off

her hair to run down her slicker. Without hesitation she rushed inside, pushed Carolyn aside as she slammed and locked the door, and then ran to the hall table where she yanked out the drawer and pulled something from it. She spun back around to face Carolyn, a .38 caliber pistol in her hand.

Carolyn gasped, unable to understand what Dolores was doing. "Where did you get that gun?"

"The drawer, Carolyn. You saw me."

Horrified, Carolyn backed away. For long seconds they stared at each other, lightning flashing and thunder rumbling above them. Then Carolyn whirled around to dart up the steps, cut off from the back entrance by Dolores.

"Wait!" Dolores cried. "I'm here to help you!"

"Not with a gun!"

"Stop! You're wrong," she called, chasing her. "A police officer said it was there."

Carolyn didn't believe that for a second. It didn't make any sense. Why would a police officer put a gun in her drawer? So how had it gotten there? She hated guns and wouldn't ever own one. She froze. Unless the gun belonged to Richard.

Suddenly terrified, Carolyn knew she had to get away from Dolores. The whole scene was surreal. The wife of her dead father was pounding up the stairs after her, with a gun in hand. The same gun that had killed Roberta?

Oh God—why? Because she was bankrupt and needed to inherit the balance of the Langdon fortune?—money that would come to her upon Carolyn's death?

Was Dolores the watcher person, everything that

had happened a part of a plan to kill her before she had children to inherit—*before Dolores was permanently removed from the contingencies of the will*? It didn't make sense. It was crazy.

But Minnie had been raped. Carolyn gulped air. If Dolores was behind it all, that meant Tony was, too.

And what about the DPeaches that might be in Richard's computer files? Damn her own computer dumbness. She hadn't found that connection yet.

Carolyn ran into her bedroom, headed for the only door with a lock, her bathroom. When she reached it, she slammed herself in and twisted the bolt, stepping into the bathtub to be out of the way of bullets that might come through the door panels.

"Carolyn, come out! My God, I'm here to help. Someone is trying to kill you!"

Duh, Carolyn thought inanely. She didn't respond, not wanting Dolores to know she had stepped to the side. A bullet through the wall could kill her as surely as one through the door.

There was a long silence.

Carolyn went over the possibilities to escape. There were none except for the door she'd come through.

She strained her ears. Nothing. Where was Dolores? Outside her door waiting for her to open it? So she could shoot her? That hardly made any more sense than Dolores saying that a police officer had told her where to find the gun. Carolyn felt as though she'd entered The Twilight Zone.

Then she heard something. What? It sounded like muffled scuffling, as though several people were shoving each other around. Nonsense, she told herself as the house went silent again. Maybe Dolores had gone somewhere else.

Had she given up and left? Or maybe the police stakeout had seen something was wrong and arrested her. Her hand hesitated on the lock. Then why hadn't the officer come upstairs to make sure she was all right?

She waited a few more minutes. The storm had moved on, the thunder gradually fading as it traveled beyond Atlanta. The house itself was absolutely silent.

Cautiously, she opened the door. Dolores was gone. Still Carolyn hesitated, her gaze quickly moving over the bedroom to make sure. Beyond the doorway the hall was shadowy and empty for as far as she could see. Outside the dark cloudy sky was bringing on an early night.

She crept forward slowly, trying not to make a sound. The hall, like the guest room and Richard's office, was silent. But the back of her neck prickled with apprehension.

Where was Dolores? Had she given up?

No, Carolyn reminded herself. She'd exposed herself. She'd have to make sure Carolyn didn't tell. Cold talons of terror clawed at her chest. She had to get out of the house.

Take it slow. Don't panic, she commanded herself. It was a mantra she repeated over and over in her mind, as she slipped through the shadowy stillness. The air was thick, stagnant. Evil hung there like fog in a swamp.

Carolyn had reached the top of the stairs and panicked. She sprinted downward, no longer concerned about the noise she made, hoping to outrun anyone that might be in her house. She hit the bottom and leaped across the foyer, her eyes on the door.

Carolyn saw the shape on the floor after it was too late to avoid it. Stumbling, only several feet from escaping, she sprawled onto the small Oriental rug in front of the entry. For seconds she lay stunned, her mind not comprehending. Then a bloody hand reached to grab her ankle.

"Run, Carolyn," Dolores whispered. "He's going to kill you."

Absolute horror slid over Carolyn like a sheet of ice. Dolores was lying in a pool of blood that was spreading on the polished hardwood. Even though the lights hadn't been turned on, Carolyn could see that she'd been stabbed in the chest. A long-bladed knife lay beside her. The gun was nowhere in sight.

Sucking in long breaths, Carolyn managed to get to her feet, but her limbs shook so hard she had to brace herself against the hall table. But her gaze darted everywhere, seeking out the dark corners.

Someone else was in the house. She had to get out.

"Hang on, Dolores." She spoke softly, aware of being overheard. "I'll get help."

But it was already too late.

A dark shape stepped from the shadowy living room into the light that shown in through the stained glass windows from the porch. A man dressed in black blocked her way to the door. Their eyes met.

She stared mutely, unable to process her feelings, what his presence meant, and why he was there. Her first response had been to go to him, but her feet moved of their own volition, backing her away from the frightening expression on his face—and the gun that was now in his hand.

He smiled coldly, as though he enjoyed seeing her shock.

"Why?" The word soared into the upper reaches of the house.

"Why? Because you were easy." His laugh was harsh. "Both you and her—" He nudged Dolores's still body with the toe of his shoe. "Were mine right from the beginning."

"You mean you had an affair with Dolores?" Her voice wobbled.

"Naw, only cyber sex."

Her eyes widened in horror as she stepped back even farther, until her heels came up against the bottom step. "It was you."

He inclined his head, his eyes glinting as lightning flashed briefly in the hall. It was getting darker. The sun was setting.

Slowly she turned one foot, positioning it for a fast getaway, speaking to divert his attention from her movement.

"How did you get here so fast?"

"How do you think, sweet Carolyn? I bet you're too stupid to figure it out."

His smug, twisted smile made her think of a mask she once saw in an art gallery that was titled, *The Face of Madness.* That's what she saw in his. How had she missed seeing it before? Because it was behind another mask, his mask of loving concern and normalcy? She'd been so fooled.

She had to save herself, and Dolores. He meant to

kill them both. Maybe Dolores was already dead.

She twisted around, screaming for help, and flew back up the steps, hearing him curse as he followed, wondering why he didn't shoot, hoping the stakeout cop would hear her above the storm. Once again there was no time for other options; she headed for the bathroom off her bedroom, with the door that locked. Twisting the bolt, Carolyn jumped to the side, shaking and gulping breaths. Then she waited, bracing herself for when he'd break in, a curling iron in her hand, the best weapon she could find.

Again, there was only silence.

With each passing moment she became more unnerved, unable to stop shaking. Richard, why? she thought. Shreds of once treasured memories scattered in Carolyn's mind like ticker tape in the wind.

The minutes mounted. She had no idea how long she'd been in the bathroom. But she knew he was out there somewhere, waiting, enjoying his sick game.

What was his game?

Then she knew. Acrid smoke began to seep in under the door. The house was on fire. God, help me! she begged silently. She could stay in the bathroom and burn, or open the door and make a run for it.

She flung the door open and rushed into the bedroom, taking him off guard. She managed to get all the way down the steps before he grabbed her. Twisting and kicking did no good. His arms pinned her so tightly against him that she couldn't move. His right hand over her mouth cut off her screams as he dragged her to Dolores who still lay unmoving on the floor. Smoke curled around her.

Beyond the hall, the fire he'd set crackled loudly from the back half of the house. The draperies in both the living and dining room burst into flames as she watched. Soon the whole house would be engulfed. She didn't want to die. Not by the fire or Richard.

So when he suddenly released her, she didn't hesitate. She ran, gaining only a few steps. The sound of the gunshot reverberated above the roar of the fire. The bullet hit her in the upper back, but she didn't realize it had until she was lying on the floor.

She couldn't move but didn't lose consciousness, aware of her cats around her. Mutely she watched him put the gun in Dolores's hand, pick up the knife and then turn toward her. She closed her eyes.

Pretend you're dead, she told herself. As he came closer she held her breath, trying to ignore the pain from the bullet wound, the sensation of blood soaking her sweater. She was certain he'd kill her if he saw her move. She steeled herself for the shock and pain.

She heard the knife drop next to her, felt a gloved hand press her fingers around the handle. He was making it look like she'd killed Dolores, after Dolores came to murder her.

Why Richard? Why would you do this? You said you loved me. I loved you, believed in you.

The *why* suddenly became clear to her. He was third in line to inherit her father's estate, after Dolores. Somehow he'd known that, maybe from the naïve Dolores who'd been searching for a man on the Internet. Instead she'd found a sociopath who'd destroyed them both.

Carolyn heard him move away and opened her eyes to watch him from under her lashes. He wasn't leaving the house but was running back upstairs. Once he disappeared she tried to get up, but fell back, so weak she felt faint.

Don't pass out. Somehow you have to get out— before he comes back. She squeezed her eyes shut, willing strength back into her body.

Above the conflagration she heard another sound, a vaguely familiar poof. Her eyelids popped open. It was the noise the door to the attic made as it closed. Richard was climbing under the eaves on the side of his office, the sloping storage area that was connected to the space above the breezeway.

God help her. He would be in the garage in seconds and out the back window, as though he'd never been there. The flames would take care of overlooked evidence. His alibi would be solid, as always.

Her mind slowed. As her reality receded, the last thing she remembered was Mayo and Mustard next to her. There was no way out for them either. They would die with her.

The smoke in the air seemed to be filling her mind with a gray mist, narrowing her thoughts to a tiny point of light. And then it snapped off, too.

Carolyn came to slowly, her cats meowing next to her, as though they'd been trying to wake her up. She could hardly breathe because of the smoke. Moving slightly, she grimaced as pain seared from her back into her left chest. Then she remembered. Her house was on fire. Dolores had been stabbed.

She'd been shot. She had to get them out of there.

It was Richard. It had always been Richard. Richard was the caller, the watcher, *the killer*.

She forced her mind away from her betrayal. She had to or they didn't have a chance. Carolyn figured that she'd been out for only a minute or so. Otherwise the hall would be burning by now.

She tossed the knife aside and crawled to Dolores a few feet away. Lowering her ear to her stepmother's chest, Carolyn determined that she was still breathing. Struggling to her knees, fighting waves of dizziness, she yanked off her sweater, oblivious to the blood, and wrapped it around her head like a mask. Somehow, she was able to get hold of Dolores and drag her toward the door, Mustard and Mayo beside her.

Abruptly her strength was gone. She knew she wouldn't make it, feeling too weak, knowing she was about to pass out again.

Moving in and out of consciousness, Carolyn didn't know if the breaking glass was because of the fire or if someone had smashed in the oval glass panel on the door. When it suddenly burst open, the flames were sucked from the back of the house into the hall.

Searing heat flashed over her as someone dragged her onto the porch. With loud, protesting yowls, Mayo and Mustard flashed past and disappeared into nearby shrubbery. Carolyn recognized Barney as he dragged Dolores from the house.

Gulping air, she welcomed its freshness, smelling the rain that still fell from the sky. She couldn't believe she was alive. She couldn't stand and her

throat ached from the smoke, *but she was alive.*
Beside her Dolores moaned.

Carolyn twisted her head to see her, grateful that
she wasn't dead. But was she dying? Hopefully, because of Barney, they'd both live. She tried to find
enough breath to thank him.

"Take it easy," he said, sounding shaken himself.
He stood with his back to the porch steps, about to
lift first her, then Dolores, away from the burning
house. He didn't see Richard step from behind the
shrubs, another gun in his hand.

"Behind you, Barney!" Her cry came out in a
hoarse croak.

Instantly, Barney ducked and the first shot
missed.

"Fuckin' bastard! You're dead!" Richard's words
were a hiss, sounding nothing like the man Carolyn
had known. He was going to kill Barney. Then he'd
finish the job on her and Dolores.

In shock, not understanding how the .38 could
still be resting on Dolores's chest, she grabbed it.
Her anger surfaced with a suddenness that shocked
her. He'd betrayed her, used her, had no compunc-
tion about killing her. She pointed the gun and fired.

She hit his right upper arm and Richard stumbled
backward. Her shot gave Barney time to rush forward, grab the gun and cuff him.

"We got you, you bastard," Barney cried. "Your
fingerprint in the blood on Roberta's door has connected you to the woman who was murdered up in
Chicago last year. You're going down for keeps,
fucker."

In the distance sirens cut through the peaceful

neighborhood of Buckhead. Seconds later her yard was lit by the sweep of blue and red bubble lights.

Vaguely, Carolyn was aware of fire trucks, and the paramedics who placed her and Dolores on gurneys to be lifted into the ambulance.

"Hang in there, Carolyn," Barney told her. "You're gonna make it fine." He hesitated, lightly squeezing her hand. "And thanks, kiddo. You saved my life tonight."

"We're even then." Her voice was hardly a whisper and he bent lower to hear her words. "You saved mine first."

"We'll discuss it later, over wine and spaghetti when you're all better. Okay?"

Behind him the walls of her house quivered like crimson tissue. Above the house that had once been her dream come true, fire bloomed like gigantic flowers against the clear night sky. It was fitting that the house die, too.

"Okay?" His repeated word was gentle, as though he guessed her sadness and disbelief.

She managed a nod, feeling the familiar grayness closing in on her consciousness. She couldn't think about Richard's treachery, that he'd tried to kill her, the man who'd been so tender with his lovemaking. It had all been a lie.

She gave in to the lethargy, welcoming it.

37

"**H**ey there, Carolyn." Barney stepped into her hospital room, looking relaxed, fit and handsome in his off-duty Levis and T-shirt. "I see you're dressed and ready to go."

"Just waiting for the doctor to get here and release me." Carolyn finished clipping back her hair into a ponytail, then turned from the mirror above the sink. "Five days are enough to spend in a hospital."

"You've got that right." He stood in a pool of sunlight that streamed in through the window and silvered his eyes. "How's Dolores doing?"

"Still critical, but gradually improving. She's lucky to be alive."

He nodded.

Carolyn knew she was equally lucky. Her bullet wound had not been life-threatening; she was assured of a complete recovery. But if not for Barney, both she and Dolores would have died in the fire. Her body was healing but she wondered if her broken heart could ever be mended.

The man she'd loved had tried to kill her. He'd never wanted her, only her money.

"The doc will check you one last time before he releases you, right?"

"Yeah." She glanced at her watch. "He should be here any time now."

"So I'll have time to look in on Dolores before I drive you home."

"Sure." Her voice wobbled. Tears were never far away these days.

He inclined his head and strode back to the door, paused and faced her again. "Carolyn, you'll find real happiness one day." He grinned. "Trust me." Then he disappeared into the hall.

She swallowed hard, and forced her thoughts away from Richard's betrayal, concentrating instead on the man she now knew him to be. No, not a man, she corrected herself. A monster.

Going to the window, Carolyn looked out, not really seeing the parking lot below her. Barney had visited her every day, and as she'd regained her strength, he'd updated her on the facts he'd uncovered. Richard was not an international land broker; his work was a con game, his money came from the women he'd bilked under his many identities. He'd met them on singles bulletin boards, then wooed them on-line with promises and cyber sex. His banker was really a female loan rep at the Chicago bank who had access to financial papers and their fax machine. His many trips were faked with the help of another lover, a travel agency owner who accessed the airline's passenger list to place Richard on the manifest. The chunk of money that was wired from Europe came from a German woman he met on the Internet; he'd flown there to meet her and propose—and borrow money, before making himself known to Carolyn. Those women survived with their lives, even though several had broken the law for him and were under investigation. The owner of the travel agency had been arrested; since the terrorist attack on America the year before, the woman's offense was serious. Other women didn't survive Richard's fatal charm.

Sudden tears blurred her vision. The money he'd repaid Carolyn for his BMW and their house had come from Dolores who'd sent it to a post office box in New Jersey. She'd considered it a loan to the man she intended to marry. Another of his computer women retrieved his mail and forwarded it on to an Atlanta address where Richard, under a different identity, maintained a cheap studio apartment.

Her poor stepmother. So desperate to find love, she'd allowed herself to believe a faceless Internet lothario, who'd wooed her several times daily with long E-mails, setting up their dates for instant-mail sex chats. He was Will Millgard, but not the distinguished older man in the photo she'd downloaded from him. All the time Richard, as Will, was really setting Dolores up to look as though she'd killed Carolyn before dying in a fire she'd set.

Carolyn turned back to the room, wishing the doctor would get there. She needed to get home.

Home? She no longer had one. Although her house hadn't burned down completely, she'd lost everything, except her cats. Dean was taking care of them at his grandmother's house, where Barney was taking her today to finish her recovery.

Antsy, Carolyn sat down on the bed. "Be patient," she thought. "Don't dwell on things. Think about the future."

It didn't help.

According to Barney, Richard designed the frightening incidents—the phone calls using a voice synthesizer, the messages in her box at NNN, even going into her elderly neighbors' condo to make an impression of Carolyn's house key while Thelma and Carl were walking Sammy. He'd been in her condo even before she met him. His aim was to throw suspicion onto Dolores and her family, beginning his reign of terror before he set up a way to actually meet Carolyn. Once, he'd even staged an incident when he was the watcher's target, to divert suspicion. When both women died he intended to be the grieving husband, not the main suspect.

Richard had learned the terms of her father's will from Dolores, that she was next in line to inherit upon Carolyn's death. If both women died the estate reverted to Dolores's family, unless Carolyn had a husband. Richard was third in line.

Dolores had shared intimate details of her family with Richard, and he began watching Carolyn on NNN, studying her, figuring out how he could win her affection. While searching Richard's apartment Barney had found a videotape of Carolyn discussing Dean's English assignment on her likes and dislikes.

Once Barney knew that Richard was the killer, he'd gotten a search warrant to enter the apartment he'd discovered from a rent receipt in Richard's wallet. The subsequent search revealed most of Richard's personal records, including his laptop computer with a complete list of his women and various names and a record of their E-mails. He determined that Richard had gone through Carolyn's purse and car to get her driver's license number, her birth date and Social Security number, and to make wax impressions of her keys for duplicating, all before actually meeting her or breaking into NNN's computer. With that information he hired an on-line investigative researcher for $250 and obtained Carolyn's personal history: financial, medical, marital and work.

Carolyn was still unable to grasp the evilness of the man. Barney said the police had yet to prove who had broken into NNN's computer but he'd found a zip disk with the list of customer and employee files, definitely implicating Richard. He also knew that two of Carolyn's fans were among Richard's cyber lovers and possible future victims. The files had given him Roberta's address, the information about Carolyn's sizable life insurance policy, even Minnie's address which Carolyn had listed as an emergency contact. Richard's concern about an insurance policy on his life was another lie. He had never taken one out on himself.

Since meeting Carolyn, Richard had not traveled except for one trip to Germany when Minnie was murdered. The trip was his alibi, should he need one. He flew over, received the fax from Carolyn, flew right back for the killing, then arranged the itinerary change through his travel agent woman.

Carolyn sighed as the doctor came into the room, a welcome relief to her disturbing thoughts. After a quick examination of her healing wound, and her promise to come into his office the next week, he left the nurse to apply a new bandage. Carolyn was buttoning her blouse when Barney reappeared at the door.

Carolyn was wheeled down to the entrance, Barney brought his car around and they were soon on their way to Buckhead.

"I have some new information." Barney glanced, a question in his eyes.

"I want to know, Barney." She corrected herself. "I have to know."

"You sure?"

She nodded, bracing herself.

"You know your house was heavily damaged but the firemen got the fire out before it burned through the whole attic."

She faced him, waiting as he maneuvered through an intersection.

"We found a computer/phone line linkup under the eaves. Each time Richard called you from one of his trips, he was actually calling from the attic. And while he was keeping track of you, he also kept up on his E-mail, using the laptop."

"You mean—he spent time up there—when I was home?"

"Uh-huh." Barney kept his eyes on the street. "And slept up there. We found a half-burned sleeping bag."

The air went out of her lungs and she squeezed her eyes closed, fighting momentary faintness. "But he had a studio apartment?"

"A twelve by fourteen unfurnished room with only a table and chair. There was no bed."

"All those times I heard noises in the night it was

him." She paused, taking in the horror of it, remembering the night she heard footsteps at her bedroom door. Her instincts had been right to pretend sleep. "He was the person in the dark sedan?" she asked.

"Yeah. It was almost identical to Dolores's car and parked in a carport at the apartment."

A long silence went by.

"What caused him to be such a monster?"

"A person like Richard sees things differently. He's incapable of having empathy for another person's pain. He's a manipulative sociopath who is totally focused on himself, and to the exclusion of any other human being."

"What else did you find in the apartment, Barney?"

He glanced, noting her upset. "It can wait."

"No, I'm okay."

There was a hesitation.

"He taped all of your calls. We found the tapes in his apartment." Barney hesitated. "Neither Minnie or Roberta had a chance once he heard their phone conversations with you about their concerns." His voice hardened. "You didn't know what they meant, but he sure as hell did, and knew they had found the thread to unravel his elaborate deception."

"And he couldn't allow that." Carolyn's voice was a weak whisper. "So he killed them."

"That's it in a nutshell."

"But Roberta left her message on my answering machine the night before her murder. He must have heard it. Why did he wait so long?"

"I think I know," Barney said. "Remember, I brought you home and had you wait by the door while I checked out the house?"

She nodded.

"I figure he got there just ahead of us, didn't dare listen to messages if he was to make his hiding place in the attic. But he switched off the answering machine, knowing you wouldn't check if the red light wasn't flashing. He had to wait until you went to sleep before he could switch off the alarm system and hear the recording."

"And then I couldn't sleep because of phantom sounds and it was probably almost daylight before he finally heard Roberta."

"Yeah, I ran that scenario past Richard when I questioned him. He just smiled, as if to say *fuck you*."

"I always thought he admired Minnie." She blinked back tears, diverting her thoughts from how her friend must have suffered.

"Minnie was a uniquely attractive woman despite her age. He probably lusted after her, hence the rape and his need for dominance before he killed her."

Poor Minnie, Carolyn thought. She knew Dolores's E-mail tag through Dean and saw it on Richard's list. His access number, the seven letters, must have been written on the paper she picked up, and she'd penetrated his private E-mail, and seen posts from Dolores and others. Then she'd called Carolyn.

"Two more things."

She waited.

"The DNA testing came up with a semen match, connecting Richard to Minnie's murder, and to a woman who was killed in Chicago. And his fingerprint is a match to the bloody print at Roberta's house." He glanced, meeting her eyes. "We have him for four homicides, the women and the stakeout officer, two counts of attempted murder and various lesser charges. He faces the death sentence."

She stared out the window at the passing scenery. She'd forgotten about the officer, mentally blocked that he'd died trying to protect her.

"What was the other thing?"

"Richard's real name was Alderman, not Crawford. He grew up in foster homes, never sticking anywhere because no one could control him, were in fact afraid of him. We don't know yet how he attained his veneer of sophistication. But we have uncovered one vital fact."

"What's that?"

"You aren't married to Richard. He already has a wife out in California."

Carolyn was stunned into silence.

By Christmas Dolores had recovered and moved to Augusta with Jessie, Tony, and Dean to a house Carolyn had bought for them with the insurance proceeds from hers. Dolores could no longer bear to live in Atlanta.

Carolyn planned to live permanently in her Buckhead house, enjoying Dean's weekly visits, and her accelerated involvement at the Youth House working with Barney. She'd gone back to work, but her stage presence was altered. She could never again be so candid with faceless viewers, and when she lost her number one sales position she was philosophical.

Another Richard could be out there . . . watching.

Tom called often but she wasn't interested in anything but friendship. Barney was a different story.

She enjoyed going out with him to various functions around town. Gradually she began to let her feelings show.

"Hey kiddo, you planning to stay single forever?" They were having a glass of wine after a movie.

"Who wants to know?" Carolyn asked.

"Me."

"Why?" She hesitated. "I've already made two bad choices."

He grinned. "You know what they say about the third time. It's a charm."

Carolyn grinned back. Some things were inevitable.